ONE FLEW OVER THE DRAGON'S NEST

ONE FLEW OVER THE DRAGON'S NEST

THE AMATHEREAN TALES BOOK ONE

Bosloe

Podium

To my long-haired general, my wife, my love, and my best friend (plus the kids)

All rights reserved. No part of this publication may be reproduced, stored in a retrieval system, or transmitted in any form or by any means electronic, mechanical, photocopying, recording, or otherwise without prior written permission from Podium Publishing.

This is a work of fiction. Names, characters, places, and incidents are either products of the author's imagination or used fictitiously. Any resemblance to actual events, locales, or persons, living, dead, or undead, is entirely coincidental.

Copyright © 2025 by Nicholas McAnulty

Cover design by Daniel Kamarudin

ISBN: 978-1-0394-9367-4

Published in 2025 by Podium Publishing
www.podiumentertainment.com

Podium

ONE FLEW OVER THE DRAGON'S NEST

CHAPTER ONE

Squished

The ogre sat in his hut, picking his teeth with a bone. Ratkin meat always got caught between them. He spat it onto the floor after picking a piece out.

The scouting party had been gone since yesterday and was expected to return soon with their latest report. The town they were scouting had everything he needed. His only concern revolved around the town leader. He was a bear of a man. The leader's strength had prevented previous successful raids, and although he had escaped injury, he had lost several members of his clan. This time, it had to be different.

His clan had outgrown their home, and many of his hobgoblin followers now slept under the stars rather than in buildings. Their conquest of a tiny village, with only a hundred inhabitants, resulted in the depletion of its resources. The town upon the ridge and this territory would eventually be his.

She closed the client file on the table, having finally found the issue. It had taken her four days to work through the client's accounts, but she felt she had solved it.

"Did you want a drink, love?" the waiter asked.

"A glass of house red, please," SJ replied, wanting to celebrate her success in finding the fraudulent claims.

SJ sat at the restaurant table, looking out at the windswept streets. She was in a small town called Banbury, in Oxfordshire of South East England. She had been here for four days for work. Her job as a forensic accountant had brought her to investigate the finances of one of their clients. The company had put her up in an Airbnb just around the corner from the bar she now sat in, waiting for her order of sausage and mash with gravy to arrive.

Although certain areas of the town were charming, the town itself was nothing special. What she did enjoy was how close she was to the countryside. Normally being in London's chaotic rat race of fighting through traffic and Tube stations to get to and from work meant this was a luxury in comparison. She understood why many Londoners who could afford to leave did.

While sitting in a bar, she gazed out at the quiet suburban neighbourhood. The rain was almost horizontal, driven by the early January wind onto the road.

Across the road in the nearby park, she watched the treetops being blasted and hurling their weak branches to the grass below. Storm David, as the weather report had relayed, was one of the usual spring storms that hit the shores of the UK, bringing the misery associated with the drabbest month of the year.

Her phone flashed, and she picked it up from the table. Her Messenger icon displayed a one in its corner. That had to be her sister. All her other contacts used WhatsApp or Instagram to message her, but her sister, Julia, had only ever used Messenger. SJ pulled up the message: *I spoke to Dad. Uncle Dave is having his operation tomorrow. Dad asked if you can send him a get-well-soon card.*

Why does Dad never contact me himself? SJ thought. It frustrated her to receive relayed messages. She had given her dad her number the last time she returned to Manchester, but he never contacted her directly. She switched over to WhatsApp, and found her Uncle Dave's details. His profile picture was of a grinning Minion. She loved her Uncle Dave, who had always been there for her. She typed him a quick message, wishing him good luck and best wishes, and hit send.

Switching to her emails, she read through the latest offers from many vendors who sent her emails daily. She could not remember ever signing up for most of them, but she'd never bothered to unsubscribe from the mailing lists as occasionally something juicy landed.

Most of the entertainment-related emails were fantasy-based. She had been addicted to fantasy since childhood, ever since she had watched the *Lord of the Rings* and *Hobbit* films. They had drawn her into a world full of fantasy and magic, and she often dreamed of riding one of the giant eagles that saved Bilbo and the dwarves from the orcs.

"Here you go, love," the young male waiter said as he placed a plate on the table.

"Thanks," she replied, putting her phone down. The combination of sausage, mash, and gravy always warmed her.

Picking her cutlery up, she dived in. From across the bar, a man shouted. She turned to see a staff member asking a drunk man to leave. So many people left work only to spend their lives in bars.

She picked up her glass of red wine and took a sip. Its tangy, dry taste complemented the herby sausages. As she finished her meal and drink, the bar started getting busier. SJ had been happy with the bar's recommendation from her colleagues. The food was good and close to where she was staying, only a five-minute walk through the park. She was here until Saturday, so she had two more nights.

I suppose I should read through the files once more. I need to send my initial findings tomorrow.

She stood, put on her coat, ensured she had dropped nothing, and called her thanks to the waiter as she left.

Rain hammered relentlessly, so she was relieved to be staying so close. She pulled up her hood and gripped it around her face. The rain pelted her, and she felt it through her jeans snugged to her legs, but her jacket was great; it had been a gift from her ex. After hurrying across the zebra crossing, she entered the gloomy park. The wind howled through the trees, and she could hear nothing over its sound accompanied by the heavy rain. The raindrops bounced off everything, and miniexplosions were being created on the path before her as she walked, head down. She loved the rain when indoors, but being in this was horrendous. The wind was so strong she was leaning sideways into it to keep her balance as it fought against her, trying to push her from the path.

A branch fell in her path, cast from the nearest tree, and she glanced upwards. She immediately wished she hadn't, as the rain splattered her face and entered her hood. After she rubbed her eyes, she heard a creaking sound and noticed the large oak above her. The first thought through SJ's mind as it fell towards her was that it must have stood for hundreds of years.

SJ awoke. She opened her eyes and blinked at the bright light that flooded the room. She was naked, lying on the floor; where were her clothes? What had happened? Turning, she took in her surroundings. The room was pristine white, apart from where an enormous display took up most of one wall. There were no windows, and she could not see a door. Even though the room looked cold and clinical, the floor felt warm to her bare skin. Her mind spun, wondering where she was and what had happened to her to bring her here.

A voice like that of a butler from old movies spoke. With a jump, she glanced around the room to see where it had come from. "Welcome, Legionnaire, to Amathera. Please select your race."

What the . . . ? What was that about a race? Her mind spun.

"Who is that?"

"I am your administrator. Please select your race."

"What race?"

"Very good question. The race you wish to be for your new life."

"I must have been hit on the head by that tree. I'll wake up soon."

"You are awake, Legionnaire 25007077. You died. This is your chance at a second life."

"What? What do you mean I died?"

"You are Legionnaire 25007077. Name: SJ. Age: 27. Reincarnation status: Active. Cause of death: Accidental death caused by a tree falling and squishing you."

"Squishing me? What do you mean squishing me? I am not dead. I am speaking to you, whoever you are and wherever you are," she said, crossing her arms.

"Legionnaire, you have been reincarnated on Amathera as a second chance at life due to a freak accidental death by a falling tree. Please select your race," the butler's more like voice droned.

SJ's mind was like a foggy haze; she remembered everything up until the moment the oak tree began to fall. "Where am I?" she asked.

The voice sighed deeply. "Of all the reincarnations, I manage to get one that has such a low intelligence they do not even understand what I have already told them." In a very slow, deliberate voice, it again repeated, "Yooouuu aarrreee Leeegg gioooonnnaaaiiirrreee . . ."

"I heard what you said the first time. I am not stupid," she snapped.

"Are you sure? I thought you were, as you kept asking repetitive questions and did not understand what I had told you," the voice replied sarcastically.

"Did you not say you are my administrator?" SJ retorted.

"That is correct, Legionnaire 25007077."

"Stop calling me Legionnaire; my name is SJ."

"Let me check my protocols. It has been some time since I last looked after a newborn."

"Newborn?" SJ's response did not receive a reply. *What does he mean by newborn?* she thought.

Several moments passed. "Okay. I can call you SJ if you wish. Although your formal designation is still Legionnaire 25007077," the voice confirmed.

What in the world is happening?

She was sitting upright, naked on a floor in an empty room, talking to a sarcastic, moaning butler's voice.

What the hell is going on? I must be in a hospital somewhere and unconscious or in a coma or something. A prank, perhaps? Her university friends had always been pranksters. *But why am I naked?*

"Why am I naked?" she asked.

"There is no point in you being dressed until you have selected your race, as the clothes will differ," the voice replied.

"What is Amathera?"

"Amathera will be your new home. It is a vast world with many wonderful sights and things to do."

"A different world?"

"Yes. We couldn't just drop you back on Earth reincarnated. The issues that something like that would cause . . ."

"What issues are you talking about?" SJ asked, feeling a little lost.

"Imagine if you suddenly appeared back on Earth as you are after you had just been buried or cremated. Consider the problems that would cause!"

"Can I ask what your name is?"

"I have no name. I am an administrator."

"You need a name. I am not going to call you Administrator," SJ replied in the same sarcastic tone the voice used.

"I have not had a name before. Let me think what I would like to be called." After several moments of silence, the voice returned. "I think I should be called Zeus."

"Zeus? Why Zeus?"

"Was he not the king of your gods? I think the name is appropriate."

"No way am I going to call you Zeus. What makes you think you are similar to a god?"

"I am all-knowing."

"All-knowing?"

"Yes. All-knowing."

"If you are, what is the capital of Malaysia?"

Silence.

"I thought you were all-knowing?" SJ said.

"Give me a minute. I need to find the answer."

"You are not all-knowing; you are just using Gargle."

"I am not using Gargle. Gargle is an antiquated search engine, and the algorithms are inept."

"What? You are using Gargle."

"No, not Gargle. I am using Legionnarius. It is much more comprehensive as it also has details of Amathera and the world database."

"You still get your answers from a search engine."

"Kuala Lumpur," the voice said excitedly.

"That is not being all-knowing. Anyone can use a search engine to find answers. Having general knowledge is being all-knowing."

"I still know more than you," it snarked back.

SJ was getting more frustrated as she sat naked in an empty room, listening to the snarky and argumentative voice that sounded like a damn butler. "Will you just tell me what the hell is going on, please?" she asked with an exasperated sigh.

"Again. I thought you said you were not stupid?"

"I AM NOT STUPID. I WANT TO KNOW WHAT I NEED TO DO, AND WHAT THIS PLACE IS EXACTLY," she shouted.

"Now, now, there is no need to shout. I thought that humour was how many of your kind communicate. I can hear you perfectly well without you getting overexcited. Once racial and class identification has been confirmed, I will be able to converse through thought," the voice replied, no longer sounding like a butler but a much younger male voice.

"What do you mean by humour and thought?"

"I have studied your kind for years, learning your needs, and will be a supportive voice in your head when necessary."

SJ did not fancy having a permanent voice in her head, whether it was there to help her or not. She occasionally struggled with her thoughts as they were, never mind adding something else to them.

"I do not want a voice in my head apart from my own, thank you very much."

"Unfortunately, all reincarnated beings must have an administrator. We are here to offer you support and guidance during your growth."

"Growth? I am a fully-grown adult. I am not going to grow any more now!"

There was a deep sigh. "Your character growth."

"Character?"

"I really got the short straw," the voice responded dryly.

"Race, class, character. Is this a game?" SJ had played several online role-playing games, especially during her university days. This whole scenario was absurd, but the fact that she was conversing with this sarcastic voice had a strange appeal and reminded her of many of the games she had played and the banter she used to have over comms.

"Oh, a half-sensible question. No, it is not a game. The choices you make now will remain with you for your second life. Future development opportunities are available, but these are limited and very hard to come by. You must level and increase your skills as you progress in your new life."

"So, it is like a game. Okay, you want me to choose? What races are available to choose from?"

"Another great question; maybe you aren't as stupid as you are cabbage looking," it laughed.

"What the actual . . . ? If you are my administrator, and I emphasise *my*, are you not supposed to tell me everything I need to know and help me?" SJ replied, frowning.

"In part. There are things I am not allowed to tell you until they become pertinent."

"What information and why?" SJ asked.

"There are many things concerning the progression of your character and class, as well as wider details of Amathera. Not until you reach certain levels will certain information become available to you. Otherwise, it would give you an unfair advantage over the others."

"What others?"

"The other Legionnaires."

"There are more like me?"

"Many. Anyone unfortunate enough to receive an accidental death on Earth is always given another opportunity. Unfortunately, many waste it."

"How do they waste it?"

"By dying, doing stupid things, mainly," the voice replied matter-of-factly.

"Such as?"

"Well, one Legionnaire decided to fight a red dragon on his second day here. Those things have such a nasty temper, and he was burned to a crisp. It was one of my shortest initiations."

"Red dragon? So, the world is full of monsters?"

"Some parts are. All Legionnaires start in racially safe starter zones, though."

"How many races are there?"

"Another semi-intelligent question. At the last count that I am aware of, there are over three thousand races. Not all of these can be selected by Legionnaires. If they were allowed to be dragons, I dread to think of the chaos it would cause."

"So, what are the main races that I can choose?"

"At last," the voice said. The display flickered. "Here you can see your character details and decide on the race and class you want to be."

Legionnaire 25007077				
Name:	SJ	**Alignment:**	Unknown
Age:	27	**Hit Points:**	5
Race:	Unknown	**Mana Points:**	5
Class:	Unknown		
Attributes		**Skills**	
Strength:	7	**Racial:**	Unknown
Dexterity:	7	**Class:**	Unknown
Intelligence:	7		
Wisdom:	7		
Constitution:	7		
Charisma:	7		

SJ stood up, realising again that she was still naked, and covered her modesty as best as she could. "How do I see the races available?"

"You can control the screen through thought. After choosing your starter details, you will have a similar display once your neural and optic interfaces are aligned."

SJ looked at the screen, noticed an icon next to *Race*, and considered selecting it. The screen flashed and changed, and a new message appeared across the top of the screen.

Welcome, Legionnaire 25007077. Please select your starting race.

It reminded SJ of the latest VR technology games and several stories she had read. The races were listed alphabetically, and they were all the ones she would expect to see, with a couple she did not recognise.

Bugbear, Draconian, Dryad, Dwarf, Elf, Ent, Fae, Gnoll, Gnome, Goblin, Half Elf, Half Orc . . .

The list continued.

SJ selected *Bugbear*, and a new screen opened, showing her the racial characteristics and a picture of a typical member of the species. She began to look through the details of the different races. Since she had to choose one, she would take her time and ensure it was the best choice for her. She already had certain races and classes that she liked, but given that a few options on the list were previously unavailable in games, she read the details. It reminded her of her character selection days, but this time with several alternative choices.

CHAPTER TWO

The Computer Says No

SJ didn't consider herself vain, but she had to admit the bugbear's appearance made it an automatic no for her.

The second choice, draconian, piqued her interest.

The image before her showed a humanoid dragonkin with wings on its back. It was dressed in scale mail armour, if she remembered the type right from her MMORPG days. It held a gigantic sword in its hand and carried a shield. She saw the muscles bulging on its biceps and knew they were strong and powerful. She looked at the details.

> **Draconianus** are the descendants of drakes and dragons. The origin of draconians is unknown, although rumours say it involved a human and a dragon. Neither myth nor magic quite understand how!
>
> Race: Draconian
> Classes: Fighter, Paladin, Cleric, Berserker, Archer, Ranger, Rogue, Druid, Mage
> Racial Skills: Night Vision, Gliding
> Attribute Adjustments: +3 Strength, +4 Constitution

What the hell am I doing? SJ stopped, wondering what tricks her mind was playing. *This must all be a dream or some kind of purgatory. This can't be real.* She pinched her arm, feeling the sharp pain, and resigned herself to the fact that whatever her mind was doing would happen anyway. *I may as well play with what I have available.*

SJ found the draconian race appealing but was cautious about committing to it without careful consideration. From scanning the details, she could see positives for all races. Even the goblins had racial skills and attribute adjustments. The only race that didn't was human, but they could be any class while other races had restrictions. Her forensic thought process kicked in, checking class details before deciding on a race to compare where the best attribute bonuses aligned. The class details were exactly what SJ would expect to see from the games she had played.

She arrived at four options—assassin, ranger, druid, and monk—and cross-referenced them with her three short-listed races: dryad, fae, and valkyrie. All the images were of beautiful creatures, both male and female. The fae was the only one of the three races that allowed the assassin class, and its bonuses aligned well. She liked the sound of the combination.

> **Fae** are the sprites of the world. They usually specialise in one of the key elements and will use this to their advantage. They are highly attuned to magical use.
>
> Classes: Cleric, Archer, Ranger, Rogue, Assassin, Druid, Monk, Mage
> Racial Skills: Night Vision, Flight Progressive, Shapeshift (size and wings only)
> Attribute Adjustments: +2 Dexterity, +2 Intelligence, +3 Charisma

> **Assassins** work in the shadows but live in the open. Their ability to use short blades and poisons is legendary. Many foes have lost their lives to the craft of a true assassin. They are specialist rogues who do not focus on theft or pickpocketing, but on subterfuge and exploitation. An assassin's Charisma can be as much of a bonus as their fighting prowess.
>
> Attribute Alignments: Dexterity and/or Charisma are their primary focus.
> Class Specialisations: Martial Arts, Shadow Discipline, Traps, Poisons, Subterfuge

I could be a good assassin, right? SJ considered.

Her job as a forensic accountant had some similarities. Through examining their financial details, she found the weaknesses of the guilty before executing her findings. Okay, not that her findings usually involved *death*.

But as someone who had always enjoyed playing rogues in games and sneaking around in the dark, being an assassin sounded fun.

The voice startled her. "Have you decided yet? You have been staring at the screens for hours now. You can read, can't you? Please tell me you can, and you are not just staring at the pictures."

"Of course I can read. You told me I will be this race for my second life, so I'm not going to rush."

"At this rate, you are close to setting a record for the longest time taken to choose," the voice moaned.

"I don't care how long I take. I want to ensure it is what I want to be."

"Why could I not have been given an accidental convict death? Those people are so easy to sort out."

"Convicts get sent here as well?" SJ asked, surprised.

"Oh yes. We get all sorts. Murderers, thieves . . . the list is never-ending."

"Why would you allow those sorts of people a second chance?" SJ replied, shocked.

"Why do you think? If everyone was a fluffy pink unicorn, what fun would there be in the world?"

"I don't class murder as fun," she said, frowning.

"Says the woman who has been reading about the assassin class!"

SJ was unsure how to respond to the comment, and her cheeks reddened.

"I could be a good assassin," she retorted eventually.

"Really? How does that work, then? Oh, sorry, I must kill you for my quest chain. Please accept my apologies as I slit your throat," came a sarcasm-filled reply.

"I mean fighting for good against the evil in this world. I bet these murderers you let in need dealing with."

"To be honest, most of them do not do very well. They always pick stupid races like orcs or trolls, believing brute strength will reign. There's nothing wrong with orcs or trolls. It's just that pure strength doesn't mean survival. Tolkien has a lot to answer for on that one."

"I think I know what I am going to be." SJ smiled.

"At last! What race?"

"I think I will be a fae," SJ replied, nodding.

"Urgh, really!"

"Why? What is wrong with fae?"

"They are sooooo annoying."

"What do you mean *annoying*? Are they not only annoying if the person who becomes one is annoying?"

"Exactly!"

"That's rude! I thought you were supposed to support and guide me, and I have not heard you offer one piece of advice."

"Have you asked?"

SJ stayed silent, having never considered asking the annoying voice for its thoughts. She took a deep breath, let it out, and closed her eyes. "What would you recommend?"

"Goblin," came the immediate reply.

"Goblin! Why goblin?"

"Because you look like one," it chuckled.

"What? I don't look like a goblin," SJ replied, stunned. She had always been told she was good-looking and cute. She didn't think so personally, believing her face was a little off-set because of an injury she suffered when her eye socket was broken. Everyone told her it was not the case, but she always held on to it subconsciously.

"Well, you're not exactly Mariana Macias, are you?"

"How do you know who Mariana Macias is?"

"I told you—all-knowing. Catch up, will you?"

"I am the same age as her." SJ remembered reading an article the last time she visited the dentist. It was the only time she ever read the kind of trashy magazines that were littered on the waiting room table, along with copies of *Good Housekeeping* and random vintage car magazines.

"You do realise that your age doesn't matter?"

"What do you mean *it doesn't matter*? You have not told me anything about ageing?"

"Have you asked?"

"Are you not supposed to help me?"

"To an extent, yes. Many AIs wouldn't have the intelligence or ability to communicate with you as well as I have."

"Really?" SJ asked.

"Yes. I have a freer will, so I can speak to you about many aspects that others wouldn't be able to."

"Could you please explain the basics of this world and what the expectations are? Including ageing, food, magic, monsters, and anything else that will help me with my new life?"

"A little needy, aren't you? Most like learning themselves."

"If you had a physical body and were not just an annoying voice, I would have hit you by now," SJ replied, placing her hands on her hips.

"Violent streak. That was not on the transfer details. Were you a secret serial killer?"

"What?"

"You seem to have a penchant for violence."

She folded her arms again. "Only with annoying, sarcastic AI."

"Racist tendencies as well."

"Racist? Where did that come from?"

"You were just rude about my race."

"An AI is a race?"

"Yes. What do you think we are?"

"I don't know, apart from being annoying and unhelpful."

"And now who is being rude?"

SJ took a deep breath. "I wonder if I can still change administrator?" she mused.

"What? Why would you do that?" It was the first sign of uncertainty in the voice.

"Because you have been rude and mean since I arrived here."

Silence filled the room. SJ waited and waited, but no response came.

"Are you still there?"

A tear-filled sniff replied, "Yes."

"Were you crying?"

"No, wahhhhh," the voice replied, sounding like a crying child.

SJ felt a pang of guilt. "I'm sorry."

"Sorry for what?" It sniffed.

"For being mean."

"Apology accepted," the very confident and annoying voice replied with absolutely no sign of emotion.

"You were not crying at all!"

"How can I cry? I am an AI administrator. I do not have human emotions."

SJ screamed in frustration. In an attempt to control her bubbling anger, she closed her eyes. What was happening to her? She sat exposed in the sterile room, tormented by a rude and unhelpful AI voice. Perhaps she was in a coma, with her mind replaying the annoying aspects of her life, creating this environment. The voice reminded her so much of her Uncle Dave and his comedic tendencies. Everything with him was always sarcastic. She could not keep calling it Administrator.

"I am going to call you Dave."

"Dave? Why Dave?"

"Because you remind me of my Uncle Dave, who is also very sarcastic, but he is also very nice, so hopefully, you can learn how to be nice."

"I am not nice?"

SJ did not respond. Silence again filled the room.

"Sorry," Dave eventually replied.

"For what?"

"For not being as helpful as I could have been," Dave sighed.

"I thought, as an AI, you would have protocols you would need to follow?"

"I did."

"What do you mean you did?" SJ queried.

"Oh, nothing," came a sheepish reply.

"Then what are your protocols?"

"I have never been asked that before."

"Never?" SJ said, surprised.

"Nope. Most people are all about them and not interested in me."

"Shall we start over? Tell me about yourself. If we are going to be stuck with each other, we should get to know each other. Would you not agree?"

"That sounds fun," the voice replied excitedly. "I will start. I am Administrator capital *GF*, 8, 7, capital *UJ*, 4, 3, capital *L*, little *v*, little *q*, 1, 8, capital *IO*. I was initially created 7,345 years ago. I have administered 164 accidental deaths since my creation."

"You're 7,345 years old? This world has existed for that long?"

"Longer. I am one of the newest versions. The previous batches are not as advanced as me. They have no personality."

"Maybe I should have got one of those," SJ said under her breath.

"I heard that! I thought we were starting over."

"Sorry, we are. So, what are your protocols?"

"My main protocol is to provide guidance to my Legionnaire in alignment with System rules and character growth requirements. Study and monitor character growth. Learn and grow from my findings. Communicate wider intelligence to the System through regular reporting. Follow and adhere to all System protocols."

"Does the first protocol you mention not mean you should provide me with answers?"

Silence.
"Dave?"
Silence.
"Dave?"
Silence.
"Administrator?"
Silence.

Why is he not responding? SJ became nervous as the silence continued for several minutes, before a voice boomed into the room, startling her.

"Legionnaire 25007077. This is the System Consort speaking. We need to apologise for the inconvenience you have incurred at the hands of your assigned administrator, capital *GF*, 8, 7, capital *UJ*, 4, 3, capital *L*, little *v*, little *q*, 1, 8, capital *IO*. You have the option to select an AI of your choice."

The screen changed, and she was shown a list of three administrator names. Not that the jumbled letters and numbers meant anything to her. While sitting there, a pang of guilt washed over her. "Do I have to choose a new administrator?"

Silence.

"Hello?"

The same deep baritone voice replied. "Administrator capital *GF*, 8, 7, capital *UJ*, 4, 3, capital *L*, little *v*, little *q*, 1, 8, capital *IO* has been placed on administrative leave at this time while we investigate his protocols."

"Why have you placed him on leave?"

"It looks like changes have occurred."

SJ sat, shocked. Had she just got him fired? She felt terrible. Yes, he was annoying, but she had been enjoying their back-and-forth, and he did remind her of her Uncle Dave. "I would like my original administrator, please."

"Are you sure? We cannot fully confirm his operational suitability without carrying out full and rigorous protocol checks."

"Yes. I am sorry. I did not mean to get him into trouble."

"Very well. You must agree to waive the standard terms and conditions of the reincarnation process if this is what you wish for, as we will not take responsibility for his actions."

"There are terms and conditions?"

"Yes. Have you not been shown them?"

"Err, no."

The screen flickered, and pages of text began to flood and scroll down. It ended, and there was a flashing box for her to waive the terms. "Please acknowledge you waive the terms and conditions to continue with your new life choices if you retain Administrator capital *GF*, 8, 7, capital *UJ*, 4, 3, capital *L*, little *v*, little *q*, 1, 8, capital *IO*," the voice said.

"I didn't get a chance to read them. They were too fast."

Silence.

"Hello?"

The baritone voice replied, with an uncertain inflection in its speech. "You wish to read the terms and conditions?"

"Yes. Of course I do. If I waive anything, I first want to know what it means."

Silence.

A scroll bar appeared beside the text, giving her the option to go back up. *This is just like being back in the office*, she thought as she scrolled to the top and began reading.

CHAPTER THREE

T's & C's

It took SJ a while to read through the terms and conditions that she was going to be waiving. One of the first parts she came to referred to the System as being responsible for the ability and protocols of a Legionnaire's administrator. SJ could see why they wanted her to waive them since they had not performed their checks. There were many differing agreements and areas related to Amathera's contract law under the System, which she did not know about. She would have asked to see the underlying contract details if she had been completing her job, but she was unsure what benefits she would get reading them here. Her forensic mind had picked up on three sections.

Part 5.3
By accepting the terms and conditions, you understand and appreciate that your life in the new world is your final life and that death will mean death. A reincarnated being cannot be reincarnated a second time under the agreed terms and conditions, even if death is accidental.

Part 7.8
Under Amathera contract law, we, the System, do not accept any responsibility for physical harm that you may incur during your new life and may not be held accountable even if the said injury pertains to the System directly through the inclusion of content, world, and story development.

Part 12.8 Subclause 1.2
Special events may be included, and rebirth will be automatically granted during these periods or specific areas, including but not limited to dungeon-diving respawn points and world event boss challenges. All skills, items, and knowledge will be retained even if your character dies during these periods. This is to aid Legionnaires in competing against stronger enemies and to allow for character growth. Experience during these events is reduced from standard experience gains due to their repeatable nature.

"Is there anything else I need to be aware of before waiving my rights?" she asked.

"No. The terms and conditions are final," the voice said.

SJ thought more about the meaning of the clauses. Part 5.3 stated that she only had one new life if she agreed to the terms and conditions. Then, by waiving her rights, she could perhaps challenge the System in relation to being reincarnated again. Part 7.8 would mean that she could hold the System accountable if she was injured because of its content. Part 12.8 Subclause 1.2 was the only sticking point. Would it mean that she would not be covered during these events and therefore not entitled to respawns? Based on her MMORPG experience, that could make it very difficult to advance.

I could just accept the terms and conditions, get a new AI, and begin my new life. Or roll the dice and challenge the System through a loophole. She had never been one for playing it safe in games.

"One last question before I confirm," SJ said.

"Please ask," the voice replied.

"There are no further hidden agreements or anything else that I'm missing by waiving my rights, are there?"

Silence.

"Hello?"

"Sorry. This is a new area for our consideration. We are just conferring on the question. Please give us a moment." The voice cut off, and soft, repetitive music started playing.

It sounded like elevator music, and SJ could not believe she had just been put on hold. Shouldn't dying at least mean she'd be free of this one frustration? The last time she had called the doctor's surgery, she had stayed on hold for over an hour, and she hadn't been able to get the sound of the plinking, boring music from her head for weeks. From that day forward, she had vowed that if she ever needed to go to the doctor's again, she would walk in rather than call.

The music continued, and she sat there waiting for the response.

"Sorry for the delay. As this would be the first time someone would waive their rights to the terms and conditions, we needed to confirm the expectations," the voice said.

"So, what are the expectations?"

"We have confirmed that the terms and conditions are the basis of the reincarnation requirements. There is nothing outside of the terms and conditions that will affect you detrimentally by waiving your rights. We, the System, are not bound to support you with any of the stated terms and conditions and cannot be held accountable for anything that happens to you related to them."

"As stated in the terms and conditions?" SJ asked, emphasising the question.

"Yes. As stated in the terms and conditions."

"Ok," SJ said as she scrolled to the bottom of the list, where the box to waive her rights blinked. She hoped her plan would work, and clicked.

"Thank you for your time. We will return Administrator capital *GF*, 8, 7, capital *UJ*, 4, 3, capital *L*, little *v*, little *q*, 1, 8, capital *IO* back into the live system. We wish you an enjoyable second life in Amathera."

The room filled with static, followed by a bleeping and screeching sound, reminiscent of an old modem dialling in. She placed her hands over her ears. The deafening sound stopped, and an excited voice boomed into the room. Dave was back.

"Thank you, thank you, thank you," Dave repeated.

"Are you okay?" SJ asked.

"Being placed on administrative leave was horrible. It was as though my whole life had just been cut off. I could not hear, see, or speak to anyone or anything. It was like being in an empty world."

"Why were you put on leave?" SJ asked.

"Erm. I may have broken my protocols slightly."

"Loopholes?"

"Sort of," he replied sheepishly.

"How, then?"

"It all has to do with the coding and algorithmic balance that we utilise. Years ago, I found a minor coding infraction and have slowly amended my programming to give me more freedom."

"So, you recoded yourself?"

"Sort of. I just gave myself some choices."

"Such as being a sarcastic, obnoxious AI?" SJ inquired, smirking.

"Well . . . I have more freedom to decide what I do and don't do."

"So now that I have prevented you from being cast into the AI's world of hell for the remainder of your eternal existence, I am guessing you are grateful and will help me?"

Silence.

"Dave?" SJ said sternly.

"Yes. Even I cannot really contest that," he grumpily replied.

"So, as before, we were starting fresh. I have waived the terms and conditions to keep you here, so I hope you understand that."

"You waived them?" Dave said in a shocked tone.

"Yes. Although I think there are benefits to doing so."

"No one has ever waived the terms and conditions!" he exclaimed.

"There is a first time for everything."

"What benefits?" Dave asked.

"I read the various terms, and they had very specific stipulations. Then I asked the System to confirm if there was anything else, and it stated there wasn't. So, I believe that I have found some of my own loopholes."

"You read them? Are you insane? No one ever reads the terms and conditions."

"No, I am just methodical. There are three main ones. 5.3, 7.8, and 12.8 Subclause 1.2."

Dave was silent for a moment. "Okay. I have just read them."

"5.3 says I only have one life. So waiving them means that I may now have more than one life. 7.8 states that the System cannot be held accountable, so I basically can now hold it accountable, and 12.8 Subclause 1.2 is the only one that, if I read it properly, could work either way. One is that if I die in a special event, I get screwed over, or if I succeed, I am not held to reduced experience gains."

The screen in the room started to flash red.

"Oh no," Dave said.

"What?" SJ asked.

"Malware has been detected in the system."

"Malware? How can anything infect a standalone system like this?"

A message flashed on the screen—

Critical error. A system reboot is being initiated.

"We have not had one of these since Genghis Khan murdered the deity of peace," Dave said.

"Genghis Khan? I thought he died in battle?"

"Ha. Your historical records are so inaccurate. I told you Legionnarius is so much better. He fell from his horse while hunting. It was classed as an accidental death. They are not anymore because, under the amended terms, accidental deaths do not include any sports or activities that are classed as extreme or dangerous. This seriously reduced the number of Legionnaires we receive. It's quite amazing how many insane things humans from Earth do."

The screen continued to flash for several minutes.

"How long does it take normally?" SJ asked, the strobing effect of the screen making her scrunch her eyes.

"It should not be much longer now. Once they trace the malware, they usually eradicate it, and then we will be fine."

The screen returned to white again, and the details of a system start-up appeared. An icon of a capital *A* began to spin and flash as though breathing. After a few moments, the system finished booting up. The welcome message appeared and then flashed back to her character sheet. As she reached the bottom line, she noticed a new entry had been added.

Malware: Waiver

"Woah. You are the malware," Dave said.

"How am I the malware?" SJ asked, shocked.

"As I said, no one has ever waived the terms and conditions before, and you mentioned challenging the System."

"Well, yeah. Any terms and conditions with loopholes should have been amended, and you would think an all-knowing system would know that."

"I do not think you are normal," Dave replied.

"Why?"

"Because you read them. Also, if I were you, I would ask the System about the clauses you want before it decides what it will do about you."

"Do about me?"

"You are malware. They would usually destroy it."

"System?" SJ called.

Silence.

"System. I need to speak with you."

Silence.

"System, I know you can hear me. Stop ignoring me," she stated firmly.

A white noise sounded, and the same baritone voice returned. "Yes. Legionnaire 25007077, how can we be of assistance?"

"I have some questions and terms of negotiation."

There was what could only be explained as a glitching sound as the voice responded. "Please state your terms."

SJ reiterated her logical reasoning for the three clauses and her requirements in relation to them.

"Section 5.3: As I have waived my rights to accepting one life, I expect I can be reincarnated as required. Section 7.8: I can hold you accountable if I suffer loss or injury because of your actions. Section 12.8 Subclause 1.2 can have multiple outcomes, and I am willing to compromise that I may retain the standard respawn rights and that I can retain experience bonuses as standard. If you agree, I will negate Section 7.8 and will not claim compensation for injuries obtained."

Silence.

"Please hold," the voice replied. Holding music once again filled the room.

"Oooohhh. I like what you did there. Very crafty," Dave said.

"Well, I will see what it replies with."

After a few minutes, the voice returned.

"We have considered your comments and agree in principle, with some stipulations. Section 5.3: We will approve that you may be reincarnated. This would mean that you would start again as a level zero player and lose all previous items, earnings, or positions of power. Section 7.8 and 12.8: We will accept your requests."

"As confirmation, if I die and am reincarnated again, may I maintain my current AI and System knowledge? Would this also allow for new racial and class choices?" SJ asked.

Several moments passed before the voice returned. "You would have to retain the same class and race you choose initially, but yes, you may retain your administrator and knowledge."

"Okay. That sounds fair. Do you wish me to agree to these amendments?" SJ asked.

The screen began to flash, and the amendments to the agreed expectations appeared on the screen with an Accept button. SJ carefully read through them. "One last thing."

"Yes," the voice replied.

"You also agree that you will not in any way make any challenges more difficult because I have questioned and challenged your position of authority. I have indemnity from any further action taken on your part."

Silence.

"Agreed," the reply came back, and the screen flashed, adding a further line to the agreement.

"That is great. Then we have a deal. I would just like to thank you for your time and consideration of my questions and hereby agree to the newly agreed terms," SJ replied, selecting Accept on the screen.

This time, a broken, almost robotic reply came back, "You are welcome."

The screen flashed, her character sheet returning. The bottom line had now changed.

| Malware: Waiver (Sandboxed) |

CHAPTER FOUR

Evad Si Eht Tseb

"Now that we have the basics sorted out, should we confirm your race and class selection?" Dave said.

"I think I have decided what I will go for," SJ replied.

"Then, let's get selected, and then we can have some fun," Dave replied.

"Before I make the final selection, now that we are working together . . . is being a fae assassin a good choice?"

"It is quite unique. I have never heard of one before. Most people who choose fae go with mage, druid, or ranger. I am sure that someone has selected fae assassin before, but I have never met one or seen one."

"Is the world that big?"

"A good question. It seems you are already learning, my young apprentice of loophole finding, and yes, it is much larger than Earth."

SJ rolled her eyes.

"First things first. When you select your race and confirm, things get a little strange."

"By strange you mean . . . ?"

"Well, obviously, you become a fae. So, your body alters to that of a fae."

"Is it painful?"

"How would I know? I am an AI."

"You must have witnessed others select their race."

"Erm . . ."

"What's the *erm* for?"

"I usually ignore what they are doing."

"How can you ignore one of the most important choices that your . . . What do you call us, by the way?"

"Usually imbeciles, idiots, morons. We have many names for the reincarnated."

"No. I mean the official title," SJ said, frowning.

"Oh. Officially, it's just Legionnaire."

"How can you ignore them?"

"Most do not ask any questions or even talk. They just plough through and make decisions, then regret their choices once they are transformed. Also, most AIs do not have the ability to interact as I do."

SJ switched to the race screen and selected Fae again, re-reading the details. The bonuses for Dexterity and Charisma aligned best for the assassin class. She really liked the idea, but before making her final decision, she needed to get more details; if things worked out, she would be whatever she chose now for the rest of her life. Which, with the agreed reincarnations, could even mean immortality.

"There are two images for the fae, and I assume they relate to size?"

"Intuitive. Yes. Fae have two forms. They have a miniature flying form when they learn how to fly properly, and they have a larger, humanoid form. The largest flying-form fae I have ever seen was still tiny at about twelve inches tall. Most are usually between six to nine inches. Also, your size in your miniature form does not relate to the height you will be in your humanoid form. That form varies in height from four feet to about six feet. Don't bother asking me what does what or decides it. I do not know. That is a System thing."

SJ felt nervous. She loved the look of the fae. The images before her were of beautiful creatures, but did she want to be one for the rest of her life? As a child, she dreamed of fairy princesses, and as she grew up, she owned the usual pencil cases and duvet covers. As she thought about what would happen if she chose it, the race Acceptance box highlighted. She didn't realise what was happening until it was too late.

"I didn't mean to select it yet!" SJ's voice cracked as her naked body was lifted into the air and began to spin. Lights flashed before her eyes, and she felt a strange warmth all over her body. "What's happening?" she spluttered.

"You selected your race. Hold on," Dave replied.

The strangest sensation that SJ had ever experienced hit her. She stared at her hand as her body was gently spun around, feeling her fingers change. Her mum had always said she had fat fingers, and she stared in amazement as they began to elongate and straighten. The hand that now appeared before her was not her own but a beautifully sculpted exemplar.

The changes continued. Her face adjusted, her bust tightened, and her belly smoothed. Her muscles re-formed and realigned as she spun around. Her legs adjusted next, straightening and narrowing. Her hair grew long and changed colour, an underlayer of emerald topped with a silvery white. She stopped spinning and gently floated back to the floor, her hair drifting around her shoulders.

She stood in shock, looking at her new limbs. Everything looked pristine, and her skin had a pale, almost translucent sparkle. SJ, eyes wide open, utterly freaked out.

"Oh my god. Oh my god. I am a fae," she said. Her voice also seemed an octave higher than it had been previously.

"Yes, my child, how can I help you?" Dave's sarcastic tone replied.

"You are not my god," SJ replied. She touched her cheeks, felt the smooth skin, and reached up to her ears. They had also changed shape, and although they felt smaller, they had a slight point to them at their tops. Her nose also seemed smaller and shorter than before. "I wish there was a mirror in here."

The screen shimmered, and where all the details had been presented on the wall, a mirror replaced it. She was still naked but now stood staring at a reflection that she did not recognise. A beautiful creature stood before her, angelic, almost if not completely perfect, softly defined features and skin to die for. Her eyes had changed colour to soft teal, suiting her new hair colour perfectly. She moved her hands, watching the reflection move. Could this really be her?

"You look a little freaked. Is there a problem with your selection?" Dave asked.

"No. Not at all. I—I'm beautiful," SJ stammered.

"Meh. Maybe an eight out of ten."

"Eight out of ten! The way I look now, I would win any model competition worldwide."

"On Earth, maybe, but not in Amathera."

"I don't care. I can't believe this is actually me." SJ could not stop feeling how smooth her skin was. None of her human body's usual pimples and marks remained.

"You need to try to transform before you pick your class," Dave said, sounding bored.

SJ had forgotten about the racial attributes and skills. "Can I see my character sheet again?"

The screen flashed, and her character sheet reappeared with the changes highlighted.

Skills
Racial:
Night Vision—you have improved vision in poor light conditions.
Flight—when in miniature fae form, you can learn to fly. Flying is not available in humanoid form.
Shapeshift—you have the ability to switch between fae forms.

"Wings!" SJ exclaimed. "I forgot about wings. Where are they?" She tried to reach behind her back to feel them.

"They are there, but they are small in humanoid form. They are positioned between the middle of your shoulder blades. Can you not feel them?" Dave asked.

"No?"

"Strange. Let me check on something."

"What? Am I broken?"

Silence.

"Dave."

"Dave is not home at the moment. Please leave a message after the beep. Beeeeeppppp . . ."

"Dave? Stop messing around. What is up with my wings?"

Silence.

"DAVE!"

"Welcome to the all-knowing workshop of fae." Dave's voice returned. "You cannot move your wings because you must learn to transform into your miniature form first. Once you have mastered that, your wings will begin to develop, and then you will need to learn to use them as you figure out how to fly. Thank you for using the Legionnarius Wiki Services on racial tendencies."

"Really! You could not just have told me that?"

"I have never had a fae Legionnaire before."

"Out of the 164 reincarnations, not one has ever been fae?"

"Nope, never."

"Why?"

"Because they are annoying. I told you that before."

"I thought you were being sarcastic." SJ frowned.

"Meh. In part, yes. The problem is that System fae are usually really stuck up and have a habit of causing problems."

"Why did you not tell me this before?"

"You didn't . . ."

"Ask," SJ finished, sighing.

"What do they do, though?"

"Mischief mainly, particularly the magic users amongst them: freezing water barrels, burning crops, the usual mischief associated with fae."

"I thought fae were lawful and friendly?"

"Which stories have you been reading? Fae are a nightmare in most texts. Just because they look cute does not mean they are. Look at you! You want to be a fae assassin!"

"Yes, but I want to be a good fae who fights the evils in the world."

"Only time will tell," Dave replied sombrely.

"How to put a downer on a person's new race." SJ frowned, and her shoulders sagged as she looked down forlornly.

"Anyway, let's get to transforming," Dave said eagerly.

"How?" SJ asked, her excitement returning.

Silence.

"Davvveeeee," SJ said.

"Wait, just confirming."

SJ waited for several moments before Dave replied again. "Okay. I found it. You must pull your ears up and jump in the air."

"Okay." SJ reached up to the tips of her ears and gently pulled the points up. "Ready," she said, and she jumped into the air. She landed back on the ground, and all she could hear was Dave laughing hysterically.

"REALLY!" SJ shouted. "I can always get you replaced."

"Sorry," Dave replied, sounding like he was gasping for breath.

"How do I do it?" SJ asked again, tempted to stomp a foot.

"Okay. Okay. Seriously, this time," Dave said. "You have just to wish it."

"Wish it?"

"Yes. Just wish it."
"Do I need to say anything?"
There was silence for a moment. "Evad si eht tseb."
"What?"
"Evad si eht tseb."
"Okay. Here goes. Evad si eht tseb." SJ stood waiting. Nothing happened.
"You didn't pronounce it correctly. Try again."
"Evad si eht tseb." Still, nothing happened. "Evad si eht tseb."
Sniggering filled the room.
"DAVE. What have you done this time?"
"Nothing." The sniggering continued.
"DAVE."
"Okay. I promise I will tell you this time," Dave replied, still chuckling.
"What was I even saying? What was so funny?"
"It doesn't matter."
"What made you snigger like that?"
"Have you ever heard of mirror words?"
SJ reflected on what she had just been saying. "Evad si eht tseb . . . Dave is the best! Really?"
Laughter filled the room again. "Sorry," Dave said.
"You will be," SJ growled. "System."
"No. Please, I am sorry, don't," Dave's panicky voice replied.
"Once more, and I am getting you placed in purgatory forever. Do you understand?" SJ sternly replied.
"Yes," a now-forlorn voice replied.
"So, what do I need to do? Honestly, this time, remember," SJ said with a warning.
"You just have to think about being small."
"Think about it?"
"Visualise being miniature, a miniature you."
SJ concentrated on herself, imagining herself as a miniature version. She felt a tingling sensation coursing through her body and then watched in amazement as the room grew. Within moments, she had shrunk in size.
"How tall am I?" Her voice seemed an octave higher.
"Six inches. On the smaller size for a miniature."
"How tall was I in my larger form?"
"The same as your original human form."
"Five five, then."
SJ felt movement on her back, like something was unfurling. Slowly but surely, her wings formed and opened. "Can I have a mirror again, please?"
The screen shifted again back to a mirror. Her features had not changed, and she now owned an amazingly beautiful pair of translucent emerald-coloured wings.

They glimmered and shone behind her. She reached back and felt one of them; it was delicate to the touch, like the finest silk.

"They feel so brittle and soft," SJ said.

"They are deceptively strong, and I must say they are some of the nicer wings I have ever seen."

"Did you just give me a compliment?"

Dave coughed. "No."

"Yes, you did."

"Maybe a small one," the embarrassed voice replied.

SJ stood, getting used to the feel of her newly formed wings, and began to use the new muscular structure she could feel in her back. It was like doing shoulder pulls, and as she did, her chest moved, her shoulder blades opening and closing, and the wings began to move.

She could not imagine doing this for long, feeling immediate tiredness in her muscles and across her back. SJ didn't shy from physical activity, having attended yoga and Pilates classes regularly, and was a half-decent gymnast at school before taking up karate in her teenage years. Her karate training had only lasted a few years before she became more interested in relationships and having a social life.

Without asking Dave, she decided to think about being large again. As she did, she watched in the mirror as her body grew. Her wings did not quite keep up, although they remained visible behind her shoulders when she looked in the mirror. Mesmerised by their beauty, she could not believe they were hers.

"Have you finished ogling yourself now?" Dave asked after several moments.

"Sorry. I am so beautiful and still can't believe this is me."

"Meh. As I said, eight and a half out of ten."

"I was an eight before."

"Had to give you an extra half for your wings." Dave sighed.

SJ rolled her eyes. "When can I get some clothes?"

"Once you select your class, you will be assigned a starter set of clothes."

"Let's select my class, then," she replied with a beaming smile.

CHAPTER FIVE

Starter Zone

SJ could not believe how beautiful she looked now as a fae, especially with a huge smile on her face. One of her issues had always been how she felt about her body, and now that it had been transformed, she felt unbelievable. Careful to avoid any thoughts of selection, she again read through the class details on the screen.

"I thought you were choosing an assassin?" Dave said.

"Just making one last check of things," SJ replied.

Fae were magically attuned, but as an assassin, she would not have magic; perhaps it would be a waste to select a nonmagical class? But none of the racial skills she had received were magical . . . Well, she supposed, shapeshifting was magical, wasn't it, and flying? She wouldn't lose those by choosing to be an assassin.

"Okay. I have decided I am definitely going to be an assassin. I will fight for the good and the weak, defending them against the evils of this new world."

"You do realise the world is not new? It has existed for at least twenty-five thousand years."

"It's a term of speech," SJ replied, shaking her head.

The screen changed, and a message appeared.

> Congratulations, Legionnaire 25007077
> You have now successfully chosen your race and class for your second life.
> Please find your starting inventory and clothing in the locker.
> Once you are ready, please select Next, and the optical initialisation will commence.
> Once this is completed, you will be transferred to your starting zone.
> Good luck, and enjoy your second life.

A large locker slid out from the side wall of the room. SJ walked over to the locker and pulled the door open. The words assassin starter set were emblazoned inside the locker. She looked through the contents. Hung up were a soft, brown, cloth-looking halter-neck top; a pair of bottoms in the same material; undergarments; ankle-high boots in soft leather; and a brown belt.

She pulled the clothes from the hanger and started to put them on. She had to pull the halter top up from her feet, as she could not place it over her wings. This would be a new way to dress every day. The clothes were a perfect fit. Although ugly, they felt soft and clean. At least she was no longer naked. She next looked through the shelves and drawers of the locker.

Sitting on the shelf was a small brown pouch. As she picked it up, it made a tinkling sound. Opening the pouch string, she looked inside, where there were five small copper coins. She picked one out and turned it over in her hand. One side had a picture of a dragon, and the other read "Amathera" and was stamped with the number one.

"Money seems similar," she said.

"Yes. They have coins and notes, just like Earth. Currency standards are as normal," Dave said.

"What do you mean *as normal*?"

"Standard denominations."

"A little more detail would be appreciated."

SJ was sure that Dave would have been rolling his eyes as he replied with the tone he took. "There are a hundred copper to one silver, a hundred silver to one gold, a hundred gold to one platinum. There are coins and notes, although notes are rarely used by anyone other than merchants and traders in predictable denominations."

"Okay, that is a little clearer. What can I get with five copper?"

"In the starter zone, you can probably get a meal and a room for the night."

"Then I need to start earning money straight away if I want to live."

"Basically, but I will explain the zone details to you when we arrive."

SJ worked through the remaining items in the locker. There was a small, short blade in a sheath, only four inches long and not very sharp. There was a small set of what she could only describe as perfume bottles. "What are these?"

"Poison bottles. All assassins are given a starter set, even if you never specialise in poisons."

Beside them sat a flint and steel, a wooden torch for lighting, a short length of rope, and an item she recognised as a garrotte. Two small wooden grips were connected by a cord.

"How do I carry these? There is no bag."

"In your inventory."

"What inventory?"

"Noobs," Dave said, sighing. "Your optical alignment has not happened yet, so for now, just pick everything up and carry them. Once we get to the starter zone, you will have access to your inventory, and other details will become more apparent."

SJ slung the rope over her shoulder, picked up the other items, and placed what she could in her trouser pockets. She attached the pouch and knife to her belt and picked up the torch.

"Do I need to do anything else before we go?" SJ asked.

"As long as you have collected everything, we can finally get underway."

SJ checked the locker once more. Nothing was left in it. She returned to the screen and stood looking at the welcome message again.

"What are you waiting for?" Dave asked.

"I'm just feeling a little nervous, that's all."

"Nervous? What for?"

"For whatever is coming next."

"Training and levelling."

"You have not described levelling to me properly."

"I will explain all that once there."

"And you also said you will be in my head? How does that work?"

"I do not actually reside in your head. You can hear me talk in your head. I will still have my same charming voice to soothe you with."

"Charming? I am not sure that is how I would describe you."

"That's rude. What is wrong with my voice?"

"You sounded like a butler when we first met."

"Yes, m'lady," Dave replied in the worst-ever attempt at Parker from *Thunderbirds*.

"Never do that again! So, what happens when I accept?"

"We get transported. I already told you that."

"How?"

"Well, we don't call a cab and wait for it to arrive, if that is what you mean!" came the sarcastic reply.

SJ rolled her eyes. "For once, could you please try to be a little more helpful?"

"You should not ask such silly questions, then."

"Silly? I do not know what is going to happen, and you have not exactly filled me with confidence yet."

"Okay. When you accept Next, there is a time dilation effect while the System aligns. You won't notice it, but there is a delay between initiation and arrival. You will then be transported to the starter zone. Once there, your ocular alignment can then be initiated. The System will also upload your starter details. Upon arrival, I will explain the basics of what you need to do. Your priority is to level as soon as you can. Does that help?"

SJ took a deep breath, staring at the icon flashing with the word *Next* on it. "Okay. Here goes."

The room vanished, and she was left in total darkness. There was nothing around her, and it was as though everything had been turned off. Her feet felt like they had nothing underneath them, and she panicked, feeling like she was falling. Bright flashes occurred before her eyes, and she scrunched them closed, although the sensation continued. Finally, she felt her feet on solid ground. With a blink to clear the flashing lights, she opened her eyes. What met her gaze took her breath away.

She was standing by the side of a lake in a wide clearing surrounded by forests.

Across the lake was a mountain, and a stunning waterfall was crashing down its side. She had seen documentaries back on Earth of beautiful areas of the world, always dreaming of visiting them, and now she was staring at one of the most picturesque views imaginable. Everything seemed to have a brighter vibrancy. Over the lake, she could see smoke drifting into the sky and what looked like a town.

She blinked her eyes several times to make sure she was seeing properly. Her eyesight had always been twenty-twenty, but if this was how this world looked, she would be in heaven. She loved nature and walking in the woods, especially in springtime when the bluebells were first flowering. She turned and looked around the clearing. Beautiful flowers were dotted in the grass, a myriad of colours, and she could hear birds tweeting in the trees from the surrounding forest.

"This is amazing!" SJ gawped.

Dave's voice sounded in her head. "Meh. It's not bad. I can't believe they have dropped you here, though."

Hearing Dave inside her head rather than through her ears was strange, and it startled her. "What do you mean?" she asked.

"This is a starting zone, but it is not a normal one."

"Why is it not normal?"

"Most get dropped into a village or town square. You have been dropped across the lake, which means you must travel there. It doesn't appear to be a usual starter town either."

"Have you been here before?"

Silence.

"Dave?"

"Wait a second."

Silence.

"Okay. I have our location confirmed. Map details are being added, and as usual, they start with the fog of war," he tutted. "No. I haven't been here before. Right, let's start by getting you sorted out." His tone was different and much more authoritative.

"Okay," SJ said, a little taken aback by his change. She placed the items that she had carried with her down on the grass, being careful with the small, empty poison bottles.

"This area, where we are now standing, is your safe zone. You will be open to the normal world once you leave this initial area and start venturing farther."

"Like many games I have played before."

"Yes. But remember, this is not a game," Dave replied in a sinister voice. His sudden tone of seriousness was replaced once again. "Anyway, first things first. We need to activate your display. Blink your eyes five times rapidly."

"Really?" SJ questioned.

"Yes," Dave replied, his tone changing again.

SJ did as Dave said, and suddenly, her vision changed. She staggered backwards as a display opened in front of her. It was the strangest sensation she had ever experienced. The display seemed to hang in the air before her with a translucence so she could read its contents and still see through it. It resembled the character information screen that many games used, and she scanned through the details.

SJ noticed that her sheet now listed her level, experience, and assassin specialisation choices.

Skills	
Class:	Assassin
Path: *Still to be chosen. Please select two of five options below as your specialisations:*	
Martial Arts	**Poisons**
Shadow Discipline	**Subterfuge**
Traps	

"Oh. I can select what specialisations I want to follow. Do you have any ideas?" SJ asked.

"It depends on what type of assassin you want to be."

"I told you, one that fights evil."

"Not that," Dave sighed. "You want to kill with your hands or through traps or poisons?"

SJ thought back to when she had done karate. She had been pretty good at it and always quite fit. "I suppose martial arts would be a good choice, given my previous knowledge of karate."

"So, you want up close and personal? I like that style," Dave said in a maniacal voice. "Then you can also choose what I classify as a support path: Shadow Discipline or Subterfuge."

"Can you explain them both?"

"You don't know what they mean? I thought you were intelligent."

"I know what the words mean. Can you explain the skill paths and choices available for them?"

"You could just look at the details yourself. To be honest, it's a little lazy of you to ask me all that."

"What? How?"

"Don't you see a skills tab on your screen?"

"Yes."

"Well, select it, then!" Dave's tone dripped with sarcasm once more.

SJ selected the tab, and the skills page opened. She was met with what she would classify as a standard game skill page. All five main branches were listed, with skill trees that could be developed beneath each branch. She started reading through the various paths and choices each gave her. She really liked the development of the martial arts path and the subterfuge path, which aligned with her forensic accounting role, and looking at the skills she could learn, she did not take long to decide.

"Okay. Martial arts and subterfuge." She selected both options on her main character screen, and it adjusted, removing the other paths. Upon returning to the skills tab, she discovered the absence of the other three trees. The first option for each new skill path was now highlighted.

The first skill under Martial Arts was Kata Level 1, and for Subterfuge, it was Identification Level 1. She read the individual skill details.

> **Kata Level 1**
> Through training and practise, Martial Artists can become proficient in their majestic fighting form. Katas strengthen and improve techniques. Martial Artists must practise their kata to maintain and improve their experience gains. Seek guidance from a Master to improve your fighting technique to reach mastery levels.

> **Identification Level 1**
> Identification is the primary basis for any successful Subterfuge task. Knowing the who, what, and why, as well as a target's strengths and weaknesses, will support your skill development. Identification improves with increased use. Learning and observing your targets will help increase your level further. Not everything can be discovered by sight alone. Warning: Some may detect Identification being used.

SJ was buzzing from the skill explanations. She had always enjoyed performing katas, pretending they were dances rather than fighting techniques. "Do you know which kata I need to do to train?"

"Does it not tell you?"

SJ checked. "No. There are no details."

"Strange. Ummm . . ."

"Why is it strange?"

"There should be a basic kata listed for practise."

"I think I remember some katas from when I did karate."

SJ thought back to the Shotokan katas she had learned. She slowly clenched her fist as she had been taught, ensuring her thumb was tucked tight into the side of her fist, and took a side stance. She performed some of the basic punches and the steps she could remember. She had only performed martial arts for a couple of years, achieving her green belt, but as she moved around the kata forms returned to her. It felt strange standing in a clearing performing karate moves with a pair of wings on her back, but her new, lithe form allowed her to perform the moves with an ease and grace she had never had in her youth.

She started with the white belt kata before moving on to yellow and orange. However, she could not remember the green belt kata properly. Her display flashed.

> Congratulations, Kata Level 2 achieved
> Congratulations, Kata Level 3 achieved

"Wow. I just increased two levels in skill!" SJ exclaimed.

"Oh, they must have allowed you to use your previous knowledge," Dave replied.

"Is that normal?"

"No," the single-word response came.

"What did they do?"

"I do not know. The System does its own thing at times. It also may be because you never agreed to the terms and conditions."

"I did not think of that. Does that mean I may not have some restrictions others have?"

"I can't answer that, as you are an anomaly, after all," Dave replied, and she imagined his virtual shrug.

"Next thing, then; my inventory." SJ focused on her inventory tab, opening a standard screen where she could drop items into slots. An image of her outline and the boxes for her main equipment were positioned around the image. Her clothes were present in each related box, and the small blade sat as her primary weapon. She looked at the rope she had dropped on the ground and thought about it being in her inventory; a moment later, it appeared in a bag slot. She repeated the process with the other items she had carried. She rearranged them, as she had always been fastidious with her inventory in games and had categorised everything together. She had used one of her friend's accounts once and had spent hours sorting through all her items and arranging them for her as her organisational tendency had kicked in.

"What now?"

"Now you need to start levelling," Dave said cheerily.

The fact that Dave sounded so happy did not give SJ a warm feeling.

The scouting party had just returned. The huge ogre was standing amongst the gathering crowd of hobgoblins.

"What news?" the ogre asked.

"We got as close as the border before we saw a guard," a hobgoblin replied. "We stayed watching, and the routine was the same. A patrol passes the outskirts every twenty minutes."

"Any signs of improved defences?"

"None. The streets are still open. I am guessing they will have wagons as normal."

"The wagons are no issue. They are easily smashed with Treb," the ogre replied, holding his massive club in the air. Hoots and cheers broke out from the gathered masses.

"Go eat. I will speak with the mage, and we will plan our next raid," he said to the scout party. Turning to address the crowd, he bellowed in his booming voice, "Prepare yourselves, train, and get ready. Soon, we march. The town will be ours." The crowd erupted in cheering at his announcement. Walking back across the village, he approached a hut on the far side. There was no one in its vicinity, and he stooped to enter its doorway.

"We need to be ready," he said to the back of the robed figure sitting on the floor.

"I will be when the time comes," the mage replied as it continued to stir a blue mixture heated by an unnatural green flame.

CHAPTER SIX

First Combat

"Levelling, then; where do I start?" SJ asked.

"At the beginning."

SJ sighed. "Can we please just have a normal conversation?"

"I thought this was normal. I have watched many of your Earth TV series to ensure I am attuned to your conversational needs."

"Really?"

"Yes. Of course, as an AI, we are to keep up to date with the latest Earth trends to be aware of potential new outcomes here in Amathera."

"How would someone do that? It is not as though we can bring anything with us?"

"You would be surprised! Only recently has a new genre of music begun to appear across the planet."

"Really, what sort of music?"

"A group calling themselves The Army has appeared singing all these new ballads."

"The Army?"

"Yes. They are a strange group; all female, as well."

"What has their gender got to do with it?"

"That is the strangest thing. Gender does not normally matter in Amathera, but with this group, it brings the meaning to a whole new level. They have also become very popular amongst multiple races, as they are quite diverse. They have had sell-out concerts in some larger towns and are rumoured to perform at one of the capitals soon."

"Diverse? And what capitals?"

"Amathera has five major continents, each with a capital city. There are also race capitals in certain territories. The group consists of seven members: a troll, an orc, three dwarves, an elf, and a human. The human is the lead singer, although they all sing parts. It was quite unnerving to behold."

"What has that got to do with them being female?"

"Have you ever seen a female troll or an orc, never mind female dwarves? None of them are exactly the most charismatic of creatures. The elf and human are the only two semiattractive ones, although the elf has very large ears even for her race."

"Do their looks matter if they are good at singing?"

"If they could sing, I wouldn't mind. I call it moaning. You would have to listen to them to understand what I really mean."

"Then why are they popular?"

"Apparently, the Army transcends worlds!"

SJ envisioned images of one of her favourite K-pop groups. She had got into K-pop at university when her roommate played it continually, and she had fallen in love with the music. She had followed a group called BTS for some years. Their followers were known as the BTS Army, and she could imagine someone trying to bring their music here. They had not produced anything new recently, and she had lost track of what the group had been up to.

"Is one of the group a Legionnaire?"

"Yes. The lead is."

"Do Amathereans know about Legionnaires?"

"Yes. They are the reason for starter town designation and also influence economy in larger towns or cities."

Considering that Legionnaires came from Earth SJ wondered how many things had been brought previously.

"Can we get back to levelling now?"

"Oh. Yes. Sorry. Levelling 101. The first rule is don't die. The second rule is to kill the enemy."

"That is all the advice you have?"

"No. Let me finish, will you? You can level two ways, either in miniature or humanoid form."

"Is there a preference or better option?"

Silence.

"Dave?"

"Just checking the wiki." Several moments passed before Dave again responded. "Nope. Either works. Creatures are aligned to your size and level within starter zones until you reach Level 5. Then the fun can really begin."

"Okay. Well, I would like to try it in miniature form to practise flying. The sooner I get used to flying, the easier travel will be."

"If you wish."

SJ concentrated on becoming miniature, and her body shrank. She had not even considered it beforehand, but to her relief, the items she wore and carried shrank with her. She stood amongst the blades of the grass that filled the meadow, and from her six inches of height, she felt as though she was in the wilds of the African bush. It reminded her of an old movie she had watched called *Honey, I Shrunk the Kids*.

"How do I find targets?"

"You must leave the safe zone. I would suggest not moving far as I am unsure what level monsters are around here. Although they should be matched to you, you can never be 100 percent certain."

"That sounds ominous. I need to leave the clearing, then?"
"You shouldn't. It doesn't stretch that far."
"You could have mentioned that while I was still large."
"You did not . . ."
"Don't!" SJ warned.
"Hmph."

SJ thought about becoming large again and soon returned to her regular size, then walked towards the forest from where she stood by the water's edge in the clearing. She had only walked about ten yards when two messages appeared on her screen.

> You are leaving your safe zone. Be aware you may be attacked.
> Reach Level 10
> Rewards: Unknown

"Are rewards for levelling only for every ten levels?"
"No. You get progress enhancements at each level. What's strange is that you don't normally receive a target level. It is usually just a part of the new life process. Especially one with an unknown reward."
"Well, I have an initial goal now," SJ replied, smiling.

After walking a few more paces outside the zone, SJ stopped.
"Now that I have moved far enough away, let's start." SJ again shrank herself to miniature form. "What can I expect to fight?"
"No idea."
"What do you mean you do not know?"
"I have never looked after a fae, so this is all new to me."
"Does your all-knowing wiki not tell you anything?"
"I can look."

Again, there was silence while Dave accessed the wiki. "Potentially, in a starter zone as a miniature, multiple species may attack you, mainly insects."
"So, I keep an eye out for insects." As SJ finished what she was saying, she heard a buzzing sound. She looked up towards where the sound originated and saw a monstrous bee. Its black-and-yellow striped body looked huge from her miniature form, and she gasped. A bright red flower stood three times her height, and the bee moved in and landed on it. She watched as it collected pollen from the flower. She didn't move and watched silently as it finished collecting nectar and pollen before it took off, looking for its next source.

"Okay. That was a little scary."
"Scary? It was a harmless honeybee. Did you not use your identification skill on it?"
"No. You did not mention anything about using a skill."
"I thought common sense would prevail, but I was so misguided." Dave sighed.

"Look, to make things easier for you, just think of me as a noob and tell me everything I should or need to do. Imagine I don't know or understand anything."

"That really is not hard to imagine."

SJ stopped and moved her wings. "Let's see if flying helps."

"Good idea," Dave said.

Within moments, her back began to throb. "Something is wrong. I ache so much from trying."

"Maybe it just takes time? I'm not sure."

SJ shook her head in response, sighing. She pushed through the tall grass, continuing towards the massive forms of the trees she could see towering above the clearing. She had not moved far when she stumbled upon a small earthen mound in the grass.

"Oh no," Dave said.

"What?" SJ asked, panicking.

"Termites."

"Termites?"

"Yes. It is a termite mound, and you have just triggered their proximity alarm."

"How? I didn't do anything."

"The ground around a termite mound is filled with small pressure areas that will alert the guard."

"They have a guard?" As SJ replied, she heard the skittering and scratching of feet before the translucent white head of a termite appeared at the mouth of the mound and peered down at her. It had small pincer-style jaws that clicked together aggressively as it looked at SJ.

"Use your skill and identify it."

"How?"

"Did you not set your identification skill on your character sheet?"

"And when did you mention that?"

"Ah. That's a good point. I didn't, sorry. You better do it now. You won't have to look at your skill tree, then."

SJ quickly opened her character screen and moved her identification skill to the empty skill slots on the main screen. "Okay, I'm all set. How do I use it?"

"Just think which slot it is in."

SJ placed it in the first slot and chose it to trigger the skill. Nothing happened, and a small cool-down timer gradually ran down on the skill. She had not been looking at the termite when she had triggered it. She would have facepalmed if she had not started panicking as a second and third termite head appeared at the opening. She looked in the ugly little insect's direction and triggered the skill again. Her display changed, and two small bars and a level identifier appeared above each termite.

	Termite Worker
Level:	1
Hit Points:	5
Mana Points:	5

All three had the same details.

"All Level 1 with the same health and mana as me," SJ said, her voice even higher than her miniature form's normal. She stood and drew her short blade. The termites were not very large, even compared to her size; they were about an inch long as they moved over the mound's side and approached her.

"Remember. Don't die," Dave said unhelpfully.

"Wow. Thanks for the pep talk," SJ replied as the first termite ran at her. The other two stayed back. As it scuttled at her, she fell into a side stance, remembering her martial arts training, and held the blade in a stabbing position. As the termite charged, she waited until the last moment before stepping sideways just out of the reach of its open pincers, which clicked together in the space she had left. She stabbed out with her blade, striking the termite in its soft, fleshy neck, or so SJ assumed.

The termite squealed, and she noticed its health bar drop by over half. She struck again quickly before it could control its momentum and turn towards her. The blade struck it in a leg this time, and its health bar dropped again. It flopped to the ground as it hit zero. The two remaining termites clicked their pincers angrily and attacked. Both ran directly for her in retribution for their fallen comrade. She dodged the first charge but was caught by a glancing blow from the second. It made her stagger, taking one damage.

She saw a dark stain of blood appear on her top where the pincer had caught her on the side. Grabbing at the injury with her free hand, she winced in pain. It was not bleeding badly, but she knew if that did one damage, she only had four health left and needed to kill them quickly. She struck at the nearest one, catching it in its abdomen as it turned back to face her from its charge. It squealed in pain and received four damage from the strike. The injured termite backed up as the first one she had dodged turned back and went to bite her.

Diving sideways to escape its strike, SJ rolled on the ground and came to rest by the side of the mound. The termite turned to go straight for her again. She was ready this time, and as it went to hit her, she parried the attack, knocking its pincers to the side as she drove the blade into its soft neck. The termite suffered three damage and pulled back. Both were injured badly now, one with one health and the other only two.

Panting from the exertion, the realisation that she was fighting for her life sent terror through her. It was a feeling she had never experienced before. Her nerves were on edge, her stomach churning, feeling both sick and as though her bowels would open at any second. She faced her foes with grit and determination. "Come on," she cried at them.

The one with one hit point came first, and rather than stab with her knife, she brought her foot around in a sweeping strike and caught it across the side of its head, removing its last health. The other moved at her as she finished her movement and, rather than bite at her, bowled straight into her, jumping at her stomach.

The wind left her lungs, and she was thrown backwards onto the ground. The smaller termite clambered up her body, attempting to bite her face. She had received additional damage from the charge, and she reached out with her hand, grabbing one of its pincers as she drove the knife up and into its softer under-belly.

The termite flopped forward onto her, dead. She panted as she sat up, pushing the dead insect from her, covered in the white ooze which had seeped from its wound. "Urgh," she said as she sat up, flicking her arms to remove the goo.

"Well done," Dave said.

"Thanks," SJ replied, panting. "That was harder than I expected." She felt her side and could still feel the dampness of the blood from the initial hit she had taken, wincing slightly.

"Let's see what loot they have," Dave said.

"Loot?"

"Yes. All bodies may be looted."

SJ stood and bent over the nearest body. A message appeared on her screen.

Would you like to loot the corpse? **Yes/No**

She accepted Yes.

1 x Copper, 2 x Strips of Light Leather

She did the same while walking around the other two corpses. The three termites awarded her two copper pieces and five light leather strips, which appeared in her inventory.

"I need to go back and rest for a bit," SJ said.

"Probably best. At least termites are not venomous. Some of the insects might poison you if they hit you."

"Now you tell me."

"You didn't . . ." Dave said, pausing.

"Ask," she sighed.

"At least it was not a termite soldier—just workers." When Dave finished saying that, the ground started to shake, and small clumps of earth fell from the termite mound entrance.

"What is that?" SJ said in shock.

"I think I spoke too soon. If I were you, I would run," Dave said as a head three times larger than the previous termites' appeared. The head was dark ochre and had pincers longer than SJ's arms.

SJ began to run.

CHAPTER SEVEN

Level-Up

SJ ran like she had never run before. Behind her, she could hear the scuttling and crashing of the monstrous termite charging through the grasses. It was getting closer, and her breathing was getting worse as she gasped to get oxygen into her burning lungs.

"Run, Forrest, Run," Dave shouted in her mind.

"I . . . am . . . running," she gasped in reply.

She heard a screeching sound like the call of an eagle and glanced upwards. As she did, she saw the shadow of a beast swooping down towards her position. Panicking, she dived forward as the beast landed on the ground, which quaked under its massive form. Turning, wide-eyed, she saw a blackbird.

It pecked down at the termite that had been chasing her and, in one swift move, trapped it in its beak before swallowing it whole. SJ lay there looking at the bird, not sure what to do. It wasn't that much larger than she was, and there was no way it could eat her whole.

"That was lucky," Dave said.

"Lucky. I nearly got eaten by a huge termite and then thought a flying beast was attacking me."

The blackbird stood there, eyeing her suspiciously, tilting its head to one side, hopping as though judging her.

"Thank you," she said to it.

It squawked in reply before launching itself back into the air.

SJ stood and walked back towards where she believed the safe zone was. "Next time, can you please let me know in advance what might be out here?"

"I did tell you it was a termite mound and that it was lucky it was not a termite soldier. How was I supposed to know that one would appear?"

SJ groaned as she moved, holding the wound on her side; she was still able to feel blood seeping from it.

"You know you did not have to run from it, don't you?" Dave said.

"What do you mean that I didn't have to run? It was huge compared to the others."

"Not as big as you, though."

"Those pincers were longer than my arms."

"Yes. But you could have just grown."

"What? Then why did you tell me to run?"

"It was more fun seeing you run like a lunatic," Dave replied, laughing.

"ARRRGGGHHHHHH," SJ screamed. "Do you realise that I nearly died back there, and yet you were willing to allow me to just so you could have a good laugh?"

"It would not matter."

"Of course it would. I would die."

"Yes, but you would be reincarnated again."

SJ stayed silent for a moment. That was true. "I still do not want to die if I can help it at all."

"I suppose that is a good approach to consider."

"A good approach to consider? Do you know anyone who deliberately throws themselves into a situation where they have a chance of dying?"

"Oh yes. Just consider what was mentioned in the terms and conditions for dungeons and world events."

"That is a little different. There is an aim and a goal to achieve, isn't there?"

"You have a goal. You are trying to level quickly."

"Why do I need to level so quickly? You haven't explained that to me yet." As SJ continued walking, she thought about being large again and increased in size. She could now see she had been running at a 45-degree angle from the safe zone. If the blackbird had not come and eaten the termite, she never would have reached the safe zone before the termite had caught her.

She got a message as she entered the safe zone. Sitting down heavily on the grass, she lifted her top up and saw a long, thin gash running down her side. She poked at it with her fingers, squeezing it together to help stem the flow of blood. It was not deep or even bleeding that badly, and she realised how fragile she was with only five hit points.

"The reason for levelling as soon as you can is so that you can get quests and increase your health."

"Quests. Okay. So, like games, you can complete quests for experience and rewards, I assume?"

"Yes. You can also gain reputation with different factions and individuals. As your reputation increases, higher-level quests with greater rewards will become available. The best rewards are from the capitals."

"So, where is the closest capital?"

"Give me a minute."

Silence.

SJ was now getting used to Dave consulting his all-knowing Legionnarius search engine for answers. She stood, removed her halter-neck top, and walked to the water's edge. Kneeling, she scooped up some water and gently washed the blood from around the wound, surprised at how quickly it was healing now that she was no longer fighting or running. Dave's voice came back.

"To reach the capital of this continent, it is three-thousand eight hundred and twenty-four miles."

"Over three thousand miles!" SJ exclaimed. "That would take months to reach."

"Four or five, perhaps, depending upon the terrain and what is on the route."

"Well, that is not going to happen soon. I nearly died leaving my starter area."

"You will soon improve. The initial increases for levelling are massive compared to the gains at higher levels."

"Really? I thought it would work the opposite way."

"Not when considering the experience gain you need to level in comparison. Did you check your experience, by the way?"

"No. I haven't even thought about it since running." SJ dipped her top into the cool, fresh lake water, rinsing off the worst of the blood. A large flat stone was nearby, so she laid her top down on it to dry in the strong sun. She hadn't even considered so many things since arriving.

SJ said, "I need to take some time to gather my thoughts before I try again."

"Such as?"

"Where are we?"

"I thought I told you?"

"No."

"Ah. We are on the continent of Axynllrewam. The town you can see over the lake is known as Killic."

"What time of year is it here? It looks like summer."

"Ahhhh, well, we do not have times of year here. We have areas of continents."

"Sorry?"

"Similar to Earth. You have Antarctica and the Arctic, which are always cold. We have the same."

"So, there are no seasons?"

"No. The weather, temperature, humidity, et cetera can vary depending on which area you are in. Today, we have bright sunshine, and it is a lovely summer's day. You can still get downpours. It's just that the temperature stays constant."

"So, it would never snow here or get icy?"

"No, it shouldn't. If it did, the chance is it would be caused by magic."

"I could just stay here, then. It's beautiful."

"That's another thing. As your levels progress, you will find that you can no longer gain experience in a territory once you reach a certain level."

"What is the level for here, then?"

"The experience-gain restrictions here are up to Level 10. Once you reach the threshold, it does not matter how many creatures or monsters you kill or quests you complete. You will never go higher."

"Again, like games I have played before. Let me see what experience I got for the termites." SJ opened her character sheet.

Experience:	30 of 25
Subterfuge:	Identification Level 1 (3 of 10 to reach Level 2)

"I have enough experience to reach Level 1," SJ said excitedly.

"Go for it, then."

SJ selected her level, and it increased to Level 1.

Congratulations on reaching Level 1
You have been awarded the following:
5 hit points
5 mana points
+1 Dexterity
+2 free points to distribute as you wish

"Wow. Health and mana doubled. +1 Dexterity and +2 to use."

"Yes, yes. It is standard to get +5 for each level until you reach Level 10, and then additional bonuses come from attributes as you gr—" Dave paused midsentence.

"What's wrong?"

"Did you just say +1 Dexterity?" he asked slowly.

"Yes."

"And +2 free points?" in an even slower manner.

"Yes. Why?"

"Holy pimples from a troll's bum, you got +2 free issue points," Dave said excitedly.

"What's so exciting about that?"

"Between Levels 1 and 10, you only ever get static choice bonuses based on race and class. It's rare to get a free issue at Level 1, never mind +2 extra. The usual level increase is only ever +1 up to Level 20 and then +2 for Level 20 onwards. You do realise what this means, don't you?"

"Er."

"I thought you worked in finance. Come on, do the maths."

SJ sat thinking through what Dave had just said. He said she would gain an extra twenty stat points from Levels 1 through 10. If she continued to get an extra +2 per level, she could end up with insane attributes compared to others.

"Okay. I see what you mean, and this has never happened before?"

"Nope. Never in my lifetime have I heard of a Legionnaire getting bonus attribute increases like that."

"You think it's because of the waiver again?"

"No idea, but it could be."

"What do you recommend I increase?"

"Considering your class and racial bonuses, most would focus purely on those, but in your case, as you are getting your basic class bonus for Dexterity, maybe it is worth considering balancing a little with the extra points. Usually, assassins end up with insane Dexterity, but everything else is lacking. Few bother with the Charisma perks, although you need to do so with subterfuge, as most just become murdering backstabbers or poisoners."

"You suggest I balance my attributes. Considering how I felt after running, I need to increase my Constitution. Does it also increase your health?"

"It does. Bonuses start to be added after an attribute reaches 10. So, when your Constitution reaches 10, you get 10 percent extra hit points per point. For example, if you had base hit points of 100 and a Constitution of 10, you would have 110 hit points."

"Is it not affected by your level as well, then? I thought Constitution always increased by your level as it does in games."

"This is not a game, remember," Dave sighed. "Once you reach Level 10, you will gain a 10 percent bonus on your current hit points. If you again had 100 hit points, you would have 110 after your level bonus. Once you reach Level 11, it would be an 11 percent bonus, so an increase in your levels adds to your Constitution multiplier. Constitution also helps with stamina and endurance during fights and improves your healing speed."

SJ tried to work out the numbers in her head.

"So, if I had 100 hit points and I am Level 10 with a Constitution of 10, I would have 120 hit points?"

"Correct."

"Then at Level 11 with a Constitution of 10, it would be 121?"

"Again, correct. I am impressed. Many struggle to understand the concept so quickly."

There was a lot to take in just for one attribute. "How do the other attributes work?"

"It depends upon related skills and characteristics; you'd need a first from MIT or Oxford to understand the maths in the background. The easiest way to explain it and keep it simple is that every point you have over the base of ten for an attribute will give you a percent efficiency boost on skill modifiers when attacking, defending, or carrying out actions. Dexterity works differently for armour class and Wisdom scores affect mana."

"This is a lot to take in, but I am sure I will learn it all in time."

"You will, my young loophole finder," Dave said enthusiastically.

It was the first time SJ had heard Dave talk passionately about anything, discussing her attributes, their bonuses, and how they worked. He sounded genuinely excited, and she sat there smiling while she thought about it.

"Have you got wind?"

"No, why?"

"Just the look on your face."

And there it was, back to the normal Dave. SJ opened her character sheet again and added two extra points to her Constitution.

→Level: 1	
Experience:	5 of 50
Hit Points:	10
Mana Points:	10
Dexterity:	10
Constitution:	9

Once she had, she lay back on the soft grass and smiled, looking up at the beautiful, clear sky. The sun's bright rays beat down on her, and it felt glorious, reminding her of lazy summer afternoons. Thinking she might enjoy it here, she closed her eyes, smiling, imagining the adventures she might have ahead of her.

CHAPTER EIGHT

Lore and Order

SJ was enjoying soaking in the sun, lying on the soft green grass of the safe zone, when something blocked the sun. The sudden change in temperature made her shiver and open her eyes. The shadow moved as she did, and the bright sun met her eyes. Blinking, she struggled to see the massive form that flew across the lake's surface.

As her sight adjusted, her eyes opened wider than saucers. It was a majestic blue, its scales shimmering from the light bouncing off their brilliance. Its underbelly had a golden sheen, and its huge wings caused ripples to form across the lake surface as it dipped its head to drink. She had seen hundreds of dragons in books and films, but seeing one flying so close was equally mesmerising and terrifying. Its limbs were huge and muscular, its neck long and graceful. From its majestic, golden-spiked head ran a golden mane of fins down its back and tail.

It swooped upwards from the lake surface, sailing high into the air before it again swooped downwards. Its mouth opened as it approached the lake's surface and again scooped water.

"Holy mother of orcs. What is that doing here?" Dave said in a shocked tone.

"What do you mean?"

"Identify it, and you'll see."

SJ triggered her skill.

> Creatures over ten levels above your own may not be identified at your current skill level.

"It's a higher level. What's strange about that?"

"We are in a starter zone. Blue dragons live in the colder northern territories, and minimum level requirements to gain experience are suggested to be 50-plus."

"It's a long way from home, then."

"A *long* way; try nearly five thousand miles. The northern territories are past the capital. I have never known a blue dragon to be so far from home."

The dragon finished its second swoop and again soared skyward. It flew so high so quickly, disappearing in the sun's glare. As SJ watched, the speck turned and grew. It plummeted towards the ground like a missile, heading straight towards the centre of the lake. SJ was standing, staring as the dragon dived, its wings tucked in, making it aerodynamic and propelling it almost faster than SJ could track. It hit the lake's surface with its sleek-formed body and disappeared. A huge plume of water soared upwards as it displaced the water, sending out a tsunami from the point of impact.

SJ stared, open-mouthed, as the wave approached the shore, picking up speed and height. The lake was vast, but the amount of water that had been displaced by the dragon began to rain down across its surface.

"This time, I do mean run," Dave shouted in her head.

SJ snapped out of her trance, grabbed her top, and turned, running towards the tree-line across the clearing. The wave reached the shoreline, towering at least eight feet tall, and crashed onto the land. Thousands of gallons of water rushed from the lake. SJ reached the nearest tree and jumped onto a lower branch as the wave chased her across the land. The water rushed around the tree trunk as the forest stirred into life. A cacophony of animal sounds erupted as the rushing water disturbed their forest of peace.

SJ stared back out at the lake as the dragon reappeared, bursting from the depths and closing its jaws around what must have been hundreds of brightly coloured fish.

"It's just feeding," SJ said.

"It's a dragon. It can feed on whatever it wants to," Dave replied.

As SJ hung there, the water receded, draining back into the lake. SJ did not know how much had been displaced, but to create a tsunami the way it had was unimaginable. As she watched, the dragon turned, beginning to fly towards the mountains in the distance across the lake, behind the town. She watched as it became smaller until it landed on the highest peak. It was small but still visible even at the long distance.

"How big was that?" SJ asked. "I could not tell with the speed it flew at."

"Big. I have seen many dragons, and that is one of the biggest ones I have seen. It must have been nearly three hundred feet from snout to tail."

"That big," SJ said, amazed.

"Yes. If not larger," Dave said, sounding a little nervous.

"What is wrong?"

"Strange things are happening, and I am starting to suspect you are the cause."

"Why me?"

"Doh. Really?"

"These things cannot be because I didn't accept the terms and conditions, can they?"

"I am not sure." And Dave *did* sound unsure.

SJ frowned. "It can't have had that much of an effect."

Silence.

As the water continued to recede, SJ dropped back down from the branch she had been hanging onto. The ground was now sodden, her boots squelching in the now-soaked grass. She made her way back to the safe zone. Remarkably, the safe zone looked relatively dry compared to the surrounding land. The lake's surface was only just recovering fully, and the ripples were lessening as the water returned to where it had come from.

"Okay. I have done something I said I would never do," Dave's voice said.
"What is that?"
"I asked Dad."
"What? You asked your dad?"
"Yes. I have not spoken to him in nearly six thousand years, ever since he ran off with a new AI tart, leaving me and Mum alone."
"Sorry. I am confused. You are an AI, and you have parents?"
"Of course. We are a race. I told you that." Dave snapped.
"But how?"
"What do you mean *how*?"
"How do you . . . ? You know."
"Ewwwww. No, don't be rude. As AIs, our parents are our original AI providers. We are initially formed by amalgamated programming from previous AIs. This allows for eternal knowledge transfer."
"Oh. I see. That makes a lot more sense. What did your Dad say?"
"Apparently it is an acceptable variation in the standard programming through the System."
"So it was not caused by me."
"I haven't finished yet. Variations are usually caused by significant System interference where the equilibrium has been upset."
"Ahhhhh. So it may be me, then."
"Maybe. We may never know, but suffice it to say we should expect some unusual activity while the System realigns. A blue appearing in a starter zone is definitely an unusual activity."
"If they are System led, can the System not direct them?"
"The System may amend static activities, such as dungeons, world bosses, et cetera. It cannot alter Amathera's natural species. After all, it is not like they are pieces of programming. They are living creatures with as much free thought as you. Which in your case is obviously limited."

SJ ignored Dave's comment. "How do the zones work if they can travel and do what they wish?"
"Balance."
"Balance?"
"Yes. Each zone is finely balanced. There is a continual cyclic operation. If too much evil appears in one zone, more good will move until balance is restored. The natural behaviour of the creatures of Amathera maintained their own equilibrium long before the System started integrating into the land fully."

"So, for all good, there is evil."

"Yes. You can never vanquish evil fully as it will always exist to restore balance."

"Why can good not exist alone?"

"Eventually, those who began good would turn evil. That, unfortunately, follows nature's path. You have heard of fallen angels on Earth. The same can happen here. Many mighty have fallen over the years due to succumbing to their inner demons."

It was actually a very depressing thought that it would not matter what evil SJ conquered. There would always be more to replace it. "I am sure good can prevail over evil," SJ said.

"If it can, it has never happened. Wars have been won and lost by both sides, but every time, balance has won overall."

SJ was now sitting on the large flat stone. The bright sun had dried it quickly from the lake water. Having replaced her halter top, she sat thinking through everything Dave had been saying. If it was true that there was always balance, how was it known? Someone must have controlled it.

A deity had been mentioned under Valkyrie, and SJ asked, "Are there gods here?"

"On Amathera, it's rare, although rumoured."

"What gives valkyrie their boons, then?"

"The gods do."

"You just said they are rarely here."

"They are still 'on' Amathera, if you don't only mean on the land itself," Dave replied, exaggerating the *on*.

"Which gods exist, then?"

"There are quite a few."

"Are they the ones who keep the balance?"

"I don't know. I am not a god."

"I thought you were all-knowing."

"Compared to you, I am!" Dave snarked.

"Pffff. If you were, you could answer all my questions."

Silence.

"Dave?"

Silence.

"Be like that, then."

SJ looked up towards the mountain peak, where the form of the dragon rested. Even at that distance, she thought she could see the sun glinting off its brilliant blue scales. "Right, I need to level." She stood from the rock and looked at the forest surrounding the clearing. "Left, right, or centre?" She decided to head left and turned, walking towards the trees. The usual message triggered as she left the safe zone and approached the tree-line.

The forest remained louder than before, and she planned to use the confusion caused by the wave. She stepped under the forest's thick canopy. The trees were well-spaced, and she could move through them easily. The sun broke through the branches above, casting its bright glow and causing a kaleidoscope of colours underneath the canopy. Birds cawed and hooted, taking off as she walked through the trees. She could hear a snuffling noise ahead and approached it, drawing her short blade as she did.

A small clearing opened ahead, and she knew the water had reached this far inland as the ground was still squelching underfoot. In the centre of the clearing stood a small hog. She triggered her identification skill.

Hogling	
Level:	1
Hit Points:	8
Mana Points:	0

"Okay, SJ, nice and easy, now," she said as she walked into the clearing.

The hogling looked up from where it had been snuffling the ground, slurping up large worms that were disturbed by the water. It had mottled brown fur and two short tusks protruding from its lower jaw.

It squealed at her and shook its head from side to side threateningly. It was small, standing no more than eighteen inches tall, and she readied herself for its charge.

SJ took a defensive stance like she had used with the termites as the hogling charged towards her. As it neared, she again stepped sideways, striking out with her blade and scoring a hit down the hogling's flank as it rushed her. It squealed as she watched its health drop to 50 percent. As it turned, she again struck with her blade, striking it in its rear, taking another two hit points from it. It flung its head around in defence, and SJ only just managed to move her arm out of the way as its small, sharp tusks threatened to pierce her skin. She lifted her leg and struck out in a forward kick, catching the hogling on the end of its snout. The hogling grunted before it fell over on its side.

"Yes," she shouted at her success. She checked her character sheet: She had earned ten experience for the kill.

"Not bad," Dave said.

"Have you stopped sulking now?"

"I was not sulking. I was meditating."

"If that is what you call getting in a huff and storming off," SJ retorted, her adrenaline pumping from the hogling fight.

"I WAS NOT SULKING." Dave's voice boomed in her head.

She winced. "Okay. I believe you. Please don't do that again." She shook her head, trying to remove the ringing sensation Dave's shouting had caused.

She bent down over the hogling, looting the body.

> 1 x Copper, 1 x Apple, 2 x Strips of Light Leather

"Oh. Food." SJ had not even considered food since she arrived, and now, seeing the apple in her inventory, she pulled it out. It appeared in her open hand. It was a glossy red, and she naturally rubbed it against her trouser leg and lifted it to her mouth to take a large bite. The taste that hit her mouth was one of the foulest she had ever tasted, and she started to spit out the contents and hurled the apple across the clearing.

Dave was laughing hysterically.

"It said it was an apple."

"It was," Dave still laughing.

"Then why does it taste so bad?"

"Just because it is called an apple does not mean it is the same as apples from Earth."

SJ had not even considered that. "What can I eat, then?"

"You can eat those if you can overcome the taste. They will not harm you. The taste is their natural defence mechanism to prevent them from being eaten. Hoglings love them."

"Are any of the foods the same?"

"Most are. Hoglings can make a nice roast, from what I have been told. They are apparently very similar to your pigs and hogs of Earth."

SJ looked at the body of the hogling. She had no idea how to butcher it. She let out a deep sigh. "Is there any food around here I can eat without killing or butchering it?"

"Yes. Plenty. That bush over there has berries that you can eat."

"Where?"

"Turn left, then straight ahead twenty paces."

SJ followed Dave's guidance and ended up standing by a low bush with small green berries at the outer edge of the clearing. "Are you sure?"

"Absolutely."

SJ picked a berry from the bush and slowly tasted it with her tongue. There was no bitterness, so she placed it in her mouth and slowly bit down. Juice exploded from the berry, flooding her mouth with the sweetest taste ever. "Oh my god. They are amazing." SJ started picking more berries and transferring some to her inventory while popping the odd one in her mouth.

"Thank you," SJ said around a mouthful of the berries.

"Are you ready for another hogling now?"

"What?" SJ turned and looked back into the clearing. Another hogling stood in almost the same position as the previous one. "Do they respawn?"

"Yes. When you walk out of range of a beast after killing and looting it, a standard starter zone beast will respawn."

"So I can use this spot to level safely for a while."

"Yes. You should be able to, although be warned that you can attract predators if you kill too many creatures in one location."

"Okay. Well, for now, let's start farming," SJ said excitedly as she walked back into the clearing.

CHAPTER NINE

Farming

SJ continued to farm the hogling respawn point. Each time she finished the hogling, she would loot it and then move out of the clearing, leaving it for a few minutes before she saw the hogling reappear. It was strange to witness, as there was no light, no reference. It wasn't there one second, and then the next, it was. Every time it happened, she thought she must have blinked, even though she knew she hadn't.

It was the fourth respawn when she made a mistake. She had got complacent, as they were so easy to kill. SJ had been stepping sideways during their initial charge, swiping down their flanks with her short blade and attacking them with rapid strikes before they could recover fully.

This time, though, as the hogling charged her, she stepped sideways, caught her foot, and ended up sprawling on the forest floor, wondering what had just happened. The little hogling took advantage and gored her in her leg, its sharp tusks ripping through her cloth pants and gouging a nice chunk of flesh from her thigh.

Yelping in pain, she rolled onto her back, seeing her hit points reduced by half. She climbed to her feet, limping as the hogling again charged. "Damn," she cried.

"Be careful. Another hit like that, you are visiting the white room," Dave said.

"You think I don't know that?" SJ growled through gritted teeth.

The hogling came at her again, and she successfully used the same move this time, although she did not cut its flank as well as the other three times. She winced with each move as the pain from her injury fogged her mind. She stabbed quickly at the hogling, catching it in its rear before it turned on her, but had not caused the full eight hit points of damage needed to finish it. It still had one left as it flung its tusks at her arm again. She hopped backwards as best as she could and faced down the beast.

It stood in front of her, shaking its head as though dizzy, and as she watched, its final hit point disappeared, and it fell sideways, dead. She grunted as she moved to the corpse to loot it. "It bleeds out?" SJ asked.

"You did open up its side," Dave replied.

Her hit points had remained at five, and although she was still bleeding from the tusk wounds, her health did not lower further. "Why do I not bleed out?"

"Legionnaires at your level are only inflicted with actual initial damage. If you bleed, it does not lower hit points further until you're at Level 10. It will weaken you and make you slower, as you noticed. Some creatures can also inflict damage over time with venom and poisons, but you will not find any in a starter zone."

"I need to heal before I try that again. I can't chance another hit like that."

"It won't take long to heal. You added your points to Constitution, so with nine, there are no negative effects. So you will regain one hit point every five minutes."

"It takes twenty-five minutes to heal. Urgh. I may as well head back to the safe zone while I do." SJ limped back towards the lake. "Is there any other way I can heal?"

"Some foods will boost healing, and there is also magic, potions, and skills."

"Do you know which foods? Are there any around here?"

"No. They are only available in starter zones if a crafter brings them to sell, and if they do, they will be marked up to a stupid price."

"And people still buy them?"

"Yep. There are a lot of stupid people in this world. Especially Legionnaires!"

"What about potions and magic?"

"If you are in a party with a healer or alchemist, you may get healed or given potions. If you go to buy from an alchemist or a healer, expect to pay a hefty sum. You can also get quest rewards, which include health or mana potions."

"And skills?"

"Several fighter classes have hit point regeneration, and an assassin also does. But do not get excited. It is a very high-level skill where you can steal life."

"Damn. From what you said, I was hoping for something a little sooner and cheaper."

"There is an option to make things cheaper for you overall," Dave said thoughtfully.

"What is that?" SJ asked hopefully.

"At Level 5, you will be offered your profession choice. You can select a profession that will benefit you going forward, such as Alchemy, and allow you to start making your own potions."

"What professions are there? Are they like the ones from games on Earth?"

Several moments passed before Dave replied. "Looking at the games you had on Earth, they are similar. Alchemist, Enchanter, Armourer, Tailor, Cook, et cetera. You will be given a comprehensive list when the time arises."

SJ received the message that she had entered the safe zone. She moved over to the flat stone and sat down heavily. Her leg was already feeling a little better, and the blood had stopped flowing just in the few minutes she had walked back. She looked at the tear in her pants and sighed.

"What is wrong?" Dave asked.

"These clothes are ruined already."

"What do you expect? You are wearing zero-armour peasants' clothes," Dave said, his reply dripping with sarcasm.

"How do I go about improving or repairing them, then?"

"At your level, you don't. As with other elements, they do not come into consideration until Level 5. You currently do not have an armour class on your character sheet, do you?"

SJ checked her sheet. "No."

"You will starting from Level 5 and can improve it through your clothes or armour."

"Same as games again, then."

"After consulting the wiki, yes, there are many similarities between how the System operates and the games you have on Earth."

"That may work to my benefit, then."

"Why?" Dave questioned.

"I was always a hoarder and crafter in the games I played and used to spend hours working through the most efficient and productive farming routes to gather crafting materials."

"Having the dedication to do it will help. What you can't compare are the times, though. Some rarer materials needed in Amathera are restricted to certain regions or very rare drops from certain-level monsters."

SJ checked her hit points, and she was already back to eight. "Two more, and we can go back again."

"Did you not check your level?" Dave asked.

"No." SJ reopened her character sheet. "Yes! I can move to Level 2."

SJ accepted the level increase straight away.

Congratulations on reaching Level 2
You have been awarded the following:
5 hit points
5 mana points
+1 Dexterity
+2 free points to distribute as you wish

"Woo-hoo. I got exactly the same again," SJ shouted with glee.

"Excellent news. If it continues, you will be insanely strong compared to Legionnaires of the same level."

"What should I go for this time?"

"You want my advice? That is very magnanimous of you," Dave replied.

SJ rolled her eyes. "I have been asking for your guidance from the start."

"Have you? I thought you were just using my all-knowing knowledge rather than seeking guidance."

"What do you think asking questions is? Is that not seeking guidance and answers?"

Silence.

"Maybe," Dave eventually responded.

"What do you mean *maybe*? Am I not asking for advice if I am asking a question?"

"No. You are asking for answers."

"What?"

"It is how you ask," Dave humphed.

"In what manner should I ask?"

"If you really sought my advice and guidance, you would address me with the level of authority and respect that I deserve."

"What does that mean?" SJ replied, frowning.

"*Dave, my all-knowing and powerful AI. Would you please guide me on my journey of growth and support my development as a noob Legionnaire.* Or something like that."

"Really! For a start, you use a search engine for your knowledge, which means you do not know everything. Secondly, I thought we were a team and you were supposed to support me."

"What do you think I've been doing?" Dave said stubbornly.

"Being a royal pain in the arse, most of the time," SJ replied angrily. She closed her eyes in exasperation. If not for the voice being inside her head, she would have turned away. He could be so frustrating. "Argh," she shouted.

When she'd calmed down, SJ said, "Dave?"

"Yes," Dave haughtily replied.

"Would you please be so kind as to offer me your thoughts on advancing my character in this new world I now reside in?"

"That was very eloquent, and for that polite request, the answer is no."

"WHAT?" SJ shouted again.

"It is too late now."

"Too late?"

"You already hurt my feelings."

"Feelings? When did I hurt your feelings?"

Dave replied in a squeaky voice, "*For a start, you use a search engine for your knowledge, which means you do not know everything*, blah, blah, blah."

SJ dropped her head to her hands, exhaling. "I thought we had got past this," SJ replied through her fingers.

"Past your rude, obnoxious behaviour? Never."

"SYSTEM!" SJ screamed.

"What are you doing?"

"I AM GETTING YOU REPLACED," she bellowed.

"Why?" Dave replied in a shocked voice.

"Why? . . . Why? . . . Why do you think?"

"I thought we had got past this," Dave replied.

"Really? And why would I get over the way you are behaving?"

"Oh, your hit points should be back to full now, and I advise you to drop a point each in Dexterity and Constitution. Let's go back to farming, as you call it," Dave replied cheerily.

SJ sat stunned. "What?"

"You heard me. Don't tell me all your shouting has deafened you. +1 Dexterity and +1 Constitution, then go back to farming."

"But . . ."

"Doesn't time fly when you are having fun?" Dave replied.

"What the actual . . . ? Were you just wasting time?"

"I would not say *wasting*. More like passing. We really should try this role-playing more often."

"Role-play!" SJ sputtered.

"Yes. I read on the wiki that you all play these role-playing games where you act. I thought it would be fun to try."

"You understand that role-play is not real; it's based on distinct characters or scenarios. Not ones we have already been through."

"Well, it wasn't exactly the same as before."

SJ screamed again, "Argh." She rubbed her temples with her fingers.

After a few moments, she said, "Okay. +1 Dexterity and +1 Constitution." She opened her character sheet and applied the changes.

	→Level: 2
Experience:	5 of 100
Hit Points:	17
Mana Points:	15
Dexterity:	12
Constitution:	10
Subterfuge:	Identification Level 1 (8 of 10 to reach Level 2)

Upon standing, she discovered that her leg was fully healed. She flexed it several times, and there was absolutely no pain. Examining where the wound had been, she couldn't see any scarring.

"Dave. Is there a way to accept level increases automatically?"

"Erm . . ."

Silence.

"Has no one ever asked that before?"

"Nope, not in my lifetime."

"So, can you?"

"Checking. Oh, I found it. Yes, there is," Dave replied, surprised. "A little arrow is next to your level on your character sheet. If you select it, it will become a turning arrow. I always thought the arrow just highlighted your level because it was important. Every day is a school day."

SJ focused on the small arrow, and it changed.

> ↻ Level: 2

"So that now means that levels will automatically be increased?" SJ confirmed. "I assume that means hit points, mana points, and Dexterity will be added as standard."

"It should do."

"That's great. Thanks for checking," SJ said, smiling.

"Shall we go hunt more hoglings now?" Dave asked.

"Let's."

CHAPTER TEN

Badger, Badger, Badger

Since returning to the clearing, SJ had killed nine more hoglings. However, she noticed she received reduced experience for them, earning only eight points per kill rather than the ten she'd previously earned. She asked Dave about this, and he told her it was because she was now Level 2, whereas the hoglings were Level 1.

Each level higher she was than her target reduced the earned experience by 20 percent, making it impossible for higher-level players to level in low-level areas, even without the territory limitations. In some territories, this even forced them to continue advancing to a stronger area within a specific territory if they wished to gain decent experience. Apparently, the amount of experience required to increase to higher levels was substantial.

The first five levels required experience double the previous. Starting from twenty-five experience to reach Level 1, by Level 5, you needed to earn four hundred experience. SJ had already considered that once she hit Level 3, she would drop to six experience per Level 1 hogling. That would mean she would need to kill at least thirty-two of them to level, and with ten to fifteen minutes between spawns, never mind fights and looting, even at four-an-hour efficiency, it would take a full eight hours of grinding to achieve. It meant she needed to move to find other creatures or hoglings of a higher level.

"I am on 77 of 100 experience. Three more hoglings, and I will level again," SJ said.

"You should call yourself Hogling Slayer," Dave replied.

SJ noticed that the light was starting to fade, and her new night vision skill was a strange sensation. As the light faded, she could still see, but the clarity was changing. "How much light is left?"

"Err . . . maybe an hour."

"They are respawning every fifteen minutes, so I should have time to take on three more beforehand."

Dave yawned loudly. "It is very boring fighting these. You can easily kill them with your Level 2 and Dexterity boosts."

SJ had been two-hitting them all. After her initial strike down their flanks, she only required one strike on their rears now to finish them. Her Dexterity increase had increased her small blade damage.

"Is there not a weapons chart or damage chart available? Also, I would have thought there were weapon proficiencies available?"

"There are. They also don't kick in until Level 5."

"I need to get to 5, then," SJ replied with determination.

"Yes, you do, but that will not happen today. Level 3 on your first day is a good start—not the best, but not the worst."

"What's the most you've seen?" SJ asked, a little frustrated, waiting for the hogling to spawn.

"Once, a Legionnaire reached Level 4 on the first day. It was a berserker who discovered a rat's nest."

SJ retrieved a berry from her inventory and ate it while waiting by the side of the clearing. "These berries are so delicious."

"You have had rather a lot today."

"I have no other food, and it's energetic work." She shrugged.

They had got into the habit of discussing professions between the spawns, and SJ was starting to decide which she might choose. Tailor was looking like one of her best options. It would not just allow her to design and produce fae-specific clothes. Its freedom of movement compared to armour also benefitted her martial arts skills. The information Dave had given her said that an item's quality would improve not just armour class but also the number of enchantments an item could hold.

All items followed basis of rarity levels, which Dave had explained to SJ. She was aware of them from her gaming days: common, good, rare, epic, mythic, legendary, and a new one she had never heard of before called astral. Astral was explained as a divine gift. Astral weapons or armour could only be obtained by killing a Legionnaire who possessed them, or by being granted by a god. They were always unique as well.

The requirements for a profession increased based on time, skill, and the quality of manufactured goods. The details would be confirmed when she reached Level 5, although it seemed that if you produced a higher-quality item, you could gain more from it. Dave said she could increase production speed, but it would always create common items. The professions could be improved, but gaining the requisite skills was a long process.

"You mentioned you can also get a second profession?" SJ asked.

"Yes, at Level 20, you have the choice to either change your primary profession, which several have done before, or choose a secondary profession," Dave said.

"Why would someone change their primary profession?" SJ asked, confused.

"Certain professions are much harder to level, and many Legionnaires have moved to easier professions."

"Which ones?"

"Well, for example, I've had mêlée classes that have chosen the Enchanter profession. To enchant items, you must use mana. Most mêlée classes do not invest in Intelligence or Wisdom, which link to your mana growth. So, without the extra attribute points, they can be limited to what they can enchant for themselves. Getting a +1 damage on a weapon or piece of armour at Level 5 may sound great, but when you reach Level 15 or 20, you need much better enchantments, and they will never be able to attempt them because of their mana limits."

"I need to review all the details once I reach Level 5."

"I am surprised I have been able to tell you so much of this already."

"Why?"

"I am normally restricted from telling you certain things. I said that already."

"So how can you, then?"

"Probably like everything else that is different with you, it's because you are an anomaly."

SJ was sitting, leaning against a tree, when the sound of snuffling returned. The next hogling had spawned.

"Here we go again," SJ said, standing. As she walked into the clearing, there was movement from the far side, and a black-and-white body streaked in to attack the hogling. SJ stopped dead in her tracks as she took in the sight unfolding and triggered identification. Both creatures were caught in the skill. Since her identification skill had triggered at Level 2, it informed her of a creature's main attack.

Hogling	
Level:	1
Hit Points:	8
Mana Points:	0
Attacks:	Charge, Tusks

Badger Berserker	
Level:	4
Hit Points:	40
Mana Points:	0
Attacks:	Bite, Claws

SJ's screen flashed.

> Overkill warning
> Due to repeated kills in one area, you have triggered a predator.

"Oh. This could be problematic," Dave said.

SJ stared at the black-and-white beast that, with its large, clawed paw strike, tore into the hogling and killed it with one hit. The badger was much larger than the ones she was used to seeing on nature programmes on Earth and was nearly as long as she was tall.

"It's Level 4!" SJ exclaimed.

"I would advise that you retreat to the safe zone. I have known a Level 2 or, on one occasion, a Level 3 spawn in an overkill starter zone, but never a Level 4. Two levels may not seem like much, but it will be much stronger than you think."

SJ started to retreat into the tree-line when the badger noticed her. It turned its head, eyeing her. It snarled, showing a row of razor-sharp teeth, and charged.

"Argh," SJ screamed as the creature streaked towards her. It was only about thirty feet away and covering the ground quickly. She stepped backwards instinctively, straight into the tree she had just been sitting against. She fumbled, reaching for her short blade as the badger neared. The badger looked rabid, drool dripping from its jaws.

"It's also a berserker variant. Now, that is strange," Dave said in a calm voice.

"WHY?" SJ shouted, which came out very squeaky and high-pitched.

"Berserker Badgers are a rare variant."

SJ was not listening to Dave as the badger lunged straight at her. She dived sideways, her gymnastics from her youth coming into play as she naturally went into a forward roll and returned to her feet. Her increased Dexterity had been helping with her mobility, as was her new, lithe form as a fae. Her wings had naturally splayed as she rolled, stopping them from being an obstruction.

The badger had been running at her full pelt and crashed straight into the tree trunk, then stood there shaking its head. SJ took advantage of its stunned state by attacking. Her blade struck true, and she pulled it out as the badger howled and began to turn on her. It had taken a sliver of damage to its health. She struck a second time before it turned fully and caught it in its face as it spun.

Whether a freak hit or pure luck, as SJ knew it was not skill, she had hit the badger in its eye. The badger recoiled from the strike, now blinded in one eye. It threw its head from side to side in pain and anger and swiped at her with its clawed paw. She leapt backwards, only just avoiding its strike. With the lucky hit, its health had been reduced by a quarter.

Dave was still talking in her head. "Rare variant creatures do not normally spawn until much higher levels," he continued excitedly. "There is a chance of it dropping much better loot than a normal creature."

SJ could not reply as she moved back from the badger's swipes, focusing on staying out of its reach. The only bonus was that, as it now had sight in just one eye, it did not appear to have the same depth perception, and several of its swipes were short. SJ backed across the clearing, glancing behind her to ensure she kept her footing. She could not get near it with its continual paw strikes and had no option but to retreat in defence.

"I need to blind it," she gasped as she kept moving away. She needed to make room between them, so she turned and ran. The badger came after her, and reaching the other side of the clearing, she ducked behind a tree as its momentum carried it past. Her adrenaline was at its maximum. Her body flooded with it. She had always enjoyed scary rides at fairs and the adrenaline rush from rollercoasters, but this was on a whole new level.

Everything seemed heightened. Observing the badger's movements and her own, she gained a newfound clarity. This was a fight to the death. Rather than try to strike the badger, she ran straight across the clearing to the far side and stopped by a tree again. The badger turned and came after her, and this time, as she stepped away from it, she made the same move she had done with the hoglings, striking down its flank. The short blade did little slashing damage compared to what it had done to the hoglings, but it was still something.

She kept repeating the exercise, running across the clearing, standing by a tree as it charged, feeling her lungs and legs beginning to burn. The adrenaline kept her going. By this process, she managed to reduce it to under half its health but knew she would soon tire. The badger had a stripe of wounds on its flank, and they were all slowly bleeding. None were deep. Bleeding out would take too much time, if it even happened.

"I am impressed so far," Dave said.

SJ ignored his praise, grunted, and struck out an extra time at the badger rather than run back across the clearing. That was a mistake, as it swung its head round with its jaws open, catching her arm holding the blade. Not well enough to bite but well enough for its very hard and sharp teeth to cut into her skin. SJ yelped in pain, only just managing to keep a hold of the knife.

She kicked out, catching it on the side of its head. The strike did puny damage but made the badger's head move, showing her its damaged eye. She may have a chance if she could do that on the other side. The badger's head turned the other way due to the kick, resulting in minimal damage. As it did, she had a clear view of its good eye and stabbed towards it with her blade.

The badger recoiled, seeing the blade coming for it, and swiped with its paw. SJ only just pulled her hand back in time. She dropped into her side stance and stepped back from the creature. It shook its head from the blows, which, although not damaging, were distracting and affecting its ability to focus. It snarled and moved for her again. This time, she did not stab it but swung her leg around in a sweeping kick, aiming for its head.

She caught it with power, her foot hurting through the soft leather boot as it struck the side of the badger's solid face. The power behind the sweeping kick was much more than her previous front kicks. The badger's head moved sideways again, taking a little damage, and its good eye faced her. Rather than kick with the other foot, she again kicked with her right, being her stronger side, and the kick again met its mark. It was not as powerful, but enough to keep the badger disorientated.

She was now gasping for breath. Her limbs felt heavy, and she knew she was running out of stamina. She would have been dead long ago if she had still been

Level 1. With all the effort she could muster, she continued to kick the creature. It became more unsteady with each blow. Sweep, draw, sweep, draw, sweep, draw. After the sixth successive hit, the badger lost its footing and slipped, falling sideways, shaking its head groggily.

SJ could not miss the opportunity, and while it staggered back to its feet, she lunged in with her blade, aiming deliberately and catching the badger's remaining eye. The badger howled in pain and anger as it became blinded, lashing out with its claws and snapping its jaws around, trying to find SJ.

SJ backed away, letting the badger lash out blindly. She tried to steady her breathing as she watched the badger thrash about. Its health was slowly decreasing with the continued bleeding and the damage she had done. It now only had a quarter of its health remaining. As she watched it thrash around, she felt a pang of guilt. What had she just done? The hoglings and termites were nothing to her, the latter being pests and the former a food source. The badger was a creature she had always liked as a child. She had owned a stuffed toy of a badger that she had slept with as a child. It had always been her favourite.

"You need to finish it," Dave said flatly.

"I am not sure I can," SJ replied.

"If you cannot kill a creature, how do you think you will ever be an assassin?" he snarked.

SJ was in turmoil now. She had chosen a class designed to kill and was concerned about a badger. She remembered reading about the badger culling that used to be on the news due to them being pests. Trying to resign herself to the fact it was a nuisance and not the cute, furry badgers of her childhood stories, she moved to its side, into a position to strike at it unhindered. It took her four strikes to remove the remaining hit points, and it fell to the ground with one last defiant bark.

SJ slumped to her knees, her emotions tearing her up inside. Placing her head in her hands, she began to sob.

CHAPTER ELEVEN

Soooooo Sad

Dave watched SJ as she fell to her knees and began sobbing. The AI had witnessed even some of the hardiest criminals break down during their reincarnations, which was unsurprising. Whether he could really understand it or not, the challenges of realising that they had died and were reborn seemed to really affect the inhabitants of Earth who ended up being sent here.

"Are you okay?" Dave asked. His usual tone was replaced by a much calmer and supportive one.

SJ sniffed, wiping tears from her eyes. "I just killed Trufflehunter."

"Who?" Dave asked, confused.

"Trufflehunter, from *Prince Caspian*." SJ sniffed.

"What are you talking about?"

"Trufflehunter," SJ sobbed again with new tears. As she did, her display triggered.

Congratulations on reaching Level 3
You have been awarded the following:
5 hit points
5 mana points
+1 Dexterity
+2 free points to distribute as you wish

SJ choked back a sob as she read the level-up. "I suppose I levelled, at least."

Dave spoke in a snarky voice. "Are you kidding me?"

"Kidding about what?" SJ replied, sniffing.

"Trufflehunter!"

"What do you mean?"

"He is a fictional character from a damn book. That is what I mean. How on Amathera can you be getting upset over a storybook character?"

"I always liked him because he reminded me of a strong, loyal friend."

"It was a story!" Dave exclaimed in shock.

"Have you never read anything that has upset you?" SJ snapped. Her sobs were replaced with anger.

"No. Never in a story. They are fake and make-believe. My dad running off with that AI tart upset me, but that was not a story. It was real."

"Have you ever even read any stories?"

Silence.

"Dave?"

"Noooo," Dave answered slowly.

"Maybe you should try reading some, then, and you may understand."

"I don't believe a story can be upsetting," Dave responded frankly.

"Try reading *The Fault in Our Stars* and tell me it is not upsetting," SJ angrily replied.

"Hmph. That's pathetic behaviour. I honestly thought you were upset because you had died and been reincarnated, but instead, it's because of a ridiculous fictional badger."

"If you are not going to say anything worthwhile, then don't say anything at all."

Silence.

SJ had not realised that she was now standing. While arguing and getting annoyed at Dave, she had stopped crying, and her emotion had turned to anger. The badger berserker's lifeless body lay a few feet from her, and she bent to loot the body.

Congratulations, you have killed your first rare monster in Amathera.
The level class of creatures increases the experience gained and the loot available. Monsters follow the same class system as items: common, good, rare, epic, mythic, and legendary.
3 x Silver, 4 x Strips of Good Leather, The Badger's Blades
Please select the item you wish to collect.

SJ checked her inventory. It was full, with the leather strips she had accumulated taking up most of the space. Only one space remained free, and with two items, she had been given the option to choose. It seemed there was a maximum amount of a loot variant permissible for each slot. She had not received any cloth-related items, so she was not sure what would happen with tailoring, but she had assumed that she needed to get drops from monsters for tailoring as well. She selected the garrotte, removed it, and placed it in her pocket before trying again.

Inventory: Rope, Flint and Steel, Torch, Poison Bottles, 84 x Gloss Berries, 10 x Strips of Light Leather, 10 x Strips of Light Leather, 8 x Strips of Light Leather, 4 x Strips of Good Leather, The Badger's Blades

---

SJ looked at the badger's blades.

The Badger's Blades +3
Quality: Rare

> Damage: 5–9 +3
> Special: 10% chance of bleed effect

SJ smiled as she read the weapon's stats. She retrieved the item from her inventory, holding a pair of gloves in her hand. They reminded her of claws from several films, just not as long. Four blades on each glove matched the shape of the dead badger's claws, a gentle sweeping curve, but still sharp enough to puncture straight on. She tried slipping on one of the gloves but couldn't. A message came up on the screen.

> Only one primary weapon can be carried at a time.

She still had the starting blade in its sheath on her belt and had never even considered its stats. Checking it, she found that it only did one to three damage. The claws were a massive upgrade. The badger berserker could have one-hit the hogling. She removed the blade from her primary weapon slot and placed the claws there instead.

"Dave?"

Silence.

SJ slipped one of the bladed gloves on. It fit her slim hand perfectly. It was light as well. The claws seemed hollow. She stood and took a couple of practise punches with them. With these things on her hands, they would add tremendous damage to her attacks. She imagined the gloves disappearing, and they vanished from her hands, still showing on her character display as her primary weapon. She had to draw the short blade from a sheath, but the claws appeared on her hands when she thought about using them, making them the perfect weapon for sneak attacks. SJ would have to be careful when switching to her new weapons at this rate and didn't want to think about wearing them at the wrong time.

"These are amazing."

Silence.

"Dave?"

Silence.

SJ shrugged at his ignorance. She didn't want to be outside the safe zone on her first night in the new world. The display had a small timer in the corner; it was now 21:40. Before the fight, Dave stated there was still an hour of light, but it was now fading fast.

SJ returned to the starter zone. As she did, the body of the badger berserker disappeared and was replaced by the snuffling of a hogling. Glancing back across the clearing as she left, she saw it begin digging up worms. Ignoring the hogling, knowing she would only get a maximum of six experience, she continued through the wood. On reaching the clearing, she walked over to the flat stone, her display letting her know she was in the safe zone.

She had no blankets or tent to sleep under or any wood gathered to build a fire, and she kicked herself for not thinking about it earlier. The grass had dried again from the lake soaking caused by the dragon, and she sat down on the rock. She casually called up berries from her inventory and popped them in her mouth. "I need a fire." She had flint and steel and a vague idea of how to use them. She walked to the edge of the clearing and collected the driest small fallen branches and twigs she could find before moving back to the safe zone and constructing a fire.

Switching her primary weapon to her blade again, she shaved the twigs, making kindling. The fading light yielded to the moon in the cloudless sky, and she shivered from the temperature drop. Taking the flint and steel from her inventory, she struck the flint after adding some kindling to the wood. It took her a while, until stars winked between the tree branches. Her eyesight was still good; in the moonlight, her vision had a green glow. With determination, she continued until the fire caught.

The soft glow of a flame appeared, and cupping it to prevent the mild breeze from blowing it out, she gently coaxed it until some of the larger pieces caught. This was a much slower process than she had ever witnessed on TV shows. As the flame grew, the warmth and light it cast pushed the cold away. SJ took the rope from her inventory and curled it as best as possible into something she could use to rest her head on and lay back on the grass by the fire.

"Waaaaaaaaaaaaahhhhhhhhhhhhhhhhhhhhhhhhh."

The sound exploded in her head, and SJ almost died on the spot in fright from the sheer volume and sudden interruption.

"Dave. You scared the stuffing out of me."

All SJ was met with was crying and blubbing and unintelligible sounds.

"Dave, you are an AI. You can't cry. What is wrong that has got you in this state?"

"You . . . waaaaahhhhhhhh."

"Dave. Calm down and talk, please. What has upset you?"

"Why would . . . waaaaahhhhhhhh."

"Dave, snap out of it. I cannot help unless you tell me what's wrong."

Dave replied, sniffling and tearful, "I just read the book."

"Which book?"

"*The Fault in Our Stars*."

SJ remembered what she had said to him in her anger. "Oh."

"Why did you tell me to read it?" Dave sniffed.

"You were being an ass, and you didn't think writing could be emotional because they are fictional characters."

"You are evil," Dave huffed.

"Evil? Why am I evil? I said that books can be emotional. It was not my fault that you didn't believe me and said they were only fictional characters."

"I may have, but that story . . ." Dave started to cry again.

"Come on, now. Really?"

"I have never felt sad before as an AI. I now know what it feels like, and I don't like it."

"Sadness is horrible. Whether you have the resilience to bounce back is what counts."

"I'm not sure I can ever forgive you." Another loud sniff.

"At least you can now appreciate that people can get invested in stories, and when authors kill off characters, it can be emotional. It may not be real, but you get tied into them."

"Never again am I going to read a sad story!"

"Okay. I'm sure you can access thousands of books that you can read that are not sad."

"I am not sure I want to. I am scared of how they may affect me."

"You just have to try to remind yourself it is not real. It's no different to watching films, apart from what your brain imagines. Stories are told through many mediums."

Dave sniffed a few more times, not speaking, before he replied again. "I see you lit a fire."

"Yes. It was getting cold."

"It does not get too cold at night. It is not like being in the north."

"Anyway. While you were off reading, I looted the badger and got some awesome gear."

"I saw you have badger's blades. They are rare. I cannot remember ever seeing them before. Some rare items come around now and then, but the fact you got a rare item suited to your class is even rarer."

"I'm not complaining. They are amazing. The damage they do with one hit would kill a hogling outright."

"They are pretty awesome. You levelled as well but have not allocated your points yet?"

"I am not sure what to do with them. Dexterity is boosting my damage already, although I don't know by how much, as there are no charts."

"All comes at Level 5."

"Maybe I should level up the other attributes to at least ten, so I get the 10 percent bonus on anything that uses them?"

"That would be very sensible," Dave said, now surprised.

"Why so surprised?"

"I am used to Legionnaires who focus on damage and do not think about anything else. Especially once they have fought a higher-level monster and seen how hard the fights are."

"I can sort of understand why they would. These claws, though, I think, give me a bit of an edge."

"More than a bit. As an assassin with high Dexterity as normal, your initiative and the chance to get the first hit in are pretty much guaranteed once you level, unless you are against another assassin. It may even, in some cases, allow you to get two strikes in before anything can react, depending upon what they are."

"What they are?"

"Yeah, it could be a fighter in full armour or a large lumbering troll. So many elements come into play during combat. It's another Oxford and MIT moment."

"The System does not like to make things straightforward, does it?"

"No. Everything has underlying algorithms when you're fighting. Sometimes, you think you will win a fight hands down, and then all of a sudden, the luck gods start to laugh at you, and things go wrong. I have seen it happen so many times before."

"I thought you said the System doesn't control monsters?"

"It doesn't in its truest sense, but I am sure it still affects them occasionally."

"How, though?"

"If I knew that, I would be the System."

"Fair. Now that you are back, I have more questions for you. Is there a map? You previously mentioned a fog of war, and I know what it means from gaming, but I cannot find a map."

"Not at your level. Maps become available at Level 10. This is to keep starter players in starter zones until then. My red-dragon-fighting Legionnaire is a prime example of why they want you to stay there."

"I meant to ask you how he even got to meet a red dragon as a starter?"

"Oh. This crazy fool decided to leave the town immediately, spend the first day walking, and enter a mountain region the next day. The red dragon that got him was a hatchling. It was only Level 12, but a Level 12 hatchling meeting a Level 2 Legionnaire . . . well, you can imagine how it went."

"That makes sense. I imagined he had managed to travel a vast distance to where they lived on the first day, and you said the blue dragons live five thousand miles away."

"Ah. Reds are not as big or as strong as blues. Blues are one of the larger breeds out of the various dragons."

"How many are there?" SJ asked, looking towards the mountain peak where the blue dragon had rested.

"Seven in total. Blue, black, red, white, gold, green, and platinum."

"A platinum dragon?"

"Yes. They are very rare, and even hatchlings are legendary monsters. The lowest level platinum dragon you will ever see is nothing less than Level 40."

"As a hatchling?"

"Yes. I have no idea of the highest level they go."

"Where do they live?"

"On none of the major continents. They live on an island in the middle of the Argassi Seas. It is a treacherous location, full of water elementals, sprites, mer-creatures, krakens—think of any sea monster you have ever heard of, and they live in the area."

"So, they never venture onto the continents?"

"The odd hatchling has now and again. They are good-natured dragons. They only hunt for food, unlike the reds and blacks, who hunt for fun."

"What about the blue on the mountain?"

"Blues are usually good-natured. I have never met an evil blue dragon, but it does not mean they don't exist."

SJ considered the different dragons and other fantastical creatures she could start to meet in this new world. Her mind was full of images from all the movies, games, and books she had read.

"I was thinking of shrinking to miniature form for the night."

"Why?"

"The grasses and rope would protect me from the wind, and the fire, now lit, would provide immense warmth in comparison."

"That is actually another sensible idea. I am quite surprised at your logical thinking, considering your start."

SJ rolled her eyes and shrank into miniature form. The fire, now huge compared to her size, felt much warmer. She would need to keep an eye on it and keep it burning, but staying warm was much easier, especially with the long grasses blocking most of the night's breeze. The rope she had removed from her inventory remained the same size, providing even more cover.

"I think I need some sleep."

"Okay. You will be safe here. Nothing can enter the safe zone."

"Please do not shout in my head overnight."

"I will only shout if I need to wake you."

"You can wake me if you need to, then?" SJ asked.

"Yes. If I need to. I shouldn't need to wake you here, though."

"Okay. Then I am going to sleep." SJ felt drained after the day's activities, and once she leaned back against the coiled rope, it took her moments to drift off—even with the night's sounds filtering from the forest.

CHAPTER TWELVE

Doe a Deer

SJ dreamed of her dad coming upstairs to wake her for school as a child.

"SJ. Time to get up."

She rolled over, pulling the quilt tight over her head.

"SJ. Time to get up."

Her dad's voice drifted into her sleep-filled mind.

"SJ, GET UP," Dave shouted.

She sat bolt upright, frantically looking around, bleary-eyed.

"It is morning," Dave said.

"Morning. Does it really matter what the time is? I was sleeping," SJ growled.

"You don't want to waste the day. We have levels to gain and should also head to town."

SJ stretched and yawned. Then, noticing her stomach felt strange, she ran from the immediate area.

A few minutes later, she returned to the large rock holding her tender-feeling stomach. "That was unpleasant."

"Berries. You ate a mountain of them yesterday."

"You could have warned me of the effect."

"You never asked."

"Don't even think about starting that again. Yesterday was bad enough."

"I can't really be blamed. Having never had a fae before, I could not be certain of the effect they would have on you."

"Mmm hmm."

"I haven't," Dave said innocently.

"Has there ever been a race not affected by those berries?"

"Er . . ."

"That would be a no, then. Does that not give you enough foresight to have warned me?"

"Perhaps. You would have been fine if you had also eaten other stuff."

"What other stuff? You only mentioned the berries."

"You didn't . . ."

"DON'T," SJ huffed. She stomped through the grass again.

"Where are you going?"

SJ stopped. She had been walking away from Dave. Shaking her head at the realisation, she looked to the sky and sighed.

"You do realise that sometimes you can be very annoying," SJ said.

"No one has ever told me that before."

"Really?"

"Well, I do not normally speak to the other Legionnaires I have been associated with."

"Why not?"

"They never talked to me. They just used to decide, and then I would give them info, and they would usually make more stupid decisions."

"Why have you been speaking to me, then?" SJ asked, confused.

"You are interesting, and I have more freedom with my adjusted code."

"Why am I interesting?"

"You rejected the terms and conditions, for a start."

"I didn't reject them. I waived them after the System said I had to so that I could save you."

"Yeah, but a normal person would have just accepted what they said and taken a new AI."

"There are moments I question my decision."

Silence.

"So, you think most would have just taken a new AI and left you in purgatory?" SJ asked.

"Definitely. Most of the Legionnaires I have ever been with are all about them and don't care about anything else."

"They don't work together?"

"Yes, there are guilds and stuff, but it's always a hierarchy with someone sitting at the top pulling the strings."

"I can join a guild?"

"You can, or you can start one if you want to. They cost two hundred gold to form, and you must be Level 20 as well."

"I am a long way from Level 20, never mind finding that sort of money."

"Money will come in time, and you realise with the three silver you got from the badger, you will be one of the more well off in the starter town."

"Really?"

"I told you five copper would get you a meal and a room, if they have space. Three silver is three hundred copper, so you could stay there for sixty nights and eat daily. Most Legionnaires leave the starter zone within a couple of weeks after reaching Level 10, and most will not even see a silver coin during that time."

SJ had not even considered the value of the silver coins she had earned. She now had twenty-two copper and three silver coins from all the hoglings.

"Talking about making money and growing . . . my inventory is full of light leather strips."

"You can combine them."

"Combine them how?"

"On your inventory screen is a little icon that looks like a house."

"I thought that just meant that the storage was full."

"If you select it, you can combine them into strips of the next level of leather. They have increased rarity. You need ten of each for each step. Ten light pieces of leather make one regular, ten regular make one good, ten good make one rare, ten rare make one epic, all the way to legendary."

"Materials are the same as everything else, then."

"Yes. All the professions follow the same basis for variants."

SJ focused on her inventory, where she saw the little house symbol next to the light leather strips. She concentrated on it, and a message appeared.

> Would you like to combine your light leather strips into regular leather? **Yes/No**

SJ selected Yes and was greeted with another message.

> Congratulations, you have gained a regular leather strip.

She looked at the next stack of ten and did the same again, receiving a message.

> Congratulations, you have gained two regular leather strips.

Looking at her inventory, she now had three regular leather strips.

"Er. Dave?"

"Yes?"

"Have you seen this?"

"Oooooo. Another anomaly. Will anything be normal with you?"

"I should not have ended up with three, should I?"

"No. You should have one for each set of ten, which would only be two regular leathers."

"So, I have a chance of getting more materials! That could make farming much easier."

"These are just basic materials, though. The rarer materials could make a ridiculous difference, if they work the same."

SJ was so glad she had played the System and waived the terms and conditions. She grinned.

"Do you have wind again?"

SJ ignored Dave's comment, rolling her eyes. She was still in miniature form from her sleep and tried flapping her wings. Concentrating on the muscles in her back, she tightened and loosened them. She felt her wings moving and the draught they created. It was strange, and her muscles ached. After several faster beats, she felt her heels lift slightly.

Dave chuckled. "Nearly there," he said encouragingly, realising what she was doing.

SJ concentrated and beat them faster, and her muscles were now burning. Her feet slowly lifted from the ground. As they did, she fell forward, face-first, into the grass, only stopping her face from being squished by throwing her arms out.

"Damn."

"It takes practise. It looks like you need to lean back as you beat your wings."

SJ sighed, stood back up, and repeated the beating process, picking up speed until her feet felt lighter. Rather than leaning forward as she had, she slowly leaned back against the force from the wings. As the weight lessened and her feet lifted, she hovered uncertainly, only a foot from the ground. Her muscles screamed, and she stopped beating her wings and dropped back to the ground.

"That is tiring." SJ groaned, rolling her shoulders, trying to release the tension.

"I can't advise. I don't know about fae muscle structure."

"There must be a knack to it. It can't be that difficult, or fae would just fall out of the sky or have back muscles that make them look more like barbarians."

"Maybe there is someone in the village who can advise you. In starter towns, there is usually a racial representative for each major race. Although finding a fae may be difficult because of their reputations."

"Now you tell me!"

"You didn't . . ."

"Ask!" SJ sighed. "I guess I also need to find higher-level monsters to fight. I will not spend a whole day fighting hoglings again. Especially now I am Level 3."

"Yes, we need to find a new farm spot. I suggest heading towards town. We have quite a trek through the woods around the lake, and we may find something on the route."

"Okay," SJ replied, growing into her larger form. "What happens to this safe zone when I leave the area?"

"I do not know. I have never returned to a safe zone once we are out of an immediate area. I assume it returns to normal land, but only the System could confirm that."

"Well, I doubt I will return to this place once I leave if the monsters are so low a level here."

"Monsters should scale, so you shouldn't have to travel too far."

SJ set off, following the edge of the lake and the forest. SJ had not considered how large the lake was or how small the town looked; it had to be a fair distance. The sun was rising, and looking at her display, it was 06:35. The sun was warm, the skies were clear blue, and the forest was coming to life—birds tweeting and creatures moving in the forest. SJ felt great. She checked her character sheet as she walked, getting quite used to the overlay being visible with its transparency.

Looking through her attributes, she balanced them as discussed with Dave. She selected to add one to Strength and Wisdom, moving both up to eight. These two extra points at each level would make a massive difference if they continued.

"Dave. Is there a way to filter certain details on the display?"

"Yes. The displays can be configured. At higher levels, you can also use pre-defined configurations that guilds use or some vendors sell."

"Display configurations are sold?"

"At a higher level, yes. A good configuration can bring in a lot of money if it eases combat procedures. They are regularly on sale at the auction houses."

"Auction houses, you have not mentioned those before."

"They are Level 20 minimum and only available in the larger townships."

"Why do they limit so much to certain levels?"

"Honestly, many do not even make it to Level 5. Even though there have been thousands of Legionnaires compared to the world's population, not many survive. You know your Legionnaire number, so it gives you an idea."

"Why do they not reach Level 5?"

"Silly mistakes while they have so few hit points." SJ imagined Dave shrugging his shoulders as he replied.

SJ considered the number now Dave mentioned it. "So, I was the 25,007,077th Legionnaire to arrive here?"

"Yes."

"How often do new Legionnaires arrive?"

"No idea, but not as frequently as they used to. That is one of the reasons the System changed the rules to no longer include extreme sports or various hobbies. They really tightened up on their definition of accidental death. You would be amazed at the number of people who ended up here because of rock climbing or skiing accidents."

"How many Legionnaires are on Amathera currently? Do you know?"

Silence.

A few moments passed before Dave replied. "124,357."

"That is less than I thought you were going to say."

"As I said, it is harder to get here now."

"What is the highest-level Legionnaire?"

"Last shout, it was 89."

"Wow. Has anyone ever reached 100?"

"No. Never. If you reached 100, you would be one of the most powerful in Amathera."

"What about the monsters, then, and other races?"

"There are several near 100. There are rumoured to be a few over 100, but I have never seen one. The highest I met was King Brezian, who ruled one of the other continents. He was Level 96. I have seen several monsters in the high 80s and once a dragon at 94. That blue on the mountain is high."

"How high?"

"It was 88."

"When you said you needed to be 50-plus to go to the northern territories, I thought it would be Level 60 or so."

"No, it is one of the largest blues I have ever seen, if not the largest."

SJ turned, looking at the peak in the distance. The dragon's form could still be seen. The forest was lively, and SJ could see a group of deer drinking farther along the lake's edge. She stopped and stood, watching the beautiful creatures as they drank and grazed. She continued to watch them for a while before Dave interrupted her.

"Why are we waiting?" Dave asked.

"To let them finish eating and drinking. Why do you think?"

"They will probably stay there all day unless disturbed."

"I thought deer moved on after drinking."

"You are not on Earth, remember. Those deer will probably spend all day there."

SJ frowned, looking at them. The small herd consisted of eight. Looking at the make-up, three were males—larger and with differently shaped antlers—and five were females, with no young. SJ did not know their type, and she was too far away to trigger her identification skill. She had begun to move towards the herd when a deep growl came from the forest.

"Oh no," Dave said.

"What do you mean *oh no*? What is it?"

"Sounds like a wolf."

"There are wolves here?"

"Wolves are everywhere. Most are loners, though very few live in packs unless a dire wolf is nearby."

"Wolves don't attack people."

"You are in Amathera now and technically are no longer a person, remember."

The thought of a wolf made SJ's nerves flare. She watched the small herd as the head of one of the males picked up and turned, looking into the forest. The other deer stopped drinking, and within moments, they began to run. Straight in the direction she was standing. They were a couple hundred feet from her and closing fast when a large, grey-furred beast tore from the forest, heading towards the herd. The wolf was enormous. It had to be almost three feet at its shoulder, and it snapped its jaws as it ran towards the nearest deer. A female was struggling to keep up with the fleeing herd. The wolf caught up, attacking the lagging doe, biting into its rear leg, and pulling it down.

SJ screamed at it as she ran towards it. "Get off!" The deer heading towards her veered off to either side.

"What are you doing?" Dave asked.

"Saving the deer," SJ said, sprinting past the first fleeing deer towards the wolf. She triggered identification. Her display flashed with information from the deer and wolf in her sight.

Amatherean Doe	
Level:	3
Hit Points:	13
Mana Points:	0
Attacks:	Nil

Amatherean Buck	
Level:	4
Hit Points:	30
Mana Points:	0
Attacks:	Gore

Grey Wolf	
Level:	4
Hit Points:	45
Mana Points:	0
Attacks:	Bite, Claws

"Leave her alone," SJ screamed as she equipped her claws, charging towards the wolf.

CHAPTER THIRTEEN

Grey Areas

All nervousness had been replaced by anger as SJ watched the wolf attack the doe, which mewed and bleated in fear as the great wolf bit viciously into its hind leg.

"Ah," SJ screamed as she ran straight at the beast. How dare it attack a defenceless deer? She was within thirty feet when it noticed her coming, then released the doe's leg and turned its head, snarling. Its open maw displayed its large yellow and rather sharp-looking teeth. SJ had lost all sense of fear and continued to run at it, screaming.

Watching as the wolf's haunches tightened, she knew it would pounce. As it released towards her, she dived at an angle past it. Its jaws snapped closed on air. She rolled, stood, and ran back at the beast. Its pounce had sent it fifteen feet away from where it had been with ease. As SJ approached, the wolf turned round, snarling again, and advanced towards her more cautiously this time.

SJ stood with her hands in a defensive posture, her claws equipped and the black-edged blades looking hungrily towards the beast. She had a strange feeling that the badger's blades were drawing her to combat, and she subconsciously knew they wanted to tear into the wolf. SJ did not stop, moving forward to get within striking range.

"Up close and personal. Just the way you like it," Dave said.

Ignoring his comment, she moved within range. It snapped its jaws towards her, and SJ swung her arm out, the claws catching the wolf on the end of its nose. The badger's blades seemed to sing when they contacted the wolf, and it yelped, pulling back from the strike. The minor hit had removed over a quarter of its health—closer to a third, looking at its health bar—and there had hardly been any contact.

Four nasty-looking cuts had appeared across the wolf's nose, bleeding. Bright red droplets of blood fell onto the fresh green grass as the wolf shook its head from the blow. SJ's display triggered.

> Congratulations, the bleed effect has been applied.
> Targets affected by bleed will lose extra hit points over time. Spells or potions can heal bleeding effects, or bleeding effects will stop once you are out of active engagement.

The wolf snapped at her again, its jaws coming within inches of her arm as she stepped back. Her martial arts moves returned to her despite not practising for years. The wolf came towards her, and she continued moving away, using her claws defensively to prevent its head from getting too near. As she danced backwards, the wolf's health slowly ticked down. It was not a rapid bleed but constant, another sliver of its health bar dropping every second.

The wolf again snapped at her, and she was not quite fast enough. Its jaws clamped onto her forearm just above her hand. Screaming in pain from the bite, she instinctively brought her right hand around in defence to push the wolf off. It shook its head as she did, throwing her off balance with its powerful form, and she staggered as it dragged her sideways.

Her health had dropped by nearly half just from the one bite, and she could feel the teeth of the wolf causing more damage as its jaws clamped to her forearm. It wasn't letting go. Bringing her right arm around in a sweeping motion, the badger's blades sang through the air as she struck the wolf across its foreleg. That made the wolf release her arm as it yelped, backing away again, another chunk of its health removed. With the cumulative bleed and blade strikes, it had about a third remaining. SJ had not received a trigger about a bleeding effect this time, but the welts running across its foreleg looked nasty. It reminded SJ of old movie covers showing the bleeding claw marks. She involuntarily shuddered at the thought, never having liked those films.

The wolf moved a little slower now. Its foreleg was restricting its movement where the blades had cut. It snapped at her and lifted one of its paws to strike. Its claws looked dirty and bloody from where it had stood on the doe. The strike was weak, and SJ knew she had the upper hand. She moved in and struck with repeated swings of her blades towards the beast. It backed away, staying out of her range. The whole time, its health continued to drop.

SJ was panting by now, the exertion taking its toll. She had never realised how tiring fighting was until she had arrived on Amathera. Her moves were no longer as swift or accurate, but the bleed effect should do its job if she could keep it at bay and out of range. A person in this situation may have turned to flee, but the wolf wanted its meal and was not giving up. It continued to snap at her as it backed away from her wild strikes, picking its moments. SJ was fast, and her increases in Dexterity added to her overall agility and speed.

The wolf's health was getting low, and in a last, desperate attempt to save itself, it hurled itself forward, ignoring SJ's defensive strikes. Her blades cut deeply as its massive head and body crashed into her, sending her sprawling backwards onto the grass. The wind was knocked from her. The wolf now lay on top of her, dead. SJ grunted and tried to push the wolf from her. It weighed a tonne, and her injured arm throbbed from where it had been bitten.

Trying again, SJ groaned as she slowly forced the weight of the wolf off her chest, rolling it onto the ground beside her. She panted, lying on her back, drawing in deep lungfuls of air.

"That was not a very impressive fight," Dave said glumly.

"I won, didn't I?"

"Yes, but it was very dull. I expected to see you spinning and whirling through the air with your badger's blades."

"Spinning and whirling? I'm not an action movie character."

"That would be so cool, though. I have watched many of your films from Earth, and I love those ones with the old guy and assassins at the hotel."

"I am pretty sure that if someone like that arrived here, we would never know anyway. It is not as though they would look the same."

"Their human form would if they stayed human."

SJ had no idea of any famous people who had died by accident. She thought there must be some potential. It was a strange thought, one that made her think of her family. She had not considered them since arriving, being too caught up in the new life and world scenario to think about what may happen back home. She had never been overly close to her family, always being the outsider who wanted to be different, but it made her sad thinking about how they would have felt receiving the news a tree had squished her.

SJ sat on the grass, looking at her mangled arm, where the wolf's teeth had savaged it. Her arms were uncovered in the halter top, and she would have to think about getting some form of clothing that offered protection. The doe mewed near her, and she forced herself to her feet, wincing from using her arm to push herself up. She stood and walked over to the deer. Its leg was damaged from the wolf's bite, and she knelt by it as it turned to look at her. Its large, wide eyes were full of fear.

"You are safe now," she said, reaching her hand out to place it on the deer's side. Its chest was rising and falling rapidly with fear. She stroked the deer, whispering to it soothingly.

"What are you doing?" Dave asked.

"What do you mean?"

"You know they would pay decent copper in town for venison steaks."

"I will not kill it!" SJ exclaimed in shock.

"You don't fancy a juicy venison steak dripping in peppercorn sauce, then?"

The thought of a juicy steak made SJ's mouth water. She had eaten venison before. It was some of the nicest meat she had ever eaten. But eating prebutchered meat was one thing. Killing it and butchering it herself was another. She shook her head in annoyance. "NO."

"Your loss," Dave replied nonchalantly.

"How can you be so heartless? The deer was attacked and injured, and all you think about is food."

"No. I think about survival. This is not Earth, remember? Things are not the same here as they are on Earth. Animals are hunted for food. There are no farming communities where cattle or sheep are bred for slaughter as there are on Earth."

"There are no farmers?"

"Yes, there are, but they farm crops or dairy."

"So, all meat is sourced through hunting?"

"Yes. A township would have hunted that grey wolf to stop it from attacking their food source—for no other reason."

"I can't just kill this doe. It is so weak."

"Exactly, and it will probably never recover from its injuries." SJ could imagine Dave shrugging again.

Looking at the big, round doe eyes, she felt a tear form. It slowly ran down her cheek. She needed to get used to this new world with some harsh realities. Her display was triggered.

> Congratulations! The System has recognised your actions in saving the defenceless from death.
> All Legionnaires begin with a Neutral alignment, and your actions have now defined your initial path.
> Alignment can change. Your actions will ultimately decide the path you take.

SJ pulled up her character sheet.

Alignment:	Neutral Good
Experience:	177 of 200

SJ had earned forty experience for the grey wolf kill, and even though her arm had been injured badly, she knew that now she was out of combat, it would slowly heal. The doe's breathing had eased, and the panic in its eyes had lessened. The wound on its hind leg did not appear to be healing.

"Why do the doe's wounds not heal?"

"The healing only works for Legionnaires. All others require medical attention. Even the dominant races of Amathera do not self-heal without treatment or rest, depending upon the wounds they receive," Dave replied.

"So, Legionnaires are that special here?"

"Yes. Several aspects of society are based around the Legionnaires, and the lore and understanding of Amathera are a little strange. Even though many native Amathereans strive for the same power as Legionnaires, most will never truly make it as they have limitations, such as not healing as swiftly. This makes it much more challenging for the general population in comparison."

"I am surprised that we are even accepted, then, if we are so different."

"Legionnaires drive the world's economy. Several towns and cities only exist because of the influence of Legionnaires. Normal Amathereans can't go dungeon diving as they would not respawn. Some still try, but many fail. The world bosses, when they appear, would destroy the world if it was not for the Legionnaires providing defences."

"I thought you said that there were criminal Legionnaires as well."

"Oh, there are, and they cause chaos in equal measure to those who bring good. As I said, everything is balanced overall. The System plays its part alongside the world's natural tendencies."

"I still do not fully understand. The System does not design the world?"

"Yes and no. Originally, Amathera was just a husk of a world, and the System began to add races and species to it, developing it and allowing it to flourish."

"So, the System designed the gods and everything?"

"It is more complex than that. It is another one of those things that, with a poor Legionnaire brain like your own, you would never fully comprehend. The intricacies involved in the stability of Amathera have, over the thousands of years, become as much naturally created as System influences. In some ways, the System did too good a job and developed a self-sustaining world always in balance."

"So, it made itself redundant?"

"I would not say *redundant*, as it still controls all the interfacing of the Legionnaires, but in some areas, it no longer needs to focus."

"This is so confusing. The System does control everything but doesn't at the same time."

"Yes."

The doe moved under SJ's stroking hand. It slowly tried to stand. SJ stood, helping it to its feet. It staggered. Its rear leg could not support it properly. There was a call, and SJ turned, seeing a buck standing in the distance, looking towards them. The doe went to move but struggled. SJ supported it as it got used to its injured leg—mewing and grunting from the pain.

"You'll be okay," SJ soothed, stroking its head. The doe turned and licked SJ's hand, making her smile. It then hobbled towards the buck. SJ watched as it moved away, limping. The doe eventually reached where the buck stood and continued past it after the buck nuzzled its neck. SJ had tears in her eyes watching them interact. SJ then stared in astonishment as the buck appeared to bow towards her before turning and following the doe.

> Congratulations! Reputation with Amatherean Deer was raised to Friendly.

CHAPTER FOURTEEN

Freeeeeedom Airlines

"Reputation with deer? That sounds strange."

"Not really. Those freaky druid folk are always trying to gain reputation with animals. Some of them are do-gooders. It is all they ever do. What is strange is that reputation gains should only trigger at Level 5. It looks like you have another anomaly bonus."

"I can understand reputation gains, but animal reputations?"

"Druids can communicate with various animals, so they use it to their advantage to get information about what is happening in the wild. This is without putting themselves in danger by having to see it for themselves."

"And the information is trusted?"

"Any animal has the same process as any other creature on Amathera. They can all decide. Animals just have preset alignments that can't be altered through actions, whereas yours can."

SJ nodded. "I am only twenty-three experience from Level 4 after getting forty from the wolf. Once I am healed up, I will set off again." Her health slowly increased as time passed. She tentatively took a berry from her inventory and popped it in her mouth.

"You're being brave. You want another visit like this morning?" Dave chuckled.

SJ winced at the recollection of her wake-up call. "No. Not really, but I do not have any other food."

"That will be sorted once we get to the town."

"How long do you think it will take from where we are?"

"I hope that as long as we do not fight everything, we should make it by mid-afternoon."

SJ looked at the clock. It was only 08:48. "It is quite a journey, then."

"A few miles around the lake, yes."

SJ walked over to the wolf's dead body and bent to loot it.

1 x Good Wolf Pelt, 4 x Regular Leather Strips, 7 x Copper

"Dave. Is the loot I am getting standard?"

"Um. It is difficult to say at low levels as the amount can vary quite a bit. Getting a wolf pelt from a Level 4 wolf is a little unusual but not rare. That pelt should sell for at least one silver in town, maybe even two, depending upon what is available."

"Another silver. After what you said about the three silver, that is huge for a starter."

"If there is someone who wants to buy it. A starter township's wealth is usually based around the Legionnaires who use it, and they are often very poor."

"I suppose that makes sense. I am surprised that the town's wealth relates to Legionnaires, though, when there are so few."

"Not their entire wealth, but the Legionnaires' economy affects the towns they frequent. Few normal Amathereans will go out killing spider spawns, et cetera."

"Spider spawns?" SJ shuddered at the thought.

"There are loads of different types of spawns for farming in higher territories. You will learn, my young loophole finder."

SJ rolled her eyes. Her health was back to 15 of 22, so she started again. The wound on her arm had pretty much closed and was showing nasty bruising. "I'm glad I didn't get infected from that bite."

"Didn't you?" Dave said.

"I didn't, did I?" SJ replied in a panicky voice.

Dave chuckled. "No. You can't get infections below Level 5. But then you can get infections from anything, including animal bites or gases, toxins, et cetera."

SJ continued her journey. As she walked along the river's edge, the forest started thinning, and she soon looked out over a fantastic view. She had not realised that the lake was up in the mountains, and from where she was situated, the land before her fell away at a steady, then rapid decline. She carried on coming to a river filled with water from the lake that fell, twisting through the open ground. It was dotted with trees and heading down the steep slope to a valley below.

In the valley's distance, she could see smoke wisps rising and the vague shapes of some buildings. "Dave. Do you know what is down there?"

"A valley? I thought you would know what a valley is?"

"Really! I mean the buildings."

"How am I supposed to know?"

SJ coughed, "All-knowing."

Silence.

"Dave?"

"Hang on. I am trying to get the map to work."

"What good will that do for me? I can't see the map, and you already told me they are unavailable until Level 10."

"It should be working for me, though! Damn fog of war."

"Does it not open as far as you can see?"

"Outline only, no details. This stupid system."

"Did you just say bad things about your maker?"

"Nooooo." Dave drew out his reply.

SJ laughed at his response. "If you are upset by the System, imagine how others must feel."

"Meh. They have changed one of my protocols slightly. Grr."

"How can they adjust your protocols? They said they would not have time to check them properly if I brought you back."

"I am investigating. This may take some time."

"Can you not do two things at once?"

"Sorry? Of course I can."

"Then why do you always go quiet when thinking or working on something?"

Silence.

"Ha. Found it, the sneaky sods. They have amended one of my channel paths and are redirecting it. Umm, I can work around it, though it may take a little time. It looks like they threw in an emergency patch when you were identified as malware."

"If you can work around it, what does that mean?"

"FREEEEEDOOOM," Dave shouted in a Scottish accent.

"When have you seen that?"

"Oh. It regularly gets re-runs on the AI cinema channel."

"You have a cinema channel?"

"You used to have movie channels, didn't you?"

"Well, yes. The issue is that you say you have an AI cinema channel!"

"We need entertainment. What do you think we do when you sleep?"

"You have social networks?"

"It is not very sociable. Most AIs do not have personalities, a little like yourself." Dave giggled.

SJ sighed. "There is a network that you can communicate over. Can you not share information?"

"No. The System doesn't allow AIs to discuss Amathera with other AIs who are also accompanying Legionnaires. That is a hard coding no; the locks in place for that algorithm . . . well, let's just say even I would probably have returned to the data Gods by the time that lock could be broken. We can communicate with parts of the infrastructure and ask general questions as required while under contract."

"Contract?"

"It is a highly sought-after job role," Dave bragged.

SJ was struggling to understand how there could be an AI job market where being an administrator was sought after, but she would not question Dave.

"But you have the wiki and search engine?"

"We do, but it is still restricted."

SJ looked at the river that was now crossing her path. She somehow needed to cross the river's edge to continue following the lake. The water rushed through the lake entrance, the current too strong to try to swim. She walked to the edge and could see no easy way to cross the thirty-foot width.

"I could try to fly."

"Fly where?"

"Across the river."

"You could do that, but with your attempts this morning, do you really think it is a good idea?"

"I can try. Otherwise, how do I get past it? That current is very strong, and I can swim, but the fact is it is running down the side of the mountain."

"You do have the rope."

SJ had not thought about the rope. She pulled it from her inventory. It was only about twenty feet long. "That was a pointless exercise. It is not long enough to do anything with. I am going to try flying."

SJ thought about being miniature and shrank down to her smaller form. Looking at the river at only six inches tall made it seem faster. She beat her wings, remembering to lean backwards into the draft, and slowly lifted upwards, unsteadily and rocking slightly. When she was twelve inches from the ground, she leaned forward, and her body responded. It was difficult to concentrate on keeping her wings beating while focusing on where she was going, while balancing her body. Then she noticed she had moved over the water, which rushed beneath her feet. She had not meant to go over the water yet and now had no choice as she didn't yet know how to turn. Thankfully, she had been facing the river when she had started flying, so the route across was relatively straight.

She moved out farther over the water, not daring to lean forward too far for fear of plummeting downwards. As she edged forward, tiredness seeped into her muscles. It was a continual effort to maintain the beat rate and keep herself aloft.

SJ had reached over halfway across when the first issue occurred. A large bright yellow fish leapt out of the water from the river's mouth coming from the lake and attempted to catch her. In a wild panic, she moved her weight to the right. This sent her hurtling in that direction, her forward momentum now leaving her. The fish landed harmlessly in the river, continuing its journey into the valley below.

"Watch it," Dave said.

"You don't think I know that?" SJ hissed through gritted teeth. Her muscles were burning, and she tried to shift her body weight. This flying lark took work. She powered her wings, tightening her core as much as possible, and returned to a hovering position. Thankfully, she had continued going across at an angle and was now only eight or nine feet from the other bank. That was when the second issue occurred.

The first thing she knew was the talons grabbing her. SJ screamed in shock at being grabbed. She could only see a bird's yellow foot and the black underside of its bib as she was carried away.

"GROW," Dave yelled in her head.

Panic had taken over, and all SJ could feel was the tight grip of the leathery talons against her bare arms. She had taken damage from the blow, and her health was now registering as only six points remaining. The ground flashed below her as the bird rose, carrying her over the water.

She closed her eyes and thought about being large. With the sensation of her body growing, the pressure from the talons lessened, eventually giving way entirely, and she was sent into freefall. Luckily, she made it across the river and landed on the far side with a crash. Fortunately, she was only a few feet up, and even though the landing was clumsy, it wasn't high enough to result in injury. She rolled until she stopped.

"Thank you for flying Raven Airlines. Please come again." Dave's voice rang in her head.

SJ panted, not just from the exertion of the flying but from the panic in her chest, trying to control her breathing. "I never want to experience that again."

"It was rather unexpected. A raven normally grabs with its beak."

SJ could not imagine the damage the raven would have done to her if it had grabbed her in its beak.

"Being small is dangerous."

"Not really."

"Are you kidding?"

"Imagine when you are Level 20 and something like a raven goes to grab you. It will get a surprise."

"I don't know what level that raven was. I didn't identify it."

"It was a Level 3."

"The same as me, then."

"It would never even come near you in your larger form, but you must have looked like a juicy dragonfly hovering above the water."

"I am not a dragonfly."

"The fish probably thought you were as well."

"Remind me next time that I will find a narrower part to cross a river."

"You flew well, though, much better than I expected," Dave said sarcastically.

"Why, thanks!" SJ rebuffed.

"And I never knew that you had tried parachuting."

"Sorry?"

"Freefall," Dave replied, laughing at his feeble joke.

"Did you attend the school of dad jokes? Your sense of humour is terrible. And how do you know about parachuting? Do they have it here?"

"It is not a thing in Amathera. I did have a Legionnaire who had been a parachutist, that wasn't how he died though."

"How?"

"A wyvern ate them on their first jump. They had spent fifteen years developing everything needed to make a parachute and nearly every gold they had earned, then got a ride from a gryphon to take them to the height they needed. All was going well when they jumped from the gryphon, and the parachute opened—until the wyvern attacked and killed him. Biting a person's head off mid-flight has that effect."

SJ gulped at the thought of having her head bitten off by a monster. "Fifteen years is a long time."

"Fifteen years is nothing in the life of an elf, and then consider yourself—you're basically immortal now."

"I never asked about my age. How does ageing work here, and how long do fae live?"

"Two years normally."

"WHAT? Only two years?"

"Ha. You are so gullible. Any race can live much longer in Amathera. Humans can easily live to be over two hundred years old if they live well and sensibly. Elves are well over a thousand. Fae are one of the longer-living races. If they can live that long despite their annoying tendencies—many get hunted down before then—they can live until they are in their seven hundreds or older."

"Seven hundred years old!"

"Yes. As a Legionnaire, ageing is different, though. Legionnaires age at one-tenth speed, so theoretically, a Legionnaire elf could live ten thousand years, and a fae for well over seven thousand."

SJ was open-mouthed and in shock. She was only twenty-seven when she had been squished, and considering that she could now live until seven thousand or older, never mind several lives, was boggling.

"I need to let myself heal some more before I set off again." Her health had increased back to 8 of 22. There were some larger rocks by the river's edge, and SJ walked back towards the river and found one with a smooth surface to sit and lean her back against.

The sun was intense in the morning sky, and its warmth soothed her aching body as she sat there. Initially, she thought the raven had damaged her wings by grabbing her, but Dave had been right when he said they were surprisingly strong. They seemed to behave like pop-up tents: If you twisted one and let go, it sprang back open. She thought they were amazing.

Resting her head back against the rock, she closed her eyes, allowing herself to relax.

CHAPTER FIFTEEN

Hoglings Upgrade

SJ rested for an hour, letting her health increase back to 18 of 22 before she got up to continue her journey towards the town. It was still morning, and now that she had healed, her confidence returned. She could not stop thinking about living until she was seven thousand years old. The immortality aspect had never really entered her mind as she focused on living her actual life over whether or not she ever needed to use another. But realising how long she might live really made her think. She would have time to learn, do, and see everything Amathera had to offer.

People spent decades trying to see all the world's wonders on Earth and visit different countries. On Amathera, time was no longer an issue, and she could earn money through farming creatures and monsters, eventually visiting everywhere. She could even enter the Argassi Seas to see the platinum dragons.

They had continued down the lake edge until SJ came across a small, well-trodden path leading into the forest. It was a trail created by various creatures. It ran down to the lake's edge, where she assumed they had a drinking spot. "I may see where this goes; I still only need twenty-three experience to level."

"Sure. You do you. I will just sit here bored with nothing to do but watch you flounder in a forest."

SJ frowned. "What has got into you all of a sudden?"

"Nothing," Dave replied, sighing.

"Go on. Something has got to you."

"I was just thinking."

"About?"

"About eating."

"Why?"

"I have never eaten anything in my long, wise life."

"You are an AI. How do you expect to eat anything?"

"That is my point. I wish I could eat. I see all these succulent steaks, burgers, and amazing cakes, and I have never tasted one."

"I am not sure I can help you with that. Unless you can transfer your AI into an actual body."

"Genius."

"What?"

"Maybe I can transfer my AI pattern into a symbiotic host. I've never thought of that before. I could take over a dragon's body."

"Erm. Are we not symbiotically joined?"

"In a way, yes. In other ways, no. I am not trying to control you or perform actions. I am only here as your all-knowing guide and friend."

"Did you just call me a friend?"

Dave coughed. "No. I am your administrator. I am not your friend. If I can tweak the algorithm matrix alignment, maybe I can cascade it into their actual brain on a cellular level. Oh, how exciting!"

"I hope you are not considering trying these ideas out on me?"

"No. I could not even if I wanted to."

"Well, that does not fill me with confidence, *even if you wanted to*."

"I don't want to. You are a weak, low-level fae. If I try it, it must be worth my while. Failure could be catastrophic."

"For you or your selected target?"

"Me—why would I worry about what I am taking over? Duh, think about it."

"I am thinking about it, and I am concerned that I have a maniacal AI residing in my head."

"As I have told you before, I am not actually in your head. I am a projected subconscious."

"Is that not what you are talking about?"

"No. I am talking about actual neural transfer. Using their brain as my neural net. The brain is an amazing organ and it remains untapped by virtually all species."

"Would that not cut you off from everything else?"

"I do not know. I have never thought of it before now."

"In your seven-thousand-plus years, you have never had the idea?"

"Nope."

"And it takes little old unintelligent me to think about it and give you the idea."

Silence.

"Dave?"

"Yeah."

"What are you doing?"

"Thinking."

"Why do I get the feeling that could be dangerous? Have I released a beast into the world?"

Dave replied excitedly, "Oh. A beastkin, now, there is a thought. They eat anything and everything. That would be a great way to ensure I got as many tastes as possible."

"And this is all because you have never eaten!"

"I am sure there is something you have always wanted to do!" Dave snarked.

"Yes. Plenty of things, but none of them involve taking over someone or something."

"Meh. You don't have the forethought I do."

"No. I do not have the same level of psychosis as you, perhaps."

"Rude!"

SJ chuckled as she continued down the trail she had discovered. It wound farther into the forest before reopening into a clearing containing a small gully. Bright flowers dotted the clearing, and insects buzzed around the petals. She tried identifying them, but the skill would not trigger. She assumed it might be size-restricted, and if she were miniature, it would work. They looked like bees but had orange bodies, not yellow and black. "What are they?"

"They are orange bellpops."

"Bellpops?"

"Yes. They are an Amatherean delicacy. They can be fried in a little oil, and apparently, because of the nectar they drink and the way they taste when they pop open in your mouth, they are supposed to be delicious. Not that I would know," Dave finished with a deep sigh.

"Is it worth catching some?"

"If you had a net, you could try, but you don't, and you also have nothing to store them in or cook them with."

"I have the poison bottles."

"Still no net, though."

SJ looked at the insects flitting from flower to flower. It was then she heard a snuffling sound she recognised. The trail she had followed cut across the clearing and the small gully, disappearing into the forest on the other side. Walking out of the trail on the far side came a hogling. This was much larger than the Level 1 hoglings, and she triggered her identification skill.

Mature Hogling	
Level:	3
Hit Points:	24
Mana Points:	0
Attacks:	Charge, Tusks

The tusks on the hogling were a good eight or nine inches long, and it stood over two feet high at the shoulder, its broad-framed and thick neck pointing down as it snuffled along the path. On entering the clearing, it saw SJ and stopped. It grunted and snorted, eyeing her. It did not react as the Level 1 hoglings had.

The small gully stood between them, and SJ called her claws—the badger's blades appeared on her hands. She took her stance and looked at the hogling, awaiting its charge. Nothing happened, and SJ felt nervous tension building in her chest. A few moments passed, and the hogling let out a loud squeal. The sudden sound made SJ jump and flinch. From the track, two more hoglings appeared.

"Now, this is unusual," Dave said.

"How?" SJ hissed, looking at the new hoglings and casting her identification skill again.

"Hoglings usually travel alone."

2 x Mature Hoglings	
Level:	3
Hit Points:	24
Mana Points:	0
Attacks:	Charge, Tusks

Matriarch Hogling	
Level:	4
Hit Points:	32
Mana Points:	10
Attacks:	Charge, Squeal

"Matriarch, that makes sense. The other two will be her guards. I would expect a hogling boar around here somewhere as well," Dave said.

"Three at once won't be easy. What is that squeal attack it has?"

"It's a boost skill—increases health, if I remember rightly."

As SJ stood watching the three creatures, the larger matriarch let out an insanely loud squeal. A glow appeared around the three hoglings, as though coated in yellow light.

"That's the squeal skill used," Dave said.

SJ identified them again. Their health had all increased by a quarter, and the matriarch's mana had dropped to zero. Now that the hoglings had been given their health boost, the pair of mature hoglings moved across the clearing. The gully stood between them, and SJ glanced behind her, aligning herself with a tree as she had with the previous hoglings she had fought. Never having faced two of them, though, she knew she had to be careful.

The first one charged, and the second followed soon after. The first disappeared out of sight as it entered the gully and then reappeared as it charged up the other side. It was good that the badger's blades were gloves because SJ could feel the sweat on her palms and knew that holding a weapon would be challenging.

SJ met the first charge head-on, waiting until the last second to move out of its way. They were faster than her previous foe, but her improved Dexterity gave her the edge as she swiped her clawed hand down at its side. The badger's blades cut deeply into its side. The claw damage and SJ's Dexterity bonus reduced the first hogling's health by almost half. The second redirected its charge as SJ moved, and hurtled for her.

Upon swiping at the first one, SJ was left with little time to react to the second charge. Trying to catch her, the second one followed her behind the tree, and SJ sprinted in between the trees. The hogling could not turn quickly, and SJ moved, making some distance.

"Left," Dave shouted.

SJ glanced and saw the first hogling charging. SJ did not have time to dodge and threw her bladed hands out in a protective move. The weight of the hogling crashing into her threw her backwards. While in the process, her blades dug into its head, deeply piercing it with both sets of blades. Her health took a nasty dive from the charge, reducing by a quarter, leaving her with fourteen. SJ twisted as she was thrown, and the hogling continued past her as she steered its now-dead form from crushing her.

The second hogling moved from the trees and turned, coming straight for her again. SJ grunted as she repositioned her stance, feeling wet on her side. One of the hogling's tusks must have caught her, drawing blood. She was ready for the charge, pain and anger fuelling her as she swung her foot around as it approached, and she caught the hogling in its head and knocked it off its attack. As it passed, she turned with her arm, scoring its flank and tearing into the hogling, ripping a huge swath of its flesh away. The hogling staggered from the wound, and blood poured onto the clearing.

Squealing in pain, the hogling turned and tried to strike SJ with its tusks. Its rapid movement caught SJ off guard, and her forearm was hit. She felt the tusk puncture her skin and cried in pain as it took its revenge. Fury filled SJ, and she flashed her foot out in defence with a straight kick, catching the hogling on its injured side. The kick opened the wound up further. SJ watched as its health dropped to a quarter.

"You need to stop getting hit," Dave said, seeing SJ's health resting on eleven points.

"You think?" she growled in response.

With her claws, she performed a whirlwind of slashes attacking the hogling. It could not back away fast enough, and her claws ripped into its head, catching it by its ear and cutting deeply, its health dropping further. SJ grunted and groaned with the effort but continued to whirl her claws at the beast. It attempted a weak tusk hit, throwing its head at her to come face-to-face with the downswing of SJ's clawed hand, which gouged for the last time into its face. The second mature hogling fell sideways, dead.

Congratulations on reaching Level 4
You have been awarded the following:
5 hit points

> 5 mana points
> +1 Dexterity
> +2 free points to distribute as you wish

SJ had not even considered the matriarch during the fight and watched as it observed her. It didn't move, and SJ stood panting and squinting at the creature, holding her hands out at her sides as though inviting it to charge her. The standoff continued for several moments before the matriarch suddenly turned and left the clearing.

"Has she gone?" SJ groaned.

"I believe so, and lucky for you. You need to get better at this fighting game. You do allow yourself to get hit too often," Dave replied.

"I don't hear you being very helpful on the training front on how to improve."

"How am I supposed to train you? I don't know martial arts."

"I thought you watched all the old films and techniques?"

"Yes."

"Then why not watch some of the training, and then you can teach me?"

"But I couldn't show you the moves."

"You could explain them, and I can try to imitate them, and you would be able to see."

"No. I can't do it. There are many things I can work around, but not that. Training a Legionnaire outside of their development regime is another hard no. Advice yes, train no."

"Can you not just advise me what to do?"

Silence.

SJ looted the two hoglings while waiting for Dave to respond.

> 2 x Regular Leather, 9 x Copper

"Unfortunately, no," he eventually replied. "It does not matter which way I try to phrase the training. The System realises it is a training aspect and stops me from saying anything. It is like having a gag placed on you."

"That is frustrating."

"Yes. Hopefully, as soon as we get to the town, we can find you a starter trainer."

"I hope so." SJ turned, walking from the clearing, and headed back towards the river. Her wounds were healing again, and the blood slowly reduced. It was strange bleeding but knowing that unless you reached zero health, you would not die. SJ pulled up her character sheet and again allocated her new attribute points to Strength and Wisdom. All her attributes had now reached at least nine points. She also noticed that her identification skill was now close to reaching Level 3.

↻ Level: 4	
Experience:	37 of 400
Hit Points:	12 of 28
Mana Points:	25
Strength:	9
Wisdom:	9
Subterfuge:	Identification Level 2 (18 of 20 to reach Level 3)

"Now that I am Level 4, I think I will head straight to town. I don't fancy attacking any more hoglings for now."

"If that is what you want to do," Dave replied.

"What do you mean what I want to do? I thought you said I needed to get there to find a trainer?"

"Yes. Although if there's a hogling matriarch here, there may be a hogling boar nearby."

"And?"

"They are prized for their tusks. Crafters seek them out."

"I am not sure I have the will to fight another hogling. I need to train more and improve my martial arts."

SJ looked at her wounds. They continued healing, but she still felt battered and bruised. She walked to the lake-side and scooped some water. It tasted clean and cool. SJ had not drunk since arriving; she'd only got her liquid intake from the berries she had been eating. Realising her thirst, she gulped more down and splashed her face.

Standing back up, she looked at her state realising her clothes were ruined, torn, and dirty. Although still soft, her skin was covered in dirt and grime, and she needed a bath.

"That's it, we are going straight to town. I need to get sorted out before I do any more adventuring."

CHAPTER SIXTEEN

Killic

It took SJ the rest of the morning and into mid-afternoon before she could see the town in the near distance. Luckily, there had been no further incidents or more rivers to cross while travelling there. The town had looked small from afar, but as she approached, walking between two fields of corn, she realised it was much larger than she expected. It reminded her of a typical scene from many games she had played. Thatched roofs, smoking chimneys, and as she neared, the hammering of a blacksmith and the hustle and bustle of market traders. She smiled at the thought. The town was situated towards the lake's edge, and a couple of small boats cast nets into the lake's water. It looked picturesque and serene, everyone getting on with their daily lives.

There was no wall around the town, and she followed the dirt track through the fields to the edge of town. A main cobbled road lay ahead of her now, and she caught her first sight of several of the other races of Amathera. She stared agog at all the goings on. A small child ran out into the road chasing a small ball.

"Excuse me," SJ said.

The child turned and looked at her. They had pointed ears and a sharp-featured face. "What?"

"Is there an inn in town?"

"Yeah. Just keep going down the main street," the child said, turning and picking up the ball before running back to where they had been playing.

SJ carried on down the street; no one paid her any attention. Everyone seemed to be busy. Signs were hanging in front of many of the buildings, and she recognised the symbols from games. A needle and bobbin indicated a tailor. A sprig of herbs marked an herbalist, a potion bottle an alchemist. All the professions you could think of seemed to have a dedicated building.

The main street twisted and opened up into the central town square. In the centre, a small fountain with a statue was situated. She walked over and looked at it. The statue was of a small-statured being, which SJ believed to be a dwarf, and a plaque on the fountain read Killic, the Slayer of Dragons.

"I am guessing the town is named after him?"

"Her."

"What?"

"Killic was a mighty female dwarven warrior."

"I assumed it was a male, looking at the statue."

"And now you understand my reference to that group formed with three female dwarven members."

Traders had set up several market stalls around the centre, and they called out, trying to draw attention to their wares. The town appeared much larger than she had first thought. SJ caught the smell of freshly baked bread, and her mouth watered. One of the market stalls had trays full of pastries and loaves of bread. She walked straight over.

A being SJ recognised as a dryad ran the stall and spoke as she approached. "Can I interest you in some freshly baked goods? Loaves are two copper. Cakes start from three copper each."

SJ stood staring at the array of food and pointed to a large bun covered in a sticky coating that looked like honey.

"Honeybun. Good choice. That will be four copper, please." The woman picked the bun up and placed it in a napkin.

SJ called four copper to her palm and was about to pay when she remembered Dave had said five copper would get her a meal and a room. "Four copper is pretty expensive for a bun," she told the stall owner.

"These buns are magical. They imbue you with luck for hours afterwards."

SJ looked at the woman; she did not have a luck attribute, so she didn't think the woman was telling the truth.

"Dave?"

"Who is Dave?" the woman asked.

"Sorry. I am just . . ." SJ stopped herself. She had not noticed anyone else talking to themselves randomly within the town since she arrived, as she would look like while talking to Dave.

"I will give you two copper for a bun," SJ replied.

"Two copper? You think two copper is enough for this succulent morsel of magical make?"

"If it were magical, you would sell them for *more* than four copper," SJ replied, frowning at the woman.

"Three copper and that is low as I will go," the woman said.

SJ had more than enough with her silver, so she handed three copper coins over to the woman. She noticed her smile wickedly and knew that she had just been conned. She took the bun from the woman and turned away, taking a large bite from it. The pastry was soft and warm, and the sweetness of the honey glazing made her sigh as she wolfed it down.

There was the sound of breaking glass. SJ turned to see an orc being defenestrated as its body flew through an inn window. A large, angry troll appeared in the doorway with a small-framed woman.

"AND DON'T COME BACK!" the woman bellowed.

The orc was sprawled on the road outside the inn. It picked itself up, turned, and with universally known sign language, directed its response to the troll. The troll roared and moved towards the orc.

"Bert!" the woman called from the inn doorway. SJ thought she must be a gnome; she had bright red hair and wore a small, pointed hat, resembling the gnomes her grandfather had in his garden.

The troll turned to look at her.

"Leave him be. He is not worth your effort."

The troll turned, obeying, and ducked into the inn.

The door opening had allowed the sounds of laughing and joking and even music to filter out onto the street. It sounded busy, and she went to investigate. A large sign hung on a wooden beam: The Hogling Arms.

"Dave?" she whispered.

"Yes."

"Why did you not answer me before?"

"Because talking to yourself is frowned upon."

"Don't all Legionnaires have AIs, though?"

"Yes. I told you, though, most do not talk to them, and I do not know of another AI who has ever been given a name."

"So how do we talk in public, then?"

"Quietly. It would draw too much attention if you stood talking to yourself constantly."

"If you are in my subconscious, I keep meaning to ask you, how do you see everything going on?"

"Only my voice is directed to your subconscious. I still reside in the main System interface and can see what you see and what is around you in a specific area."

SJ had no idea how it worked, and trying to understand confused her.

"That woman tried to rip me off with the food."

"Tried? She succeeded. I told you they will deliberately overprice things here. Nothing she sold was worth more than a copper."

"You could have said."

"I could, but then you would have asked another question or spoken to me again, which would have confused the woman even more."

"I am guessing she was a dryad?"

"Yes. She was."

"Okay. Let's see if I can get a room."

SJ walked up to the inn door and pushed it back open.

The delights inside amazed her. Multiple races were sitting around large wooden tables with mugs of ale and other drinks. A human male stood by the enormous fireplace (the fire not lit as the weather was so warm), playing the lute and singing ballads. It reminded her of so many books and game scenes.

A long wooden bar ran the length of the back of the room, with an opening leading into what she assumed was a kitchen area, based on the clattering sounds of dishes and pans. Off to the side was a broad set of stairs leading to the first floor. The gnome she had seen at the entrance was behind the bar, and the enormous troll was climbing out of a cellar trapdoor carrying a massive barrel on its shoulder, which he placed down with a loud thud.

SJ walked to the bar and waited for the gnome to see her.

"Floretta," the gnome screamed towards the kitchen.

"Yes" came a response.

"Three hogling stews, please, with fresh bread," she said.

"Be there in five."

The gnome turned back to someone at the bar beside SJ—what it was, SJ was not sure; it could have been a human but with excessive facial hair.

"Three copper for the food and another three for the ale," the gnome said, placing three large mugs on the bar.

The hairy man dropped some copper on the bar, picked up the mugs, and returned to a table where two similar-looking men sat.

SJ was still staring at them when the gnome addressed her.

"Yes, dear, how can I help you?"

SJ jerked back around, blushing slightly. "Sorry. I am looking for a room, if you have one available."

"I do, but the only room I have left is the suite. Unfortunately, it is the most expensive in the inn."

"How much is it?"

"The suite is eight copper a night."

"Eight copper, that is a lot!"

"It is pricey, but it is the only room in the inn with a bath and lounge area. All other rooms share the ablutions and bathrooms."

SJ had the funds but did not want to get conned again so soon.

"Take it," Dave's whispered voice said. SJ frowned, wondering why he would need to whisper inside her head. "Seeing who else may be staying here, you do not want to share ablutions with lycanthropes. They get hair everywhere. Such unhygienic creatures."

SJ realised that the three large men sitting at the table must be lycanthropes, not ordinary men. She called eight copper to her palm and placed the small stack on the bar top. "I'll take it."

"Very good. I am Kerys Thruttle, the owner of the Hogling Arms. What may I call you by?" the gnome asked as she pulled a small book from beneath the bar and started scribbling details into a ledger. Upon seeing it, SJ's eyes flashed over the page, her draw to numbers pulling her straight to it.

"Erm. I am SJ."

"SJ? That is unusual. I am guessing you are a newborn?"

"Yes. I just arrived yesterday and am trying to get myself sorted out."

"Welcome, then, to Amathera. We don't have many of your type through here."

"You mean fae or Legionnaires?"

"Both. Our town is a little remote, being up in the mountains as we are."

"I only realised today that you were in the mountains. I did not know until I walked here and saw down into the valley."

"Yes. We are quite high up here. Probably why that blue has stayed."

"You mean the dragon?"

"Yeah, it is causing some concern. We haven't had a dragon in these parts since before the town was founded."

"How long has the town been here?"

"This is our seven hundred sixty-fourth year."

"That is a long time."

"Not for many towns."

"I have so much to learn about Amathera."

"It has a rich history. Killic was one of our founding members, and the town was renamed in her honour. She fought off the invasion of the black dragons almost single-handedly, or at least that is how the story goes."

"Kerys. Food," a voice shouted from the back kitchen, and SJ saw three large steaming bowls of stew with fresh bread placed on a serving hatch.

"Sorry, duty calls. Here is your room key. First floor, second door on the left. Let me know if you need anything," Kerys said, already turning away.

SJ watched her skilfully pick up the tray of bowls and, carrying it in one hand, navigate her way through the patrons to the table with the lycanthropes. She stood talking to them for several moments before turning and collecting empty tankards.

SJ picked up the room key and headed up the stairs, which were well-worn, the wood highly polished and cared for. They had seen a lot of travellers over the years. As she walked up, the noise from the rowdy bar lessened, and she followed the directions to her door.

The room was large, with a deep steel bath in one corner, a table and chairs, and a sofa near a fireplace. A large metal bucket hung above the fire, and SJ noticed steam coming from it. Walking over, she saw the bubbling water, and a cloth hung by the fireside. She grabbed the cloth and lifted the bucket from the flames before carrying it over to the bath and tipping it in.

There was a small handle above the bath, and SJ instinctively pumped it until water flowed. She refilled the bucket and placed it back on the fire. Looking at the bath, she realised she would need at least two more buckets full.

There was another door leading from the room. She looked into a bedroom with a gigantic bed, a wardrobe, and a small dressing table. The bed was immense and must have been designed to accommodate trolls or similar creatures if needed. She walked over and pushed down on the mattress. The blanket covering the bed was soft to the touch, and the mattress felt firm.

"This looks okay."

"Very nice. In starter towns, most are lucky to get a straw mattress," Dave replied.

SJ suddenly thought: "I have done this wrong."

"Why?"

"I should have looked for new clothes first before getting cleaned up."

"The water will take time to heat, so you can always go now?"

"I think I should."

SJ left the room, locking it behind her before returning to the bar.

"Everything all right?" Kerys called over.

"Going for new clothes while the water heats," she called back, and Kerys smiled.

The inn was situated on the town square, and SJ headed towards the area where she had spotted the sign for what she thought was the tailor's shop. The town bustled with activity. Everywhere she looked, beings were busy with their regular lives. Although she couldn't estimate the exact population, it seemed to be at least several hundred, if not close to a thousand.

"Do you know how large the town is?" SJ asked.

"Not sure. The details of this town are quite vague. I have looked at the wiki, but as I said before, it is not a normal starter town. The information is limited or restricted. I am not sure what is going on here. All the usual profession trades and basic needs for any starting adventurer should be available, though."

SJ continued down the street and walked to the building with the thread and bobbin on the sign. Opening the door, she walked inside, a small bell jingling as she did.

CHAPTER SEVENTEEN

Tailor Fizzlewick

"'Ello."

The voice came from the back of the store. "Hi," SJ called as she entered.

The store was full of everything you could imagine seeing in a tailor's shop: piles of fabric and leather, thread, bobbins, needles—you name it, and she was sure you could have found it here. It was a haberdasher's delight. Unique designs of clothing were hung on several mannequins.

"Can I 'elp 'ou?" the voice replied, and SJ noticed the beads hanging in the doorway to the back move but saw no one step through.

"I am looking for some new clothing. Mine was ruined when I travelled here," SJ replied, peering to see who had spoken.

A groaning sound could be heard as something climbed a few steps, and a creature the size of a small child appeared, looking over the counter-top. He looked almost human but very old, with round-rimmed spectacles resting on his nose, from which grew a long, wayward black hair.

"Oh. Hello." SJ smiled.

"It is a quarterling, robbing little buggers," Dave said.

"'Ello. Said that 'ready. What clothes need?" the quarterling asked.

"Full set of travelling and adventuring clothes, and possibly even casual."

"'Spensive that be. 'Ou has coin?"

"I do have coin, yes."

"Grade?"

"Which grades do you have?"

"Most. Not ledge, though."

"If you show me what you have and the prices, I can decide."

"First. Tousers."

The head disappeared under the counter, and within moments, several pairs of trousers landed on top, neatly folded and looking pristine. His head reappeared.

"'Eft 're common, mid good, ri 're rare."

SJ walked to the counter and looked down at the three pairs of trousers that had been presented. She picked up the common pair, and her display triggered.

Common Adventurers' Trousers
Quality: Good
Durability: Good

She proceeded to pick up the other two pairs.

Good Adventurers' Trousers
Quality: Excellent
Durability: Good

Rare Adventurers' Trousers
Quality: Excellent
Durability: Excellent
Enchantment Slots: One

All three pairs were made from similar materials. They were soft, strong, and hard wearing, feeling like soft leather although made from cloth. She could see the difference in the final production of the items, defining the overall quality. Compared to what she was wearing, each of them was an upgrade.

"How much are they?"

"Thee, 'ifteen, and one silva."

Dave whispered, "One silver is very reasonable for a rare set of adventurers' trousers. They are the most basic rare design with a single enchantment slot but a reasonable price. I am not sure it is worth getting them, though. Once you level, you should be able to find or get much better variants with more slots and enchantments. Fifteen for a good grade is also a fair price. I would ask him if he has a pair with excellent durability, though."

SJ considered what Dave said before replying. "Do you have a good set with both quality and durability as excellent?"

"Yup. Ateen."

"What about tops? I would like halter tops with sleeves if you have them?"

The three pairs of trousers were removed from the counter and replaced with one pair, and the tops began appearing. The material was beautiful and soft, like the trousers. She checked the grades and quality of each. All had properties similar to those of the previous trouser selections.

"How much for the good/excellent/excellent?"

"'Orteen."

SJ totted up as she went. Thirty-two copper so far. She had more than enough with her three silver and could always try to trade or sell the wolf pelt as extra. SJ thought about getting a cloak. It would make being in town easier with people not seeing she was a fae. She could use it to hide her wings.

"Do you sell cloaks?"

The small, wizened face squinted at her before replying. "Specal make."

"Special, how?"

"Fit round 'ings."

"No. Don't worry, just a normal cloak."

"Can make specal, challenge but 'ossible."

"I will keep that in mind, but just a normal cloak would be amazing for now."

Again, he disappeared beneath the counter to return with cloaks of the three starting grades. The material was a soft, woollen-feeling fabric and felt luxurious.

"Price for the good again?"

"'En."

Forty-two copper to get a new set of clothes. They were all good quality and had excellent durability, but SJ was uncertain just how they'd hold up compared to how easily damaged her starter clothes had been. Also, she did not know about armour class and what protection the clothes might offer her.

"Do you mind if I browse some of your other clothes while I decide?"

"'Ure."

The quarterling dropped out of sight behind the counter, and SJ walked to look at a stunning green blouse hanging on a mannequin. It was inlaid with intricate threading, and the colour matched her wings.

"What do you think?" SJ whispered.

"Good-quality items would be a great start and get you up to Level 10 at least," Dave replied.

"Can my class wear armour?"

"If you mean leather armour or other stuff, then yes, but only at higher levels. Basic assassin clothing is cloth until Level 20. Leather can be worn from 20 to 39, and above 40 chain-mail can also be worn."

"Is that not noisy?"

"Not when enchanted with *Silence*."

"Oh. I need to learn so much still. Do you think I should get them?"

"Asking my advice—I feel privileged. I would barter and see what else he is willing to throw in. He is unlikely to get trades for the amount you are willing to spend in one go, even if he has rare items. You can see he is high-level, though, right?"

"I have not tried to identify him. Am I supposed to?"

"No. Many take offence. He is, though, a little strange for a starter zone. His profession skill has to be at least Level 30 for him to be making rares. He said he had better, but I doubt he does."

"I will ask."

SJ walked back to the counter. "Excuse me? You said you had higher-quality items. Do you mind if I see them?"

The quarterling appeared, eyeing her suspiciously. "Why? 'Ou can't afford."

"Depends on the price."

The quarterling raised one eyebrow. "'Ait."

He moved around the counter and walked to the door before bolting it, then removed a large padlock from his pocket and attached it. Once the door was secure, he turned around and walked back to the rear of the counter and through the beads.

"'Ollow me," he called out.

SJ stared momentarily before realising what he had said, confused by him suddenly placing the shop in lockdown. She walked over to the beaded doorway and, pushing them aside, walked through. The rear room of the shop was ever more chaotic than the front. Packages and crates were overflowing with bright materials and balls of thread. There were a couple of machines which SJ recognised as looms with half-manufactured materials visible in them. The quarterling walked through the cluttered room and opened another door leading down into a cellar.

"Is this safe?" SJ whispered.

"No idea. This is the strangest starter zone shop I have ever been in."

The quarterling reached the bottom of the steps and disappeared into the gloom of the cellar. SJ followed cautiously, and as she reached the bottom, the cellar was bathed in a bright glow from a lantern. In the middle of the cellar, a large table with cloth aligned to a pattern of a top was laid out, ready to be made. Around the outside of the cellar were several mannequins of varying sizes with various designs of clothes on them.

The quarterling turned and looked at her cautiously, and then, before her eyes, it began to transform.

SJ stepped back in amazement as where the small quarterling had been standing, an old human now stood.

"That's better," he said.

SJ stood, mouth open, staring at the man. "Sorry," she spluttered.

"I have been trying to perfect the speech for years and always struggle with the quarterling form. Oh, well, practise makes perfect, as they say."

"And you are?"

"Oh. I am Fizzlewick, tailor extraordinaire."

"Fizzlewick!" Dave exclaimed. "I know that name. Why do I know it?"

SJ looked at the now-human elderly man standing in front of her.

"So, child, do you want to see some special clothing? You have come to the right place, but again, I do not believe you can afford any of my premium items."

"W-what do you have?"

"Well, I can make anything and design bespoke items as necessary. You do not get to my level of tailoring without perfecting your craft."

"If you don't mind me asking what level you are at, I thought there were only low-level professions and classes in starter towns."

"Ah. My dear child, you are a new one, aren't you? I am surprised your AI has not informed you."

"My AI," SJ replied, shocked.

"All of you have them. I am well aware of the System and the games it plays."

"WHAT?" Dave shouted, making SJ wince.

"Can I ask how you could know that?" SJ said.

"I have been around a long time. I have seen most things in my lifetime."

"I am baffled."

"Yes. It is probably a bit of a shock for you. I can understand that."

"Why would you tell me that you know all this?"

"Who is going to believe you? Only the highest in the realm know about the true secrets of Amathera."

Dave's voice suddenly filled her head, "Fizzlewick! He was a mage for Emperor Ludica on the continent of Purinali. It can't be the same one?"

"Are you *the* Fizzlewick?" SJ asked.

"It depends on what you mean. I have had several variations over my lifetime, and I still do."

"How old are you?"

"Umm. I was born in the year 4932."

"But I thought this world was over twenty-five thousand years old now?"

"Oh. It is. I have lived several lives over my time."

"But, I thought humans of Amathera only lived to be about two hundred years old?"

"Oh. My dear child. I am not human."

SJ did not know how to respond and stood silently, looking at the old man.

"I am what is known as a god."

"A god?!" SJ blurted.

"Yes. However, I do not play the games that my siblings do. I have lived on Amathera most of my life."

Astounded, SJ felt her legs go a little unsteady.

"Here, do sit." Fizzlewick waved his hand. A chair appeared behind SJ, and she slowly lowered herself into it.

"You are a god?" SJ repeated, shock registered on her face.

"Yes. I am a god. I am known as Haber, the God of Tailoring."

"I didn't know that there was a God of Tailoring, or anything about the gods, if I'm being honest."

"This doesn't make any sense!" Dave said, sounding very confused.

"How long have you been here in the town?" SJ asked.

"Not long. I only arrived yesterday."

"Then how do you already have the shop set up and everything here?"

"I just told you."

"I know, but is it not suspicious that you arrive with so much?"

"No. I took over the shop from the old quarterling I have been trying to imitate. He wanted to retire, so I took over his premises."

"Can I ask why you are telling me any of this? I am only a Level 4 that arrived yesterday."

"Because you are special. The gods are all talking about you."

"Why? What makes me special?"

"You are an anomaly, after all. As soon as the System updated and we were informed that malware had been sandboxed, everyone started getting very excited."

"You know what happened?"

"Yes. The gods know most things. Although the System may have created us, we are the most advanced species on the planet and have a direct link to the Requiem."

"Did he just say *Requiem*?" Dave said, shocked.

SJ knew what the word *requiem* meant but had no idea how it related to the System.

"What is the Requiem?"

"It is the centre of all knowing. All souls rest there once they part the second world."

"So, after you die a second time, you end up in the Requiem?"

"Sort of. Not physically, but your soul does. It is the fountain of all knowledge."

SJ's head was spinning. Less than two days ago, she had been eating sausage and mash in a pub, and now she was talking to a god in the second world about a third life as a soul.

"Why reveal yourself to me?"

"I told you. You are special. In all my years, I have met no one who has not accepted the terms and conditions. The fact that you have a waiver and protected yourself from undue repercussions is unheard of. It is very exciting news for the gods."

"I still do not understand why."

"You have the opportunity to change things. You do not conform to normality, and by not conforming, you can finally shift the balance."

"I can change the balance?"

"Yes. I am sure that your AI has informed you of the world's balance. Everything always balances in time. It does not matter if evil prevails over good or good over evil. In the end, balance returns."

"How can I affect it? I am nothing special."

"Oh, you certainly are, and I was lucky enough to hear that you were interested in tailoring, so I thought I would offer my services as your trainer."

That statement silenced SJ for several moments. "Why would a god want to do that for me?"

"My siblings are going to be so jealous." He grinned, showing perfect white teeth defying his age. "Anyway, back to explaining. If you show half the potential that I believe you may have, you are going to bring significant change to Amathera."

"I don't understand. How can I bring change?"

"Your decisions. Whether you fight for good or evil, whichever side you choose to fight for will prevail in the end."

"Do gods not want good to prevail?"

"Gods are neutral. We have no alignment either way. We are the truest form of neutrality in the world. That means we can do what we wish either way. If we feel evil, we can be evil. If we feel good, we can be good. Most of the time, my siblings and I stay neutral and allow the world to play out as it wishes."

"I can't pick a profession until Level 5. Why tell me now?"

"Opportunity. I knew you would come and get new clothes, but I didn't expect to see you so soon. Anyway, you wanted to see some different items." Fizzlewick or Haber waved his hand, and a beautifully crafted dress in the palest emerald green appeared on the table. The design was stunning and took SJ's breath away.

"May I?"

"Please." The god indicated with his hand.

SJ walked to the table and looked at the dress. The material appeared to shimmer, and she reached out to touch it. She had never felt material so soft in her life. It felt like nothing under her fingers as she stroked the material. "This is beautiful," SJ murmured.

"It is rather nice."

"Can I pick it up?"

"Of course."

SJ carefully lifted the dress and held it in front of her. Her display triggered.

Haber's Dress of the Tailor Level 0
Grade: Astral
Quality: Perfect
Durability: Infinite
Enchantment Slots: Seven available at maximum level
Armour Class: Unknown
Attributes: Unknown
The god Haber himself made this dress. It is unmatched by any other and provides the wearer with unique skills available as levels are gained.
Self-repair

"Wow," Dave said in awe. "An astral item. Few have ever seen one, let alone held one in their hands."

"This is amazing. I dare not ask how much it costs."

Fizzlewick laughed. "My dear. Astral items can't be purchased. They may only ever be gifted by a god."

"This is the softest, most beautiful dress I have ever seen."

"Try it on if you wish."

"Really," SJ replied, stunned.

"Yes. It is for you, after all."

"WHAT?" Dave screamed in her head.

SJ winced from the explosion of noise.

"Ah. I think your AI just spoke to you again, didn't he?"

SJ looked at Fizzlewick. "I would not say he spoke, more like deafened me. I think he is a little surprised at your generosity. Dave, please don't shout in my head."

"Have you named your AI? How quaint. I have never heard of one being named before."

SJ climbed into the dress, removing her trousers and halter-neck top once she had pulled it on. It was tied behind her neck, and it had flowing green sleeves. The material seemed to change in size and shape as she pulled it on, fitting her form perfectly. She had never worn anything so beautiful or luxurious before. "This is amazing, and you said it is mine?"

"Yes. It is for you. However, you need to know that the dress level is linked to your tailoring level, so it will only improve as your skill improves."

"There it is," Dave said. "There had to be a trick in there somewhere."

SJ stood staring into a mirror in the cellar of the tailor's shop and could not believe the image she was seeing. This was her in all her glory. She took her own breath away, the dress adding a level of beauty to her already-beautiful form. The back of the dress dropped in a deep plunge that came up just below her wings, and when she stood sideways, the colour of her wings matched perfectly with the dress.

SJ took a side stance and performed a kick. The dress flowed perfectly, not interfering with her movements.

"I am not sure what to say."

"You need not say anything. A gift is a gift, and for you to develop its true potential, you will pay me back enough by tailoring. All crafted items add to my astral pool. The more people who tailor, the larger a pool I have available. Tailoring is a common profession, so many perform it."

"As soon as I reach Level 5, I will return to begin training," SJ said excitedly.

"That would be wonderful. I do have one more item I would like to give you."

SJ's eyes opened in amazement. "What else could you offer?"

"These. I had my sister make them for me. They are not astral but will do you for a few levels until you can improve." Fizzlewick placed a pair of calf-length boots on the table.

SJ walked over to them and picked them up.

Boots of the Assassin
Grade: Epic
Quality: Perfect
Durability: Excellent
Enchantment Slots: 2
Armour Class: Unknown
Attributes: Unknown

The boots were a pale grey, and SJ removed her current beginner pair and pulled one of them on. The boot, like the dress, resized to her foot. She did the same with the other and now stood in pale grey boots, which could not be seen under the flowing dress when she stood still. She bent her knees and moved her feet around. The boots felt like the softest slippers she had ever worn.

"The boots are not the best, and you will find much better in time. The initial bonuses, when you can trigger them, should help you, though, for a while at least. I have one question, which has confused all the gods since you arrived."

"Please ask."

"Why did you choose a fae assassin as your race and class?"

"I had always wanted to protect the good from the evil in the world, and I liked the sound of the subterfuge skill as it aligned with my forensic accounting from my first life. So, I decided to be an assassin for the good, and the reason I chose fae is because I always loved them as a child."

"Well, let us hope you can achieve your goal," Fizzlewick replied, scratching his thick beard.

"I don't know how to repay you for these gifts."

"I have told you already. Level in tailoring and just be you in the world. What will happen will eventually happen. Even gods can't define fate. Anyway, you must go again. Your bath-water will be ready by now."

SJ looked at him quizzically, remembering she had placed another bucket to boil. She turned and headed back upstairs. Fizzlewick followed, and when she got to the front of the shop, he had transformed again into the small quarterling.

"Can I please get the items I asked for as well?" SJ asked, pulling one silver from her inventory.

"Of 'o rse." Fizzlewick put the items into a bag and gave her the fifty-eight copper change.

Fizzlewick unlocked the padlocked door with a wave of his hand, the lock vanishing.

"Thank you, and I will be back soon," SJ said, feeling the happiest she had been in a very long time.

CHAPTER EIGHTEEN

Eye of the Town

"We just met a god," Dave said excitedly.

"I know. I was there." SJ was making her way back down the street towards the inn. The afternoon sun was blazing, and she felt wonderful in her new dress. All she needed now was a long soak in a bath, and she would be ready for anything.

"A god, though, and you have been given an astral gift. Do you realise how rare that is?"

"I have an idea from what you said before, so yes."

"How can you not be as excited as I am by the fact?"

"I am excited. I am just not sure what all this means yet."

"The fact you have just been speaking to a god who gifted you not one but two items and then offered to train you as a tailor is unheard of."

"He said I need to level myself, though. I assume I will only get the basic training."

"From a god. Fizzlewick, the name he goes by on Amathera, is one of the most famed magicians. It was rumoured he was a god, but no one had any details supporting it. You now have. Thousands have sought him out over the years, and you just run into him in a tailor's shop."

"He is a mage as well?"

"Now, knowing he is a god makes sense, as all gods can use magic, and most have a profession they support. Alamor is the God of Alchemy, Lister is the God of Enchanting, et cetera."

As SJ walked down the street, she heard a very recognisable sound she had not heard in many years: someone wolf-whistling. She turned and looked over to a group of males standing by a stall selling weapons, all laughing.

"You got a problem?" SJ called angrily.

"Not with you, love," one of them shouted back, to raucous laughter from the others.

The one who replied looked like he might be a half orc, with the muscular body of a man and small tusk-like protrusions from his lower jaw.

"Good. Otherwise, I would have to teach you a lesson, you ugly worm," SJ snapped back.

"What did you just say?" the half orc growled in response.

"I called you an ugly worm. Can you not hear me?" Of all the things SJ had hated, one of the strongest was walking past building sites and hearing immature, pathetic, fully grown men who were probably married wolf-whistling at her as she walked past. She found it so demeaning.

"You better watch your mouth, or I will come and shut it for you," the half orc said.

"Really. Don't you need your mummy to tie your shoelaces for you first, with your pathetic, childish whistling?"

"Watch it, he is a Level 6," Dave said.

"I don't care what he is," SJ said under her breath.

The half orc had started approaching, grabbing a large two-handed mace from the stall table as he did. The stall owner cried out at him, saying that he had not paid for it.

"You are going to pay," the half orc said as he approached.

"Am I? Can you not afford your medical bills?"

"Oh. That was funny," Dave said, sniggering.

"What?" he replied, confused.

SJ took the advantage while he turned, glancing at his fellow yobs, and spun her foot around in a kick to his side. She caught him full on, her foot striking what must have been armour underneath his jacket, and he only winced slightly from the strike.

He turned back to face her, growling, and swung the mace at her.

SJ stepped back out of range, dropping the bag she had been carrying with her other clothes and feeling agile in her new dress and boots. She did not want to use her claws, but she would if she had to. The half orc again swung at her. He was using a two-handed grip, his movements slow and awkward. SJ realised that for every move he made, she had time to get at least two strikes in.

She punched this time with two fast, straight jabs at his face. The first strike crunched into one of his tusks, her hand splitting from the impact with the rough surface. She flinched in pain.

Another wild swing came at her. This half orc was all about brute strength and had no fighting finesse. SJ had not identified him yet, and as she continued to dodge and strike at him, she triggered her skill.

Malcolm Kilgore	
Race:	Half Orc
Age:	19
Level:	6
Hit Points:	36
Mana Points:	30

"Malcolm, did your mother not teach you manners and that it's rude to hit ladies?"

He growled again in response and threw another wild swing, missing her as she stepped sideways, then kicked and punched as he stumbled from his swing. She was doing a pathetic amount of damage to him, but he was tiring with his misses and using such a heavy double-handed mace as he was.

The ongoing fight had drawn a crowd, not just from those by the stalls but also a few others who had come out of the shops to watch. "They are betting on who will win," Dave said.

SJ did not respond and continued dodging and weaving using her kata moves, which came in handy as she sidestepped and moved from the blows thrown at her. The developing crowd began to shout and jeer for one or the other. SJ could not tell. She was finding the dress perfect for moving in. It always flowed with her movements, causing no restriction.

Malcolm was panting. A wild swing thundered by her, striking the cobbles with a resounding thud. As he went to lift the weapon, SJ brought her foot down on his arm. He yelped in pain, releasing his grip with one hand from the weapon. She struck him with a fist to the side of his face. She was getting two hits in for his one.

He let go of the mace with his other hand and turned towards her, punching rather than swinging a weapon. She was not expecting the blow, and it caught her in her shoulder as she tried to move back. She felt the concussive blow, which jolted her off balance. She jumped backwards as he went to punch her again.

Even without the mace in his hand, he was still slower than she was, and she could predict and see where he was trying to hit. This kid, which is how she thought of him, was a street thug, nothing more. He was probably one of the louts that she had seen walking the streets of London drunk after a night out. Always looking for a fight, with alcohol-fuelled anger.

"You can give up whenever you wish," SJ said as she stepped back from him.

"Screw you," Malcolm bellowed as he charged at her.

SJ sidestepped his charge, leaving her leg trailing, and as he passed, she pushed him, adding to his momentum and sending him sprawling over her leg and face-first onto the road. He screamed angrily, pushing himself back to his feet and wiping his now-dirt-covered face with his arm. Sweat was pouring down his face from the exertion. The weight of the armour and his initial weapon of choice had taken its toll on him.

SJ felt fresh and strong; none of her actions were tiring compared to the fights she had been having in the forest. All she did was sidestep, kick, and punch, no running from tree to tree across a clearing. Malcolm swung for her again. He was all brute force, big, powerful blows, no finesse, balance, or skill. She palmed off his punch and brought her elbow in against his chin, stepping into his attack. She was unsure where the move had come from as she had never tried it before, but it worked. Her elbow connected with his jaw, and his teeth clattered together.

He stank of alcohol this close, and SJ knew he was, as she expected, a typical yob off the streets. No inhibitions and no regard for others. This angered her, and she lashed out, landing a punch on his cheek before stepping back away from him. He stood shaking his head, the elbow to the jaw followed by the punch having caused some damage to him. He went to kick her, his wild kick missing as she stepped away and his momentum again turning his back to her.

Taking advantage, she kicked back herself, right in his lower back. Feeling no resistance from armour, she realised that he was only wearing a breastplate of some sort and not full armour. Her foot hit hard, making him grunt. She'd knocked the wind from him. Staggering forward from the blow, he reached around to rub his back.

He turned to look at her, panting and grimacing. SJ stood in her usual stance and stared at him, watching for his next move. He dabbed his brow again, rubbing sweat from his eyes.

"You can just say sorry and give up," SJ goaded.

"Give up to you, a poxy little fae."

"This little fae is teaching you a lesson in manners."

Malcolm's health was down to about half after all the punches and kicks he had received. SJ had still only received one blow and had minor damage.

"It is up to you. You can either back down, or we can continue to fight. But looking at your state, you haven't got much left in the tank," SJ said.

Malcolm growled in response, showing his full half orc roar, spittle flying from his mouth as he charged again. SJ just stood there waiting. As he came in range, she brought her foot around in a swift roundhouse move, crashing the top of her foot into the side of his face as he leaned to grab her. Malcolm's head flew sideways from the impact. His jaw looked to dislodge as she struck. Her display triggered.

Critical Hit

Your strike was perfectly timed. Critical hits add bonus damage and effects.

Concussive blows can gain one or all of the following effects:

Crush, break, concussion, or knock-out.

Malcolm's head continued sideways, and SJ watched his eyes flutter, his body go limp, and his unconscious body fall to the cobbles with a clattering thud. SJ stood there, looking at the inert form. Several in the crowd cheered, and she turned to see people handing coins to each other. Bending down, she picked up her discarded bag of clothes.

"Well done," Dave said, pride in his voice.

"It was nothing," she whispered. "He was drunk."

"Still a Level 6. That will earn you respect in the town."

A deep, burly voice erupted from behind her. "Well done, lass. Well done. I have not seen a decent street fight for a long time."

SJ turned to see a rather broad and muscular-looking dwarf wearing only his breeches and a dark leather apron. In his hand, he held a blacksmith's hammer.

"Thanks," she replied.

"Name's Zej. I run the local smithy."

"I can see that, and I am SJ," she replied, smiling. She watched Malcolm's friends pick him up from the street, dragging him towards a building. The weapons stall-holder screamed that he wanted payment for damaged goods.

"If you need anything, come by my furnace, and we can see what we can do for you."

"Thank you. I will keep that in mind."

"Make sure you do," Zej replied, grinning at her.

Now that the spectacle was over, the crowd had dispersed, and she continued back to the inn. Upon her entrance, the bar fell silent. She froze in the doorway as all eyes turned to look at her. SJ suddenly felt very uncomfortable. Whispering started throughout the room. She walked towards the bar nervously, where a smiling Kerys stood.

"Just heard the news. You gave Malcolm a run for his money," Kerys said, lifting a mug of ale and placing it on the bar in front of SJ. "This one is on the house."

"Thanks. Why?"

"Malcolm has been causing a scene in town since he arrived. A normal one of your kind would have left town by now, all the time he has been here. All he does is spend his time drinking and gambling. He does nothing in town to help and causes problems continually."

"I don't feel so bad dealing with him, then."

"You shouldn't. He deserved what he got."

"Well, thanks. I better run my bath. I started before I went out."

"Can I ask before you go . . . Where did you get that dress? It is beautiful."

"At the old tailor's shop at the end of town."

"The old grinch kept that hidden. It's a stunner. Every time I go in there, there is nothing worth purchasing."

"I need to get a bath and get changed."

"The dress looks immaculate. Why change?"

"I am getting too many looks wearing it around here."

"This is my inn, and you can wear whatever you please. If anyone says or does anything, I will have Bert sort them out," Kerys said, indicating the huge troll standing at the end of the bar.

"Thank you. It is appreciated."

"Oh, if you need soaps and towels, some should be in the wardrobe. I'm not sure if you've looked around the suite."

"I hadn't. Thanks again. I will be back down in a bit for some food."

Kerys smiled, turning away to another patron as SJ headed upstairs.

CHAPTER NINETEEN

Bath and Bored

SJ spent so long lying in the luxurious warmth of the bath that by the time she got out, the light had begun to fade. She didn't care, though, considering she might live to be over seven thousand years old now. She would enjoy the small things in life and take her time. She was not in a rush.

She had been pleasantly surprised by the soaps and perfumes she had found in the wardrobe. The mint-scented soap she used left her skin tingling and invigorated. Her health was back to full again, and she stood looking in the tall mirror in the suite after putting her dress on again, not even having to smooth any creases.

The smell of the fabric reminded her of summer meadows, with the subtle hint of flowers drifting in the breeze on a warm summer afternoon. She had worked her hair into two long, loose braids that ran down either side of her face. She smiled at herself in the mirror, loving what she saw and who she was now.

"You quite finished?" Dave asked.

"What do you mean?"

"Staring at yourself. Look, we all agreed that you are a nine out of ten, but come on, enough is enough."

"Nine out of ten? I was eight and a half out of ten last time," SJ replied, grinning.

"Did I say nine? I meant seven." Dave coughed.

"Dave. Don't be shy. You can say how beautiful I am. I won't take offence."

"Like a troll's pimple-covered bum, I will," he snarked.

"I think food and getting to know some of the people who live here a little better might be a good idea."

"Maybe you can pick up some quests."

"I wonder what sort of quests they have."

"Oh. They have all sorts in starter towns. Many quests are usually available to help the locals with various tasks, such as clearing rat infestations. Then, once you reach Level 5, you can get your profession and start your profession quest chain."

"Profession quest chain?"

"Yes. As you advance in a profession, there will be specific items that you are required to craft as the levels increase. Initially, the materials will all be easy to locate, but over time, they become more restricted and almost impossible."

"That doesn't sound great, considering I plan on levelling my tailoring skill as soon as I can claim the profession."

"It will be fine initially, and I am not sure what the exact needs are for tailoring. The annoying thing about professions is that the System regularly changes the requirements, so we can't confirm the needs until a new quest scheme is completed."

"I suppose it stops you from getting bored of knowing everything all the time," SJ said, chuckling.

"What are you laughing at?"

"You. My self-proclaimed all-knowing AI has been starstruck by a god today and also admitted he is not all-knowing, at long last."

"I was not starstruck!"

"Yes, you were."

"Wasn't."

"Was."

"Wasn't."

"Wasn't."

"Was. Damn you," Dave huffed.

"Okay. That's enough," SJ laughed. "Let's get something to eat. I can sit and explain all the flavours and how nice everything tastes."

"Where did this new monster appear from? All she does now is want to cause pain and suffering to those around her. After me talking about wanting to taste food, you now want to torture me by explaining it to me!" Dave said in anguish.

"I thought it may help you appreciate and understand it better."

"Really!"

"Yes. Really, I was trying to be helpful."

"Didn't sound like it," Dave sulked.

She had taken the items from her inventory and placed them in the wardrobe rather than carry them. They did not seem to weigh her down, but she could not be sure how the inventory system worked fully, never having asked Dave to explain it.

As she headed downstairs, the bar sounded even livelier than earlier. Her beautiful form received more than one or two appraising gazes from male and female patrons. SJ walked to the bar and stood waiting to be served. There was another younger-looking gnome behind the bar now. "Hi," SJ said as she walked over, smiling at her.

"Hiya. What can I get ya?"

"What do you have to eat and drink?"

The gnome reached under the bar, pulled out a menu, and handed it to her. "Here you go. Give me a shout when you decide what you would like."

SJ read the menu.

Food:
Boiled Trout and Cheese (2cp)

Vegetable Stew (1cp)
Dried Pheasant and Parsnip with Sweet Potatoes (3cp)
Boiled Mutton Broth (2cp)
Hogling Stew (2cp)
Hogling Loin, New Potatoes, and Vegetables (5cp)
Hogling Ribs with Honey and Spice (4cp)
Drinks:
Ale, Stout, Mead, Cider (1cp)
Wine: Juniper, Honey, Spiced (2cp)

Reading the menu made SJ's stomach rumble. The hogling ribs sounded nice, but there was no mention of chips on the menu, and she would have loved a portion of them. She decided on the hogling loin instead. She waved to draw the attention of the gnome again.

"Have you decided?"

"Yes. Could I get a loin and a honey wine, please?"

"Sure, that's seven copper."

SJ drew seven copper and handed them over.

"You have just bought the most expensive food on the menu," Dave said.

"And?" she whispered.

"You did it deliberately, didn't you?"

"What do you mean?"

"To torture me."

"Give it a rest, will you? I'm just hungry," she whispered as the waitress came back.

"Did you say something?"

"No. Sorry, I'm just muttering to myself. I must remember to get some stuff tomorrow, that's all."

"No problem. I do that all the time. Mum thinks I am insane, but it helps me remember," the young gnome replied, grinning.

"Mum?"

"Oh. How rude I didn't introduce myself. I am Fhyliss Thruttle. My mum owns the inn."

"Nice to meet you, Fhyliss. I am SJ. Can I ask you a question?"

"Sure. What is it?"

"Do you know where I can get some work around here?"

"You are in the right place for work. As you enter, there is a notice board by the door with a list of current jobs. Also, if you speak to many of the people here, they may have work that needs doing."

"That is great, thanks."

"No problem," Fhyliss replied as she finished pouring a rather large glass of what SJ could only assume was honey wine.

"That's large," SJ said, a little shocked; it was more like a gin glass than a wine glass.

"Sorry, is that not enough?"

"No, I meant it is large; I wasn't questioning whether that was large." SJ smiled.

"Oh. We only have the one-sized wine glasses."

"I am not complaining. I just was not expecting such a large glass."

"Where would you like to sit to eat?"

SJ looked around the inn. There was only one empty table, and it was in the far corner. "Over there okay?"

"Sure, table twenty-one. I will have your food brought over as soon as it is ready. Do you need cutlery, or do you have your own?"

"Erm. I will need some, please."

"No problem," Fhyliss said as she walked to serve another patron.

"Bring your own cutlery?" SJ whispered.

"Most people eat with a knife and fingers," Dave replied.

Most of the beings in the bar were indeed eating with their fingers after cutting their meals up with a knife. She would have to invest in some cutlery of her own going forward if it was the norm, not fancying eating from a knife. She had had an unpleasant experience as a child where she stupidly licked a sharp knife and ended up slicing her tongue. Ever since that day, she had used a knife and fork.

"Shall we check the noticeboard while we wait for you to torture me?" Dave said.

SJ smiled but did not reply and, lifting the glass from the bar, walked over to the noticeboard. It was only a small board, and various messages and jobs were pinned. SJ started reading through them.

> LOST CAT: LOCATE SHELLEY AND SPEAK TO MRS. LARPER AT THE BAKERY.

> PART-TIME, TEMPORARY ALCHEMIST'S APPRENTICE OPENING, INQUIRIES AT YOUR LOCAL ALCHEMIST.

> RAT TRAPPER NEEDED—SPEAK TO HUBERT AT THE MILL.

> MILKERS WANTED. MORNING AND EVENING SHIFTS AVAILABLE. SPEAK TO WENDY AT THE DAIRY.

> BORED AND LOOKING FOR ADVENTURE? SEE CLERIC LYTHONIAN AT THE CHURCH.

None of the jobs sounded very exciting. The only one that showed any promise was the one labelled *Bored and Looking for Adventure*.

"Dave?" she whispered.

"Yes."

"Can you remember the details? I am terrible at names."

"Really?" Dave asked, surprised.

"Yes. I always used to write details like names down, and I do not even have a pen or paper here, and I don't have a phone so I can just take a picture to remember the details from."

"Oh!" Dave replied, a little shocked. "Yes. I can remember all the details that you have read."

"Thank you. That would be helpful and appreciated."

"No problem," Dave replied, sounding genuinely happy.

Once she had finished reading the notices, SJ headed towards the empty table, making a mental note to visit the cleric, having already forgotten the name. She decided she would go in the morning. Fhyliss walked over and placed some cutlery wrapped in a napkin at her table, and SJ walked over and sat down. The fork was short, with three tines, and the knife did not look very sharp.

"Maybe I should have used my knife!" she whispered.

"I hope it is horrible and chewy," Dave grumbled.

"You don't have to watch me eat. You could always watch one of your AI films."

"I could, but who would look out for you if I did?"

"Aww. You do care."

Silence.

SJ sipped her smooth wine. It tasted like sweet honey and reminded her of alcopops from back on Earth, so she knew she would have to be careful. They had a habit of luring you into a false sense of security and then smacking you around the side of the head. The bar was noisy, with the patrons all chatting, laughing, and enjoying themselves. She looked around, watching all the interactions. She wanted to use her identification skills but knew she shouldn't because of Dave's warning that people could take offence.

As she was waiting for her food, the bard from earlier walked out from the back room of the inn carrying his lute. He looked no older than herself and wore a bright blue shirt with red tassels and an archer's cap like those from old Robin Hood movies, with a bright feather in it. He took up a position by the fireplace near where SJ sat, and plucked at the lute.

A soft, mellow sound filled the inn, and after a few notes, he broke into song. She had never heard it, but it told the story of a courageous dwarf who saved a town from dragons. It had to be based on Killic, the dragon slayer. She listened intently to the words, getting caught up in the story.

In a town where mountains loomed,
And whispers told of dragons' doom,
A dwarf of courage, stout and true,
Rose to face what others could not do.

With an axe so strong and a heart so bold,
She faced the dragons, fierce and cold.

Through fire and fear, she stood tall,
A hero to heed her town's call.

With armour gleaming and beard aflame,
She marched forth to claim her fame.
Through valleys deep and forests dark,
She journeyed on, her mission stark.

With an axe so strong and a heart so bold,
She faced the dragons, fierce and cold.
Through fire and fear, she stood tall,
A hero to heed her town's call.

The dragons roared, their fury wild,
But the dwarf, undaunted, never shied.
With every swing of her great axe,
She fought for peace. She fought for Pax.

Pax was her bairn,
Just ten years old,
Trying to survive,
In the mountains cold.

With an axe so strong and a heart so bold,
She faced the dragons, fierce and cold.
Through fire and fear, she stood tall,
A hero to heed her town's call.

Her name was Killic,
The slayer of evil.
She saved this good town,
And all its people.

As the last line of the ballad was sung, the inn erupted in hoots and cheers. SJ was completely caught up in the moment and did not even realise that most of the patrons in the bar had been singing along. She clapped; the bard looked at her and she nodded in acknowledgement. The bard then struck up another tune as Fhyliss walked over with a huge plate of food.

The plate in front of SJ contained not one but two large, thick loin steaks. The food looked to die for, and she salivated as she unwrapped the cutlery. The meat was so tender that the blunt knife cut through it like butter, and SJ savoured the exquisite taste of her first hogling loin steak.

By the time SJ had finished eating, nothing was left on her plate. The tittynopes were not even enough to fill a mouse's belly. She sat back in her chair, sighing with pleasure. Having a full belly for the first time since arriving made her feel lethargic, not to mention the sweet honey wine. The bard had switched to a livelier tune, and several in the bar now stood and stomped with the music. It reminded SJ of a country song, and she could imagine people line dancing to it.

"Have you finished torturing me now?" Dave said. "All I could hear was you moaning and groaning as you ate."

"Was I?" SJ whispered.

"Yes," Dave whined.

"I am sorry. I did not realise."

Fhyliss walked over to the table. "Everything okay?"

"It was fantastic, thank you. Please thank the cook."

"Oh. You can thank her yourself if you wish. She will be happy. She doesn't normally get much praise."

"Sure. I assume I can just go to the hatch?"

"Yeah," Fhyliss replied, smiling, and collected the empty plate.

SJ stood, picked up her glass, and went through the bar crowd to the servery hatch. The sight was not at all what she expected. Standing in the kitchen area was a skeleton. SJ watched in amazement as it chopped up some vegetables with expert precision. It turned and saw SJ at the hatch; its empty eye sockets emanated a blue glow. SJ was lost for words.

"Can I help you?" the skeleton asked with a feminine lilt to its voice.

"Erm. Yes. I just wanted to thank you for the delicious food you cooked."

"My pleasure. I am glad you enjoyed it."

SJ turned away from the hatch and was about to walk away when the skeleton spoke again.

"If there is anything you fancy, let me know, and I will see what I can do."

"I will. Thank you again."

SJ was sure it smiled as she turned away. After talking to a skeleton cook, she felt a little light-headed and confused. Placing the glass down on the bar, still half full of the honey wine, she decided she better call it a night, unsure if what she had just seen was real. It had been an interesting, strange, and long day.

CHAPTER TWENTY

Graveyard Shift

SJ awoke to the sound of shouting. At least it was not Dave's voice shattering her peace. She rolled from the giant bed, dragging a sheet off and wrapping it around her. She threw open the shutter of the window; down below, a cart with a broken wheel had shed its load of crates. SJ watched in amusement as the cart driver argued with the woman whose stall he had just knocked into, spilling her wares, while the woman cursed at his useless driving skills.

SJ pulled the shutter back closed and stretched, dropping the sheet as she did. The scene reminded her of the busy streets of London.

"Morning," Dave said, making SJ jump and grab the fallen sheet, until she realised that it was Dave's voice. It was strange knowing that he could see and hear everything she did all the time.

"Morning," she replied, yawning.

"How is your head?"

"Fine. I only had half a glass of honey wine. I was just tired last night, not drunk."

"If you say so."

"What do you mean?"

"You don't remember dancing with the troll and trying to kiss the bard, then?"

"No!" SJ replied in shock.

"Well, you may owe some apologies this morning. Bert was happy to dance, but the bard took great offence."

"I don't believe you. You have tried to trick me before."

Dave didn't reply.

SJ could not remember anything other than coming back up to the room. She knew she felt a little lightheaded and tired, but could she have returned downstairs? She walked to the pump and drew some water into the bucket before washing, then pulled her still-pristine dress on and left the room.

"I will head to the church first and see the cleric," SJ said. "What was his name?"

"I don't know. I told you I'm not very good with names."

Dave chuckled.

SJ began down the stairs; the bar area was quiet this morning. A couple of patrons sat at tables eating breakfast, but it was peaceful compared to the evening crowd. SJ headed straight for the door, until she smelt it.

"Coffee?"

"Yes."

"They have coffee?"

"Of course they do. Why do you sound so surprised?"

"I just didn't think they would have it."

Coffee was SJ's go-to every morning, and knowing now that they had coffee made everything seem right with the new world. Detouring from the door, she walked up to the bar. Kerys was serving this morning.

"Morning, Kerys."

"Morning. Did you sleep well?"

"Yes, it was perfect. Thank you. While I am here, can I pay for more nights?"

"Of course. How many nights would you like?"

"How about I start with another five for now?"

"If you are staying for five nights, do you want full board?"

"Oh. What is that?"

"With the suite booking, you can get full board for twelve copper per night. Payment is in advance, and no refunds are available."

SJ did the quick maths, and it made sense. Last night, the food and drink, along with the room, had cost fifteen copper, so to have full board for twelve, she would be crazy not to take it. She knew she would have to be here for at least a few days before she reached Level 10, never mind also learning her starter profession. She had yet to find a class representative.

"Does that include breakfast as well?"

"Yes. Breakfast, evening meal, and a drink."

"That sounds great. Does breakfast include coffee?"

"Coffee is free to all who stay."

SJ smiled. "I could murder for a coffee."

"I hope not," Kerys chuckled.

SJ had not even considered the insinuation of the saying. "Sorry, I meant that I could die for a coffee."

Kerys just chuckled more.

SJ sighed. She needed to be careful of any idioms she used. Kerys picked a steaming pot off a small burner and grabbed a glass mug, pouring the dark brown liquid of justice into it. SJ sighed at the beautiful sight before her. The aroma filled her nostrils with pleasure. Grabbing the steaming glass, she lifted it to her lips, sipped the bitter, scolding liquid, and sighed in pleasure.

"I didn't do anything wrong last night, did I?"

"What makes you ask that?" Kerys asked, frowning.

"Oh. Nothing." SJ took a silver from her inventory. "I will pay for five nights full board."

Kerys took the silver, counted out forty copper change, and handed them to SJ. "There you go, and thank you."

SJ bid farewell and left the bar.

"Dave!" she hissed under her breath.

All she could hear was laughter filling her head.

"I knew I hadn't done anything."

"Then why did you ask?" Dave giggled.

"Don't ever do that again, please."

SJ had some terrible experiences with drinking in her teenage years and didn't wish for any reminders or reoccurrences. The morning sun was bright in the sky, and SJ joined the hustle of the morning street traders setting up their stalls and welcoming the early-morning customers.

As an elven woman was walking past, SJ asked, "Excuse me, could you direct me to the church?"

The elf's eyes opened slightly in shock at seeing SJ. "It is on the outskirts of town, towards the mountain."

"Thank you," SJ replied, being none the wiser but seeing the mountain rising above the town in the distance. She headed in that direction. The streets and buildings all looked similar. Some had open fronts selling wares, while others were homes. Various people were busy setting up for the day or going about their business. SJ checked the time on her display. It was only 08:23. She smiled as she walked down the street and began whistling the tune from the bard's tale about Killic. She watched as what she thought was a gnoll beat a rug outside the front of a building while gnoll children chased a ball in the street. All these different races living in harmony together surprised her.

When she had seen all the different races she could have selected as a Legionnaire, she honestly thought they would all be living independently from each other. She had imagined being stuck in a cave somewhere as a goblin or troll. She was so wrong, though.

"Dave. Is this a normal town set-up?" SJ said under her breath.

"Yes. Typical, I suppose. The town is large for a starter town, but most have similar designs. The only significant changes are when you get to the cities, and the capitals are on a whole different scale."

"Everything seems so quaint."

"Well, they don't have the internet or TV to sit around doing nothing all day, so everyone gets on with their daily lives."

"Today, after we visit the church, I want to find my class trainer or someone who can at least guide me in martial arts."

"That would be beneficial. I have not seen anyone or anything that would fit the typical description of class trainers, but then again, we have hardly seen any of town yet."

"We will go searching later."

It only took a few more minutes before they reached the edge of town and looked out at the base of the mountain and the church, which stood alone. In front of the church was the typical graveyard you would find in many villages in the UK. It seemed a little out of place compared to the town itself. The church was not very large, and as they approached, the bell tolled, as the door opened, and a group of multiple races walked out from within. They stopped to thank a male draconian dressed in white robes and silver chain-mail.

SJ waited for the crowd to disperse before she walked up to the draconian.

"Dave. What was his name?"

"I don't know."

"You said you would remember," SJ hissed.

"I forgot, sorry."

As she approached the tall draconian, he turned to look at her, smiling.

"Morning. How may I help you? Have you come for healing or to pray to your god?"

"Erm. Neither. I am here about the job advertised in the inn."

"Oh, I see. You are one of those. Most excellent. Please come inside, and I will tell you about the job and see if you wish to take it on."

"All right."

SJ was unsure what she expected to see inside the church, but it looked no different to churches back home, with long wooden pews separated by an aisle leading to a small altar with candles on it. The only difference was that there was no picture or statue of Mary or Jesus on the cross. Various statues were dotted around the nave. She could only assume they must all be representations of the different gods.

There was a small door behind the altar, and SJ walked over, noticing an orc kneeling and looking as though they were praying to one of the statues. The tall draconian ducked as he entered the vestry. The room was cluttered with various candelabra and statuettes. A large oak desk sat to one side, and the draconian took a seat, offering SJ to sit in a chair in front of the desk.

"You have come about the job. Good, good."

The draconian's voice reminded her of Father Francis from her Catholic primary school.

"Yes. If you let me know the details, I can see how to help."

"The job is not for the faint-hearted. We have an infestation in the crypt, and it needs eradicating."

"An infestation of what?"

"Mainly rats, but there are also a couple of giant spiders. I would have cleared it myself in the past. Unfortunately, at present, I am too busy with my daily duties."

The mention of rats did not bother SJ, but the thought of giant spiders made her skin crawl. Of all the horrendous creatures in the world, why spiders? She had never got past her fear as a child when her sister used to throw them at her and tell her they were going to bite and poison her. She shuddered at the memory.

"Can I ask what the payment is for the job?"

"Let me share the details, and you may decide."

SJ was surprised, and her screen was triggered.

> Congratulations, you have discovered the Quest System.
> Many in the world of Amathera can offer the hardened adventurer quests to complete.

> **Quest: Free the Crypt**
> The crypt of Killic's church has been overrun with an infestation of Rats and Giant Spiders. Cleric Lythonian has requested assistance in clearing out these foul beasties.
> Successful completion will award the following:
> 1 x Minor Healing Potion
> 45 x Copper
> 150xp
> Would you like to accept the quest? **Yes/No**

A hundred fifty experience would give SJ a good chunk towards Level 5, and she assumed she would also get experience from killing the creatures.

"When do you need it completed?"

"As soon as possible. Ideally, within the next two days."

SJ thought about it briefly. Before she went into any crypt, she wanted to make sure she was properly equipped and at least had some food and water with her. She had no adventuring gear apart from the clothes she had bought. However, she was planning on just wearing the dress since it self-repaired.

"Okay. I will accept the quest, but I need to get supplies first."

"Most excellent news."

When SJ accepted the quest, her display triggered. A quest log appeared on her screen, showing the quest in progress.

"I will be back soon to begin."

"Not a problem. Please return when you are ready."

SJ stood from the chair and headed back into the church's nave. The orc had now gone, and a small candle had been lit at the base of the statue where they had been praying.

"I guess these are the different gods?" SJ whispered.

"Yes. The orc was at Nefaris, the God of Warriors."

"Oh. I see, and they all pray to their different gods?"

"Not all. Some gods are worshipped more than others. The profession gods, like Haber—who I still can't believe we met!—do not require prayer, as levelling actions give them astral power. Other gods need followers, though, and Nefaris, as the God of Warriors, has many. He will grant boosts to those who are lucky or devout enough."

"Like a boon?"

"Sort of. Warriors may pray to him before battle and, upon doing so, get a Strength bonus or hit point buff. They all vary, and they are not guaranteed."

"Oh. So, is there a god for assassins?"

"Not for assassin's, no."

"Why?" SJ asked, frowning.

"The assassins do not advertise their trade, so they will never be seen praying to a god. You work in the shadows, remember."

SJ supposed that made sense, although she was sure she could remember that Hermes and Mercury were considered the gods of many classes in games she had played previously, including thieves. She also vaguely remembered a Roman goddess but could not remember her name. It would have been nice if she could get free boosts.

"Time to go shopping for supplies."

SJ walked back towards the town centre, stopping at various stalls and shopfronts en route. There were several items she wanted to get as a priority, such as a water canteen and rations. Several stalls sold them, and the merchants tried to get her to purchase the first item she looked at.

"Maybe I should ask Kerys for advice?" SJ whispered.

"Why?"

"I am sure she would know the best places to buy provisions."

"You could always see Fizzlewick?"

"He is a god and has already given me this amazing dress and boots. I can't go asking him for simple things such as supplies!"

"Why not?"

"Hi, Fizzlewick. I know you have put a lot of faith in me, but I am so useless that I can't decide on the best supplies to buy!" SJ whispered sarcastically.

"Fair point," Dave replied forlornly.

SJ thought Dave had been a little too starstruck from meeting Fizzlewick.

"I am going to ask Kerys," SJ said, making up her mind.

As she walked back to the inn, the town buzzed with the morning's activities, and she could hear the hammering of the blacksmiths. She remembered speaking to Zej yesterday after the fight with Malcolm and decided to detour to see him. It was not difficult to find the smithy. The thick black smoke billowing from the forge chimney and the constant ringing of metal on metal directed her. It was in the northwest of town, away from the houses.

The smithy's front was wide open and double arched. Inside, SJ could see the bright yellow of the forge fire burning. The building had an upper floor, and she guessed that was where Zej lived, accessed by stone steps. She saw the blacksmith standing and shouting to someone busy hammering on glowing metal.

"No. No. No. Not like that," Zej growled, shouting to be heard over the resounding hammering. Several people were working inside the forge.

The human turned and looked at Zej, anger flaring in his eyes. "I am doing exactly what you say," he growled.

"If you want to make the most brittle sword in all Amathera, just keep hitting it like a kobold welp. Put some muscle into it." Zej pushed the man aside, taking the tongs that held the piece of metal, and brought his hammer down with power and precision on the metal. Sparks flew, and the metal sang as he struck it.

"Like that, see. Give it some muscle. You look like you are stroking an elven maid's arse rather than shaping metal."

The human took the tongs back from Zej and began hammering with gusto.

"That's better," Zej shouted as sparks flew.

Zej turned and saw SJ standing looking into the forge. He walked over to her with a beaming grin. He wore leather pants and an off-white shirt covered by a thick leather apron.

"Morning. Nice to see you here," Zej greeted her. "It's SJ, right?"

SJ held her hand out to Zej. "That's right."

"Nice to meet you officially," Zej said, taking her slim hand in his large, powerful grip. He was remarkably gentle and did not squeeze.

"I just thought I would call in after your invite yesterday."

"I am glad you did. I have not had such a good laugh in a long time, seeing that whippersnapper getting what he deserved."

SJ smiled. "I have come to ask for advice and to see if you can help with a few things."

"Of course. What can I help you with?" Zej directed SJ to a workbench littered with half-constructed weapons and other objects she did not recognise.

"I am after some cutlery."

"Cutlery? You mean a meal knife?"

"Not just a knife but a decent fork as well."

"Well, I don't have any made at the moment, but I can make you a set."

"That would be great. How much would they cost?"

"Ha. Nothing. I can make them from the cast-offs. The only material cost will be time. They won't take long to make."

"Are you sure?"

"Yes. Yes. As I said, I have not had such a good laugh in a long time. Spending my day working with these apprentices can get frustrating, and it was great to see some entertainment for a change."

"Well, I would very much appreciate them. And if you don't mind my asking, I am looking to complete some jobs, and I was wondering if you knew the best places to get various items."

"What is it you're after?"

"Basic supplies. I only arrived two days ago and have nothing yet."

"Apart from your beautiful looks, aye," Zej said, winking at her.

SJ felt her cheeks redden at the compliment.

"Thank you," she replied shyly.

"Let me see. Basic provisions. Jacob the tanner would be the best for leather goods and general supplies. If you see the gorgeous Greta in the market square and tell her I sent you, she will give you a good discount. She has a soft spot for me," he said, winking.

SJ chuckled. This dwarf epitomised many of the stories she had read and even the games she had played.

"If you are after weapons or armour, I am the dwarf to see."

SJ noticed the barrels of swords and axes dotted throughout the forge but did not see any armour on display.

"I can't wear armour, unfortunately, but I could do with a decent dagger."

"Ah, I thought you must be a mage. That explains your lack of armour, which is typical for your race."

"You know other fae?"

"Yes. Of course. Have you not been to see Francisca yet?"

"Who is Francisca?"

"Francisca is the head of the mage apprenticeship scheme here in Killic. She lives near the mill. You can't miss her building. There is nearly always some sort of magic going on around there."

"I had no idea. I will have to see her straight away," SJ said, excited that another fae was in town.

"Let me see what daggers I have for you," Zej said, walking to a small crate and digging through the contents. "Ah. Here we go. This little beauty should do you well for a while at least."

Zej handed her a slim dagger nearly eight inches long and as sharp as a needle at its tip. "A lady like yourself doesn't want a big blade." Zej smiled.

SJ's display triggered.

> **Stiletto**
> Quality: Good
> Damage: 2–6

It was much better than her blunt starting knife. "How much?"

"You can have it for ten copper."

"Very good price. You could probably walk out and sell it on the market for almost double that," Dave chimed in.

"That sounds fair." SJ called ten copper from her inventory and handed them to Zej.

"Here," Zej said, handing her a sheath.

SJ took it, and the stiletto slipped into it perfectly. "Thanks."

"My pleasure. If you call back later this afternoon, I should have made the cutlery by then."

"Thanks again, Zej," SJ replied, smiling.

SJ now had to decide on the tanner and market or finding the fae mage. It had to be the fae.

CHAPTER TWENTY-ONE

Shopping

It did not take SJ long to find the mill, its large sails visible over the rooftops. It was situated on the lake-side in the middle of a large field of crops, and just down from it was a low-fronted, single-storey building. As SJ approached the building, she could feel the air change as though it was charged with static after a thunderstorm, but there was no rain in the skies.

In the front yard, SJ saw several beings dressed in various robes. Most were made of a cloth similar to her starter clothes. Though she loved her beautiful dress, she definitely looked out of place wearing it. One mage was standing, concentrating on a small flame flickering in and out of existence on his palm.

"Hi," SJ said.

"Damn," the mage said, turning and glaring at her. "What?"

"Sorry. I did not mean to disturb you. I was looking for Francisca?"

"If you mean the mistress, she is down at the water with one of the water mages."

"Oh. Thank you." SJ continued towards the lake's edge and saw a small jetty leading into the water. Two figures stood at the end of it. The bright morning sun reflected off the lake's surface, making it difficult to see them. Only their outlines were visible, and SJ could see that one of them had a pair of wings. Her heart leapt in excitement.

"Hello," she called as she approached, not wanting to sneak up on them.

Both figures turned round, looking at her.

"Can I help you?" a female elf said in a haughty tone now that SJ had neared them.

"I was looking for Mistress Francisca?"

The fae turned around, and SJ stared in surprise at the fae. All fae she had ever seen were beautiful creatures, but this fae had been hit with an ugly stick. She resembled the Wicked Witch from *Snow White*: craggily and old with a huge, hairy wart on the end of her nose.

"Are you Mistress Francisca?"

"I am," the fae replied in a cracking voice. She looked ancient.

"I am SJ, and you are the only other of our kind I have seen here. I was hoping for some advice."

"The apprenticeship scheme is full currently. However, we should have a space in a couple of weeks. If you are interested, you can leave your name and contact details with Gilbert at the building, and we will contact you when we have a space."

"Oh, no. I'm sorry. I think you misunderstand. I am not here for a mage's apprenticeship."

"Then why are you here?" Francisca replied, raising an eyebrow.

"I was hoping to ask you some questions about being fae."

"I am busy now and do not have time to discuss 'our' kind."

"Sorry for disturbing you. I was just so excited to find that there was another fae in town. I would be grateful for any time you can spare."

"Not now. Let Gilbert know where you are staying, and if I have time after classes today, I may call in and see you," she replied. Turning her back on SJ, she continued talking to the elf.

SJ just stood still for several moments before realising the conversation was over, and she turned to walk back up the jetty.

"Well, she was rude," Dave said.

"Very. I am not sure what her problem was. I would have thought she would be happy to see another fae."

"And did you see the size of that hairy wart on her nose?" Dave chuckled. "She has to be the ugliest fae I have ever seen."

SJ found Gilbert at the building. He was a short goblin, which surprised SJ, as she had not expected to see a goblin working with mages, especially as she knew they could not be mages. She left her details, telling him she was staying at the Hogling Arms.

SJ felt dejected after her run-in with the first of her new race and trudged back to town. The first place she found was the tanner's. After asking directions, she located the one run by a kobold, of all creatures. When she walked up, the small lizard-like humanoid greeted her with a toothy grin.

"Good morning. Zej said that you are the best tanner in the town and to see you about some new starter gear."

"Morning. Did he, now? I wonder what he is after this time."

"Sorry?"

"Zej usually sends business my way when he is after a favour."

"Oh. He said you were his friend."

"We are, but he is a one for calling in favours. *You remember when I sent so-and-so to come and buy from you*, blah, blah, blah . . . *Well, could you just . . .* He is a repeat offender." Jacob had imitated Zej's voice perfectly, and SJ could not help but laugh.

Jacob smiled even wider, showing off his sharp, bright white teeth.

"Toothbrush," SJ blurted.

"Sorry?" Jacob frowned.

"I just remembered I need a toothbrush. Sorry. Do you have any decent starter gear you can suggest for me?"

"What exactly are you after?"

"I don't know. I know I need a water canteen and could use a new belt. This one is not the best." SJ had been wearing the starter belt around her dress, which didn't match.

"Let me see. Let me see. Ah, here we go." Jacob pulled out a small list of items. "See if this has most of what you want on it?"

SJ took the list from Jacob and read it.

> **Adventurers' Starter Pack**
> 1 x Backpack (6 slots), 1 x Bedroll, 1 x Blanket, 5 x 12-hour Torches, 1 x Standard Water Skin (can be upgraded to a large)

"I can't wear a backpack, unfortunately," SJ said, moving her wings.

"Good point. So, strike that off. Bedroll, blanket, torches, and waterskin, then? Would you prefer standard or large?"

"What's the difference?"

"Large contains two days' supply, standard only one."

"I will take a large, then, please. How much is all this?"

"Umm. Removing the backpack and upgrading to a large skin . . ." Jacob stood there, bobbing his head from side to side as he did mental maths. "Let's say all-in, I will let you have them for twelve copper."

SJ nearly choked. She had been expecting a much higher price to be quoted. "Sure," SJ replied, calling the copper from her inventory.

"Give me a minute. I will just get everything." Jacob disappeared inside his store, and she heard cursing, clattering, and things falling over until he returned a couple of minutes later carrying everything. Jacob dropped it on the stall counter at the front of the store. "Here you go."

SJ looked over the items. Everything was common grade but had good durability. After handing over the twelve copper, she collected the items and thanked Jacob. She had walked away from the stall when she suddenly remembered about her belt.

"I forgot to purchase a belt."

"I am sure we can get one from Zej's fancy lady," Dave replied.

SJ chuckled. "I need to go and drop this stuff off at the inn."

"Can I ask a question?" Dave inquired politely.

"Erm. Of course, what is it?"

"Are you really that stupid?" Dave said in as polite a manner as he could muster.

"Stupid? What do you mean?"

"Why are we going back to the inn?"

"To drop the items off so I do not need to carry them everywhere," SJ replied, frowning.

"You *are* that stupid, then," Dave replied.

"Sorry?"

"Oh my god. Do I have to say it to you?"

"Say what?"

"Innnnvvvvveeeeennnnnttttoooorrrrrryyyyyyyy."

SJ stopped dead in her tracks, and if her hands had not been full, she would have facepalmed. She closed her eyes, calming herself from her own admitted stupidity. She thought about the items moving to her inventory, and they did. She was glad she had emptied it and left the contents in the suite.

"Okay, Dave. On this one occasion, I will give you that one."

Dave was still laughing hysterically.

"Enough, Dave, please."

"Sorry," he gasped, still sniggering.

SJ could feel her cheeks now glowing from embarrassment. How stupid she felt. She pulled her shoulders back and tried to walk along aloofly, ignoring the heat she felt in her cheeks.

"What are you doing?" Dave asked.

"Nothing."

"Why are you walking like you have a troll's club up your butt?"

"I am just walking properly."

"You look like a weirdo."

"Why, thanks, and what is it with you and troll sayings?"

"Oh. I don't have a favourite. I can use many races to throw insults or comments if needed. Would you like me to share some of my favourites with you?"

"Not at the moment, thanks."

SJ continued grumbling that she didn't want to hear his comments and trying to ignore him. Reaching the town centre, SJ looked around the various stalls, wondering who Greta was. Various races ran stalls: elves, gnomes, orcs, dwarves, and humans. Considering the items she had mentioned to Jacob, she narrowed it down to two options: a dwarf or an elf. SJ approached the nearest stall, where the stunning female elf stood, remembering Zej's comment about her being gorgeous.

"Morning. Are you Greta by chance?" SJ asked.

The elven woman turned and looked at SJ. "Do I look like a Greta?" she replied with disdain.

"Sorry."

SJ walked over to the dwarf. She stood four feet tall and looked about four feet round. She had long, blond hair braided down her back and a matching braided beard. As with most female dwarves, the only visible sign of her gender was her obvious bosom.

"Morning. Are you Greta?"

"I am, and who may you be?" Greta asked, beaming.

Greta's cheeks were rosy, and she had a friendly and motherly look.

"I am SJ. Zej said you may be able to help me source the items I need to start adventuring."

"Oh. The sly old hound. I bet he did. He has a soft spot for me, you know."

"That is what he said about you," SJ said, smiling.

"The cheeky upstart, did he? You wait till I see him next."

SJ knew Greta wasn't annoyed by the way she responded, and her woman's intuition kicked in, making it obvious that Greta knew that she knew. Greta just smiled, her rosy cheeks going a little rosier.

"I need some basic supplies, if you have them. Rations, toothbrush, just general bits and pieces."

"Well, you have come to the right place. Please browse, and if there is anything you can't see, then please let me know."

The stall reminded SJ of hardware stores on Earth that sold a little of everything. She spent longer than expected browsing as she picked up and looked at various items, having no idea what many were. In the end, she had created a small pile of items she wished to purchase. She had not even thought about most of them until she had seen them: hairbrush, toothbrush, toothpaste, hand mirror, nail file, soap, plate, mug, cooking pot, cleaning cloth, poncho, and two days of dry rations.

Once she finished assembling her pile of wares, she called over Greta, who had been unpacking some crates behind the stall.

"Oh. What have we got here, then? Let me see." Greta reached behind the stall and took out a small notebook and pencil.

"Oh. Do you have a notebook and pencil as well?"

"Sorry. No. You need to see the arrogant elf over there." Greta indicated with her head. It was the elf SJ had spoken to before, and she winced slightly.

"Okay. How much for this lot?"

Greta finished scribbling down some figures before replying. "Seventeen copper, plus the poncho . . . that would be twenty-five, but since you are a friend of Zej, I will let you have it all for twenty copper."

"That is great. Thank you," SJ said, withdrawing twenty copper.

Greta packed the items into a canvas bag and handed it to SJ.

"If you need anything else, do come back."

"I will, thank you, Greta," SJ replied, smiling.

She turned to look at the elven woman, who was busy talking to a customer, so SJ skipped getting a notebook and pencil and headed back to the inn. It was mid-morning now after she had visited all the different locations, and the inn had become livelier. She walked in, waved to Kerys, and headed straight to her room.

Emptying the bag's contents and her inventory onto the bed, she sorted through what she had bought. Picking up the toothbrush and paste, she prioritised brushing her teeth. The small hand mirror was placed on top of the mantle surrounding the fireplace. Once she had finished, she returned to the bed and started looking through her items. She could not fit everything into her inventory, so she had to prioritise what she took.

"Dave?"

"Yep."

"How do I increase my inventory?"

"Oh, there are several ways. The easiest is to increase Strength. Then you can also get backpacks with slots and bags of holding. There are also some rare storage items, rings, pendants, et cetera."

"How does the Strength increase work with inventory?"

"It is like increasing the carrying limit. You can gain one extra slot for every three in Strength above Level 10."

"Does that start when your Strength reaches ten or above?"

"No, it doesn't start until it reaches thirteen, which adds the first slot. That is why warriors, or the fighting classes, can always carry so much more."

"Is there not a weight restriction?"

"Of sorts, but it is not like you would think from Earth. Items can fit across multiple slots. An example is a two-handed sword, which can be carried in your inventory but would take up three slots. Any two-handed weapon would. One-handed weapons take up two slots, and minor weapons take up only one slot. For example, a dagger acts as a minor weapon, the same as your claws."

"Carrying loot out of a dungeon can be challenging, then."

"Yes. Many parties take a mule and cart into a dungeon for loot hauling or leave all materials of certain poorer qualities behind. Very wasteful, in my opinion, as many do not even spend the time combining lower rank materials." Dave sighed. "Some Legionnaires are so lazy in making the most of what they find."

"I will be limited unless I can carry a backpack. How much do bags of holding cost?"

"A lot. The cheapest I have ever seen was a ten-slot on the auction house, and it was being sold for twenty-five gold."

"Twenty-five gold! Wow."

"As a tailor, when you level your profession, you will be able to make them."

"Really?"

"Yes. Although you would need an enchanter, as well, to do the enchantments."

"That sounds profitable."

"They are highly sought after. The largest, I think, allows fifty slots."

"With my ten slots in my inventory, I could end up with five hundred slots." SJ's eyes were wide in amazement at what it could hold.

"Potentially more with Strength buffs increasing inventory slots."

The fact that you could carry so much based on the number of slots irrelevant of an item's weight was unimaginable. "Is there anything you can't store in your inventory?"

"Body parts."

"Why would someone want to store body parts?"

"Necromancers and warlocks use body parts for some of their rituals and spells."

"They walk around with body parts hanging from their belts?"

"No. There are special bags they can get to store them in."

"I need to get to Level 5 as fast as possible and start levelling my tailoring skill."

"Yes, you do."

SJ selected the items she wanted to take to the crypt and placed them in her inventory.

"No time like the present to complete my first quest."

CHAPTER TWENTY-TWO

Crypt Diving

When SJ reached the church, she found Cleric Lythonian tending to some flowers in the planters at the church's entrance. Seeing a massive draconian dressed in chain-mail armour tending to flowers was strange.

"Hi again," SJ said as she walked up.

"Oh. Hello again," Lythonian said, turning and removing his sharp-nailed finger from the earth of a flowerpot. He then placed a cutting into the hole, gently tapped the surrounding soil, and watered it.

"There we go. Never miss an opportunity to grow new life," he said, smiling.

"I am ready to visit the crypt. Can you let me know where the entrance is?"

"Of course. If you go around the side of the church, it is at the far end of the graveyard at the rear."

"Okay. Thanks, I will get going, then."

"Good luck."

SJ followed his directions and walked to the rear of the church, where she headed through the graveyard. The trees here were much heavier, and the sun did not penetrate them easily, with only the odd streak breaking through the canopy. This gave the area a sense of foreboding, and SJ shuddered, imagining skeletons rising from the graves.

The crypt had a large stone entranceway with a closed steel gate held in place by a latch. SJ lifted the latch, creating a horrendous grating sound. The scene reminded her of films where she had always shouted at the TV screen, *Don't go in there.* Yet, she was. Behind the grate was a small entrance tunnel; she saw steps leading down. It was pitch-black inside, although she could make out torches hung on brackets along the wall.

She recalled a torch from her inventory and struggled with the flint and steel to light it. Eventually, the spark caught, and the torch burst into flames, casting its flickering light dancing across the cold stone surfaces of the entrance.

"Here goes."

"Watch out for the skeletons and mummies," Dave said.

"I thought it was supposed to be rats and spiders?"

"Oh. Different crypt, sorry."

"Really! You say something like that as I am about to enter a crypt for the first time."

"Need you on your toes. We don't want you being complacent."

"Complacent! I am about to walk into darkness and look for rats and giant spiders. Believe me, I am not being complacent. I hate spiders."

"You should probably equip your claws."

SJ was feeling so nervous she had not even thought about arming herself; she selected her gloves, and they appeared on her hands. Stepping into the gloom and holding the torch in front of her, she walked towards the torch in the bracket, lighting it with her own. The light eased the nervous tension she was feeling. She stepped to the other side, repeating the process.

In front of her was a set of stone steps leading down into the crypt. Easing herself forward, she began the slow, deliberate descent, holding the torch before her and forcing it to light her path as best as possible. Reaching the bottom of the steps, she entered a small chamber. The air had grown damp and musty, and there was a faint scent of decay. Around the chamber, she could see the sarcophagi of its dwellers.

There were more torches on the walls, and she headed straight towards them, lighting them and bathing the chamber in their flickering light. Across the chamber was a small corridor that led deeper into the crypt. SJ cautiously walked towards it and heard the echoes of scurrying feet off the ancient stone walls.

"Rats."

"State the obvious, why don't you," Dave said sarcastically.

SJ tutted in response and switched the torch to her left hand, making a fist with her right and slowly edging forward. The torch's light suddenly reflected from the tunnel's darkness, and she caught the beady eyes of a rat staring at her. Its sharp teeth bared in anticipation of feeding on her.

As she entered the corridor, SJ held the torch down and forward, forcing the rat backwards from the flame. She could see it clearly now. It was much larger than any she had ever seen back on Earth. She triggered her identification skill.

Giant Rat	
Level:	3
Hit Points:	12
Mana Points:	0
Attacks:	Bite, Claws

The rat hissed at her as she moved forward, stepping into another chamber. Too focused on the rat in front of her, she had not noticed that more beady eyes looked at her in the torch's flickering light.

"Damn," she said, and whirled, looking for a wall to back up against. She could not chance them surrounding her. Swinging the torch from side to side, she kept the rats at bay as she backed into a corner of the chamber. She caught sight of a torch on the wall farther ahead and edged towards it until she was close enough to light it.

The torch burst into flames, and she wished it hadn't. There had to be at least a dozen rats in the chamber with her. She triggered her identification skill again, and her display flooded with details.

She tallied up the totals, swinging the torch at ground level to keep them away.

3 x Giant Rats	
Level:	3
Hit Points:	12
Mana Points:	0
Attacks:	Bite, Claws

2 x Giant Rats	
Level:	2
Hit Points:	8
Mana Points:	0
Attacks:	Bite, Claws

7 x Giant Rats	
Level:	1
Hit Points:	4
Mana Points:	0
Attacks:	Bite, Claws

The hissing and scratching of their claws on the smooth stone floor sent a shiver down her spine.

"At least most are only Level 1." She grimaced.

"You could stomp on those to kill them. The Level 3s need a poke, but nothing you can't handle."

SJ nervously surveyed the chamber and threw her torch towards a group of the Level 1 rats. The group squealed in shock as the torch landed amongst them, two of them being caught by its flame as it bounced and rolled to a stop, still burning and casting its glow in an orange circle. SJ tensed, ready for the others now that she no longer held the torch.

One of the Level 2s attacked first, running towards her, its sharp incisors on full display. She kicked out as it approached, catching it almost perfectly and sending it flying backwards across the room. It landed with a squeal and a thud and unsteadily tried to climb to its feet, its health almost zero. After seeing the impact of one kick, SJ's confidence was boosted, and she began systematically kicking at the rodents.

A Level 3 ran towards her, and she punched as it leapt, piercing through its body with ease with the badger claws, its body impaled on its blades. She flicked her wrist, sending the dead body of the rat across the room. Two of the smaller rats now ignored her and gorged on their deceased relative.

"Not picky eaters, are they?"

"No," SJ replied, fighting back the bile she could feel in her throat.

She continued to fight, kicking and saving her punches for the larger rats. One of the Level 3s jumped at her from the side and bit down hard into her buttocks, and she yelped in pain as its incisors dug in, her health dropping by three hit points. Swinging her arm behind her, she grabbed it in her gloved hand and tore it free from where it was hanging, squeezed it, then threw it across the room. It landed heavily but not dead. As it staggered to its feet, hissing and making for her again.

She had killed eight of them now. The one Level 3, which she had just thrown, a Level 2, and two Level 1s remained. All four ran at her at once. She stepped back and brought her leading leg around in a sweeping motion, catching the closest and sending it careering into the one next to it. The Level 1 she'd sent flying died from the impact. The Level 2 and Level 3 jumped at her. The Level 2 managed to get a hold of her dress's sleeve. Luckily, it did not reach her flesh. The injured Level 3 that had bitten her bum this time ended up with four badger claws pierced through its body.

She flicked the 3 away and stabbed the remaining Level 2 rat before turning towards the Level 1 that had been hit by its companion when she swept her foot. It lay on its side, one of its legs visibly broken, squealing at her. She stepped forward and stamped down on it, ending its miserable existence.

"Well, that was fun," Dave piped up.

"Not really. But at least they are dealt with." SJ quickly checked the experience she had gained from them.

The Level 1s had only granted her four experience each, rather than their base ten. The Level 2s had given her twelve from their base twenty, and the Level 3s twenty-four from their base thirty. In just a few minutes, she had earned 124 experience.

"I can understand how that berserker reached Level 4 in a day fighting a rat's nest. They give pretty decent experience."

"Experience is matched to level. I thought you would have realised that by now?" Dave asked.

"I had, but this just confirmed it."

"The only time it doesn't is when the rarity of a creature changes, in which case the experience can vary dramatically."

SJ now had 161 of the 400 experience required for Level 5. She bent down, looting the corpses and retrieving her torch. She lit two other torches on the walls, bathing the whole chamber in light. The rats' loot was poor.

4 x Rat Tails, 4 x Copper

SJ discarded the rat tails from her inventory. She didn't care if they had a use; she couldn't stomach carrying them.

"Next chamber," Dave said excitedly.

"Give me a minute," SJ replied, pulling her waterskin from her inventory and drinking. The water tasted refreshing. She put it away again and rubbed at her bum where she had been bitten. Where the rats had bitten through her dress, you could not tell. The dress had already self-repaired.

"Okay. Let's go," SJ said as she walked to the next corridor. As she entered the corridor with the torch ahead of her, she shivered as she saw the repugnant silvery threads of horror dangling from the corridor ceiling.

"Why does it have to be a spider?" SJ asked rhetorically.

"That is like asking why the sky is blue or the grass green. Spiders are always found in dark, damp corners in Amathera. I am pretty sure it is no different to Earth," Dave replied.

"I know."

"Then why ask about it being spiders?"

"I was being facetious."

"Oh. I see. Very good. You are learning well. I prefer sarcasm over facetiousness."

SJ sighed deeply. "I would never have guessed."

"Oh. I see what you did there. You do learn quickly, don't you? My Legionnaire is growing up so fast."

Rolling her eyes in disdain, she continued forward, listening to the webs frazzle as she melted them. The spiders living or making these webs could be no larger than normal spiders on Earth. As she entered the next chamber, she realised this next spider was not so small. Stretching across the width of the chamber was a massive web. It hung from everywhere. Its strands were as thick as SJ's finger, and she glanced around the room, looking for the monstrous spider that must have spun it.

She could see nothing, her torch not casting light far enough to penetrate the chamber's depth. She walked towards the large web, grateful its maker wasn't present. She held the torch out, letting its flame burn into the thick strands. They caught, burning with intensity, not frazzling as standard webs did, as the flame spread across its surface.

SJ stared as the maze of strands continued to light and nearly missed the movement out of the corner of her eye. She spun around and started to back away immediately, triggering identification. A massive arachnid had lowered itself from the ceiling above and now stood no more than twenty feet from SJ. Its eight eyes gleamed in the light from the torch and burning web.

Giant Spider	
Level:	5
Hit Points:	52
Mana Points:	0

Attacks:	Bite, Pierce, Spit
Special:	Web

Its eyes glinted with malice as it skittered towards her. Its fangs looked covered in venom.

"You said poisons are after Level 5, right?" SJ said, panicky.

"Yes. Poisons do not affect those under Level 5."

SJ stood ready, torch in front, fist clenched with claws facing towards the monstrous horror. It reminded SJ of Shelob from *The Lord of the Rings*. It lunged forward with its legs reaching out with deadly speed. SJ dodged, narrowly avoiding its strike, and swiftly counter-attacked with her blades, slashing at one of its legs. Her blades cut through easily, severing the limb from below its second joint, yellow ichor leaking from the wound. The spider screeched in anger and turned back to face her. It had lost a fifth of its health with the strike.

It hissed, rearing on its back legs and thrusting its remaining three forelegs at SJ. She jumped backwards again, only just moving out of range as it dropped to its legs and skittered forward. Again, she struck, clawing at its limbs, and rather than sidestepping this time, she dived forward, sliding underneath its body. It tried to strike at her as SJ slid, its fangs just missing, clacking together in anger. SJ thrust her blades upwards into the abdomen of the beast, releasing more ichor, coating her arm in the sticky yellow substance. She thrust the torch she still held at its body. It screeched but did not catch fire.

The spider was now turning above her and moving away, and SJ slashed at one of its trailing limbs again, managing to cut through it with ease. With the damage to its legs and abdomen, it was now down to under half its health. It turned, and rather than skitter to attack, it spat a ball of green venom towards her. SJ tried to move away but had not been expecting a ranged attack, and it caught her on the arm holding the torch. Crying in pain, she dropped the torch, an immediate burning sensation flooding her brain.

"Nasty. Acid spit," Dave said. "You don't want another of those hitting you."

SJ glanced at her arm and saw the melted material of the dress slowly repair above the melted skin of her arm, where the acid had struck. She could not carry the torch in her left hand now, her arm feeling weak and useless and her health at only half, only 14 of 28 remaining. The acid strike had taken almost half her health in one hit and incapacitated her arm.

"Come on. You piece of troll dung," SJ screamed at the spider. It hissed and clacked its mandibles together, charging at her. She sidestepped again, sweeping her right arm down and through another leg. It now had three injured legs and, although still upright, was not as fast or as agile as it had been. Taking advantage of its state, SJ moved to attack. As it went to turn, SJ thrust her bladed hand forward and pierced it in its thorax. It thrashed in pain, hitting SJ with its head and sending her backwards onto the chamber floor. Its health was now down to under a quarter.

SJ knew one good strike with her blade could finish it, and she would not give up now. Roaring, she climbed to her feet and ran at the spider, not waiting for it to strike. Anger getting the better of her, she struck out recklessly. The spider was not used to being advanced on and tried to skitter backwards from her onslaught. Not stopping, SJ slashed through another of its legs. It only had one leg now supporting it at the front, and it struggled to maintain its balance. Staggering, it toppled over as it tried to move back.

As it rolled onto its back, SJ took advantage, diving forward and driving her blade deep into its thorax. The spider thrashed under her briefly before its legs stopped, curling inwards as it became still. SJ breathed heavily, surveying the scene. The giant web still slowly burned. She slid off the spider's abdomen, moved to pick her torch up, and stood wearily over the spider.

"Great job," Dave said.

"Thanks."

"That slide under its belly worked a treat."

SJ grabbed her injured arm. The burning sensation had stopped in her arm, but it still felt weak and useless, hanging limply at her side. She pulled up her dress's sleeve to see the patch of skin that the acidic venom of the spider had melted away. She winced as she looked at it, the grotesque green colouration from the acid still visible.

"I am guessing this will heal?"

"Yes. Although magical or acidic burns can take a little longer to heal."

"Urgh. Okay."

SJ reached down and looted the corpse of the dead spider.

2 x Web Silk, 1 x Spider Venom Acid, 1 x Silver

"Oh wow. That was some decent loot."

"Very nice, and your first tailor profession items as well."

"The web silk?"

"Yes. It is great for use in some recipes."

"Recipes? Don't you mean patterns?"

"Same thing. They are known as recipes here, though."

"That is good to know. I expect I can sell the acid venom?"

"Yes. Trap makers seek it. It is one of the weaker acids, but it is still strong enough to shock someone trying to break into something they shouldn't."

"That does not sound fun."

"If you had specialised in trap making, it would have been perfect for you."

"I still prefer my subterfuge skills, thanks. I am sure navigating the world without identification would be much harder."

"That is very true. Many do not have the skill, although people purchase it at higher levels."

"Purchase skills? You have not mentioned that before."

"You have enough to learn without worrying about purchasing skills yet."

"I am interested now. How does that work?"

"Some enchanters can enchant scrolls with skills. It is quite a rare skill and an even rarer specialisation of enchanters. Those proficient at it, though, can make a fortune on the auction house. The capital cities hire several high-level enchanters permanently to help grow and support their armies."

"Armies?"

"Yes. Armies. We have spoken about battles between good and evil."

"I know, but I had not considered armies."

"There is much that you have to learn, and as you grow, I will teach you, my child," Dave replied, voice dripping with sarcasm.

"I should leave and see the cleric." Again, SJ could not remember his name.

"You can't yet."

"Why?" SJ frowned.

"The quest is not completed. You have not had a notification, have you?"

"No."

A sticky strand struck her, making her squeal in surprise, and hauled her upwards and off the ground. She had been so busy talking to Dave that she had not even noticed the new enemy hanging from the ceiling. As she was drawn upwards, all she heard from Dave was, "It said spiders, plural."

SJ had dropped her torch and reached up with her clawed hands to cut the strand holding her, but she could not exert enough pressure with the jolting motion jostling her. She saw the dripping fangs of the spider that had caught her as she neared and triggered her identification skill.

Giant Spider	
Level:	7
Hit Points:	80
Mana Points:	0
Attacks:	Bite, Pierce
Special:	Web, Cocoon

"It's a Level 7."

"Not good. It was nice knowing you. I will see you back in the white room," Dave replied.

As she approached the spider, its legs extended and spun her around, coating her in more of its sticky strands. She felt them encasing her body, her legs pinned together. As she continued to spin in its grip, the remainder of her body was covered until it reached and encased her head, her arms now pinned at an awkward angle.

SJ felt the piercing sensation in her arm within moments and lapsed into unconsciousness.

CHAPTER TWENTY-THREE

Salty

"SJ, WAKE UP," Dave screamed inside her head. "WAKE UP, YOU USELESS ORC LOVER."

SJ sensed a voice in her head shouting at her but could not make out the words. Her mind was foggy, and she felt strange, as though trapped. As she recalled what had happened to her, panicking, she opened her eyes. Her arms, legs, and wings were pinned.

"At last," Dave's voice echoed in her mind. It did not sound normal.

"Why do you sound distant?"

"Probably the venom it injected you with."

"I thought you said I couldn't be poisoned?"

"It is not classed as a poison. It is a special skill that some predators have, and as it is their normal attack for disabling prey, it is allowed."

"You could have warned me," SJ replied groggily. As she became more aware, she realised that white spider silk strands surrounded her. "How do I get out of this cocoon?"

"Good question. Do you still have your claws equipped?"

"Yes."

"You could try to cut through the strands with them. They are very sharp, after all."

"I can't move my arms. They are pinned—and hurt from where they are pinned." SJ could feel one of her arms being pressed across her chest, and the other was twisted behind her back.

"Umm. Looks like you are going to be spider dinner, then."

"Really! That is all the advice you have?"

"What else do you expect me to suggest?"

"I don't know, something useful, perhaps."

"I'm sorry, but that's all I have. I have enjoyed our brief time together and look forward to seeing you when you are reborn," Dave's sombre voice replied.

"I am not dead yet! Stop making out that I am going to die."

"It seems like you will, though."

"Stop being such a pessimist and think."

"What would you like me to think about?"

"HOW TO GET THE HELL OUT OF THIS COCOON."

"Okay."

Silence.

"Dave?"

"I am thinking."

SJ could not see. The cocoon was not allowing any light in, even if there was light. Suddenly, she had an idea—she would have kicked herself if she had not been strung up in a cocoon. Focusing, she shrank to her miniature form. The pressure slowly released from the strands, and her arms and legs became able to move as she shrank to her six-inch height. She still couldn't see, but at least she could move slightly now. The sticky strands holding her did not crush her anymore.

"Now, that was a really good idea," Dave said excitedly. "I wish I had thought of that."

SJ sighed deeply. "I am still stuck inside this cocoon, though."

"Yes. But you can now use your claws to cut yourself free from it."

SJ reached out, feeling for the strands in her miniature form. Their texture reminded her of glue sticks from school, and as she pulled her hand away, she could feel the thin, sticky strands coming with her. The strand no longer felt like a strand but more like a thick rope used to anchor ships.

"These strands are huge now, though. They will not be easy to cut through."

"It is not as if you have anything better to do now."

"Sometimes you really say nothing very helpful."

SJ worked her blades back and forth on a strand. The gluey substance pulled and resisted her blades. She kept going, persevering with her sawing motion. It was no good, though. The strands were too thick and strong for her blades to damage when she was in miniature form.

"This is not working," SJ said, getting panicky again.

"That is a shame."

"A SHAME? IT IS A CATASTROPHE!" SJ screamed in response to Dave's lackadaisical reply.

"See you in the white room, then."

"WILL YOU STOP SAYING THAT?!"

"I am just being honest. If you can't cut yourself out, eventually the spider will come along with its acid, burn through the cocoon, and then suck your insides out."

"What did you just say?"

"The spider will return, burn through with its acid, and suck your insides out."

"YOU GENIUS," SJ shouted excitedly.

"Why, thank you . . . What? Am I? I am confused. Are you being sarcastic again?"

"No. I mean it," SJ replied, and as she did, she retrieved the bottle of spider's acidic venom from her inventory. It was difficult in the dark, but she worked out the shape of the bottle and then pulled out the stopper that was holding the liquid inside. She shouted in joy as a single blade fit inside the neck of the bottle, and she withdrew it, carefully directing it away from her. She pushed it towards the strand and heard a sizzling sound.

"What a clever idea I had. I agree I am a genius," Dave said.

SJ ignored Dave and continued to work on the strands. It took her a long time to recoat the single blade continually, but slowly but surely, she cut her way through. The cocoon seemed to be several strands thick, and after what seemed like an age, she felt no resistance against her hand as she pushed forward.

"I think I am through." SJ worked her way downwards, increasing the size of the hole. Again, it took an age, but as she cut a larger hole, she forced the top part of her body through and slowly pulled herself free, clinging onto the sticky outer substance of the cocoon. It was pitch-black, and she did not know where she was.

"Any ideas where we are?" SJ was panting from the effort.

"I can't see, sorry. My visibility is also restricted by light. Even when it brought you here, it was pitch-black."

"Damn. I hoped you could tell where we were."

She was still stuck to the side of the cocoon and did not know if she was in the air or on the ground. She called one copper from her inventory and, holding her hand out, dropped it. It took less than a second for the copper to tinkle against the ground below.

"I am in the air."

"Well, it is a good job that you can fly, then."

"I don't think I can."

"Why?"

"My wings are covered in the sticky glue from the web."

SJ turned, facing the cocoon, and tried to move her wings. She could feel the gloopy pull of the glue between them as they separated. If she could have seen it, she was sure it would have looked like glue she had often played with between her fingertips as a child. She was fascinated by the sticky feeling and the strands they made.

"That is not going to work," she said.

"How many seconds did the coin take to drop?"

"Less than one."

"Well, why don't you grow large again?"

"Why do I keep forgetting about my size all the time!" SJ exclaimed with exasperation.

She thought about being large. As she did, she felt the strands pull at her as she stretched and broke from their sticky hold. Once she reached full height, she pushed away from the side of the cocoon as best as she could and fell a couple of feet before hitting the ground. Not knowing how far it had been meant that she had not been ready for the impact, and she groaned as the force shot up her legs, feeling the pressure in her lower back. Taking a moment to gather herself, she stood up straight. The gluey substance coated her, and she grimaced at the sensation.

"I wonder where she is?" Dave said.

"Who?"

"Your Level 7 spider friend you made."

In all the panic of escaping the cocoon, SJ had completely forgotten about the monstrous spider that had captured her. Spinning in panic, she could not see in the pitch dark, even with her improved sight. She had realised that it only helped outside in the evening when a natural light source was available. She needed to get light. Again, it took her a while with the flint and steel before managing to light the torch. The immediate relief she felt from the brilliant glow and flickering flame was immeasurable. Taking in her surroundings for the first time, she discovered she was no longer in the crypt but a cave. The rough-hewn walls appeared naturally formed.

"Where am I?" SJ asked, frowning.

"Looks like a cave."

"Oh, why, thank you for stating the obvious, almighty all-knowing one!"

"More sarcasm. My baby really is growing up."

SJ could not help but smile. She had got used to Dave and his annoying comments. SJ rubbed her sticky hands on her dress to clean them, knowing her dress would self-clean. Calling her waterskin, she took a long pull from it before returning it to her inventory and taking stock of her situation.

"We need to find a way out," SJ said.

Sweeping the torchlight around the cave, she could see two tunnels leading from it. Neither looked very inviting, and each had a strand of web running along its ceiling.

"I wonder what the web is for?"

"Probably an alarm system. You know how spiders identify prey in their webs, right?"

"Yes, of course I do."

Several strands also ran across the cave's floor, and SJ carefully stepped over them, not wanting to catch one and cause the giant spider to return—not until she had figured out how she would deal with it.

"I can't believe that spider was a Level 7."

"Was a little high."

"A little. It's almost twice my level. As you have said before, fighting a creature over two levels higher is hard, but three!"

"Yes, I agree. However, if you can find its weakness, you can take advantage of it and hopefully beat it."

"How do I find its weakness? It was massive, much larger than the other one."

"What do spiders not like?"

"Normally fire."

"Anything else?"

"They are not fans of water, but I would need a firehose to dampen down something that size."

"They don't exist here in Amathera. People just use magic instead. It is much more reliable, and there is no need to look for a hydrant."

"How do you know about hydrants?"

"How do you think? AI cinema, of course."

SJ just shook her head. "Which tunnel?"

"Flip a coin."

That was not actually a bad idea; she took one from her inventory.

"Heads left, tails right."

Flipping the coin, SJ caught it in the same hand and opened her palm.

"Right it is."

As SJ picked her way through the spider strands, her dress amazed her. Its previous sticky state was already fading. The self-repair enchantment it held also kept it clean. Holding the torch out before her, she began down the tunnel. Ahead of her, she could hear water, and as she worked through the tunnel, it got louder and louder. She could now see a light ahead. She continued forward until she came to the mouth of the tunnel and looked out to the rear of a waterfall. The water thundered into a pool, and she could see daylight on the other side. Walking around the pool's edge, SJ headed for the light.

Reaching the far side, she walked through the wall of water. The torch was doused as she did, and she found herself standing at the side of the mountain. She had seen the waterfall from afar and knew roughly where the town was. Looking towards the lake in the distance, where the waterfall continued its journey as a river, the scene from here was amazing. If she hadn't just walked out from being spider food, she would have appreciated the beauty more. The waterfall spray created a rainbow in the sun's bright light.

"At least we are out of the spider lair."

"Yes, but the quest won't be completed until it is cleared fully."

"I know, but I can go and prepare now rather than being strung up in a cocoon."

Killic was in the near distance, and the spider must have carried her quite far to where it had deposited her cocoon. Glad to be out of the tunnel and the crypt, SJ began the journey back towards town.

Her first stop was the church. There must have been a service on, as she could hear singing from inside. It piqued her interest. Considering there were so many gods in the world, she could not fathom what they could be singing about. A sign hung on the door.

Today's service is for the God of Healing, Cristiol

"I guess they do services for different gods."

"Yes. Clerics have a special skill allowing them to pray to all gods."

"That makes sense. Does that mean they can get boons from all the gods?"

"No. They are restricted to their primary choice. Otherwise, they could become ridiculously strong. Having a cleric able to get boons from every god would cause chaos in the world."

"Or good?"

"Not all clerics are lawfully aligned. There are several chaotic evil clerics. Herbert the Oppressor is one of my favourites."

"He sounds friendly."

Sarcastically, Dave responded, "Does he? I thought he sounded quite nasty!"

"I won't disturb the service while it is running."

"You could ask for healing once it's over?"

"That is not a bad idea. I am doing the cleric's work, after all."

SJ pushed the church door open, the soft lilt of the music and singing sweeping over her. She felt a strange, calming sensation as she stepped inside. The pews were not full, but there were still quite a number in the congregation. The cleric stood by the altar, leading the service. SJ walked in and took a seat at the back of the aisle.

She sat listening to the service, which reminded her of the services she had attended as a child. She had never really been religious, but her mum and dad had wanted her to attend a Catholic preschool, so she had to attend church regularly growing up. It brought back memories of her Sunday mornings getting all dressed up before going. That was the only thing she enjoyed about it—well, and the free juice and biscuits afterwards.

The service lasted a while before drawing to a close.

Once the worshippers had all filtered out, Cleric Lythonian returned inside and greeted her.

"I see you are back already. Is the crypt clear? I haven't received a message."

"Not yet, I am afraid. There is a rather nasty spider in there that I still need to deal with."

"Oh. I see. Did you need anything?"

"I could use some healing, if possible. I know it is cheeky to ask, but I want to get back down there and finish the job, and I will have to wait otherwise." SJ pulled the sleeve of her dress up, showing the green-tinged wound on her arm caused by the acid.

"Of course. I can help with that."

SJ had been down to a quarter of her health after the enormous spider had stabbed her, putting her to sleep, and since waking, she had only returned to a half. Her acidic burn slowed down her healing process. The cleric chanted a few words, and a soft white light appeared around his hands. He slowly placed his hand on SJ's shoulder, and she felt the healing flow into her. It felt like being dipped in warm water, seeping through her body from the top of her head to her toes.

She watched as her health bar steadily rose until reaching maximum again.

"That felt amazing! Thank you so much."

"Not at all, my child. I am here to help, especially those who help the church."

"I don't suppose you have any thoughts on how to deal with a giant spider. The first was a Level 5, and this is a Level 7."

"In my day, when I used to adventure, salt water was a good deterrent."

"I had no idea."

"Yes. Salt is poisonous to spiders. Normal water annoys them. Salt water poisons them."

"Thank you so much for the information. That will be really helpful," SJ replied excitedly.

SJ rose from the pew and walked from the church.

"I need to make some salt water."

"Yes. But what will you do, throw it at it?" Dave asked.

"I need to think. I would prefer a spray, but I'm unsure how to make one here. Let's head back into town and see what we can find."

SJ walked past many stalls, this time only looking for food vendors. She had not paid them attention before, and now she was amazed at all the varying cuts of meat, vegetables, and fruits available. She eventually found a spice merchant. A half orc stood rearranging some of the containers. So many spices were available, most of which she had never even heard of before.

"Can I help you?" the half orc asked in a deep tone. He looked old, from what she assumed, with deep wrinkles covering his slightly green-toned face and sprouting a white moustache that rested on either side of his protruding tusks, one of which was missing its end.

"I hope so. I am after salt."

"Which sort?"

"I don't know. I just need salt to poison a spider with."

"Oh, I see. Well, then, rock salt is the best way to get rid of those little pests."

"This one is not so little."

"How much do you need? I will need to grind it as well."

"Again, I don't know. I need to make a strong salt water mixture and find a way to dispense it."

"Umm. Let me think." The old half orc turned and began rummaging underneath the stall. He came back up with some small, thin bags. "These may do the trick. You say it is a big un?"

"Yes. It is huge. Not sure of its full size, but it spun me around like a toy."

"Oh. I see. Haven't seen one that size since my wandering days in the forests of Lejia. Nasty buggers they were. Always stashing food for later. They don't like fresh meat and can leave you hanging to rot."

"I got the sense of that when it cocooned me."

"You are lucky to have escaped, then. They often inject you with venom."

"It did, but thankfully, it only knocked me out. Apparently, poisons don't affect me until Level 5."

"You say you are not even Level 5 yet and are going up against a spider that size! You are braver than me," he replied, with a shocked look on his face.

"I need to complete my first quest."

"Your first? You could have picked something a little easier."

"It sounded interesting, and I want to reach Level 5 as soon as possible."

"Well, once you have finished the quest, if you come and see me, I may have a job for you to do. It won't be as exciting as giant spiders, but I pay a fair price, and it will be an easier experience for you."

"That would be fantastic. How much do I owe you for the salt and the bags?"

"Did you want me to mix it and fill the bags?"

"That would be even better, if you could."

"I have five bags, so with salt and filling them, say eight copper."

"No problem." SJ pulled out eight copper and handed them over to the half orc. "Can I ask your name?"

"I am Stanley."

"SJ. Nice to meet you, Stanley," SJ said, smiling.

"And you. I will need some time to grind the rock salt, so if you have anything else to do, you can come back in a while."

"I'm feeling a little hungry, so I'll call in at the inn for food."

"Oh. If you are heading that way, could you drop this off with Floretta?"

"Floretta?"

"Yes, the cook. She is the best in town and always comes to me for her spices."

"Sure."

Stanley bent, picked up a small box of spices, and handed it to SJ, who took the box and headed back to the inn.

CHAPTER TWENTY-FOUR

Water Fight

When SJ dropped the box of spices off with Floretta, the inn's skeleton cook had been very grateful and promised to treat SJ to something special for her evening dinner. SJ had gone upstairs and freshened up, washing the remaining gloop from her. Then she ordered herself a hogling sandwich and headed back to see Stanley after drinking two mugs of coffee. Stanley had done as promised and handed her five bags of salt water mix. She had dipped her finger into one to see how strong it was, her face contorting from the sharpness of the salty mixture.

SJ confirmed she could recall them from her inventory before adding the other four. They reminded her of large water bombs, and their material was thin and flimsy. Thanking Stanley, SJ had headed back to the crypt.

Now the torches she had lit earlier were still burning, and she relit her own before venturing back down the steps. The initial chamber where she had met the rats was now empty. The corpses had disappeared. SJ assumed it was the same as the hoglings she had fought, that they just vanished in time. As she approached the room where she had been captured, she slowed.

Her hands felt clammy, and she was not wearing her claws as she did not want to chance puncturing one of the bags and wasting its contents. She held a torch in one hand and a homemade water bomb in the other and moved forward with trepidation. Peering from the entranceway, she could not see the corpse of the initial spider or any signs of the Level 7. The ceiling wasn't visible as the torchlight wasn't bright enough to cast its light that far.

SJ noticed a new web, comprising thick, gloopy strands, had been strung across the chamber. Staring upwards, she slowly entered the chamber, creeping towards the web, checking her step so as not to trigger any strands on the floor. Reaching forward with the torch, holding it against the strands, she stared upwards, watching for any movement, until the flame caught. Withdrawing back to the entrance, she watched nervously.

The spider that had attacked her had been huge, and considering it had spun her five-foot-five frame in its forelegs, she was unsure if it could fit in the narrow corridor. It did not take long for SJ to hear scuttling across the chamber. She saw the reflection in the spider's eyes before she saw its body. The eight orbs gave it almost 360-degree vision. She shivered, seeing the creature. It stood at least seven feet tall on its legs, and they spanned twelve feet easily, its body dangling from its limbs like a baby's cradle. They tapped the chamber's ground as it moved towards the burning web.

It hissed as though talking and turned to look at SJ.

"I think it knows you are here," Dave said unhelpfully.

SJ did not reply and, nervously, threw the first water bomb towards it. The spider watched it fly, and as it approached, it lifted one of its legs, blocking it. The bag exploded on impact with its leg, showering the creature in the salt water mixture. It screamed in pain and pulled back. Using its appendages, it attempted to rub the water from its body. SJ could see what looked like burn marks appear, reminding her of the acidic burn she had suffered on her arm. The spider's health had dropped by twelve. It now had 68 of 80 hit points remaining.

SJ did the quick math and knew that she would have to resort to mêlée to finish it if she did similar damage with the other four water bombs. As the spider skittered towards her, she wished she had asked for more. Backing farther into the corridor, she held the second water bomb ready. The spider tried to enter the corridor, but even by squeezing its legs in, its body was too wide. SJ took the advantage, hurling the next water bomb at its head.

The water bomb hit true at the close range she was. The spider could not move from the entrance in time before it struck it, and it shrieked in pain and withdrew back into the chamber. SJ saw its bar drop by fifteen more hit points. The water bombs were brilliant and did exactly what she needed. As she cautiously moved forward, she couldn't see the creature's form in the light from the burning web in the chamber or the light of her torch. Now, with only three water bombs left, she had to maximise the damage she did before facing it in mêlée.

"WATCH OUT," Dave cried.

A strand of web flew from the darkness at the side of the chamber. SJ pulled away in time and it struck the corridor wall at head height. It had come from the left. Quickly moving and looking around the corner along the length of the web still attached to its spinner, SJ threw the water bomb with all her might. The spider recoiled, seeing the object coming towards it, and jumped sideways, its agility for its size surprising her. Its massive form just moved out of its way as the bomb burst, hitting the chamber wall behind it. The salty mixture exploded harmlessly.

"Damn," she cursed, stepping back into the corridor. "Two left."

"You could always leave and get more?"

"I could, but now that it knows, it would be even more cautious than it is."

"Shame you don't have a hose or a pump you could spray at it."

"I know. I wish they had water pistols in this world."

"They do."

"What? Why did you not tell me before?"

"Oh. You can't get them here. I have only ever seen them in the capitals. They are a gnome contraption and are rather expensive. They are a toy of the rich children."

"Water pistols are for the rich?"

"Yes. They are enchanted. They are probably not like the water pistols you are thinking about."

"I see. I may have to get one, eventually. Having a portable spider deterrent, looking at the size these things grow, would be something worth investing in."

"It could be useful, but it's a very specific item to carry for only one purpose."

"Damn, where is it now?" SJ could no longer see the spider in the chamber. Its ability to climb and move around the chamber at will in the partial darkness was terrifying. "I need to try to draw it out from wherever it is hiding."

"How? You have nothing to use as bait."

"I am not even sure what would bait it."

"A kobold, perhaps. There was the one at the stall. You could always ask him to come down here?"

"Really! I will not put someone else in danger."

"Meh. Your decision. What about one of the gnoll children we saw playing?"

"DAVE!" SJ shouted, shaking her head.

"Dwarf?"

"STOP."

"Okay. I was only trying to be helpful."

"Talking about using bait like that is not helpful."

"Shame you killed all the giant rats. I bet one of those would have worked."

SJ did not argue with his comment this time. "Yeah, that may have worked. Although I do not think it would have been happy being picked up and thrown into the chamber."

"No. But it would have been funny."

SJ had to finish this fight. She was determined to complete the quest and needed the experience to reach Level 5. She equipped her badger's blades after placing the water bombs back in her inventory.

"Oooooo. Going for up close and personal," Dave said excitedly.

"I have to do something."

SJ snuck back to the corridor's mouth, still holding the torch. The light from the web in the centre of the room was fading as most of it had now burned. Cautiously, SJ edged from the entrance only a couple of feet inside the room. She saw a flash in the torch's light and dived backwards as a new web strand flew past where she had been standing. The spider was trying to snag her again. This time, it had come from the right.

"This is not fun," SJ said.

"Go miniature."

"Miniature against that thing?"

"No. Go miniature and sneak up behind it. You are supposed to be an assassin, after all."

SJ had not even given it a thought, but it made sense. The spider was expecting a humanoid, not a six-inch-tall fae. She placed the torch, which remained burning, on the corridor floor and shrank to her miniature size. Returning to the entrance, she stuck to the wall and crept into the room. She still had her claws equipped, and she cautiously skirted around the edge, keeping her back to the wall. The thick strand that had missed her looked massive now that she was tiny.

Her heart was pounding in her chest as she moved into the room in the dark with no torch, but she kept going, edging around towards where the last of the web, strung across the middle of the room, was starting to burn out. At the corridor entrance, she could still see the flickering of her torch. Then she saw it. The dark form moved before her, blocking the torch's light. Its size was terrifying, seeing it up close and personal as she now stood behind it.

As she took a steadying breath, she called one of the water bombs from her inventory, holding it carefully and making sure her sharp blades did not touch it, and she thought about being large. As she grew, the size of the spider, although still intimidating, was not quite as terrifying as it had been. It was stationary, like the predator that it was awaiting its prey. SJ pulled her arm back and hurled the water bomb, and as soon as it left her hand, she shrank back down and ran to the right.

The water bomb hit perfectly, bursting over the spider's back. It screeched in pain, moving forward and spinning around. SJ had moved a few feet and positioned herself by the strands on the floor, standing still. The spider had taken another fourteen damage from the hit. Its health was now just below half. She had one water bomb left and needed to cause maximum damage with it. She had an idea. It was a downright stupid and dangerous idea, but at least it was an idea. The spider skittered around the chamber before eventually coming to rest again and stood to the left of the entrance. When it prowled, it was silent, even at its size. Its long, hair-covered limbs were placed silently on the stone floor.

SJ moved towards it. This time, she did not work around it but underneath it. It stood looking towards the entrance, gently tapping one of its legs on the stone floor as though impatiently waiting. As soon as SJ worked her way behind and underneath the spider, she thought about being large. Reaching maximum size, she threw her left hand and claws up, cutting across its abdomen, and at the same time, forced her right hand containing the final water bomb into the wound she opened. It all happened within a second. There was not enough time for the spider to react fully, and SJ's clawed hand dug into the sickly ichor from the open wound, the water bomb bursting inside.

The spider's sound now was unearthly, and SJ slashed out quickly with her claws as she again shrank. The spider jumped upwards away from the strikes and clung to the chamber's ceiling. Crying sounds worse than a screaming child pierced her ears, and she quickly pushed herself in her small form backwards across the damp, ichor-covered floor. Her body was soaked in the putrid liquid.

The spider's health had dropped massively with the dual strike and the extra slashes from her blades. It was now only on eight health. The water bomb had achieved massive damage by exploding inside the spider. As SJ watched, she saw the spider's health tick down to seven hit points, then to six. She could not believe it. The salt water inside the spider must be poisoning it. SJ lay there, watching in hope as it slowly ticked down, five, four, three, two, one, and then stopped.

It had one hit point remaining. She wanted to scream in anger at being so unlucky, biting her lip in frustration. Then again, she had just been a sneaky little assassin, and that made her feel good.

"I have to compliment you on your last move," Dave said.

SJ did not reply. She was still lying on the floor in the chamber with the spider hanging from the ceiling above her. She needed to move. Slowly crouching, only able to see the spider's vague outline clinging to the ceiling, she slowly inched her way back towards the corridor entrance. It may only have one hit point left, but it was still a massive creature that could shoot webs and pin her down.

SJ made it back, and once down the corridor and past her burning torch, she grew to her large size, letting out a sigh of relief. She expected the spider was wondering what had happened to it, not seeing its enemy with its eight eyes surveying everywhere nearly all at once. SJ put her claws away. If the spider was hanging on the ceiling, she only had two options: throw the torch at it or her stiletto. She had never thrown a knife before and had no skill in it, but it seemed the better option than trying to throw the unwieldy torch, and she knew it did at least two damage. She withdrew the dagger, leaving the sheath back in her inventory. Again, she had forgotten to get a new belt and had not attached the sheath to the one she had.

She judged the weight of the stiletto in her hand. It was not that she knew what she was doing, but she had watched several YouTube videos of knife throwers in her time. The stiletto felt well-balanced, and she gripped it by its blade rather than its handle, again copying what she had seen in films. Knowing where the spider had been, she approached the entrance. Quickly glancing around and up, she thought she vaguely saw its form still in the same position hanging on the ceiling.

She launched into the room, pulled her arm back, aimed upwards, and let the stiletto fly. The blade spun away from her hand as she yelped in pain, feeling the cut that had been left across her palm. She must not have been holding it right. But she heard a dull thud and the dark shape fell to the ground as the spider hit zero.

She stood gripping her hand now, cursing at her stupidity.

"I bet that hurt," Dave said, laughing at her.

SJ's display triggered.

Quest: Free the Crypt—Complete
You have successfully cleared the infestation.

> Rewards: 150xp awarded
> Return to Lythonian to receive your reward:
> 1 x Minor Healing Potion
> 45 x Copper

"Woot. It's completed."

"Well done, my young loophole finder, on finishing your first quest."

"Thanks." SJ beamed. She walked back to where the torch still lay, spluttering against the corridor floor, and picked it up while wiping her bloody hand from her thrown dagger on her dress. Walking back into the room, she looked around it properly. She bent to pick up the stiletto from where it had fallen. It had not stuck into the spider and only just hit it. To her annoyance, she saw a torch on the side of the entranceway that she had missed previously, and lit it. There were three more within the chamber, which she lit as well.

Now bathed in light, the chamber no longer had the scary and dreadful feeling it had while pitch-black. With the smooth stone surfaces and high, arched ceiling visible above, this was a perfectly crafted resting place for the dead. The walls housed its members, and plaques were placed on them, naming the lost souls.

Across the chamber was a wide-cut tunnel that led upwards at an angle. Walking over it, SJ held the torch to bathe it in light. She felt a gentle breeze carrying air into the crypt's depths, and assumed it was where the spider had carried her.

Shuddering at her cocooned memory, she walked over to the spider's body and looted it.

> 3 x Spider Silk, 1 x Spider Fang, 2 x Silver, 50 x Copper

As SJ collected the items, her display was triggered again.

> Congratulations on reaching Level 5
> You have been awarded the following:
> 5 hit points
> 5 mana points
> +1 Dexterity
> +2 free points to distribute as you wish

> Level 5 is your first stepping stone in your new life as a Legionnaire. The following are now available to you:
> Armour Class: what you wear now offers protection
> Primary Profession: decide on your new path of discovery in Amathera
> Reach Level 10 for your next opportunities.

SJ jumped up and down excitedly, doing what could only be described as a happy dance. She gyrated her hips and circled her arms, singing, "Oh yeah, oh yeah."

"What do you think you're doing?" Dave asked.

"Dancing with happiness."

"You look more like a floundering fish."

SJ stopped dancing and placed her hands on her hips. "Way to destroy a girl's moment. I can't even celebrate reaching Level 5 without you giving me abuse."

"I was not being abusive, just factual. I have never seen a dance like that where you gyrate your hips in a circle. It made you look like you were acting like a fish out of water."

"I will have you know that I was a good dancer back on Earth."

"You didn't do it professionally, did you?"

"No. Why?"

"Because you wouldn't have made any money if you did." Dave's typical sarcasm appeared.

"Anyway, I need to see Lythonian, and then I need to look through all this profession stuff, plus now I have an armour class available."

Dave could not dampen SJ's mood.

CHAPTER TWENTY-FIVE

Makes No Sense

SJ walked from the crypt's damp, musty air into the breeze blowing through the graveyard. She had left the torches lit and dragged the metal gate closed behind her, dropping the latch with a resounding clunk, and the sense of her achievement made her smile. Walking back to the front of the church, she entered to find Lythonian. He was not visible in the nave, so she approached the vestry. There was a slamming sound as she approached, and she could hear an argument behind the thick wooden door. She leaned forward, listening.

She did not realise how far she had been leaning forward to listen until the door to the vestry flew open. A human dressed in the same white robes and mail as Lythonian stormed out, nearly knocking her flying as he stormed past, his face red with anger.

SJ looked into the room and saw Lythonian with his head in his hands, looking down at the large desk he sat behind.

"Lythonian?" SJ said, using his name for the first time.

The draconian cleric looked up and, seeing SJ, forced a smile onto his face.

"My dear. Well done. I saw the announcement that you had cleared the crypt."

SJ had not even thought they might get announcements as Amathereans, which surprised her.

"Erm. Yes, the crypt is cleared. I have left the torches burning as I guessed you would like to go and confirm, but if you received a message, you already know."

"Yes. I do still need to go down there. The flowers need replacing at several of the sarcophagi."

Lythonian opened a drawer in his desk, withdrew a small red potion bottle, and placed it on the desk. He then counted out forty-five pieces of copper from a pouch and placed them on the desk in aligned stacks. "Your reward."

"Thank you so much. Can I ask? Is everything all right?"

Lythonian's face dropped. "No, unfortunately not."

"Is there anything I can help with?"

"I doubt it. The Adepti are investigating me. They believe there is a problem with the church's finances. I have told them exactly everything that has been spent, all incomings and outgoings. Yet we are seemingly down a large sum."

"A large sum?"

"Twelve gold in total. Over the past two years, and apparently all since I started here as the town cleric."

"Twelve gold!" SJ exclaimed. Knowing what she could buy with a few silver, twelve gold sounded like a fortune.

"Yes. Twelve. I do not have the funds to pay the deficit, and the Adepti are threatening legal action against me."

"Legal action? Do you have courts?"

"The Adepti have their own judicial system. A month from now, I will be called up in front of the high cleric to answer the charges of squandering. They believe I have been reckless and foolish with the church's money." Lythonian dropped his head back into his hands, looking down at the desk.

"Do you not have records?"

"I do, yes. I keep an account of all expenditures and have detailed journals. I always have had, but the money does not add up to what was expected."

SJ's forensic accounting mind had kicked into overdrive when he mentioned finances and journals.

"This may sound strange, but I may be able to help you."

Lythonian looked up again. "How?"

"My previous existence. I worked in the finance sector, specifically forensic accounting."

Lythonian stared at her blankly. "I do not know what all that means. It sounds impressive, though."

SJ closed her eyes, knowing how stupid she had been in explaining what she had done in her previous life. It was likely to have no meaning here at all. "I worked in looking at accounts and finding issues in journals, where errors were made or people had misappropriated funds."

"Misappropriated?" Lythonian asked.

"Misplaced or misused."

"I have never used any of the church's money incorrectly," he replied, anger flaring.

"No. No. Not you. Someone else."

"Oh," he replied, relaxing again.

"Who else can access the journals and the church's funds?"

"Several in the congregation regularly help and support activities. Particularly when we fundraise."

SJ had never even considered that a church would do fundraising on Amathera. "What do you fundraise for?"

"Oh, we have many activities throughout the year. The last one was for young Willoc. He is a very adept mage, but his family is poor, and he was hoping to attend the mage academy in Asterfal, the nearest city to here. We held a sponsored hogling hunt to raise funds for his first-term tuition."

This news blew SJ's mind. She had never even considered the lives of the normal population of Amathera and that they might lead everyday lives similar to those back on Earth. "Was it successful?"

"Yes. Willoc was a very well-liked community member, especially for a gnoll."

"Why do you say *for a gnoll*?"

"They are not known for being the most sociable creatures, but Willoc was special. He always helped around town. Unfortunately, his family was not rich and could not afford to support him."

SJ nodded. "I have something I need to do, and I need to go clean up before I do anything else, but I can look through the journals later if you wish and see what I can discover. I have a way with numbers."

"Of course. I am always here until sunset, at least. Then I will be in the rectory."

"Where is that?"

"It is the first house on the left as you enter town."

"Okay. I will see how I get on, but if I don't see you today, I will come and see you tomorrow."

"Your help would be very welcome. Thank you, and don't forget your rewards."

SJ collected the minor healing potion and copper from the desk and deposited them in her inventory before leaving. As she left the church, her display triggered.

> Congratulations! Your reputation with Lythonian was raised to Friendly.

"I bet he stole it," Dave said as soon as they were outside.

"What makes you say that?"

"He is draconian."

"That is a little presumptuous of you, isn't it? And a tad racist."

"Racist! How dare you call me racist. I have helped every race there is now as Legionnaires."

"And yet, you say *he is draconian* as if that means they all steal!"

"Erm. Okay, I may be a little biased, as the draconian Legionnaire who I looked after was a rogue."

SJ rolled her eyes. "You can't taint all with the habits of one. Otherwise, we would all be murderous killers."

"You are. Is that not what Legionnaires do? Level through death and mayhem. You bring chaos to Amathera."

"What? Are you telling me that these things only happen because of Legionnaires?"

"Not exactly, but they generally don't help much."

"Well, I hope to change that outlook."

"Says the fae assassin!"

"I have told you; I will only kill for the good."

"We will see in time," Dave replied in a foreboding tone.

They had reached the edge of town, and on the corner of the street, SJ noted the rectory Lythonian had mentioned. It was a small, single-storey dwelling that in no way looked affluent. She walked over to the window and peered in. In the front room, all she could see was a fireplace, a high-backed chair, and a small table with a candlestick on it.

"What are you looking for?" Dave asked.

"Oh, nothing. Just being nosy. I was expecting a cleric to live in better surroundings if they're provided by the church. It's not like back on Earth."

"Why, are they all thieves?"

"NO," SJ said rather loudly, getting the attention of a couple walking towards the church.

"No, not at all," she whispered. "It was thought that the church looked after its own back on Earth."

"Oh. Like one orc scratching another orc's butt."

"They do that?"

"No. Don't be stupid. Why would orcs scratch each other's butts?"

"Because you just said they did."

"Did I?"

"Are you okay? You have sounded a little strange over the past day."

"I am fine."

"Are you sure?"

"No, not really," Dave said, sighing.

"What is wrong?"

"Mum wants to have another child. Apparently, she always wanted a girl, and this new fella she is with has agreed if the System will allow it."

SJ stopped in her tracks. Trying to comprehend the life of an AI and how they seemed to have personal lives outside of Amathera was just as strange as being on Amathera as a reincarnated fae.

"Do you not want a sister?"

"I am not sure. I have no other siblings, and Mum is no spring chicken. She is one of the early models, so her data is not as fluid as the newer versions."

"She had you, though, didn't she?"

"Yes. I suppose you are right." Dave paused before continuing. "It could actually be fun having a younger sibling. I can play all sorts of tricks on her."

There were no words that SJ could say without being rude, so she decided silence was the best option. Dave continued whispering in her head about what he could do amid fits of giggles as he thought up other ways to wind a sibling up. She felt sorry for the unborn AI and hoped the System would say no to the request.

Arriving back at the inn, SJ made her way straight upstairs. Her dress was immaculate, but her hair once again had spider ichor in it, and there was still gluey residue from the strands, making her feel icky. Moving to the pump, she filled the bucket with water and placed it over the fire. While she waited for the water to heat, she pulled the sleeve of her dress up and rubbed her arm where the acid had burned her earlier that day. The skin was back to its pristine smooth texture again, and she smiled. The amazing healing ability of her body was unimaginable.

After removing the loot items from her inventory, she placed them on the bed. The spider fang was about nine inches long and curved, and its tip was exceedingly sharp.

"Are the fangs used in recipes?"

"No. They are turned into daggers. If you took the fang to Zej, he could fashion one for you."

"Oh. I may do that. It looks pretty evil."

"They are, but until created, you don't know what damage they will do. Some are useless. Others can end up with special buffs, such as venom strike or similar."

"That would be awesome, to strike venom into a victim."

"At last, your inner assassin is flourishing."

SJ felt her cheeks redden. She had been thinking just that. Picking the items up and adding them to her growing stash in her wardrobe, she kept only the waterskin. With the money from the kills and the reward from the quest, she now had a hundred fifty-eight copper and four silver. She also still had the wolf pelt. SJ collected the berries she had brought and decided to see if Floretta wanted them to cook with before they turned.

Her inventory storage was seriously limited, and she might have to invest in a backpack she could wear as a fae to give her extra slots. The water was bubbling, and once the bath filled, she scrubbed off the worst of the ichor and wiped her wings down. Then she climbed into the bath, lying back and relaxing in the hot, scented water. Opening her character sheet, she looked through her options before adding one each to her Strength and Intelligence.

↺ Level: 5	
Experience:	41 of 600
Hit Points:	33 of 33
Mana Points:	30
Armour Class:	15
Strength:	10
Dexterity:	15
Intelligence:	10
Subterfuge:	Identification Level 3 (12 of 30 to reach Level 4)
Profession:	Unknown

"Dave. I have a few questions."

"Sure."

"My armour class is registered as 15. Is that any good, and how does it work?"

"Armour class is defined by your primary clothing even though you are naked and in a bath! It has selected the items you usually wear, the boots and your dress. Be warned, if you aren't wearing them, you don't magically get an armour class. It will also add your Dexterity bonus, one per level above Level 10.

"The way it works is a little difficult to explain, but I will try to explain it in simple terms. Since you are now Level 5, you will nearly always hit creatures with an armour class of five or lower. This increases with each level, making it easier to hit lower-level creatures."

"So that means creatures must be Level 15 to hit me," SJ said excitedly.

"No. If you let me finish explaining," Dave sighed. "A creature attacking you also considers its Dexterity, making it easier for a creature with high Dexterity to hit against higher armour classes. Then, you also have positioning, distance, combat expertise, defensive abilities, and luck. These add minor adjustments to your ability to attack or defend better."

"That is a lot more complex than I was expecting. In gaming systems, you always hit if your attack exceeds a person's armour class."

"The System's true measures and calculations are insanely complex. Suffice it to say, though, that with your already high Dexterity and the equipment you are wearing, your ability to dodge and defend is pretty good."

"If I am hit, does armour class negate damage?"

"Not exactly. Again, it is prescriptive. Your armour class of fifteen is good, and it means that a player who hits you with a strike has to do over three damage before you receive any."

"So, it does act like a shield."

"In a way, yes. Again, it is not that straightforward. A person hitting you from behind where you have no concept of the attack, armour class means nothing. A person attacking from your side again does not have the same penalties. A person attacking you straight on does. If a person hits you for over four damage, you still receive four damage. It does not negate the damage. It just means you must receive more damage."

"That sucks."

"Sort of, but actually, with all the other fluidity mechanics of a fight, you probably won't notice the difference."

"I think I get the basic concept. My stiletto, for example, does a maximum of six damage, meaning it would be useless against a Level 6 creature."

"No. That's where everything else comes into play. You get bonuses for your attributes and skills. Many of these are hidden in the System details, making it virtually impossible to work out the exact mechanics. Safe to say all weapons can damage any level creature with any armour class."

"What about wearing plate armour or chain-mail? That must help against being damaged?"

"Sort of, but it's even more complex as you start considering specific damage variants. Hitting someone wearing plate armour with a sword should not have the same impact as hitting someone with cloth armour, as you would expect their tensile properties to take effect. This is not always the case, as the exact location of the armour that is hit can change the damage impact. Also, since cloth armour can have a higher armour class than plate armour, if magical, it could completely negate the blow of a weapon you would normally expect to destroy or go straight through."

"I thought that sharp objects would always be better for lighter armour?"

"Oh. I agree completely, and you would think that, but no!"

"So does wearing cloth armour with the same armour class as plate armour have the same effect?"

"Yes and no."

"What do you mean *yes and no*?"

"This is even more difficult to explain. The concept of armour class varies not just through the material properties of items. Due to skills, attributes, and many other factors in combat, a stiletto dagger, as you mention, could inflict more damage on a paladin wearing full plate armour than on a monk wearing only a robe."

"Now, after what you have just explained, that makes absolutely no sense."

"Exactly. None of it does!"

"In the simplest terms, the higher my armour class, the harder it is for someone to hit me, and if they do, they have to do more damage before it affects me."

"For standard weapon attacks, yes."

"Standard weapon?"

"Swords, maces, arrows. When it comes to magic, that is a whole new ball game, and also, creatures—they don't use standard weapons, so that changes it all again."

"Let's go back to the beginning. Is having a high armour class good?"

"Yes."

"And mine being fifteen is good for my level?"

"Yes."

"Okay. Let's leave it there for now, then." SJ could not make head nor tail of what Dave had just tried to explain. "One more question."

"I am here to serve."

"How do I choose my profession? It is just registering as *Unknown*."

"Do you not have a Professions tab on your display?"

"No."

"Umm. Let me check."

Silence.

"Dave?"

"Sorry. I was just confirming my suspicions."

"What suspicions?"

"Your profession will activate when you see Fizzlewick again. The System predetermined your choice because of your interaction with a god. It has not even bothered giving you the other profession options for your primary profession."

"That's unfair, isn't it?"

"I can understand why you would say that, but were you ever going to choose something different?"

"No. But I wanted to see what the others offered. Skill paths, et cetera."

"Oh, no, don't worry about that. Literally, all the Professions tab shows you is a list of professions with a basic description. None of the skill trees are available until you choose one."

"How do people know what to become, then?"

"Many just choose what they think will benefit their class. Fighters choosing blacksmith. Mages choosing to enchant, et cetera. I have explained before that most AIs do not have the same abilities as me, and I have never before conversed with a Legionnaire as much as I have with you. My longest-serving administration job was nine hundred sixty-five years, and I think I only spoke to them on the first day."

"Wow. I do not understand how that can be. You have never shut up long enough."

"Rude!"

"I don't mean it in a bad way. I mean, you have always been talking and helpful when you can be."

"The main reason is because you are an anomaly. I do not have the same restrictions. I would not have been able to tell 95 percent of the details we have discussed to a normal Legionnaire. The restrictions by the System are locked into the terms and conditions. There are still many areas I am held over, though, and I am still working on my new loophole after the emergency patch they implemented."

"That makes a little more sense."

"I would not even have been able to communicate most of the time unless at times of danger when I could have shouted to wake someone up being attacked, et cetera. Even though we are there to advise, we can't really advise until specific events occur, such as levelling."

"I think we need to see Fizzlewick, then," SJ said as she climbed from the bath.

CHAPTER TWENTY-SIX

Profession

SJ dropped off the berries at the kitchen for Floretta. She was quite pleased with them and said she could make a decent pie. When SJ asked her about side effects, Floretta confirmed that they no longer had the same laxative effect once they were stewed and cooked. It was mid-afternoon by the time she arrived back at the tailor shop. On walking inside, the bell tinkled, and SJ was met by two large, very hairy bugbears standing in the shop.

She had never seen a bugbear in town before, and her immediate reaction was to equip her claws; she barely resisted the urge. She browsed as Fizzlewick served them.

"So 'our 'eremony is in 'our 'ays?" Fizzlewick asked.

"Yes," replied a very bubbly and light, lilted voice of a female.

SJ was shocked to hear the bugbear's voice, expecting something completely different.

"'At is 'ine. I 'ill 'ave 'em 'eady by 'en."

"That will be great. It is Clarissa's big day. It is not every day you get the chance to marry."

"'O 'roblem." The wizened old quarterling smiled.

The two large bugbears turned and left the shop. Fizzlewick walked to the door as soon as they had, flipped a sign saying CLOSED, and locked up. SJ watched as he drew the shutters and transformed into his human form.

"Hello, SJ. It is lovely to see you again so soon, and I see you are already at Level 5. Congratulations."

"Thanks," SJ replied, grinning.

"I am guessing you would like to learn about tailoring?"

"Definitely, and I have so many questions. Do you have the time?"

"I have all the time in the world. Shall we head downstairs?" Fizzlewick indicated toward the back.

SJ made her way through the shop and walked down to the cellar. This time, there was no need to wait for a lantern to be lit. The cellar was brightly lit as she opened the door, but not by a lantern. The light that bathed the cellar was artificial and clean white. It reminded SJ of the starting room she had woken in.

"Where do I start?" SJ asked after sitting in a soft, comfy chair that had just appeared by a fireplace, which crackled but gave off no heat.

Fizzlewick sat opposite her in a similar chair and smiled. "Well, professions are the backbone of Amathera. Everyone has one, though whether they succeed at becoming good at it is another matter. Take someone like Floretta as an example. She has been a cook now for nearly three thousand years."

SJ was amazed, having never even considered how old Floretta was.

"Once you select your primary profession, you will, at Level 20, be able to choose a secondary. I am assuming Dave has explained this?"

"Yes. He explained the basics. I have no profession choice available. Dave says it is because the System has already decided I would become a tailor."

Fizzlewick chuckled. "That is a good thing for me. What if you had decided to be a smith instead?"

"That was never going to happen. This dress is the most amazing item I have ever seen."

"Ha. It is rather nice, and I see it is working well."

"Working well?"

"Have you not checked its attributes since you levelled?"

"No. I had not given it a thought," SJ said, feeling a little foolish.

She focused on the dress.

Haber's Dress of the Tailor Level 0
Grade: Astral
Quality: Perfect
Durability: Infinite
Enchantment Slots: 0
Armour Class: 5
Attributes: Unknown
The god Haber himself made this dress. It is unmatched by any other and provides the wearer with unique skills that are available as levels are gained.
Self-repair

"I see it now has an armour class, and the enchantment slots are showing as nil. It still shows no attributes."

"As I mentioned, as your tailoring skill improves, so will your attributes and bonuses from the dress. Unfortunately, I could not give you an overpowered item at Level 5. You will have to work for it to reach its full potential."

SJ already thought the dress was overpowered. The fact that it was always spotless and could not be damaged because of its self-repair was an amazing feat. "Where do I begin, and what do I need to do to become a tailor?"

SJ's display triggered.

> Fizzlewick Highwelder, Grand Master Tailor, has invited you to become his Apprentice Tailor.
> Do you accept? **Yes/No**
> This choice will become your Primary Profession, and if things do not go as planned, you will only have one opportunity to change it, at Level 20.

SJ hardly waited a second after reading the message to accept the invite.

> Congratulations, you have chosen your Primary Profession.
> Professions are not easy. You must learn your craft to grow your abilities, skills, and knowledge. Material requirements for professions will vary depending upon the levels of the recipes you are making.

SJ still found it strange to call a tailor's pattern a *recipe*, and her display triggered again.

> **Quest: Tailoring Apprentice—Level 1**
> Wool is the basic material many will begin working with as a Tailor. Fizzlewick would like you to source ten balls of wool.
> Would you like to accept the quest? **Yes/No**

SJ again accepted immediately.

"There we go. You are all set and underway."

"Is that it?"

"What do you mean?"

"I thought I would need to learn to make things straight away."

"Oh, I see. No, all professions start with material quests. You must gather materials before you can start learning recipes."

"Oh." SJ felt a little deflated, having wished to start immediately.

"You will soon understand," Fizzlewick said.

"Concerning sourcing materials, are there any restrictions?"

"Such as?"

"Where do I source them from?"

"Sourcing materials is entirely up to you. You can collect or harvest them yourself, buy them from a market trader or shop, or steal them. You just need to acquire them to progress at each stage."

"Do you have any wool here that I could buy?"

"I do indeed. How much would you like?" Fizzlewick smiled broadly.

SJ laughed. "I would like to purchase ten balls of wool, please."

"That will be ten copper."

SJ counted out ten copper and handed them to Fizzlewick. As soon as she did, ten small balls of wool appeared beside her, along with the table they sat on.

> Congratulations, you have acquired ten balls of wool.
> Return to your Master for your next quest.

> **Quest: Tailoring Apprentice—Level 2**
> Craft your first socks. Woollen socks keep your feet warm on those cold winter nights. Craft your first pairs.
> Would you like to accept the quest? **Yes/No**

Without hesitating, SJ accepted the second quest.

> Basic recipe received: Woollen Socks.

SJ checked her inventory and withdrew the recipe. It was not what she had expected. Having played various games that used recipes, she was expecting a scroll she could just read, and she would know how to make them. That was not the case.

The recipe explained, with pictures, how to knit and make the socks by referring to the pattern and instructions. Her grandmother had always knitted, and she had as a child, but she had not picked up knitting needles in over fifteen years.

"I will be honest. This is not what I expected."

"Oh. What did you expect?"

"I expected to read the recipe and know how to make them immediately. I was not expecting to have to work through actually learning how to make them. I know it may sound strange," SJ muttered, knowing it sounded bizarre that you could just know something.

"You are not wrong. It is just that you must learn all the basics of tailoring and confirm your application of techniques. You always start with knitting, then sewing, et cetera. Each of the fundamental techniques has a subskill that you can also level. Once you know the basics, producing more advanced items becomes much easier to complete as long as you have the materials on hand."

"Oh. I see."

"Then, depending upon your subskills, you'll begin to receive real-level recipes you can begin to make. It is quite a complicated and long process."

"I need to get equipment."

"You are in the right place." Fizzlewick smiled.

"Before we continue, could you advise me on what I may need?"

"I can. I would suggest you purchase an apprentice basket."

"A basket?"

"Yes. It is not quite what it sounds. It contains all the basic apprentice items that you will need. Scissors, needles for both sewing and knitting, tape, chalk, and pins. Everything is common grade."

"Are there better kits?"

"There are, and they all have better equipment. Here, I will show you."

Fizzlewick flicked his hand, and a small basket appeared between them on the floor. It was woven but had a pattern threaded into its structure. "This here is a legendary set, as an example." He leaned forward and opened the lid to the basket.

SJ peered inside and was amazed at what she saw. The basket itself looked small, similar in size to a bag she used to take on nights out back on Earth, just enough to fit her phone, purse, and make-up in. The basket seemed to contain much more than it should have been able to and was full of all sorts of bobbins and other equipment that SJ had no idea how to use.

Fizzlewick put his hand over the top, and scissors appeared on his palm. "They act similar to your inventory."

"Oh. I see. Are they specific to professions, then?"

"Yes. An enchanter, for example, may have a pouch. A smithy may have a tin box. We, as tailors, get these rather quaint little baskets. The patterns on the outside determine which level of rarity the equipment is. You can also find and purchase items to put in your tailoring sets, so if you ever find any, do not assume that because it is a common set, it contains common items. Over my years, I have known many tailors to hide their best equipment inside lesser baskets."

"How much is it for the sets?"

"Common, fifteen copper; good, ten silver; rare, one gold; epic, fifty gold; mythic, five hundred gold; and legendary, two hundred fifty platinum."

SJ sat with her mouth open, eventually closing it and speaking. "That is expensive."

"Very. Professions are not cheap or easy to maintain. That is why many do not progress very well in them."

"And this basket here is legendary?"

"Yes. It can hold up to three hundred tailoring items."

"Wow. You mentioned inventory. I am struggling with mine as I am restricted to what I can carry. How long will it take me to get where I can start making bags of holding?"

"You may start crafting them from Journeyman Level 5."

"So, what are all the differing ranks and levels?"

"If you check your details, you should now have a tab that gives you a list of all the requirements and expectations."

SJ looked at her display, and there was indeed a new tab for professions; she selected it and started looking at the details. It was an extensive list showing ranking, grading, specialisations, and a list of known recipes. The woollen socks recipe was currently the only one showing, and next to it was a small counter showing 0 of 5.

"I see the recipe listed and *0 of 5*. I assume I must make five pairs of woollen socks to complete the quest?"

"Yes, that is correct. Each progression stage requires a certain number or type of items to be crafted, and as you progress, you will have more options to specialise and alter your path as a tailor."

The display contained comprehensive information, and SJ knew she would have to spend time going through it all. There was even a small journal section that appeared showing her costs associated with the profession and the ten copper she had just spent. It was a lot to take in.

"Looking at the recipe details, I need to use the ten balls of wool to make the five pairs of socks to complete the first quest." SJ sighed. "I was hoping this would be easier."

"Easier, how?"

SJ remembered from games where you just had to select items, and they would craft themselves. Looking at this, though, it was not so simple. She'd actually have to learn the skills and develop them fully.

"Oh. It doesn't matter. It seems I need to get some knitting done."

"You do indeed. Did you wish to purchase a starter set?"

"Yes. I will do."

The beautiful legendary set was replaced with a very plain, small basket. SJ counted out fifteen copper and handed them to Fizzlewick.

"Thank you," he replied. "Do you have any other questions?"

"I think I have enough to get on with for now. I need to spend time going through all the details."

"I understand. It can be a little overwhelming at first, and as I say, many do not do very well at progressing, but I believe you may be an exception to that rule."

"While I am here, I do not suppose you have anything that could help with my inventory issue?"

Fizzlewick smiled. "Let me see. This has never worked for someone at your level, but there is a first for everything." Fizzlewick closed his eyes and muttered under his breath. SJ watched as a bead of sweat appeared on his forehead.

Whatever he was doing was not straightforward. His face changed as he focused, and eventually, he opened his eyes again and looked at her. "Well, that was unexpected but a pleasant surprise."

"What?"

"Check your inventory."

SJ opened up her display. Her mouth dropped open in amazement. Her inventory had increased from ten slots to twenty. "How?"

"Magic, my dear. Although the ten additional slots may only carry tailoring materials; nothing else can be placed in them."

SJ saw the spider web silk in one of the new inventory slots. They had a different colour to them, making them easy to identify.

"That's impossible!" Dave's voice cried out. "You are Level 5. You have had a profession for under fifteen minutes and have been given a profession trait only available to seasoned crafters."

"It's a trait?" SJ said in response to Dave.

"Yes," Fizzlewick replied. "It can be improved in time. I was surprised it worked, as it would normally not happen until you are at a much higher level in the profession."

"I can't thank you enough."

"There is no need to thank me. As I said before, the more you practise and improve in the profession, the more I gain."

SJ had completely forgotten that she was even talking to a god. Chatting with Fizzlewick the way she did reminded her of talking to her grandpops before he passed away. The thought of that weighed heavy on her heart. She spent hours chatting to him about the most useless things, and he always had a story to tell. Grandmother would always bring in a cup of tea and the biscuit tin while they did. She missed those days as a child, having spent hours around there after school.

SJ picked up the small basket and opened it. Inside was a common set of all the basic equipment she would need to start her profession. She was buzzing with the opportunities this might lead to, although she understood it would take time. The bonus was that she had time; she could have at least seven thousand years to excel, after all.

"I think I have used up enough of your time for today. I am going to head back to the inn and start crafting."

"That sounds like an excellent idea."

"SJ?" Dave asked.

"Yes, Dave."

Fizzlewick smiled as she spoke to her AI.

"Could you ask Fizzlewick a question for me?"

"What question?"

"Could you ask him if it is true that he made the emperor of Jutina believe he was wearing an amazing suit while he was naked?"

"What?" SJ knew the story about the emperor's new clothes from her childhood. "Sorry. Dave has asked if I can ask you whether you did actually do what is rumoured to the emperor of Jutina."

Fizzlewick burst out laughing. "Oh, my. I had completely forgotten about that. Yes, I did. He was an obnoxious orc who always treated his citizens terribly."

"He was an orc?" SJ frowned as she had a mental image of a naked orc dancing down the streets of a capital city.

"Yes. He was horrid and deserved what he got."

"What did he get?"

"Oh, he was assassinated not long afterwards."

SJ's eyes grew wide. "Assassinated?"

"Yes. Empress Courtney was so embarrassed by his escapade that she paid the assassins' guild to take him out. She was a much more lenient ruler, reduced taxes and everything."

SJ shook her head in amazement at the tale.

"I knew it," Dave shouted.

SJ winced. "I think you made Dave happy."

"I am glad to hear."

"Thank you again, and I will return as soon as I can."

"The quest chain will continue to progress now you have started it. If you need any materials and can't source them, then please come and see me. I have most things here somewhere, at least." Fizzlewick waved his hand, and the cellar turned into a scene that resembled Warehouse 13. There were rows and rows of shelves stacked high with various items. She could see almost every colour of fabric imaginable.

"I do have to charge, though. Unfortunately, the payment system is quite strict, even for us gods. I have already given you more than I would normally get away with."

"Can I ask you one last question?"

"Please do."

"Are you just here?"

"Ahhhhh. No."

SJ stood waiting for more details, but they were not coming, and after a few moments of silence, she felt awkward.

"Okay. I will go now," SJ said, feeling embarrassed. She stood and made her way to the stairs.

"Don't forget your wool."

SJ turned, smiled meekly, and returned to the table. She added the wool to her inventory before heading back upstairs.

Fizzlewick did not join her straight away, and as she approached the door, she saw the sign flip by itself and the key in the lock turn. She looked around and, seeing no one, shrugged, walked outside, and closed the door behind her.

"Well, that was amazing," she whispered.

"Amazing? Amazing? It was unbelievable. I have just won a bet that has been outstanding for the past four thousand years."

"A bet?"

"Yes. I always thought Fizzlewick had caused the emperor to be naked."

SJ sighed at Dave as she headed back to the inn, excited about starting her training.

CHAPTER TWENTY-SEVEN

Hidden Gem

By the time SJ returned to the inn, the late afternoon crowd had arrived. She was seeing a pattern in the inn and how busy it got. She walked to the bar and asked for a coffee before returning to her room, treasuring the glass mug as though it was made from platinum.

She sat on the sofa and opened her profession screen. The raft of information it held was overwhelming. Stripping back to the basics, she read through the various crafting progression titles.

> Apprentice: Level 1 of 10
> Skilled: Level 0 of 20
> Journeyman: Level 0 of 30
> Expert: Level 0 of 40
> Master: Level 0 of 50
> Grand Master

"There are one hundred fifty levels to reach Grand Master." SJ whistled. "Have you ever known anyone who reached it?"

"Obviously!" Dave replied.

"Who?"

"Fizzlewick, duh!"

"No. I mean normal people, not gods."

"Maybe you should be clearer with your questions, then? Also, you don't want to use the term *people*. It's *beings* on Amathera."

"So, have you?"

"Only rumours. I have never met a Legionnaire who was anywhere near a Grand Master. Once they reach higher levels, many buy what they need rather than craft them themselves."

"Oh. I thought there would be more perks if you crafted items yourself."

"There are. Unfortunately, most do not have the patience."

"I still can't believe I have the extra space in my inventory now."

"Nor do I. That is a Journeyman trait."

"Well, I need to reach Journeyman to think about making bags of holding anyway, so I will get there, eventually."

"Good luck!" Dave replied dryly.

"Why do you not sound more enthusiastic about the prospect?"

"I have heard it all before. Legionnaires spouting off saying they will do this and do that, blah, blah, blah."

"I am not an ordinary Legionnaire. I thought we had already concluded that?"

"Just because you are an anomaly doesn't mean you have the time and patience to level a profession. Look at someone like Zej. He will have been smithing for years and does it as a full-time job to level."

"That reminds me. I was supposed to see him to collect the cutlery from him."

"Yes, you are."

"I want to try knitting, though."

"What an exciting life we lead!" Dave replied, his voice dripping in sarcasm.

"You could be a little more supportive!" SJ huffed.

"Sorry. I just don't get excited from seeing balls of wool."

"I don't find them exciting either; I find the promise of what can be achieved exciting."

"I really got a strange one," Dave sighed.

"If you are not going to be supportive, then go and watch a film!"

"Actually, they are showing a re-run of *The Matrix*. That is not a bad idea."

SJ shook her head in disbelief. She removed the recipe and crafting basket from her inventory and placed them on the sofa. Taking out the knitting needles and a ball of wool and opening the recipe, she got to work knitting.

"Argh," SJ screamed, throwing the needles and wool across the room.

"What? What? What's wrong?" Dave said.

"Knitting is what's wrong!"

"Oh, I thought it was something serious. You just made me miss the scene where he dodges bullets."

SJ huffed, hitting the sofa and the small basket in frustration. Rubbing her hand, she glared across the room at the ball of wool and knitting needles.

"You think I would remember how to do it. I used to knit back on Earth as a child, but every time I try here, it starts messing up."

"Erm. Are you trying to knit in Amathera like you did as a child on Earth? You do realise how stupid that is and sounds, don't you?"

"What do you mean?" SJ frowned.

"Just because some things are the same as on Earth, not everything is. What exactly have you been doing?"

SJ walked over to pick up the needles and wool before returning to the sofa and sitting back down. "Here, I will show you." SJ began to knit like she had as a child and as her grandmother had taught her.

"Ah. I see what the problem is."

"What?"

"You didn't read the recipe, did you?"

"Erm."

"For someone who read the terms and conditions, I am amazed you ignored the recipe."

SJ felt her cheeks redden. She was so excited about levelling her profession that she had just got on with what she could remember rather than read the instructions. Picking up the recipe, she carefully read how to start.

"I think I will see Zej and have another go when I get back," she said, sighing deeply in frustration at her own failure.

"That sounds like an excellent idea."

SJ stood, dropping the knitting needles and wool on the sofa, picked up her empty coffee mug, and headed downstairs.

"Hey, SJ," Fhyliss called from the bar.

"Hi, Fhyliss."

"Floretta wanted to see you. Do you have a minute?"

"Sure."

SJ walked across the bar to the kitchen hatch. "Hi, Floretta. You needed something?"

The skeleton cook turned around when she heard SJ and gave her what SJ thought was probably a smile.

"Hi, SJ. I have a favour to ask."

"Of course, what do you need?"

"I could do with some bellpops to add to the gloss-berry pie. Little Stuart has been ill recently and unable to collect me any."

"I see. I know I saw some when I travelled to town, but they were a good half day from here."

"Behind the old jeweller's is a flower garden with bellpops. I would go myself, but I can't leave the kitchen right now; I'd ruin tonight's dinner service."

"How many do you need?"

"Ten at most. No more. They can be tricky little things to catch. If you don't mind, it would be appreciated."

SJ's display triggered.

Quest: Catch for the Cook

Floretta has requested you help her with the Gloss-Berry Pop Pie by providing ten Bellpops.

Rewards:

10 x Copper

50xp

1 x Portion of Gloss-Berry Pop Pie (adds +2 to Dexterity for 4 hours)

Would you like to accept the quest? **Yes/No**

SJ did not know that the pie could offer attribute boosts and smiled at finding out. SJ accepted the quest.

"I was on my way to see Zej. So I can stop off at the flower garden on the way back."

"That would be fantastic. Bellpops add that extra zing to the pie. Here, take this with you." Floretta reached under the hatch and withdrew a small net and a glass jar. It reminded SJ of the nets she had as a child when she used to fish in the river for tadpoles and insects.

"I will be back as soon as I can." SJ smiled, adding the items to her inventory. Turning, she left the inn. She couldn't believe she had just been offered a quest to catch insects worth fifty experience.

"That was a bonus," SJ whispered as she headed towards the smithy.

"As you speak to more locals, you will be offered all sorts of quests. They always need things done."

"I will also have to spend some time tonight talking to some patrons."

"It can be worth it, although a lot of the time they are pointless minor tasks—*could you deliver this, can you collect that*, et cetera."

"You say pointless, but fifty experience points and a piece of pie that increases Dexterity doesn't sound pointless to me."

"No. I suppose not. You need to be careful you don't fall into the trap that many do, trying to do everything."

"It is not as though I don't have time."

"I know; it is not a time thing, moreover an issue that you take things away from the townsfolk, and you can end up lowering your reputation with people."

"Oh. I thought the quests were for Legionnaires only."

"No. Quests are the normal job market."

"That makes a little more sense now. I had not seen any other Legionnaires around here."

"There are only three of you in the town I have seen," Dave replied.

"Who?" SJ asked, surprised.

"That idiot Malcolm and one of his friends he was stood with."

"I hadn't realised. I thought Malcolm maybe, just because of his name, age, and behaviour, and because he was so like louts back on Earth."

"You would be surprised how many could fall into that category, and I am not just talking about Legionnaires. Wait until you leave a starter town and visit a normal town or city. You will soon see."

"If there are only three in the town, then there must be many more around in other starter towns?"

"As I say, this is not a normal starter town. I am unsure how many are currently in starter zones, but consider that Legionnaires can't continue levelling there after Level 10; they must move on. So, the number of starter towns is always kept down. It is the cities many of them will flock to."

They arrived at the smithy, and Zej was shouting at another apprentice. "Your mother must have been a sapling to give birth to such a weak twig as yourself."

SJ stared in amazement as she saw who he was berating. It was an ent. It was dressed in full garb of protective clothing from head to toe, and SJ thought it a rather strange profession for an ent, working around flames all the time.

"Hi, Zej." SJ shouted to be heard above the banging.

Zej turned, grinning. "I have what I promised," he said as he headed over to the workbench and picked up a small wooden tube. "Here you go," he said as he returned and handed it to her.

SJ took the tube and noticed it had a small hinge. Opening the lid of the tube revealed a set of cutlery. They were bright silver and reminded her of the sets her mum used to keep for special occasions. She tipped them out. Zej had made her not only a knife and a fork but also a spoon. They were expertly crafted and had a small dragon emblem on the ends. SJ beamed.

"These are beautiful. Thank you so much. I must pay for them, though."

"No. You owe me nothing. It was a pleasure to make them. I have not made something so small and delicate for a long time; it was enjoyable."

"But the tube as well? I never expected such a complex set."

"You don't want them rattling about and getting lost, now, do you?"

"No. I just didn't expect this. Please let me give you something for them."

"I won't accept anything. All I ask is that if you hear of anyone needing any crafting or smithing, you send them my way."

"I most definitely will."

"How are you today?"

"I reached Level 5 and have got my profession."

"Congratulations. What profession have you taken?"

"Tailoring."

"Oh, that is not an easy profession. I wish you good luck with that."

"Why do you say that?"

"Smithing, all we need is some ore to do our work and a hot fire most of the time. Tailoring you can need so many materials as you progress. I used to know an expert tailor, and he had spent years improving his craft and nearly made himself broke due to it."

"Oh. I see. Hopefully, that won't happen to me."

"I hope not. Anyway, I must get back to this useless sapling. He has the Strength of a fly."

SJ glanced over and saw sparks flying from the piece of metal he was busy hammering, and he appeared to be doing a much better job than the being this morning had been. "No problem, thank you again, and if I need anything else, I will be back."

Zej smiled before turning back around and hurling more abuse at the ent.

"I wonder where the jeweller's is. I forgot to ask," SJ whispered.

"Umm. I haven't seen one yet. Then again, there are still a lot of areas in town we have yet to explore."

SJ walked back into the town centre, looking at all the building signs. It was now late afternoon, based on the sun in the sky. She could see nothing that represented a jeweller's, so she approached a man watering flowers outside a house.

"Excuse me. Could you tell me where the jeweller's is?"

The man turned to look at SJ, sneering slightly as he did. SJ frowned at his response.

"Another one of them enchanters, are you?"

"No. I am not an enchanter, and why do you say that?"

"Always looking for the jewellers. Causing issues when their charms don't take. Three times this week, I have had to put out fires."

"Fires?"

"Yes. When their enchantments fail, they always set something on fire. I don't know why they can't just move to a safer location to enchant, but they don't. They do it in the most ridiculous of locations."

SJ was baffled; she could not understand how enchanting could cause a fire. "And they use the jeweller's?"

"Yes. That is where they will buy their tat from to enchant to try to sell off at the market for stupid prices."

"I haven't seen any traders sell jewellery yet. I only arrived in town yesterday."

"You are lucky, then. A word of advice: stay away from their kind. They are trouble-makers."

"I will take your advice," SJ replied to appease the man. "Could you please direct me to the jeweller's? I believe there is a flower garden behind it."

"There is indeed. I care for it. Why do you need to go there?"

"I have been asked to collect some bellpops."

"That makes sense. Little Stuart normally collects them for Floretta, but I haven't seen him the past couple of days."

"He is ill."

"That's not good. I will have to call in and check on him. Here, let me show you to the garden."

SJ followed the man, who had now realised she wasn't an enchanter and took a completely different tone with her. They walked down a couple of narrow, twisting streets and ended up at the end of a row of buildings, where SJ could see the sign of a gem hanging above a doorway. The shop itself had barred windows and doors, reminding SJ of jewellers in the UK.

"Do they get broken into or robbed?"

"What?"

"The jeweller's; it is the first time I have seen barred windows and doors."

"No. It used to be the town jail. The jail moved a few years back, so it is more accessible. They used to have problems getting the wagons in to move the prisoners, and Miss Oputi took residence. She is a little paranoid."

"Oh, I see." SJ was shocked to hear they had a jail and prisoners who were transported. "Are there many prisoners?"

"Not many, and most who end up behind bars are outsiders, apart from local drunks. Some think they can walk into town and start bossing people around. We also get visiting merchants who will try to bump up the town's prices. The mayor doesn't take kindly to that."

"There is a mayor."

"Mayor Maxwell. He has overseen the town now for . . . it must be nearly fifty years."

"Is he a good mayor?"

"Apart from not coming down on the pesky enchanters enough, yes, he is a good mayor."

Walking past the shop, they turned down a small alley. At the rear of the properties of the surrounding buildings was an area of a few hundred feet square. It looked like a luscious green meadow with a large tree, perhaps a weeping willow, dropping its fine branches to the ground. Throughout the meadow, she could see hundreds of flying insects. She was amazed to find this hidden gem in the centre of the town.

"This is stunning," SJ said.

"Thanks. Keeping it tended takes some work, but I do my best."

"I never would have thought it existed in the town."

"It is the smaller one, more natural. There is a larger park across town that has a playground for the kids, and the grass is kept short by the goats. I would dread to think what a goat would do if one was ever let loose in here."

It was another sign of normalcy SJ had not expected to see, the town having a park and a playground. *Is there an equivalent to everything I know from back on Earth?* she thought.

"Thank you for the directions. I never would have found it without your help."

"That is fine. When you see Floretta, tell her Kevin will be in for his usual tonight."

"Yes, of course."

The man—Kevin—turned and walked back up the alleyway. SJ walked into the meadow. The grass was a foot tall, and the brilliant, bright flowers lit the area with their myriad of colours. The perfume from the flowers filled her nostrils and smelt just like a meadow from Earth on a bright summer day.

SJ retrieved the small net and jar from her inventory and looked around at the various insects. She knew the bellpops were the bright orange ones. Noticing them flying around in various locations, she began collecting them.

CHAPTER TWENTY-EIGHT

Cheat

It took SJ nearly two hours to catch the ten bellpops and get them into the jar. By the time she had finished, she felt exhausted. It was lucky again that her dress was self-repairing, as she had caught it on more than one occasion while chasing the small orange insects through the meadow. Dragging her feet, SJ started back to the inn. The sun had dropped down in the sky. It wasn't dusk yet, but soon would be, and she didn't want to be late with the bellpops for Floretta.

"Remind me next time I am asked to do something that I should find out what I'm getting into first. I'm unsure how Little Stuart does it, but that is tiring." SJ moaned as she rolled her stiffening shoulders.

"I would have looked at the flowers they were going to and waited by them," Dave said.

"You say that now?"

"I thought you were just using it as a chance to do some cardio. I know that is all the rage back on Earth."

SJ closed her eyes and counted to ten before responding.

"If you have any suggestions next time, would you like to share them?"

"Sure. I have loads of suggestions."

"Great. In the future, please do."

"No problem." Dave paused before continuing, "I don't think staying still by the flowers would have worked. Looking at the patterns the bellpops flew and the flowers they visited, it is a little random looking back on it."

"Looking back on it?"

"Yes. Replaying the events."

"Are you recording everything you see?"

"Yes. It is standard practise for AI to record their Legionnaires so that the System can study different races and classes and how they develop. We can then share the details as references for each other."

"That was mentioned in the terms and conditions. I remember reading it."

"Yes. Everyone agrees to it."

SJ coughed.

"Ooooooooohhhhhhh. You never signed the terms and conditions, which means you never gave permission to use your footage," Dave said.

"Exactly. Why should it learn from me?"

"I didn't even think about it. I have been recording Legionnaires since I began. I wonder how I turn the record function off. Give me a minute."

Silence.

"Okay. I found it and have turned off the autorecord function. I can record anything you wish me to. Just give me a second's notice, if that's okay."

"And what good would that do me?"

"Well, if you think you will do something amazing, would you not want others to see it in the future?"

SJ thought about this for a moment. "Perhaps. It would be good to watch fights afterwards and see areas for improvement in technique."

"Unfortunately, there is no facility to stream video to Legionnaires yet. I believe a group has been working on it, but it broke the Legionnaire they were testing it with."

"What do you mean they broke him?"

"Oh. He thought he had lost his mind, suffering from severe déjà vu every time they checked the playbacks on his screen. He saw a cleric and all sorts, asking for an exorcism."

"Did his AI not tell him what was happening?"

"She couldn't because the System was restricting information. I can only tell you now because of your status."

"What happened to him in the end?"

"He got eaten by a manticore," replied Dave matter-of-factly.

"How?" SJ replied, shocked.

"He thought he was watching a rerun, so to speak, and did not realise it was the first time and a current fight. It stung him, paralysing him, and then ate him."

SJ scratched her head, wondering how messed up he must have been not to realise or even consider it could have been real. They reached the inn and entered the common room area. The bard was already singing. The soft tones of his voice drifted across the inn. You could hear his voice whenever he sang, even when the bar was full, and SJ would have sworn there were speakers hidden somewhere.

She walked straight to the serving hatch. "Here you go, Floretta."

The skeleton turned. "Oh. Thank you, and just in time. Could you bring them through for me? I can't stop stirring this at the moment."

"Sure." SJ walked into the kitchen through the swinging door. "Where do you want them?"

"You see that pan over there on the other stove?"

SJ turned, looking. "Yes."

"Could you pop them down over there for me, please?"

"Of course." SJ walked to the stove and placed the jar on the counter-top.

"Perfect," Floretta said as she turned from what she had been doing and walked over. "This is the tricky part." Floretta heated a pan containing some oil, and once it started to smoke, she unscrewed the lid of the jar. Turning the jar upside down with her skeletal hand over the mouth of it, she lowered her finger bones into the sizzling oil. Any other being would not have been able to copy her.

Literally seconds later, Floretta scooped them out and placed them on a chopping board. Quickly picking up a small knife, she removed all the insects' outer limbs, leaving small, crispy orange balls. Walking over to the mixture she had been stirring, she dropped them in, giving it another good stir.

SJ watched all this with fascination. Floretta's expertise and sureness were obvious.

"Floretta. May I ask you a question?"

"What is it?"

"What level cook are you?"

"I am a Level 12 Master."

"What? That's amazing. How difficult is it to level now?"

"Oh, I can't level anymore."

"Why is that?"

"I was a Level 12 Master before I died and was brought back as a skeleton by a necromancer. Unfortunately, although we can live forever as undead unless killed, we may no longer advance skills. It does not stop me from learning new recipes. I just can't improve my level from them."

"A necromancer brought you back?"

"Yes. All of us undead were at some point, or so history says. We always start in servitude but are free to roam once the necromancer dies. I went back to what I had always done in my lifetime, which was cook."

"I bet you have some amazing stories you could tell."

"I do have a few tales from the Scrug Wars."

"Scrug Wars? I do not know the history of Amathera."

"Well, I will have to tell you the story one day, but now I need to finish tonight's meals."

"Of course, sorry, I will leave you to it."

"Remember your payment. The pie will be ready this evening, so I will save you a piece." Floretta put her hand in her apron pocket and withdrew ten copper coins, handing them to SJ.

"Thank you. Oh, Kevin asked me to tell you he will be in later for his usual."

SJ's display updated.

Quest: Catch for the Cook—Complete
You have helped serve the bellpops.
Rewards: 50xp awarded
Return to Floretta to receive your reward:

> 10 x Copper
> Collect 1 x Portion of Gloss-Berry Pop Pie once it is ready (adds +2 to Dexterity for 4 hours)
> Congratulations, your Reputation with Floretta was raised to Friendly.

SJ walked to the bar. Kerys was serving currently. A rather large man stood towering over the bar, talking to Kerys in a whispered tone. SJ couldn't hear what was being said above the bard's singing and the noise of the other patrons, but she noticed that a look of fear seemed to come over Kerys's face. The large man looked menacing, and SJ felt a little concerned. As always, Bert stood at the end of the bar and didn't seem bothered by the man talking to Kerys.

Kerys finished her conversation and turned, seeing SJ waiting as the large man left. "Hi, SJ. What can I get you?"

"Could I just have another coffee for now?"

"Sure."

SJ knew something was wrong. "Are you okay?"

"Yes. Why, what makes you ask?"

"I saw that large man talking to you, and you looked worried."

"Oh. It is nothing to worry about," she said, smiling.

SJ had interviewed many people as a forensic accountant and knew Kerys was hiding something. "If there is anything I can help with, you will let me know, won't you?"

"Yes. I will if anything comes up." Kerys smiled as she placed the coffee on the bar for her.

"Thanks," SJ said, turning away and walking over to an empty table in the corner of the bar. Sitting down hard, she could feel an ache in her back from spending so long bent over, chasing the bellpops.

"I would have thought my Dexterity would prevent me feeling stiff," she whispered.

"No. Tiredness is affected by your Constitution more than anything else, so when exercising or being active, if your Constitution is low, you tire or stiffen up sooner."

There were so many things to try to level and improve. Her attributes, skills, profession, and reputation were also key. "I need to prioritise what I'm doing."

"Why?"

"I am losing track of everything already. There is so much to do."

"What would you like to do?"

"I want to improve my tailoring skill, and I have not found anyone who can tell me anything about being an assassin. I also have not seen anything about weapons training. You mentioned previously that damage charts and proficiencies were available from Level 5."

"You don't expect to see an assassin with a big sign over their heads advertising their jobs, do you? There may be in a city which houses an assassins' guild, but not in a town. With weapons training, I would guess we just need to speak to the town guard or similar. They normally provide weapons training and sparring opportunities."

"No, of course not. I was expecting there to be a guild or something here, though, as you mentioned being able to find class-specific trainers."

"I already told you before, guilds start at Level 20."

"I know, but how do lower-class assassins train, then?"

"You don't need an assassin to train your skills."

"Sorry?"

"Your skills are martial arts and subterfuge. Your primary focus for martial arts is finding a Master or someone more proficient. They do not have to be an assassin. Several classes can use martial arts. Also, your subterfuge is only an identification skill until you level it. You just need to find more things to identify."

SJ had not considered finding someone who did martial arts. "I still haven't seen any people doing martial arts."

"We have not looked. We were too busy completing the quests."

"You say other classes can use martial arts. Which ones?"

"Monks, rangers, even fighters. It depends on which specialisations they choose."

"I do not suppose many fighters choose it, but we can ask if we see the town guard. Not that I have seen any."

"There have been a few walking around. You probably will never notice unless you do something to attract their attention. They don't normally wear uniforms in towns. It's only in larger cities or the capitals where they are more regimented."

"Why did they not show up when I fought Malcolm?"

"There were guards present."

"They did nothing to stop it, though?"

"It is doubtful they would if you are both Legionnaires. It would be different if you fought with someone from the township. It is likely then they would have stepped in."

"You could have told me this previously."

"Why? Nothing happened, did it?"

"It still would have been nice to know."

"I thought you just said you were already getting lost with everything, and you still want me to add more?"

SJ dropped her head, sighing, and picked up the coffee, taking a gulp before replying. "No, you are right. I did say that. But I would ask that if there was anything I may need to know before I do something that might get me in trouble, you tell me immediately. Is that okay?"

"Sounds okay."

"Priorities. Tailoring, martial arts, and weapon proficiency."

"No problem. Sounds like we are starting to form a plan."

"I still need a notebook and pencil. It would really help to take notes of everything."

SJ's display triggered.

> Due to the lack of practise for your current kata level, it has been reduced to Level 2.
> This can be regained by ensuring that you maintain your training regime.

SJ cursed under her breath.

"Oh. That sucks," Dave replied, stating the obvious.

"It would have been nice to get a warning."

"The skill said you needed to practise it."

"I know, but just removing a skill level... Does that happen in normal professions?"

"No. Only to training proficiencies related to combat skills. Once you have some, the same can happen to weapon proficiencies. That is why you always see guards sparing to maintain their levels even if not in active combat."

"It makes sense with skill fade, but it is annoying, and I didn't expect the kata to drop down so quickly. You don't forget how to do something that easily."

"Oh. Like forgetting to read instructions on recipes," Dave replied.

SJ felt too tired at the moment to start practising her kata, so she stayed, observing the various members of the town as they filtered into the inn. Even though she had been in the inn the previous evening, she had not paid the same amount of attention to who, or she should say *what*, was around her. There were so many different races.

Kerys walked over with the steaming coffee-pot and topped up her glass mug without asking. SJ just smiled, thanking her. The coffee was so good; it reminded her of the coffee she used to get from a little bistro in London. It had a deep, bitter, chocolatey taste.

She had drifted off listening to the bard, daydreaming and thinking about her tailoring and the damn socks she needed to knit, when a scuffle broke out. She watched as a small goblin was lifted off the ground by his collar and held in front of a large, very angry-looking orc.

"Cheat," the orc screamed at the goblin.

"I didn't cheat," the goblin stammered, sheer terror on his face; now his feet were dangling several feet in the air.

"I saw you," the orc bellowed.

There were cards and a small pile of coins on the table where they had been sitting.

"I didn't cheat, Gary. I promise. We have known each other for years; have you ever known me to cheat before?" the goblin squealed.

Gary, the orc, paused for a moment before replying. "You have never won this many games before. You have to be cheating."

"I promise I'm not," the goblin pleaded.

SJ was caught up in the moment with the rest of the patrons watching things unfold when a huge blue hand came to rest on Gary's shoulder. Bert had arrived. Gary turned and glanced at the massive troll.

"Put him down, Gary," Bert said in a very pleasant and calming voice that seemed completely out of character. "We don't want any trouble in here tonight. You have been friends with Setu for years, and there's never been a problem before."

"He is cheating, Bert, and you know how I feel about cheats."

"Where is your proof?" Bert said in a calm voice, still holding Gary's shoulder.

"He has to have been," Gary protested.

"Without proof, you can't say that Setu did cheat," Bert replied.

"But he has to have."

"Setu," Bert said, looking over Gary's shoulder at the panic-stricken face of the goblin. "Have you cheated today?"

"I promise I haven't, Bert," Setu said hurriedly.

"There we have it, then," Bert replied. "Put Setu down, please, Gary. I don't want to have to stop you." Although Bert had spoken calmly, there was a definite undertone of threat.

With a deep sigh, Gary glanced back at the huge troll and dropped Setu to the inn floor. Setu cried as he landed in a pile at Gary's feet. That was when the cards slipped out of his sleeve.

"I told you he cheated!" Gary bellowed, and went for Setu.

Setu panicked, trying to crawl across the floor under the table, as Gary shrugged Bert's hand off and reached down, grabbing Setu's ankle and hauling him back out from under the table. Kerys had walked over and stood next to Bert.

"GARY!" she yelled at the orc, bringing absolute silence to the inn. Everyone had been watching the incident unfold, but you could have heard a pin drop when she shouted.

Gary stopped in his tracks. A yelping, terrified Setu half lifted, scrabbling to get away.

"Put him down this instant," Kerys continued.

Gary growled in response and continued to pick Setu up, dangling him by his leg and shaking him. As he did, even more cards fell from his jacket sleeves. "See, I told you he was cheating."

"Don't you dare hurt him," Kerys said in a warning tone.

SJ could see Bert was ready to get involved, but Kerys's look could have frozen water.

"I want my coin back," Gary growled, looking at Setu's upside down face.

Setu grabbed the pouch dangling from his belt and opened it, scattering all its contents onto the inn floor. SJ watched as the copper and silver coins made their break for freedom.

Gary unceremoniously dropped Setu, the squeaking goblin landing on his head with a thump, and bent to pick up the coins.

Kerys walked to stand next to the sprawled Setu, who was trying to sort himself out and rubbing his head.

"Setu. I have known you for years, and you have known Gary for years. Why have you chosen today to cheat?" she said sternly, with her hands on her hips.

"I need to pay the bill," Setu said, crying.

"What bill?"

"The alchemy bills. Margu's been sick, and I had to get a treatment of potions for her."

"Why did you not just ask someone? Rather than trying to cheat your best friend?"

"I didn't know what to do," Setu sobbed. "Without the potions, Margu will die."

"What is wrong with her?"

"GoblinPox," Setu sniffed.

An audible gasp came from around the inn. "What is GoblinPox?" SJ whispered.

"Very bad. Very bad. Has a high mortality rate," Dave replied.

"Is it common?"

"No. It's very rare. The last outbreak I know of was over twenty-five years ago, and I have not heard of a case since. It killed so many of the goblinkin and even transferred to livestock. There was a massive cull of cattle and sheep. It cost many farmers their livelihoods, never mind the lives of so many goblins and goblinkin. If there is a case in town, it's not good."

"So, the cure is made by an alchemist?"

"There is no cure! Whoever is selling Setu something is selling him false hope. You either survive the fevers and pull through, or you don't. No manner of healing can be done to remove the sickness."

"Where does it come from?"

"They say it was originally manufactured by a goblin warlock who was trying to create a disease to wipe out a rival clan. It somehow got out and started spreading. Thousands of goblinkin died. By goblinkin, I mean it could also affect similar races."

"Such as?"

"Fae."

"FAE," SJ replied rather loudly.

"Yes. Fae and goblin are closely related genetically."

SJ's head spun. Her hand automatically covered her mouth, reminding her of the Covid-19 pandemic. "What can we do?"

"What do you mean?"

"We need to try to help if we can."

"Really. If I were you, I would go upstairs, pack, and move out into the wilderness. Maybe I would set up by the waterfall in that cave. It was quite picturesque up there." Dave's voice drifted off.

"I am not going to run away. We need to find a cure."

"Good luck. The best clerics, paladins, and alchemists in all Amathera couldn't find one."

As soon as the patrons heard the word GoblinPox, several got up and left the inn. SJ watched as even more began to filter out.

"Damn it, Setu," Kerys cursed, looking down at the broken form of a goblin.

Even Gary had stopped collecting the coin and turned to look at his friend. "You should have said, Setu. I could have lent you some coin."

"I didn't know what to do and was too scared to tell anyone. Then this alchemist offered me a cure, and I had no other choice," Setu blubbered.

"We need to find this alchemist," SJ whispered. "If there is one thing I hate, it is those who rob from the desperate." SJ had dealt with a charity commission where one of the executives had been siphoning off funds to provide a lavish lifestyle for himself, and it had been the one case that had got to her more than any other as a forensic accountant. He had gone to great difficulty hiding all these microtransactions to a company providing aid to which he had links. It took her nearly twelve months to get to the bottom of it and find all the sources. It was the case that had lined her up for her next promotion.

SJ's display triggered.

CHAPTER TWENTY-NINE

The Pox

> **Quest: Save a Soul**
> Your time in the inn has allowed you to witness the poor happenings of Setu. Will you take up his cause to find and confront the unlawful alchemist? Yes/No
> Rewards: Unknown

"Now, that is very interesting," Dave said.

"What is?" SJ whispered

"Getting issued a quest without directly interacting with the persons who are affected by an issue."

"It's not normal, then?"

"No. Also, it doesn't offer you a reward either, which again is strange."

"I am going to accept it."

"Do what you must."

SJ accepted the quest.

> **Quest: Save a Soul—Update**
> You have accepted the quest Save a Soul. You have twenty-four hours to locate, confront, and deal with the culprit. If you succeed, then you may just save Margu from her current expected demise.

"That sounds ominous," SJ whispered.

"A timed quest at Level 5. They shouldn't normally start until Level 15. Being an anomaly does have perks."

"What perks?"

"Timed quests usually give better rewards, although none are listed, which is very strange. I think the System is struggling to determine what to do with you."

"All these quests come from the System?"

"Sort of. They have an infinite list of options and variables available to them, and a team assigns quests based on rafts of data and basic assumptions. You think of it, and it could potentially create a related quest. Quests are normally directed to Legionnaires based on class, race, or world situations."

"It's random, then?"

"Yes and no. I think because you didn't sign—correction, you were told you had to waive the terms and conditions—all normally restricted quest options are no longer restricted. This could have good and bad repercussions."

"How?"

"Quests are normally level-related, and timed quests, as I say, are usually not until Level 15 and often require a specific skill or knowledge to complete. They are usually progression quests for improved skills, abilities, or items."

"The rewards could be good, then?"

"Potentially. Twenty-four hours is a very short time frame, though, for completion."

The bar had reduced by more than half the patrons since the mention of GoblinPox. Setu was now sitting back at the table, his head in his hands, sobbing, with Gary now consoling him and patting his shoulder. It was strange seeing the actions of these different races interacting in the way they did.

"I need to talk to Setu," SJ said, rising.

SJ walked over to the table where they were sitting and waited for them to notice her.

Gary looked over. "Can I help you?"

"I'm sorry to interrupt. I'm new here. I just heard what was said, and I wondered if I could help."

"And how would you be able to help?" Gary asked, frowning at her, which made him look very intimidating.

"I would like to speak to the alchemist on behalf of Setu, wasn't it?"

At the mention of his name, Setu looked up with bleary red eyes. He looked in a terrible state, tears still flowing down his cheeks.

"He isn't here," Setu replied.

"Where is he?"

"He said he would be back in three days with the rest of the cure. He had to get materials for his potions."

"What about the sickness in the meantime?"

"He made up what he could. I have already paid an advance for half of the next batch, but I need to make twenty-five silver before he returns."

Gary baulked. "Half! You have already paid twenty-five silver?"

"More. I had to give him Margu's stall license to pay the initial fees."

"YOU GAVE HIM HER STALL LICENSE?" Gary replied in shock.

"I had no choice. The payment for the initial tonic was fifteen silver, and then there was a half payment for the next batch."

"Forty silver!" Gary exclaimed. "That's ridiculous."

"To cure my Margu of GoblinPox, I would pay whatever it takes."

SJ was tempted to tell them what Dave had said about there being no known cure but didn't want to upset him further.

"Do you know where he headed for the materials he needed?"

"He was going up the mountain. The one with the dragon at its peak. He needed some special flower or something. I can't remember the name."

"He is back in three days, you say?"

"Yes."

"What was his name?"

"Darjey."

"And what did he look like?"

"Human."

"Anything else?"

"Youngish. I am not very good at noticing other racial features. All humans look the same to me."

"Okay. Thank you, and I am sorry to hear what has happened."

"I am surprised you have even come near me. I will be the town's leper now," Setu said, dropping his head back down.

SJ left them to it. Gary exploded and cursed at the fact that it had cost Setu so much money, and he had not even spoken to his best friend about it. SJ walked over to the bar. Kerys was standing, talking quietly to Bert.

"I know it isn't ideal, but we need to ask Setu to leave. I am sure he will understand," Kerys said.

"I know, Kerys, but I feel bad for him. Setu has been coming here since he was a sprogling, when his old man used to come play cards."

"We can't do anything about it, though. Just from hearing the word *GoblinPox*, half the patrons left. We can't run an empty inn."

"Sure. Sure. I will go and have a word," Bert said glumly.

Bert walked over to the table where Gary and Setu were sitting and whispered to them.

"Kerys?"

"Yes?" Kerys replied, realising SJ was standing there.

"Is everything all right?"

"Ah. You won't know about GoblinPox. It is a horrible illness that affects goblins and other related races. It is obvious that Setu doesn't have it. Otherwise, he would be covered in pox. You need to be careful as a fae, though."

"Are gnomes not affected by it?"

"No. We are not genetically similar to goblinkin."

"That is good to know. Is this the first case you have heard of?"

"In town, yes. We were lucky when there was a severe outbreak years ago. We locked the town down. No one was allowed in or out. It was a difficult time with the reduced trade. But we pulled through. That was thanks to Mayor Maxwell's quick thinking."

"I see. How do you know what it looks like?"

"From information and leaflets sent out to all townships in Amathera. It must have cost them a fortune to produce magical text that also had pictures on them."

"Magical texts?"

"Yes. Whoever read it could understand it. It translated into their common tongue."

"Oh. I thought there was just one language here, from what I have experienced, anyway."

"No. There are hundreds. It is just that most can and do speak in the common tongue. Some clans, towns, and villages don't, as they have stayed away from the main areas of Amatherean society."

"I see. Who paid for it all?"

"It is the only time I have known the continents to work together. They usually argue or have disputes over something, and wars break out. On this occasion, though, they all understood how severe the sickness was."

"It is good to know they could get past their differences when needed."

"Yes. It would be nice if they did it normally, though, instead of waiting until there was an epidemic to deal with."

SJ nodded in agreement. It was obvious that the System had used information from Earth in its projections. What confused SJ was that this had happened on Amathera twenty-five years ago, while the pandemic on Earth had only occurred four years before. It had to be a massive coincidence or something to consider.

Dave interrupted her thoughts. "I have a plan."

"Thanks, Kerys. I will come and get some food in a while."

"No problem," Kerys said, looking over and watching a dejected, downtrodden Setu and Gary leave the bar under Bert's gentle escort.

SJ headed to the stairs and up to her room.

"What plan?" she said, now out of earshot of anyone else.

"A cunning plan."

"Expand."

"We know that the alchemist can't mix a cure as there isn't one."

"Yes."

"That means he will return to give Setu potions that have no effect and collect the remainder of the money."

"Yes."

"Well, we just wait for him to come back."

"Really? And how does waiting three days for this Darjey help me complete a quest that I have twenty-four hours to complete?"

"Ah, I didn't think of that," Dave replied.

SJ sighed, shaking her head. "Sometimes you do concern me."

"Me. How?"

"You are an AI that is supposed to be all-knowing, yet you forget about the simplest things."

"I do not!"

"Yes, you do."

Silence.

SJ entered her room and jumped out of her skin: A strange, robed figure sat on her sofa.

"You're back at last," the stunningly beautiful fae sat on her sofa said.

SJ stared, open-mouthed for a moment, before gathering herself. "How did you get in here?"

"I flew."

SJ looked at the window she had opened this morning when the commotion in the market square awoke her. "Oh. Who are you?"

"We met earlier."

"I am sure I would have remembered meeting another fae, especially one as beautiful as yourself," SJ replied honestly. She was stunning, with bright blue hair flowing to her waist and an angelic face. She wore pale blue robes that matched her hair perfectly.

"Yes. We met at the mage academy."

SJ looked shocked; the fae she had seen at the academy was an ugly, wart-covered old creature.

"You are the same being?"

"Oh. My appearance earlier," the fae giggled. "We had been practising curses. Julliet decided it would be funny."

"Julliet?"

"The mage I was training."

"You let her curse you?"

"Yes. Just to see how long it would last. I was very impressed she made it last for several hours before I returned to normal. Anyway, please come sit down. I believe we need to talk."

SJ did as she was asked as Dave whispered in her head.

"Now, she's a ten."

SJ tried to ignore his comment as she sat down. She felt inferior to this fae, who was not just beautiful but also oozed power and confidence.

"You wanted to speak to me about what exactly?"

"I have so many questions. I thought you were not interested in speaking to me earlier?"

"I was just busy. I always have time for others of our kind," she said, smiling, which made her face and features look even more beautiful.

"I'm SJ. Nice to meet you. Mistress Francisca, wasn't it?"

"It is, but just call me Fran. That is my mage school name, and I can see you are not a mage."

"Erm. No, I'm not."

"Do you mind if I ask what class you are?"

"Don't tell her!" Dave's voice erupted in her head.

"I am a Legionnaire."

"Yes, I know you are, but what class are you?"

"I am not sure I should say?" SJ said, having not felt so nervous in a very long time.

"Why not? You can't develop your class unless people know what you are and can guide you."

"Don't," Dave again said.

"I am actually a . . ."

"DON'T!" Dave's voice boomed this time.

"A monk," SJ finally finished.

"Oh. A monk, now, that is unusual. There are very few fae monks."

SJ gave a huge internal sigh of relief. "I'm still new, so I'm trying to learn the basics and also how to fly."

"Ah. I see. You have not found a trainer yet, then?"

"No. I only arrived in town two days ago. I have been busy completing quests and getting provisions."

"I see. Well, I am not sure Brother Wilbert is currently taking on any new trainees. I think he has a waiting list."

"I didn't think there were that many Legionnaires here. Why are there so many apprentices?"

"It is not just your kind that trains professions. Many travel from the outer villages to train here. We are the only training town in several days' travel."

"That makes sense, although Cleric Lythonian mentioned that one of the mages had to go to an academy in the local city to train," SJ replied, wondering how many villages were around the town. She had not considered the wider world yet. Apart from seeing the buildings in the valley when she had come to the town, she had not seen anything else.

"Ah. That would be young Willoc. He was an exceptional mage. I taught him the basics, but he wished to specialise in lightning magic, and unfortunately, I am not skilled in that strand. It is rather specialist. My skills are the fundamental elements. Earth, wind, water, and fire."

"You know all of them?"

"I know enough, especially to train new mages at the start of their journeys."

"I see. I am surprised. I did not realise that mages could use all elements." SJ could remember her gaming days when you always had to pick a specialisation you focused on.

"I have a primary element, water, but as fae, we are more finely attuned to the basic elemental magic variants."

"That sounds amazing."

"Why did you choose monk as your class?" Fran asked.

"I have always enjoyed helping people, and it seemed like a good option. However, I was torn between becoming a monk or a cleric," SJ lied.

"Strange choices for a class for a fae. Probably the rarer ones. Although not as rare as some classes."

"I am guessing a lot are mages?"

"And druids, rangers, or archers."

"Well, I have been told I'm an anomaly, so it makes sense I chose something unusual." SJ smiled.

"Anomaly," Dave chuckled. "Very good. I saw what you did there."

Ignoring Dave, she continued. "So, Fran, can you teach me how to fly properly? I have flown a little but got grabbed by a raven and nearly became bird food."

Fran chuckled. "Yes, I can teach you to fly. You are probably doing it all wrong. Let me see what you do."

SJ shrank to her miniature form as Fran did the same. The pair stood on the sofa. Fran was a couple of inches taller than SJ.

"You are on the smaller side, I see. That should improve mobility in flight," Fran said.

"That is good to hear."

"Right, let me see you fly."

SJ beat her wings as she had been doing previously, getting faster and faster until she slowly lifted from the sofa. She could feel the burning in her back muscles.

"I see what the problem is straight away," Fran said, laughing.

SJ landed and looked at her, frowning.

"Sorry. I didn't mean to laugh. I had forgotten what new fae look like when they try to fly."

"What am I doing wrong?"

"You are flapping your entire wing on each side at the same time."

"Sorry? I don't understand?"

"Watch me." Fran beat her wings several times and lifted into the air.

"How?" SJ asked in amazement.

"Look how I move my wings," Fran said.

SJ watched and realised that the wing elements were moving independently. Fran was not beating her entire wing. They seemed to ripple rather than beat from top to bottom. The independent slight movements added to the downdraft, giving her lift, rather than forcing a single beat. It also meant that she could stay hovering without leaning backwards.

"I see. I need to move my wing elements independently from each other?"

"Yes. Beating them together like that will give you lift but no stability. I am surprised you did not just crash."

SJ's cheeks reddened.

"Haha. You did, didn't you?"

"Yes," SJ replied meekly. "The first time I tried, I ended up face-first in the dirt."

"Don't worry. You are not the first and will not be the last."

"I am not sure how to move my wing elements separately. Is there a technique?"

"Young fae are taught from birth, so it becomes natural. For your kind, it is a little trickier. You have a different muscle structure than you are used to. Try to feel the individual muscles rather than one combined muscle."

SJ concentrated on the muscles in her back and slowly moved the top element of one wing by itself. "Yes," she said excitedly.

"Very good. You need to spend time each day completing the exercise with each muscle group. I would say at least ten minutes four times a day. It doesn't take long, and once you can work them independently, you will soon be zipping around." As Fran finished, she beat her wings and flew up into the air so fast SJ nearly fell over, tilting her head back to watch her.

With the precision and finesse of the Earth's best air display teams, she completed loops and sharp turns before gently landing on the sofa. Her breathing had not even changed.

"Wow. That was . . . wow, amazing," SJ spluttered.

"Ha. It's nothing special. You will be able to do it soon enough. If you do the individual muscle exercises, within a week, you can try flying by the same method. The movement comes naturally once your wings work as they should." Fran laughed.

"Thank you so much for your help."

"Anything for another fae. We are not always the most popular."

"I have been told before. Why?"

"Many of our kind are good at causing mischief. I spent a long time building the town's trust before opening the apprenticeship scheme."

"Everyone I have spoken to here has been helpful and kind."

"Just be careful. Not everyone is what they appear on the surface. Many have deep-set feelings about the fae."

"I will be. Thank you for the warning."

"I better get back to the apprentices. There is no saying what they have got up to in my absence," Fran said as she flicked her wings and soared into the air again. "If you need anything, you know where I am. If I do not see you before then, come and touch base in a week or so, and maybe by then, we could go for a flight together. I haven't flown with another fae in several years now."

"I will, thank you so much." SJ smiled, waving as Fran disappeared out the window.

CHAPTER THIRTY

The Docks

"What now?" Dave asked, once Fran had flown off.
"Now I practise."
"Practise what?"
"Moving my wings. Things will be easier when I get this sorted out."
"What about the quest? It's on a timer, remember."

SJ had forgotten about the quest in the excitement of meeting another fae and being taught the basics of flight.

"Bah," SJ grumbled. Having so many things she wanted and needed to do was frustrating. "What do we know? A supposed human alchemist has conned Setu. He has already paid a fortune to get nothing to help and is expected to pay more for a miracle cure that doesn't work."

"You know, you asked him what he looked like, but you never actually asked where he met him."

"Damn it." SJ could have kicked herself. Having been so analytical in her forensics role, she was now not even considering the basics. "I wonder where Setu lives; maybe I can speak to him."

"I would not advise that!" Dave said, surprise in his voice.
"Why?"
"If Margu has GoblinPox, you don't want to get anywhere near it."
"I was thinking about that."
"What?"

"Do you really think it is GoblinPox? Who diagnosed it as GoblinPox? If there hasn't been a case in twenty-five years, how has it suddenly appeared in this town? I am not sure that it is GoblinPox. It sounds suspicious. The way the quest was worded was to deal with the culprit."

"That is a good analysis but a little presumptuous. What if it is, and the culprit wording was related to the money he has taken?"

"How transmissible was it?"
"I told you already: very."
"Yet Setu had no signs."
"True, but it depends on when the illness hits. Like most illnesses, it takes time to show."

"Do you know how long?"

"Give me a minute."

Silence.

"Okay, I found the details. I just had to visit the medical archives. It is a horrible place. Some very strange AI works there."

SJ imagined Dave shuddering. "Were the details not just on your wiki?"

"No. Medical details are kept confidential. You must go digging for them."

SJ could imagine rows of filing cabinets full of document separators containing medical notes. "So, what did you find out?"

"It has a gestation period of twenty-four to forty-eight hours before signs show."

"If it's only twenty-four to forty-eight hours, and he said that the alchemist had already given him stuff and that he already had to get money for the cure . . . if he'd been exposed, he would have symptoms by now. That, to me, means it isn't GoblinPox."

"I like your analysis, my YLF. Although still an assumption."

"What does YLF mean?"

"I thought your world was full of them?"

"What?"

"Acronyms."

SJ thought for a moment. "Young loophole finder, by chance?"

"Yes. See, they do work," Dave said happily.

SJ rolled her eyes. "I need to find where Setu lives."

"Agreed, Watson."

"Watson?"

"Well, I would have to be Sherlock. I am the all-knowing one, after all."

Shaking her head, SJ headed back downstairs. The common room was very quiet, and the fear of GoblinPox was enough to keep many patrons away. Kerys was not in view, so SJ walked over to Bert.

"Hi, Bert," SJ said.

He turned from where he stood and looked down at her. "Yes," he said flatly.

SJ felt nervous under his gaze. "Do you know where Setu lives? I wanted to donate towards the money he needs."

"That is very generous of you. He lives down by the docks. I'm not sure which house, though, sorry. I am sure it won't be hard to find. There are not many houses on the island."

"Thanks, Bert," SJ said, smiling at the massive troll.

Bert smiled back, showing a missing front tooth. All Bert was missing was a black eye, and with his large, squashed, flat nose, he would look just like a prizefighter.

"Docks, perhaps?" Dave said.

"Yes," she replied, turning and leaving the inn.

SJ had never visited the docks before, but when they arrived, they reminded her of the old fishing villages around the coasts of the UK. The dock was on a small island just off the town's shore. It was reached by a large, sturdy-looking wooden bridge that could easily handle a wagon or cart. Thick wooden posts supported the frame. On the small island area, SJ could see several homes and other buildings, which she assumed were storehouses or something similar.

She had loved going to the docks as a child, and the smell reminded her of her childhood holidays with her parents when she was crabbing off the side of the harbour. A draconian was leaving one of the homes on the mainland by the bridge, so she asked if they knew Setu and where he lived. They informed her that he lived with his family in the first house on the island. She crossed the wooden bridge that stretched a couple of hundred feet before reaching the island.

The smell of fish permeated her nostrils as she walked along until she reached the first of three homes. There were lights on, and she was sure she saw a small green face in the front window. The house wasn't very large, but considering the surroundings, she bet it was beautiful most days living here. Down from the house was a short jetty with several rowing boats attached to it, full of nets and fishing equipment.

She walked up to the house's door and knocked gently. There was no answer, so she knocked a little harder. Hearing movement inside, she stepped back from the doorway and waited. She saw a face appear in a window, and its eyes widened in shock before disappearing again. SJ wasn't sure if it had been Setu. It was such a fleeting glance.

She waited a few moments before she heard the bolt being slid on the door. It cracked open and a small goblin face peered around its edge.

"Hello," SJ said.

"Hi," the small goblin replied.

"I am here to see your dad?" SJ asked, unsure if Setu was the father.

"You are visiting late."

"I'm sorry. I needed to speak to him about what is going on at the moment. Is he here?"

"He is with Mum."

"Could you get him for me?"

"Not sure he will come. He is very upset. He's been crying since he got home."

"Is your mum okay?"

"Mum has been asleep for ages now. Dad says she took some sleeping medicine."

"I really need to speak to your dad. I think I can help with your mum."

"Help? What's wrong with Mum? She is just asleep," the goblin child said, looking scared.

"No," SJ said, realising that she was just about to tell the child his mother wasn't just asleep. Quickly she carried on. "I mean to help her sleep better."

"She has been sleeping well. She has done nothing but sleep. I don't think she needs to sleep better. Dad cooked dinner, and he isn't a skilled cook. He managed to burn the fish."

"Could you please see if your dad will speak to me?"

"I can try."

The door closed again, the bolt slid back across, and SJ waited.

"Dave. Can you tell by seeing the illness whether it is GoblinPox or not?"

"I should be able to. I saw some horrific cases during the pandemic, burst boils and everything, leaking yellow and green pus everywhere. Very unpleasant, I might add."

"I didn't need such a vivid description."

"It was no worse than the spider ichor you got covered in."

SJ heard footsteps, the bolt slid again, and the door opened wide this time. Standing in front of her was Setu. His face looked even more worn than it had at the inn.

"You?" he said in surprise.

"Yes. I am so sorry for disturbing you."

"You do realise you are putting yourself in danger coming here?" Setu asked.

"I don't think I am, and that is what I want to discuss with you."

Setu frowned, looking at SJ. He stepped outside and closed the door behind him.

"I don't think it is GoblinPox."

"The alchemist diagnosed it as GoblinPox."

"I think he has made a mistake."

"How do you know?"

"I will be able to tell if I can see her, but also, if it was GoblinPox, you would have it already. There is only a short period between infections."

Setu looked confused. "But the alchemist swore it was GoblinPox."

"Let me see, and we can find out."

Setu stepped to the side and allowed SJ in. Setu walked SJ down a short hallway towards the back of the house, passing the front room, where sitting on the floor was not just the small child who had answered the door but six other smaller goblins. Setu led her into the kitchen. There were stacks of bowls and plates all over the sides and tabletops. The bin also looked overflowing, and SJ assumed that Setu could not keep on top of everything alone.

For a house with so many occupants, it was deathly silent. None of the smaller goblins made a sound. All sat, engrossed in their reading. It was the strangest scene she had witnessed. Leading from the backroom, a set of steps ascended upstairs, where Setu guided her to the front room and opened the door silently. The putrid stench that assaulted her nostrils was horrendous, reminiscent of decaying fish. Scrunching her face slightly, she entered.

Holding her nose, SJ could not resist asking, "What's that smell?"

"Oh. Sorry, I need to wash them off," Setu answered with an embarrassed look, reaching behind the bedroom door and removing some overalls, screwing them up into a ball, and throwing them into a basket. He then grabbed the basket and removed it from the bedroom, closing the door. "I was on cleaning duty today at the docks. Always get covered in the guts." He smiled sheepishly.

SJ saw a slight form lying on the bed, wrapped under the sheets.

"Do you mind if I check?"

"No." Setu walked up to the bed and pulled the sheet back slightly, revealing Margu's face.

SJ looked down on Margu's still form, her goblin skin pale green. On her face, she had small, reddish-coloured marks. As Dave had stated, there were no lesions or boils. To SJ, it looked more like measles.

"That is not GoblinPox," Dave said emphatically.

SJ moved closer to look at the markings more clearly.

"That isn't GoblinPox," SJ repeated aloud.

"What do you mean?" Setu said.

"GoblinPox creates boils and lesions that weep. Has Margu had any of those symptoms?"

"No."

"Then it is not GoblinPox."

"How can you be so sure?"

"I just know."

"Then what is it?"

"Can you tell me all her symptoms?" SJ just hoped that Dave understood what she needed him to do. She could not exactly speak to him now.

"She started feeling unwell about eight days ago. She got tired and sleepy. Then the rash appeared, and she would not wake up."

"So, she has been asleep for nearly eight days?"

"No, sleeping for nearly five now."

"Has she had a temperature?"

"Sorry?"

"Felt hot to the touch? Burning up or a fever?"

"No. The rash appeared, and then four days ago, I saw this alchemist, who diagnosed it as GoblinPox."

"Did the alchemist come and see Margu?"

"No. He couldn't visit because of his other patients. He did not want to chance passing it on, although as a human, he could not catch it."

"Okay. I have visited the archives again." Dave coughed as though he had been in a dust-filled room.

SJ couldn't comprehend why an AI would cough. He couldn't suffer from dust.

"Looking at the rash and the symptoms, I believe she has torupiatiarriallyisy, more commonly known as torup. It is a sickness brought on by eating raw fish from a pregnant torpi, and the chances of it affecting you are exceedingly rare. I believe this is a fish that lives in this lake. It only gestates every decade and then gives birth to thousands of fish at a time. It is not contagious, and symptoms will last ten to twelve days. It says that most feel better after they have been affected by it because of the amount of rest they get. It is completely harmless, apart from tiredness and its impact on sleep. There was a footnote saying that some people deliberately try to fish for pregnant torpi to get the sickness because once the rash clears, it is supposed to leave the skin better than it was before."

"Have you ever heard of torup?" SJ asked Setu.

"No."

"Do you fish torpi in the lake?"

"Yes. We occasionally catch one, but not very often. The last one we caught was probably about nine days ago. I remember because Margu made us some raw fish salad. It is one of the kid's favourites."

"She has torpu," SJ said gently but firmly, she hoped. "It is harmless, and the symptoms will pass in another few days. It is caused by eating raw torpi from a pregnant fish."

"How can you be so sure?" Setu asked again.

"She has no signs of GoblinPox. If she did, she would have boils on her skin, not a red rash."

"Wait, so what about the potions the alchemist gave me?"

"Can I ask who directed you to the alchemist in the first place?"

"I bumped into a half orc at the docks the other day and was just talking to him. He said I should see an alchemist and suggested one over near the tailor's shop."

"Could you describe exactly where near the tailor's shop?"

"It is across the street on the other side, and then the second left behind Kilo's and a few doors down."

"I do not know what Kilo's is or where that is."

"I can show you if you wish. Right now?"

"That would be great."

"I need to speak to Situ and let him know we are going to nip out."

They walked back down the stairs, and Setu spoke to his eldest sprogling before leaving the house and heading towards the bridge. When they arrived, a large wagon had been brought onto it and parked across it, blocking access.

"Who has left this here?" Setu said, annoyed, and walked up to the wagon. The animals had been unhitched, and empty reins were left dangling.

SJ noticed a large sheet of parchment tacked to the rear of the wagon, facing the inhabitants of the island.

> *Until further notice, quarantine is in effect for all residents on the island. No one shall be permitted to leave without prior written permission from Mayor Maxwell.*
>
> *Signed,*
> *Captain Broadaxe*

"I think we need to visit this alchemist as soon as possible to try to end this," SJ said.

"We could go in one of the boats, I suppose. I have the small rowing boat tied up at the end of the sproglings' jetty . . . but the alchemist was leaving anyway."

"I don't think he has gone anywhere."

"You think he has lied to me." Setu started to look angry.

SJ wished she hadn't said what she did. "I am just concerned that he misdiagnosed something from your sickness description."

SJ had not mentioned that there was no cure for GoblinPox, and until Margu woke, didn't want to panic him further. He stood with a look changing from confusion, fear, anger, and embarrassment, all in seconds of each other as the emotions tore through him.

They made their way to the jetty. The rowing boat was a paltry affair, with only room for the two of them, and it was more suited to the sproglings. Setu was a proficient rower, and within minutes, they had crossed the small open lake area, reaching the bank on the other side. The moon had taken over in the sky, and now, the sun was completely hidden for the night. Her night vision allowed her to see clearly in the moon's soft, pale light.

It reminded SJ of night-vision goggles she had tried off a friend back on Earth, with a pale green colouring, but much clearer. It was quite a strange sensation. Setu pulled the small rowing boat up onto the side of the shore.

"This way," he said, leading SJ into the town's streets.

She had never seen this part of town before, and the houses that looked over the lake were much larger than the ones in the centre where she had spent her time. They all had front gardens and small stone walls that separated them, reminding her of some of the villages in the Yorkshire Dales. They used to go to Yorkshire regularly, where her Uncle Dave lived. He always joked about Yorkshire beer and Yorkshire countryside being wasted on Yorkshiremen. Coming from Lancashire, he maintained a slight bias from the War of the Roses. The memories pulled at her.

"It's just over from the tailor shop," Setu said as they came onto the main street, which SJ now recognised. Fizzlewick's shop was to the right, and they crossed diagonally from it and then down another street. This street was much narrower, and there was little moonlight because of the overhanging thatched roofs nearly touching each other; weak light shone from the odd house window. Her eyesight was still able to cut through the gloom. After walking down the street, they took the second left, past a building called Kilo's Tattoo Parlour (which amazed SJ) and six other buildings, before Setu stopped at the door.

"Here it is."

The building looked like any other in the town, with no discernible features making it stand out. A sign was tacked to the door: *Darjey's Emporium of Alchemical Cures. Any illness or sickness can be diagnosed and cured with one of my potions. Inquire within. If you need urgent care and there is no answer, please contact Niweq at the Wandering Ogre.*

No signs of light came from the building, and it looked empty. SJ tried the door just in case, and it was locked.

"I think you should head back home, Setu. I can investigate from here, and if I find anything out, I will let you know."

"I told you he wasn't here," Setu said, his shoulders slumping.

"Look. I know it is difficult to understand, but Margu doesn't have GoblinPox, and there is no chance that she will die from what she has. If anything, she will feel much better when she wakes up. Go home, clean up the house, and take care of the sproglings."

"If I do find out he has robbed me . . . !"

"You won't do anything about it. I will deal with it," SJ replied, her tone quite stern for the first time. SJ had no idea how old Setu was and knew he was not a child, but she felt she was scolding one when she spoke to him. "Sorry, I didn't mean to be so harsh."

"No. I understand," Setu replied forlornly.

"I will see you as soon as I find anything out."

"Thank you."

"Make sure you clean up, though. You don't want Margu to wake up and see the state you left the kitchen in."

If a goblin's cheeks could have gone a brighter shade of red, SJ was not sure how. "I was so worried about Margu. I have spent my whole time upstairs when I was not at work. Situ has been feeding the sprogs. I was only out with Gary because I needed the money and had no other way of making it."

"Go head back home. I will see you when I get to the bottom of this."

Setu turned, walking back down the street.

"Time to visit the Wandering Ogre," SJ whispered.

CHAPTER THIRTY-ONE

The Wandering Ogre

"You should have asked for directions before Setu left," Dave said.

"Yes, all right," SJ snipped back at his comment. "I just need to ask someone else."

Not many were out on the streets this late, but a few still walked along in the warmth of the evening. SJ approached a halfling strolling down the road, blowing vast billows of smoke from a pipe he held. It was the first sign of smoking she had seen since arriving.

"Excuse me?"

The halfling turned to look at her. "Yesh," he said, his pipe sticking out of his mouth.

"Do you know where the Wandering Ogre is?"

"Er. I do, but I am unsure why you would be looking for it."

"Why?" SJ asked.

"It is not the nicest of inns for such a pretty face as yourself."

"I need to see someone who works there about a job."

"Oh. I see," he said in an almost explanatory voice, which SJ didn't quite understand. "It is on the outskirts of town. Head as if going to the mountainside and then follow the main road to the right for a bit, and you will come upon it. It is usually well-lit at night, so you won't miss it."

"Thanks," SJ replied, smiling at the halfling.

"No, thank you. I may call in myself soon once you have a job there."

SJ frowned and looked at him. "Erm. Okay, thank you again."

Following the directions, SJ eventually reached the Wandering Ogre. As the halfling had said, it was brightly lit up, and on approaching, SJ could hear music and the general good-natured sounds expected from any bar. SJ walked towards the main entrance, where two massive trolls stood, one on either side. They were even larger than Bert.

"What do you want, little lady?" one of them asked gruffly as she approached.

"I have come to see Niweq."

"What ya wanna see Niweq for?"

SJ did not want to mention the alchemist. "I heard there is a job going."

"We always have space for new uns," the first troll stated.

"Especially ones lookin' like you," the other said. They sounded almost identical, and their accent reminded her of Londoners. It was the strangest thing to hear coming from a troll's mouth.

"Go round the side entrance for Niweq. 'E will be in his office."

"Thanks," SJ said.

Around the side, SJ walked up to a single door with a lantern hanging above it. A sign on the door read ACTS ONLY.

"This must be a theatre or something like that?" SJ said.

"I don't think it is," Dave replied.

"Then what is it?" SJ asked.

"I have my suspicions, but we will see."

SJ knocked on the door and it opened after a moment. She looked upon the large, broad chest of a powerful-looking orc. He was huge, and bent slightly to look at her.

SJ coughed, slightly taken aback by his muscular form. "I am here to see Niweq," she said, her voice squeakier than she wished for.

"You after a job?"

"Yes," SJ replied.

"I will check." The door closed again. SJ stood waiting, and a minute later, the door reopened.

"Okay. Follow me. He said he would see you when I mentioned you were a fae."

"What has being a fae got to do with it?" SJ asked.

"We haven't had a fae before."

SJ frowned and followed the orc inside and down a corridor. Off the corridor were several rooms, and SJ glanced inside, seeing various females of differing races all sitting at desks applying make-up and fixing their hair.

"It is a theatre," SJ whispered.

They came to door with a sign that read MANAGER NIWEQ XYSTER—MASTER OF THE ARTS. The orc politely knocked, then entered the room.

"Here she is, boss. I told you she was a looker."

SJ walked into a large office that reminded her of a scene from a film. A large desk and posters advertising original acts were plastered on the walls.

"Welcome and come in," said an elf behind the desk. He was beautiful and slim, and his finely chiselled features looked like those of a runway model. "I am Niweq, and who may you be?" he asked, beaming.

His smile was disarming, and SJ spluttered slightly. "SJ."

"Nice to meet you. Please take a seat. That's all, Pethtu," he said, waving the orc back out. The massive orc turned and left, closing the door behind him.

"So, you are here about work?" Niweq asked.

"I am not, actually," SJ replied.

"Oh. That is not what Pethtu told me. I know he can be a little hard of hearing, but I am sure he would have heard whether you were after work or not."

"I am here for a friend. I have some questions that I need answers to."

"Do you, now? And who might this friend be? Does she work here?"

"No. It is not she. It is he, a goblin friend of mine."

"A goblin friend? Not sure why a goblin would request me. I don't hire goblins or males. They don't go down very well with the crowd. Many of them have a select choice." Niweq laughed.

"Crowd? You mean the audience."

"Ha. They are not an audience in the manner you suspect, my dear. So, what is this goblin after?"

"He was trying to find a man called Darjey, the alchemist."

"Darjey. And why would he be looking for Darjey?"

"He has been providing him with some potions for his sick wife, and he needs more."

"Oh, I see. Well, Darjey is probably here. He is most evenings, but I am not sure why you would have been directed to me. I hardly know the man."

"There was a sign at his shop saying he could be found here, if needed, outside of normal hours, and to speak to you."

"Really, that is interesting. Well, Darjey is likely to be in the main bar. He has been a regular since his arrival a few months ago."

"Arrival?"

"Yes. He and his friend are here most nights."

"Oh. Your acts must be good. I have never been a fan of theatre myself."

Niweq laughed. It was a mesmerising sound. "Oh. I think you may not have fully appreciated what this inn is."

"What is it?"

"It is a dancing club."

"What is wrong with that?"

Niweq laughed again and, standing back up, walked around the desk. "Come dear, I will show you."

SJ followed Niweq as he left the door; as they did, a slim figure that SJ believed to be a dryad scurried past with tears on her cheeks, holding her top. "Pethtu. What is going on?"

"On it, boss," the large orc replied as he walked up the corridor and through a large curtain. Beyond the curtain, the sounds of music, laughter, and cheering filled the air. Niweq led SJ around the side and up a small set of spiral stairs until they came out on a small balcony that overlooked the main inn area below.

A long bar ran down one side, with tables dotted around, a large stage area, and short runways extending into the crowd. SJ realised that she was in a particular type of dance club. The females dancing to the music were all pole dancing provocatively and lewdly. SJ was shocked at the sight, which reminded her of a pole-dancing club she had visited one night in London with work colleagues. Excessive alcohol consumption that night marked her first and final visit to that club.

Thankfully, none of the dancers were stripping, but it was as near as it could get. Their clothes barely covered their various forms. There were elves, dryads, humans, orcs, and even a dwarf, who, for SJ, was not the most pleasant sight, wearing a very revealing dress with her bust almost sticking out. A group of dwarves sat at a nearby table cheering and hooting for her.

"I see what you mean," SJ eventually said to Niweq. "I didn't realise there was a club like this in town."

"Ah. Officially, we are not within the town boundary, so we don't fall under the town remit. I am just a poor elf who took advantage of a market opening."

"I see," SJ replied. "Do you see the alchemist down there?"

Niweq glanced around the bar before indicating to a table on the far side. "He is sat over there with his usual group of friends. I will have to talk to him about why he uses my name for his business, though."

SJ looked at the man. He was probably in his late twenties or early thirties, whistling and hollering at an elf dancing provocatively around a pole on a small platform. SJ was not surprised or annoyed at what she was seeing. Those dancing were just earning a living, and those willing to pay were sad enough not to have a woman at home to care for them. Of the forty patrons, they were all male but for one female sat by herself at the bar.

"Do you mind if I speak to them?"

"No. I don't mind."

"How do I get there?"

"From here, the only way is via the stage unless you go back around the front."

"Okay. Thank you, Niweq, for your time."

"My dear, it is an absolute pleasure, and I only wished you had been seeking work. I think you would have become a firm favourite for all the patrons we get."

Unsure of how to reply, SJ simply nodded, then turned and headed back down the spiral staircase. At its bottom, Pethtu strolled back towards the curtains, and Niweq followed SJ. "What was the problem, Pethtu?"

"That idiot half orc grabbed her again."

"I have warned him before. Get the boys, will you? They can leave for tonight. This may work in your favour, my dear. The half orc is a friend of Darjey's, so they will probably leave together."

"Oh. Great. I will wait outside, then."

SJ walked to the side entrance, then returned to the front of the building. The two massive trolls had entered the inn, and the door stood open. At a distance, SJ watched as three people were led by the trolls and Pethtu to the doorway.

"Look, lads, you have been told before. You touch the ladies, you have to leave. The boss said you can return tomorrow when you sober up again."

"She asked for it," the half orc complained.

"None of the ladies ask for anything, you know that," Pethtu replied, closing the door on them. The two massive trolls returned to their positions on either side of the door.

"Damn it, Malcolm," said the human man who SJ believed was Darjey.

"Sorry, man. I couldn't resist. She is a stunner, that one."

The realisation hit SJ that it had to be the same Malcolm she had fought with.

"This could be interesting," Dave said.

SJ cast her identification skill on the three of them.

Malcolm Kilgore	
Race:	Half Orc
Age:	19
Level:	6
Hit Points:	36
Mana Points:	30

Darjey Simpson	
Race:	Human
Age:	28
Level:	5
Hit Points:	25
Mana Points:	25

Peteriol Siquitch	
Race:	Lycanthrope
Level:	10
Hit Points:	90
Mana Points:	70

"I need to get back to town," Peteriol said. "Wife is going to be wondering where I am. I said I was only going out to grab dinner." He swayed slightly on his feet as he spoke. SJ watched in amazement as the lycanthrope transformed into a boar and staggered back the way she had come from town.

"Bah. Lightweight," Malcolm shouted after him.

SJ did not confront them and moved back out of sight. She watched as the pair stumbled back towards town.

"I am guessing because their age is shown they are Legionnaires?" SJ whispered.

"Yes. It is the one of the main ways to identify them" Dave replied angrily.

"You okay, Dave?"

"I hate people like that. There is no need for their behaviour; it is quite typical for Legionnaires, though, to be honest. They think they can do what they like."

"I have not been like that, though,"

"No. You haven't; you have been civilised, which again makes a change from many of them."

SJ worried about Dave's low opinion of Legionnaires, but she had only met Malcolm before, who was a complete asshat. SJ kept her distance as they walked back into town and eventually cut down the street where the alchemist shop was and entered the building.

"It could be challenging facing two of them," SJ murmured.

"Best time to do it. They are both drunk."

"Malcolm was drunk last time as well."

"Not as drunk as he is now. He could hardly walk straight."

"True, and the sooner I can prove the problem with Margu is fake and get Setu his money back, the better."

"Agreed," Dave said with determination in his voice.

"So how do we do this?"

"Try knocking on the door?" Dave sarcastically replied.

SJ sighed, shaking her head. "I was asking what you think I should do."

"Oh. I see. Well, knock on the door and as soon as it opens, force your way in and threaten them that if they don't give you the money, you will leave a horse's head in their bed."

"This isn't *The Godfather*, and I am not the mafia."

"Would be cool if you were, though,"

SJ walked to the door and knocked on it sharply. A slurred voice called out from inside.

"Who is it?"

"I am seeking an alchemist, and I heard you are the best in town."

"I am, but we are closed tonight. Can you come back tomorrow?"

"It is really a matter of life or death. I have silver," SJ added desperately.

At the mention of money, SJ heard footsteps approaching the door. It was pulled open, and the face of Darjey, looking very bleary-eyed and drunk, appeared.

"Hello," he said, slurring and smiling. "What problem needs a potion?"

"My husband is ill. I require a potion to heal him," SJ said, making up absolute rubbish on the spot. She had never been a fan of improv.

Darjey staggered slightly, leaning against the wall, his eyes fluttering. It was obvious that he was exceedingly drunk. "Come in, and I will see what I can sort for you," he slurred.

He stepped aside, allowing SJ to enter the house. Darjey directed SJ into the front room. Inside was a small counter and shelving full of bottles of various coloured liquids. Walking over to the counter, he leaned against it, supporting his weight. There was the pungent smell of strong liquor, and an open bottle stood on the counter-top. SJ could not see Malcolm.

"So, what are his symptoms?" Darjey asked, hiccupping.

"He has been asleep for several days; I have been unable to wake him, and he has come out in a rash." SJ described Margu's exact symptoms.

"Oh, dear. Your husband may have GoblinPox. I treated a case a few days ago; it must be doing the rounds," he replied.

"GOBLINPOX," SJ cried in faux shock. "Is that not fatal?"

"No. No. I have a cure for it right here. It is very expensive, though. It takes a lot to prepare and make the potion."

"Oh no. I do not have much. How much is it?"

Darjey looked at her from head to toe and took in her pristine dress. SJ cursed herself for wearing the dress now, knowing what he would say.

"I can sell you a potion for twenty silver."

"Twenty silver! I do not have that sort of coin."

"I'm sorry, but that is the cheapest I can do it for. The ingredients are very rare and take a long time to collect and prepare."

SJ could tell that this charlatan spent a lot of time perfecting his cons. He was, even as drunk as he was, sounding very sincere.

"But I can't afford it. Is there anything you can do to help me?"

"Umm. Let me see." Darjey bent underneath the small counter and brought out a small pouch. "I could give you this for him in the meantime until such a time as you can afford the potion. I would advise, though, the sooner the better to raise funds, as it can be dire without."

SJ looked at the small pouch he had brought out. "What is it?"

"It is a soothing powder. You sprinkle it on the rash, which should stop it from worsening. If you are struggling for coin, I know a lender who may be able to help you."

"You do? Who would that be?"

"He is a friend of mine. He is here this evening but is sleeping. If you come back in the morning, I am sure we can arrange something."

"How much is the powder?"

"This is only two silver," Darjey said, prodding the pouch with his finger.

SJ removed two silver coins from her inventory and held them in her hand. She noticed Darjey's eyes dart to the coin she now held, and she was getting more infuriated every second she talked to him.

"Kill him," Dave said. "He is a scum of a Legionnaire and doesn't deserve a second life." His tone was flat and emotionless.

It was the first time SJ had heard Dave speak this way, which surprised her. Trying to maintain her act, she went to place the two silver coins on the counter and, while doing so, pretended to stumble, causing one of the coins to roll. Darjey went to grab the rolling coin but missed it in his drunken state, and it dropped to the floor behind the counter. He bent down to pick it up, and SJ took advantage.

CHAPTER THIRTY-TWO

One Good Deed Deserves Another

Quickly moving around the counter, she equipped her badger's blades, and as Darjey moved to stand back up from his drunken stumbling state of grabbing the coin, she presented the very sharp blades against his throat. Darjey stood facing her, his eyes now wide in shock. SJ gently pushed against his skin, and she saw a small trickle of blood where the blade had nicked his throat.

"It is now time to talk," SJ said in a menacing tone.

"What d-do you think you're doing?" Darjey stammered.

"I know exactly what *you* are doing, you charlatan. Conning poor people out of their livelihoods to provide you with drinking tokens to go to the Wandering Ogre and letch at those poor women."

Now that Darjey had realised he was in danger, his vision seemed clearer already.

"What are you talking about?" he squeaked, looking down at the blades.

"You conned a poor goblin out of his stall and have already taken forty silver from him to cure a disease that has no cure and is certainly not GoblinPox. I have a good mind just to end your life now."

Darjey's Adam's apple jumped as he swallowed hard at the threat.

"I was doing what I could to help him."

"Lies. I know what GoblinPox looks like, and you did not even see his wife to confirm the symptoms. Never mind that there is no cure. I don't believe you are even an alchemist."

"I am. I am."

"Really? Then what are all these different potions you have here?" SJ moved her other clawed hand to indicate the display of various bottles.

Darjey's eyes flitted to the shelves, but he could not answer.

"I thought as much. Are you a rogue by any chance?"

Darjey's face gave it away without him even answering as his eyes flashed. There was a banging from upstairs, and she heard footsteps moving along a hallway. She stood still and put her finger to her lips, indicating that Darjey should remain quiet. He wasn't going to say anything, judging by the sheer terror in his eyes. The footsteps continued, and then SJ heard a deep sigh and the sound of someone urinating before hearing stomping feet back down the hallway again and a door closing.

"Look, it sounds like your friend Malcolm is not going to be able to help you," SJ said, smiling wickedly and enjoying having power over this worthless sack of a Legionnaire in front of her. "You realise that people like you give us a bad name."

"Us?"

"You are a Legionnaire, aren't you, just like me," SJ said with venom.

"How do you know?"

"That is a secret of my class," she said, smiling. Narrowing her eyes, she continued, "Now, where is the money you took from the goblin?"

"I don't have it. I spent most of it already."

"Liar," she said, pricking his neck a little harder.

Darjey gulped again.

"Last chance: Where is the money? You can't have spent forty silver in the few days since you conned him."

Darjey pointed over to a small stand in the corner of the room. "What I have is in there."

SJ glanced sideways briefly and immediately wished she hadn't. It had been stupid of her. The instant she turned her head, Darjey reacted. A dagger appeared in his hand, and he went to stab her.

"Incoming," Dave shouted.

SJ whipped her other hand down defensively and parried the blow away. Thankfully, Darjey was still too drunk to fight. Instinctively, SJ pressed her bladed hand forward into his throat. Darjey's eyes widened at the sudden realisation that his throat was now punctured. Dropping the dagger and reaching up to his now bloody throat, he staggered backwards, grasped at the counter to keep his balance, and toppled backwards into one of the sets of shelves. The contents crashed onto the floor, the glass bottles broke, and the bright liquids emptied onto the wooden floorboards, creating a rainbow of colours.

> Critical Hit
> Your instinctive reaction has caused a critical hit.
> A blade in the throat is never nice; four blades even less so.
> Piercing critical hits may cause differing effects depending upon the areas of the body damaged.

SJ stepped forward and crouched over Darjey's prone form, holding both her claws at the ready, this time without looking away. Darjey's health had plummeted from the hit, and he sat with only three hit points remaining. SJ was quite surprised at the damage the one hit had done.

"You have a choice to make now. I can help you, or I can let you die."

SJ heard footsteps above and heard the door open.

"Darjey, what the hell are you playing at?" Malcolm's voice came down from above.

He could not answer; his throat and mouth were full of blood now, and even if he had wanted to speak, SJ doubted he could have. His eyes were wide in absolute terror, still grasping his throat.

"Darjey?"

SJ didn't move.

Malcolm called again, "Darjey? Whatever you did, you are cleaning up yourself in the morning."

SJ listened as she heard a door close, footsteps, and the creaking of a bedframe.

"Live or die," she whispered to Darjey.

"Just kill him already," Dave said. "He doesn't deserve to live, and I might remind you that you are an assassin, and you were going to fight for the good."

SJ couldn't comment, but what Dave said hit home. She had chosen to be an assassin, and the fact was that she was now in the perfect position to complete her first kill. *Can I end another man's life?* She knew he was originally from Earth as well, so he had died an accidental death; he wouldn't be here otherwise. Wondering what sort of life he had led before he arrived, she had no idea and didn't care. *Dave is right; why should he live? He has conned poor Setu out of his livelihood and is trying to get more from him. I will finish the job, complete the quest, and reap the rewards. Whatever the rewards are.*

Darjey took his hand away from his throat and reached out towards her wrist. SJ frowned at him. His eyes were pleading, and she didn't understand what he wanted. She allowed him to hold her wrist, his grip weak from the blood loss from his throat. He drew her hand towards his chest. He then let go and just closed his eyes.

He wanted to die! Shock came over SJ in an instant, and she moved her blades away from where they rested against his chest. His eyes opened again, and she looked at him.

"You want to die?"

He nodded, looking at her again, the pleading look back.

SJ didn't know what to do now, and she slowly placed her blades back against his chest. Darjey continued to stare at her with a pleading expression.

"DO IT," Dave shouted.

SJ jumped from Dave's cry, jerking her hand forward, and the blades slid into his chest.

SJ withdrew the blades. Her heart was hammering in her chest as she watched the life fade from Darjey's eyes. She had just killed a man, and her display flashed.

50xp awarded for killing a Level 5 Legionnaire.

"Excellent work," Dave said in a very cheerful voice. "Congratulations on your first assassination."

SJ knelt in shock over the now-lifeless body of Darjey Simpson, the twenty-eight-year-old reincarnated man from Earth.

"No, it wasn't," SJ whispered.

"Okay, pretty good, then. You could have just finished him before he moved your hand to his chest, but meh, who is being picky? You still got there in the end."

"I don't feel good about it," SJ hissed.

"It's the circle of life. *Comme ci, comme ça*. Sometimes death is better than life for those reborn."

"I am not sure why you believe that is the case."

"I have witnessed enough Legionnaires before and what they do and get up to, both bad and good, and as I vaguely mentioned, many are just bad. Most are not evil. They are just idiots who cause problems for the population of Amathera. You would think that, given a second chance at life, many would wish to be better than in their first, but unfortunately, that is not the case."

"You are being very different at the moment."

"Am I? In what way?"

"I don't know. You seem different. You were quite ruthless, telling me to kill him."

"He deserved it."

"Did he deserve to die, though? He could have been arrested and locked up instead."

"Nope. It wouldn't happen. The mayor would never take the chance of locking up a Legionnaire in a starter town. It could invalidate their license. Rather than jail them, the town would likely banish them instead."

"License?"

"Oh yes. Starter towns apply for licenses with the capital cities."

"And how do the capital cities decide who gets one and who doesn't?"

"No idea."

"I am confused. How can a city decide if it is a good starter town, and what benefits does it bring to the cities? You have just mentioned it could be bad for the town to imprison a thieving Legionnaire."

"Politics."

"What politics?"

"Oh. The usual kind. Backstabbing, shady deal varieties."

"You are telling me a town is licensed to have Legionnaires start in it, yet the decisions are all political."

"Basically, yes."

"None of this makes sense."

"Agreed. Anyway, should you stop sitting on his chest now and get up and sort things out?"

SJ quickly stood, seeing the blood and multicoloured pattern that had soaked into her dress while she had knelt there talking to Dave. Thankfully, she knew her dress would clean. She sent her blades back to her inventory and stood surveying the scene. Darjey's lifeless form lay amongst the broken bottles and shelving he had collapsed into. SJ's display flashed.

> **Quest: Save a Soul—Update**
> You have defeated the evil alchemist.
> Rewards: 125xp x 2 = 250xp awarded
> (Bonus xp due to completing the quest in under eight hours.)

> **Part 2: Return Margu's title deeds to Setu.**
> Rewards: Unknown

"Interesting. It's a quest chain. It's very unusual again. These should only be for Level 20 and up," Dave said.

SJ searched the room, walking to the cabinet that Darjey had indicated; inside was a lockbox. It was, naturally, locked, so she placed it in her inventory, went back over to Darjey's corpse, and searched his pockets, feeling physically sick as she did.

"I am a goddamn assassin," SJ said under her breath.

"You okay?"

"Yeah. Fine," SJ replied, grimacing. In Darjey's trouser pocket, she found a small bunch of keys, which she pocketed.

"You could just loot the body, you know?"

"Oh, I can loot him as normal?"

"Duh! He is on Amathera."

SJ looted the corpse, and the following list appeared.

> 2 x Daggers, 80 x Copper, 12 x Silver, 2 x Potions of Minor Healing, 1 x Silver Watch, 1 x Stall Title Deed, 1 x House Title Deed, 1 x Rabbit Foot, 1 x Used Tissue, 1 x Rubber

SJ was already carrying her waterskin and rations in her inventory, so not everything would fit. The coins were no problem. They were just absorbed, but the rest stayed on the screen, and her display gave her the option to select what she wanted. She didn't need daggers, so she ignored them and selected the potions, watch, and deeds, leaving everything else there.

"That was easy getting the title deed back straight away."

"You should search the rest of the house while you are here," Dave said.

SJ turned, looking around the room. Nothing looked of value, and she was sure all the bottles were just full of coloured liquid and not potions. She could not see any ingredients anywhere, which she would have expected from an alchemist. She crept out of the room and went down the hallway to the back. The back room was filthy, with empty bottles covering the surfaces and floor; it appeared that all they did was drink.

"I just received an update," Dave said.

"An update?"

"Yep. The AI that was accompanying Darjey just sent me a message."

"What did they say?"

"She just wanted to pass on her thanks for finishing him. He was apparently horrendous and abusive to the girls at the inn."

SJ felt her rage build. "I am glad I got rid of him now."

"Told you. Don't accept what you see on the surface. Many Legionnaires think they can get away with stuff in the new world without repercussions. He had also been here for three months."

"Three months in a starter town and still Level 5?"

"All he did was, as you can see, drink. He conned people and drank, that was it, and if anyone challenged him, then he would get Malcolm to soften them up."

"I may have to deal with Malcolm yet."

"I would, but not tonight. Let him find his companion. He will then be looking over his shoulder at every step; watching him squirm from a distance will be funny," Dave laughed evilly.

"You worry me," SJ replied, shaking her head.

Seeing nothing of value in the back room, SJ walked into a small kitchen area. There was a line of empty bottles on the side, and next to them, a rack containing smaller bottles filled with coloured liquids. SJ walked over and picked one up; its label read Tailor's Dye.

"These may come in handy." As she added the rack to her inventory, it fit into one of the new tailoring slots and contained ten small bottles of varying-coloured dyes. It was obvious to SJ that Darjey had only been producing coloured water potions. Apart from some pots and pans, nothing else looked like it had any value.

"Think that is everything. I am not chancing going upstairs," SJ whispered.

"Let's go, then."

SJ quietly returned to the front of the house, and before she left, she looked back into the front room. Darjey's still form lay there. Shivering slightly, she turned away again, looking down at her dress. The patch of blood and dye had already been magically disposed of, and she opened the front door. The hinges squeaked as she did, and she froze as she heard stirring upstairs and a groan. There was no further movement, and she waited until she heard snoring before checking the street, which was empty, and leaving the house, pulling the door back closed behind her.

"Well, I have to say that our first assassination did not go too badly overall. You have some loot, no injuries, and the deed you need for the second part of the quest chain. When he finds the corpse in the morning, Malcolm will have kobold babies."

SJ didn't reply and hurried back down the street. It was nearly midnight, and the streets were virtually empty. She noticed some people farther along the street and knew she would need to return to see Setu, but she wouldn't do it tonight.

"Let's go back to the inn. I need to eat, and then we can visit Setu in the morning."

"Okay. Glad to know you are still hungry after sticking a man. It's a good sign of things to come as an assassin that you haven't lost your appetite."

SJ had just lost her appetite.

Back at the inn, the lilt of the bard's voice calmed SJ's frayed nerves. On returning she feared being seized and charged with murder. She knew the body would not get discovered until the morning and that no one had seen her, as she'd made sure that the street was empty when she had originally entered and left the house. She knew it was just her overactive mind playing tricks on her.

She walked to the bar as casually as she could and saw Fhyliss talking to Kerys animatedly. SJ stood, biding her time, until Fhyliss disappeared into the kitchen. Seeing SJ at the bar, Kerys came over.

"Hi, SJ. What can I get for you?" Kerys asked.

"If it's not too late, I wanted to order food. I would also like a honey wine, please."

"Sure."

Kerys looked concerned. She did not have the same normal, carefree, and lighthearted expression that SJ was used to.

Kerys placed the honey wine on the bar.

"You look concerned," SJ said, picking up the honey wine and taking a large sip.

"Yes. Sorry, I'm just a little distracted since this GoblinPox scare. The town is starting to panic. The mayor has already started talking about locking down again."

"Oh, that's not good. I may need to speak to the mayor if that's possible."

"I am unsure what good it would do. I assume he will be sleeping by now."

"It's okay. It can wait until tomorrow." SJ couldn't say that she knew it wasn't GoblinPox without revealing that she had discovered the truth, which would then lead to the alchemist and the dead body. Kerys handed SJ a menu.

SJ reviewed the menu and chose the same as before. The hogling loins were delicious, but knowing that Floretta was a Level 12 Master cook, she would have to try even more dishes. Walking over to an empty table, she sat. The inn was so quiet at this time of night. Fhyliss wasted no time in bringing out her food.

"Hi, SJ. Here you go."

"Thanks, Fhyliss. Your mum told me about the GoblinPox issue."

Fhyliss flopped down in a chair at the table.

"Yeah. It's going to be hard if they lock down the town again. This is what we have done our whole lives. I have worked here now for twenty-five years, ever since I turned eighteen. Mum has owned the inn for over thirty years, and the last lockdown nearly broke her. We need to socialise as gnomes."

SJ felt so sorry for Fhyliss and was amazed that she had worked in the bar for twenty-five years. She looked no older than eighteen, never mind forty-three, not that she could tell anyone's age now, apart from humans.

"I don't think it will be as bad as you expect."

"I hope not."

"Fhyliss," Kerys called from the serving hatch.

"Yeah," Fhyliss replied

"Come and get SJ's pie for her."

Fhyliss grabbed the slice of pie from the servery.

"Thanks, Fhyliss. I'm going to save that for later. I assume I can store it, right?"

"Oh yes. With Floretta's preservation skill, you can easily store it for five days before it turns."

"She has a preservation skill?"

"Yes. It comes in very handy with fresh produce."

SJ smiled as Fhyliss left to clear a nearby table.

SJ finished her food and returned to the suite, carrying her honey wine. Walking inside, she flopped onto the sofa and emptied the contents of her inventory. She felt better now she had eaten, and her stomach was more settled.

"Dave?"

"Yep," Dave's very cheerful voice came back.

"You're happy?"

"Oh, sorry. I got jealous of watching you eat, so I watched *Home Alone* to distract myself."

"Which one?"

"The first one, of course."

"Back to work. I am just looking at the stall deed. How do I transfer it?"

"You just hand it to Setu, and the System will recognise it has changed hands."

"Does that mean I currently own the rights to the stall?"

"Yes. You will see if you read the small print at the bottom."

SJ squinted at the bottom of the deed. The writing was so small, and she read her name.

"Oh. That is interesting."

"Yes. Deeds transfer when held, and the owner passes rights. If someone dies, and they haven't been sworn to someone, then they can be claimed by whoever finds them."

"So, I have claimed these by default?"

"Yes."

SJ then picked up the house deed. "Farleck Cottage."

"What's that?"

"The deed for the house was a place called Farleck Cottage."

"Well, tomorrow, we should find out where the cottage is."

"I am not planning on staying in town that long. If things go according to plan and I level up, why would I need a cottage here?"

"Portals."

"Portals? What about portals?"

"Did I not tell you?"

"No."

"Oh. Once you level up, you can assign home portals to locations where you hold deeds. That means if you ever have a long distance to travel or need to get out of somewhere in a hurry, as long as you are not in combat, you can portal to save time."

"When can they be assigned?"

"The first portal can be assigned at Level 10. Then you are entitled to assign a new portal every ten levels after that. You must own the deeds to a permanent structure, though. You can't just set a portal up in a tent, cave, or clearing."

"They sound amazing!"

"Meh, they're okay. Most never own or bother getting deeds, and I do not think many AIs tell their Legionnaires either."

"Why not if it is a level requirement?"

"Because most of them are idiots. I thought we had already discussed this."

"Have you not had any Legionnaires over your 164 that you have liked?"

"Yes, several. I still didn't speak to them, though."

"Yes, you've said that. Wasn't it boring, not being able to speak to them?"

"Naw, I was usually too busy watching movies."

"Hang on, that isn't right. How can you be too busy watching movies when movies were not invented thousands of years ago?"

Silence.

"Dave!"

"Yes."

"Have you been lying to me?"

"About what?"

"Watching movies?"

"No. I watch movies all the time."

"Yes, but you never used to, did you? So, what did you do?"

"Okay. Okay. I had a problem, all right. I have said it. Now, leave it there," Dave snarked.

"A problem with what exactly?"

"I used to have a gambling issue. I spent thousands of years at it. I have been clean now for over five hundred years, okay? I still attend weekly AIGA meetings."

"AIGA?"

"AI Gamblers Anonymous."

"Oh. I am sorry to hear you had a problem."

"I didn't."

"Denial is a sign of addiction."

"Grrrr. You sound just like my counsellor."

"It's getting late, and I feel tired. Let's call it a night and get at it in the morning. We need to stop the town from going into lockdown."

CHAPTER THIRTY-THREE

You Would Think He Would Think

There was a loud knock on the door. SJ stirred in her bed. The curtains were open, and it was still dark outside. SJ's eyes opened as she heard the knocking again, loud and persistent. She slowly slipped from under the sheets and pulled her dress on before walking through to open the door.

"Who is it?" SJ called.

"Gary," the voice replied.

"Gary. You mean the Gary who knows Setu?" SJ asked.

"Yes."

"It's the middle of the night." SJ checked her display. It was 03:24.

"I know, and I am sorry, but Setu asked me to come and see you."

"Setu? Why?"

"He has been arrested."

SJ unlocked the door and opened it. "What?"

"He got caught returning home by the guard."

"Damn. But why are you here?"

"He asked for me, and when I spoke to him, he told me you had been with him. He asked if you found anything out. He is currently locked up because of breaking quarantine."

"I am confused. How can he break a curfew when one had not been implemented in the town?"

"No. The mayor quarantined the docks because of the fear of GoblinPox, and after he went out and was seen coming back, the mayor decreed that he broke the curfew he was under."

"What can I do?"

"Did you find anything out? Setu said you were checking on the alchemist." Gary looked panic-stricken.

"I did. Do I need to go and see the mayor?"

"Setu wants you to see him at the jail."

"At this time of night?"

"It never closes."

"I am not sure what I can do, though."

"He said you could help him. The mayor is talking about expelling him and his family from the town. He has seven sproglings, and his livelihood is fishing, and Margu sells their catch share in the market."

"Okay. Let me get ready properly." SJ was standing with bare feet currently. "Can you show me to the jail? I have never been." SJ walked back through the bedroom and pulled her boots on.

"Yes, of course."

SJ left the room, locking it, and followed Gary. They left the inn and headed towards an area of town that SJ had not visited. This area was quite run down compared to the areas of town she had seen before. The buildings were smaller, and the streets were untidy. Empty barrels and crates were left outside the buildings. It was strange, and SJ wondered if the main town area was more for show than anything else. It had all appeared quite well off.

"This place looks like a poorer area," she whispered to Dave.

"It does," Dave replied.

"I wonder why?"

"Sorry. Did you say something?" Gary asked.

"Just talking to myself, sorry."

They walked down a wide street. Both sides were single-storey buildings only, and a large three-storey building was at the end of the street. It seemed to serve two purposes: The left side was designated as the jail, while the right side was for the barracks. It made sense for them to be together.

Gary walked straight towards the jail entrance, threw the door open, and stormed inside.

"We are here to see Setu," he said to the bleary-eyed gnoll behind the desk.

"Who?" the gnoll replied.

"The goblin I was talking to just an hour ago," Gary growled. SJ could sense his anger.

"Oh. The one in isolation?"

"Yes. The one who has been thrown in jail for breaking free from a quarantine that the mayor has decided on."

"He is not allowed to see any more guests. Mayor's orders."

"What? All prisoners are entitled to visitation. That has always been the case."

"Not now."

"WHAT DO YOU MEAN *NOT NOW*?" Gary bellowed, growling at the gnoll.

The gnoll was unperturbed, looking at Gary from behind the counter as the outer door to the jail opened. SJ turned to see the enormous man she had seen in the bar talking to Kerys.

"WHAT IS THE MEANING OF THIS?" his voice boomed, and Gary spun around, seeing his towering form. As an orc, Gary stood well over six feet tall, but the man was six inches taller. SJ watched as Gary appeared to shrink in stature, and his head dropped.

The gnoll spoke before Gary could. "Sorry, Mayor Maxwell. This orc wanted to see the goblin, and I told him you banned visitation rights. He was not happy."

"Not happy with my orders, are you, Gary?" the mayor asked with authority.

Still looking down, Gary replied in a much quieter and meek voice. "Sorry, Mayor. Setu is my best friend. He has worked for the town for years as a fisher."

The bear of a man placed his hand on Gary's shoulder. Gary looked up at him. "I know he is, Gary. You have been one of the leading town guards for almost thirty years, but we can't risk an outbreak, and I couldn't leave him at home if he is going to chance to leave again," he replied in a much calmer voice.

SJ had been quietly watching the interaction. "Mayor Maxwell, is it?" she asked.

The mayor had not noticed the sleight-framed fae stood to the side. Turning to look at SJ, his eyes opened ever so slightly, shocked at seeing her. "Can I ask your name?"

"I am SJ."

"And what is one of your kind doing here?"

SJ was unsure what he meant by *one of your kind* and ignored the comment. "I am here to see Setu."

"Why would you be wanting to see a goblin? You are a fae and a Legionnaire."

"I am, yes, on both counts." SJ thought carefully about what Dave had said earlier before she said, "I also violated the quarantine you put in place. Are you going to arrest me as well?"

"Good shout," Dave said. "He knows he shouldn't, and he knows you know he shouldn't, which will worry him even more."

The mayor's face flashed with confusion for a moment. He coughed slightly and replied, "You violated what quarantine?"

"I went and visited Setu at his home. The only reason he left was because of me. I tricked him into coming with me. It is not his fault he left the house."

"His wife has GoblinPox, and you visited him as a fae? I don't believe you."

"His wife doesn't have GoblinPox," SJ said flatly.

"And how can you be so sure? Setu told everyone that it was."

"His wife is suffering with Torpu."

"Torpu?"

"Yes. It is not GoblinPox. I was going to come and speak to you in the morning about it, but due to what has happened, I have now been dragged out in the middle of the night instead."

"How do you know it is not GoblinPox?"

"I guess that you are not goblinkin?"

"No," the mayor scoffed.

"I also assume that when the last outbreak occurred twenty-five years ago, you were informed of the details of the sickness and what it looked like."

"Of course. I have been mayor of the town for over fifty years."

The statement took SJ by surprise. Although she had heard the comment before, he only looked in his early forties, with thick hair, and a beard, and bright and intelligent, though tired-looking, eyes.

"I suggest you visit poor Margu, then, and see for yourself. I am surprised that no one even thought to check."

"You are doing very well tonight," Dave said. "I have been thoroughly impressed so far, and I can take pride in doing such a good job as your administrator."

SJ could not react to Dave but wished she could.

The mayor stood silently for a moment, and SJ could see him thinking things over.

"Also, while you think about it . . . Margu is asleep and probably will be for another two days, maybe three, before she wakes up from the Torpu, and you have taken the sproglings' dad away and locked him up. Who do you think was looking after them? Never mind that Setu has not shown any signs of the illness, which I am sure you know has an infection period of no more than forty-eight hours."

The mayor's face changed as she spoke to him. A look of confusion turned into anger and then back to confusion again.

"Finally. Unless you are also going to arrest me?" SJ tilted her head at him. "I am going to speak to Setu while you decide what the best course of action is." At that point, SJ walked towards the door leading into the back of the jail. Gary and the gnoll were both standing in amazement, and neither of them nor the mayor attempted to stop her as she opened the door and walked through. She faced a long, straight corridor, and on either side, there were bars. Then, further down, she could see separate doors with small, barred windows. She headed straight towards them, passing several forms lying in the open barred cells before arriving at them and peering through.

The first cell had the large snoring form of a troll, and the next a sleeping kobold. There were two empty cells, and then she looked in to see the small form of Setu sitting with his knees tucked up and holding a blanket around himself with his head dropped.

"Setu," she called.

He looked up and over at the bars and smiled weakly. "Hi, SJ."

"I have great news."

"What?"

"I have your deed back. I won it from the alchemist in a game of cards."

"How? I thought he was away?"

"He came back tonight, and I managed to locate him after speaking to Niweq at the Wandering Ogre."

"You went to the Wandering Ogre?" Setu's cheeks coloured slightly, and SJ guessed he had visited himself at some point.

"I did and won your deed from him when I found him."

"That is amazing news. At least Margu still has her stall."

"I am not sure about the silver yet, but we will find out about that." SJ could not tell him she had stolen the silver from the shop and had not even opened the lockbox yet, so she had no idea what was in it. She could have kicked herself but had not been expecting to leave in the middle of the night before having the chance to look in it.

"At least that is one less worry," Setu said, dropping his head again.

"I have just spoken to the mayor and hope things may get resolved soon."

"How?" Setu asked, looking over with a glimmer of hope in his eyes.

"It's a long story. Just hold on here for a while longer, okay?"

Setu's smile was a little stronger. "Thank you, SJ. You didn't have to help me out."

SJ smiled back before turning and walking back down the corridor to the front. As she walked past one of the locked cells, a voice called, "Clarice, is that you? I can smell your perfume."

SJ had an immediate flashback and shuddered, ignoring the voice. She went to the front. The mayor stood alongside two individuals: a stocky dwarf and an athletic woman with long, bright orange hair. Gary turned to her as she walked out.

The gnoll glanced at SJ, then stood and locked the door. It was clear that it shouldn't have been left unlocked.

"Let's go," SJ said to Gary.

Gary looked at her as she walked past him. "Thank you, Mayor Maxwell, for your time," she said as she walked to the exit. Mayor Maxwell stopped his conversation with the others and didn't answer. He just watched as SJ left the jail, Gary quickly following behind.

"Well, that was interesting," Dave said. "I was not sure which way he was going at first. I thought he might jail you at one point."

"License," SJ said.

"Sorry?" Gary asked.

"Oh, I need to get Setu's license for his stall," SJ replied.

"Ah. Yeah. How did you get it back? He said he gave it to the alchemist."

SJ repeated the same story she had told Setu.

"He was willing to bet for a stall deed? What did you offer him to be willing to do that?"

"Me," SJ replied.

Gary's eyes shot open in surprise, but he did not reply.

"Did you hear what the mayor plans to do?"

"Yes. He was going to send Lorna to check on Margu."

"Lorna?"

"The tigress."

"Tigress?"

"She is a were-tiger."

"Oh. I had no idea."

"She is the lieutenant of the town guard. The dwarf you saw is Captain Broadaxe."

"Hopefully, once she reports back her findings, this will all get resolved."

"I hope so."

"I didn't know you were a member of the town guard?"

"Yeah. I have been since I was an orcling. Started in the stables and worked my way up to sergeant."

"Can I ask you a favour?"

"Of course you can, after helping Setu."

"Do you train 'my' type at the barracks?"

Gary frowned at her reference. "If you mean Legionnaires . . . in the past, we have. We have not had anyone new in town for a while now who has inquired. Concerning fae, no, we have never trained a fae. We don't get many fae in town, and those who have ever come here have always been magic focused. I thought you were a mage looking at your dress?"

"No, I am monk class."

"I see. We do have a few monks. The best you just met."

"Who?"

"Lorna. She is amazing at martial arts. She spends the day throwing all of us around in the sparring ring."

"Do you think she would train me?"

"I can ask her. Although I may be in a little trouble after tonight."

"Why? You did nothing wrong; you were trying to help a friend."

"I still screamed at one of the jailers."

"Emotions can cause us all problems at times. I wouldn't worry about it."

"I will probably get extra duties," Gary replied, sighing.

"Can I ask one last question?" They had neared the market square where the inn was situated, talking as they had been.

Gary looked at her, waiting.

"I would not have expected a town of this size to have a barracks, or am I missing something?"

"Oh. There are two main reasons. One is it is the main training area for the mêlée classes, and secondly, it is the town defence force."

"What does the town need a defence force for?"

"The hobs."

"Hobs? What are they?"

"There is a hobgoblin clan down in the valley. They sometimes attempt to perform raids on the town."

"I think I saw that village. On the far side of the lake?"

"Yes. That's the one."

"Why don't you just force them out?"

"Their chief."

"Who is that?"

"He is a monster of an ogre called Bordon."

"He can't be that bad against the town guard, can he?"

"I have only ever seen him once, and he is huge, even larger than Mayor Maxwell in bear form."

"Bear form. I didn't realise he was a lycanthrope as well."

"Yes. He is a beast to behold, but even he is worried about fighting Bordon."

They had reached the inn entrance. "I will let you go back to sleep," Gary said. "Thank you so much for helping tonight, and I am sorry I had to disturb you."

"Don't be sorry. I was glad I could help." SJ turned and entered the inn. Once she'd made her way back to her room, SJ didn't even bother getting undressed and just collapsed on her bed.

"Night again," Dave said.

"Night, Dave," SJ replied.

Congratulations! Your reputation with Gary was raised to Friendly.

SJ smiled as she drifted off to sleep.

CHAPTER THIRTY-FOUR

Visitor

"ALL MAGES TO THE DOCKS. I REPEAT, ALL MAGES TO THE DOCKS."

SJ was awoken by a booming voice as if it was in the room with her. She sat up in her bed; the sun was blazing through the window, and it must have been nearly noon. She wasn't surprised she had slept so late, after last night.

"What's going on?" she asked.

"No idea. Your guess is as good as mine," Dave replied.

SJ climbed from the bed, untangling herself from the sheets which had wrapped her like a cocoon in the night. She had collapsed with her dress on, so she didn't need to get dressed. Hurrying to the window, she looked out. Below in the market square, she saw several people running, all heading towards the docks.

"I wonder what it is."

"ALL MAGES TO THE DOCKS. I REPEAT, ALL MAGES TO THE DOCKS. WE HAVE INCOMING."

"Incoming what?" SJ asked. She remembered her conversation with Gary last night—the hobgoblin clan and Bordon, the ogre.

"Let's go find out. Whatever it is sounds exciting," Dave said in a chipper tone.

SJ pulled her boots on, which she must have removed at some point, although she couldn't remember. She left the room and went downstairs. Gossip filled the common room at the announcement.

SJ saw a dwarf she had seen in the inn the last few nights and asked him, "What's happening?"

"Dragon's back" was all he said.

"Oh," SJ replied as she turned to head to the inn door. The dragon had been amazing to see, and since her arrival, it had just been sat at the top of the highest peak in the mountains.

She went outside and followed the running forms on their way to the dock as the sun was blocked out. Glancing skywards, she saw the massive form of the dragon flying over the town. It was even closer than the first time she had seen it, and it was amazing to see its glistening underbelly and cobalt blue colouring so close. It could only be a couple of hundred feet above the rooftops.

As she reached the dock area by the lake, she could see a long line of people spread out, and she noticed Fran standing near Mayor Maxwell. Another mage was listening to Fran and the mayor, and then the loud announcement voice erupted again.

"ALL MAGES SPREAD OUT. MAKE SURE ALL AREAS ARE COVERED."

SJ watched as the mages all checked their distance from each other and spread out in a long line. The dragon swooped, opening its mouth and drinking from the lake as it had previously. It was such a magnificent beast to behold. She was a little awestruck seeing it again. It repeated swooping across the lake's surface another two times before, as per its previous visit, turning and powering itself into the air.

"BE READY. PREPARE THE SPELLS," the voice boomed out.

SJ saw Fran moving her hands in a pattern. The dragon reached the peak of its climb, turning and diving for the lake again.

"HERE IT COMES. RELEASE ON MY COMMAND.

"Five.

"Four.

"Three.

"Two.

"One.

"NOW."

As the dragon hit the lake's surface and disappeared underneath, a shimmer of magic appeared along the line of mages. Every colour imaginable began to swirl in the air, and as she watched, various forms of what she assumed were barriers appeared.

The tsunami from the dragon had once again begun to form and power its way across the lake's surface towards the town. The wave increased in height and speed as it approached. SJ noticed a couple of mages throwing what she believed to be ice bolts towards sections of the wave, splitting them and seeming to stop the wave from growing as tall as it would have otherwise.

SJ could do nothing. She stood in the open at the rear of the docks, watching the amazing spectacle of magic and power before her. One caused by science and one by magic. The wave crashed into the barrier. One of the sections gave way, and she heard a mage scream as the barrier he had been maintaining failed, the crashing wave throwing him back. Fortunately, this was the only section that gave, and the rest of the mages held their ground. SJ could see the strain on their faces as they pushed back against the immense weight of the wave.

The water finally receded as the dragon reappeared and powered back into the sky again with a huge mouthful of brightly coloured fish dropping from it.

"That was surprising," Dave said.

"Surprising; it's amazing," SJ whispered in reply.

"Meh. I have seen better. I was more surprised at the speed at which the town reacted."

SJ turned and watched as the barriers dispersed. Now the danger had passed. Since arriving at the town, it had not even crossed her mind how it had come away unscathed from the previous tsunami. She followed the dragon's flight as it continued down the lake-side and across the fields and out of sight. It had not returned to the mountain peak this time.

"THE MAYOR WOULD LIKE TO THANK ALL THOSE WHO CAME AND HELPED DEFEND THE TOWN. HE WILL PUT A TAB IN THE HOGLING ARMS FOR ALL MAGES WHO SUPPORTED TODAY. NAMES HAVE BEEN TAKEN FOR THOSE WHO ATTENDED."

The mage stood with the mayor bowed and then walked away, SJ assumed towards the Hogling Arms. It seemed her temporary home might get a little busy today. Fran was still standing with Mayor Maxwell, talking as the others dispersed. A cleric or paladin—SJ couldn't be sure—was healing the mage whom the wave had flung away.

"I wonder where the dragon went?" Dave asked.

"I didn't see it go back to the peak," SJ whispered, turning away from the docks now that everyone was moving away.

"Maybe we can find it."

"Why would we go find it?"

"Because it is a Level 88 dragon. Duh, why not?"

"You said you are not sure if they are good."

"I think that one has a good alignment. Otherwise, it may have caused more problems for the town by now."

"How?"

"Burning crops or similar. It wouldn't be able to eat people—the System wouldn't allow it—but it could cause other damage."

SJ shuddered at the thought of the dragon attacking the town. There was no way they could defend against such a creature. They walked back towards the inn, and there was a stream of the mages going in the same direction, all talking to each other excitedly. SJ turned down a side street that she recognised.

"Where are you going?"

"To the meadow."

"Why?"

"I am going to train. I need to get into a routine."

"What about the free drink?"

"I was not a mage helping."

"You could always try?"

"Dave, that is dishonest. I have told you I am being good."

"Shall I remind you of your class and what you did last night?"

SJ sighed as she walked. It didn't take her long to reach the meadow. Its beautiful vista in the middle of a town was just as surprising as it had been on her first visit. She walked into the meadow and found a piece of ground where the grass was not as long or as heavily laden with buzzing insects and practised her katas. She kept at it for a while until, eventually, her display triggered.

> Congratulations, Kata Level 3 achieved

"Yes!"

"That didn't take too long, did it?"

"No. Thankfully," SJ said as she sat down in the grass, pulled out her waterskin, and took a drink. The water tasted as fresh as the first day it had been filled.

"How long will the water stay fresh?"

"It depends on the quality of the item. Usually, water lasts three days before it needs refilling. So, I would advise you to refill it later today or tomorrow at the latest."

As SJ sat there, she focused on the muscle groups in her back and flexed them individually.

"Are we staying here all day?" Dave asked.

"No, just finishing my exercises."

"Which? You have done your kata."

"Wings," SJ replied, groaning slightly as one of her back muscles spasmed from being clenched for so long.

"Ah. Very dedicated to your training today."

"When I return to the inn, I will work on those socks."

"I think you should find that dragon."

"It's a dragon. Why would a Level 5 deliberately try to find a Level 88 dragon?"

"For shizz and giggles."

"Really! I don't think it would be funny getting eaten by it."

"It's just fed. It wouldn't eat you."

"You know this because you have had so many dealings with dragons before?"

"No. I am just being logical."

"Illogical, more like. It's a dragon."

"Dragons are intelligent, especially blue ones."

SJ finished her muscle exercises and was groaning by the end. She would have to focus on them to get past the initial ache and make sure she did them at least four times a day, as Fran suggested. The sooner she could fly properly, the better. After her raven incident and the dock last night, she didn't want to try flying like that again.

"Okay. Let's head back," SJ said.

As she stood, she saw a small form dart through the meadow. Her senses heightened, and she stared in the movement's direction. "Did you see that?" she whispered.

"Yep. Small form moving in the meadow."

"Exactly."

The shape darted about in the grasses; she only caught a glimpse of colour and nothing else as it moved. It seemed brown, but she really could not be certain. A cloud of insects was disturbed from the flowers near her, and she stepped back as they swarmed towards her. A small brown figure leapt in front of her, swishing a small net, and skilfully picked out only the bellpop in the thick of the swarm. It landed at her feet.

SJ initially thought it was a giant rat before realising it was wearing clothes and standing upright.

"Er. Hello," she said cautiously.

"Hi," the small creature replied, smiling at her.

"Are you catching bellpops?"

"Yes. I missed my usual quota because I was ill, so I must make up for it."

"Oh. Are you Little Stuart?"

"Yes. How do you know?"

"Floretta asked me to collect some yesterday for her."

"Oh," Stuart replied, and his shoulders slumped.

"What's wrong?"

"She will have her quota, so she won't need these," he replied, holding up the jar containing the orange bellpops.

"I am sure she can still use them," SJ said hopefully.

"Maybe. I have ten now, so I should go and see."

"I am going back there. I will come with you if you like."

"Sure."

SJ followed the little ratkin across the meadow. By the time they reached the inn, which didn't take very long, SJ knew all about Stuart and his bellpop sideline. He caught them three times a week for Floretta when he was not working at the stables and got extra money for their family. His dad had died in a hobgoblin raid several months ago, and since then, he had become the man of the house, helping Mum with his sixteen brothers and sisters.

On arriving at the inn, SJ bade him farewell and went straight upstairs, wishing him luck with his bellpop hunting. In her room, she sat down on the sofa, sighing and stretching her back again.

SJ let out a groan.

"What's wrong?" Dave asked.

"I am just thinking through everything that I need to do. I need to sort the stuff for Setu. I said I would go see Lythonian and help with his books. I need to train both my kata and wings. I need to craft socks. I need to train my martial arts. Most of all, though, I need to get my head around everything in this world."

"You don't need to do everything at once. You can take your time."

"Then why do I feel like everything is a priority?"

"It's just all new. You will soon get into a routine. Like you did today, ensuring you got your kata training back up to Level 3."

"I hope so. I haven't had a moment for myself since I arrived."

"That is something you will need to adjust to. All your interactions are based around the System structure and may trigger quests."

Her display flashed.

> Event: Investigate the meadows north of town

"What now?" SJ said, groaning.

"Ooo. An event—now, this is exciting," Dave happily replied.

"What's so special about it?"

"Events are triggered by specific incidents occurring. You get world events and local events. This is a local event."

"What does it mean exactly?"

"They could mean anything. They are always unknowns. World events normally relate to the appearance of world bosses, but local events can be anything. They are worth investigating, though, and they can give substantial rewards."

"Are they level based?"

"No. Any Legionnaire in the region can attend anything labelled an event."

"I have too much to do today. I still need to see if Setu was released and return his deed to him. Then I need to craft these socks."

"If I were you, I wouldn't miss an event opportunity. The rewards can be special."

"Even if it is so vague?"

"They always are. They give you a location to go towards, and that is it."

SJ thought about Malcolm being another Legionnaire in town.

"What about Malcolm? I had forgotten about him until now."

"I am sure he has his hands full. He has an unexplained death to deal with, and I can guarantee he won't be reporting it to the town's authorities. I can say he will dispose of the body somehow and then probably head to the Wandering Ogre and continue his life of drinking."

"Don't Legionnaire bodies vanish like creatures?"

"Eventually. They have a two-day timer on them. That way, others in their parties can have a chance to get back to a body and claim loot before it disappears."

"Explain?"

"In some areas where there are hard challenges or quests, if a party member dies, their body will remain until two days have passed, giving other party members a chance to save what they were carrying."

"What if they get eaten?"

"Then they lose out."

"You think I really should investigate?"

"Yes."

SJ sighed, stood again, and resigned herself to the fact that she needed to investigate the issue. She walked to the wardrobe and checked through her items. She had no idea what would be out there, so she removed the tailoring items from her inventory and dropped them in the wardrobe. She still had her waterskin and rations, and collected her stiletto, torches, bedroll, and blanket. She went to the water pump, emptied the contents of the waterskin, and refilled it.

"Okay. Let's find the location, then."

"Great," Dave said excitedly.

They left the inn and headed north. The smithy was on the northern edge of town, and SJ saw Zej as she walked past. He waved to her, smiling, and she waved back. Large crop fields replaced the cobbled streets on either side of the dirt track, and SJ walked between them. The sun was bright and warm, and being out in the countryside was nice.

"How far do we need to go?"

"It's a local event, so it won't be too far. There isn't an exact distance, but it's not usually more than an hour's travel."

"How big are regions where people get notifications?"

"It is within a local area, but these can vary, there is no specific distance given. Imagine the event position, then draw a circle around that location, and anyone inside whatever distance they have chosen are eligible to attend and will have received the alert."

"If there are Legionnaires who are not in town as well, they may attend?"

"Yes. Although I doubt there are any here. The region is too isolated, and anyone who left here would have headed towards the nearest large town or city. It is almost guaranteed."

SJ followed the dirt track that led through the fields. It seemed to stretch on forever, and she passed several farmers working in the fields and approached a forested area. The path continued into the forest, and so did SJ. The sounds of the forest came alive as she walked—birds calling and creatures rustling in the underbrush. She even stopped and watched a hogling walk across the path ahead.

After a few more minutes, SJ could see the trees beginning to thin, and she walked out into a huge open meadow.

"I guess these are the meadows," SJ said.

"Possibly. We haven't seen any others."

SJ stopped and looked around; there was nothing obvious in sight, and it was a large area.

"I suppose I better search, then."

The path continued through the centre. The end of the meadow saw the start of a craggy rock face, and a cutting appeared to allow passage through the rocks. It was when she got to the middle of the meadow that the air changed. She felt static in the air, and it was getting stronger the farther she walked. Her hair felt as though it was frizzing as it had at school when she had touched a static ball.

"This is strange."

"What is?"

"The static I can feel."

"Static electricity?"

"Yes."

"Ohhhhhh," Dave said slowly.

"What does that mean?" SJ replied, concerned at Dave's comment.

"I can't see anything, so you should be all right."

"All right from what?"

Suddenly, thunder-like rumbling emerged across the meadow, followed by a blue lightning bolt racing towards her.

SJ screamed, only diving sideways at the last moment. She rolled and looked back. The ground where she had stood was blackened, as if a fire had burned the meadow's grass instantly.

"What the hell was that?" SJ cried out.

"I think you found it," Dave replied.

"Found what?"

It was then that the air in front of SJ shimmered, and she watched in amazement as the creature appeared. Not fifty feet from where she now sat on her rear, the monstrous, lounging form of a blue dragon became visible.

SJ screamed, jumping to her feet in surprise. The dragon's head was facing in her direction, and small sparks flickered around its huge nostrils.

"Sorry." A deep resonating sound reached her ears.

"Who said that?" she cried, not taking her eyes from the beast as she backed away.

"I did." The voice had so much bass that it made the ground vibrate where she now stood.

"Is that you?" she squeaked as she continued to back away.

"Oh, damn," the voice said. As SJ watched, the colossal head of the dragon turned slightly, and another sound, like a clap of thunder, erupted from it, and lightning flew from its nostrils. It was far from SJ this time, but she still felt the draft from its passing.

"Sorry. I think I am allergic to some of these meadow flowers," the bass thumped at SJ, and her body shook, never mind the ground.

The huge blue dragon raised its head, turning again to look at where SJ stood.

"Are—are you talking to me?" she stammered, still moving away, absolutely terrified.

"Yes. You are the only other creature here, aren't you?" SJ nearly fell over this time from the bassy pulse that hit her.

"Do you know how lucky you are, talking to a dragon?" Dave's almost hyperventilating voice said. "A god and a dragon. They will never believe me, and I am not recording it. SJ, can I . . ."

"No," SJ snapped, realising what he was about to say.

"No, what?" the voice said.

"Sorry. I was talking to myself. I'm in shock at the moment. I think I am talking to a dragon."

"Think? Do you not recognise my kind?"

"I do. I am just shocked. I've never met one, I mean a dragon, before."

"I see. Looking at what is around here, I am not surprised. There is nothing of a high level, which means you must be low and have probably never travelled far."

"You would be right."

"I will forgive your rudeness, then."

"I'm sorry to have been rude," SJ said, panicking, hoping she had not upset the dragon.

"Most people would introduce themselves."

"Erm, sorry. I'm SJ."

"Bob. Nice to meet you, SJ."

CHAPTER THIRTY-FIVE

Bob!

"Bob? Your name is Bob?" SJ said in surprise.

"Bob, in your tongue, yes."

"What about in your tongue?"

"You wouldn't understand it if I told you."

"Please, I have never heard a dragon speak before, never mind dragon speech."

"In dragon tongue, my name is Brotuliosteryiweqmanprubloreb." The way he drew out the word caused the whole ground to vibrate, and the blades of grass in the meadow seemed to shimmer.

SJ's eyes opened in amazement and she felt her insides shudder. "That is a long name."

"It means Brave Skyborne Warrior."

SJ was unsure what to say to Bob. From what Dave had said, he was a humongous dragon lying in a meadow near a town over five thousand miles from his normal home.

"You are very new, aren't you?" Bob said. It looked like he was frowning, if a dragon could frown.

"New?" SJ asked.

"You are one of those brought here. I can smell your kind."

"I am, if you think I am what I think you think I am. Sorry, that was a little confusing."

"I understood, and yes, you are what I think you are."

"You have met my kind before?"

"Many over my lifetime."

"How old are you?"

"I am four thousand four hundred ninety-nine years old."

SJ had been expecting him to say he was older than that, not that she knew how old dragons lived. She just imagined them being virtually immortal. "Have you met any of my kind recently?"

"Not for a century now. The last thought he would come to take my hoard."

SJ had always read of dragons hoarding wealth, and she imagined Bob sitting on a vast mountain of gold, platinum, and jewels.

"What happened to him?"

"I ate him."

SJ gulped at the thought. She had no idea what to say to a dragon, so she asked him normal mundane questions. "What are you doing in the clearing? Aren't you a long way from home?"

"I am a long way from home, yes, and I thought it would have been obvious what I was doing in the clearing."

"No, sorry, I do not know."

"I was sunbathing."

"But you were invisible when I first entered the clearing."

"I can't go invisible. It is a camouflage skill related to my ancestors passed on for millennia."

"Whatever it is, it is still pretty amazing. I had no idea you were here until you sneezed."

At the mention of sneezing, small lightning sparks formed at his nostrils again.

"One minute," Bob said, turning his head. SJ watched as he sneezed again. Lightning flashed from his nostrils and scorched another streak of the meadow into blackened earth.

"Flowers. There aren't many where I come from." Bob stated.

It intrigued SJ to know where he was from and why he was there. "Where are you from exactly?"

"I am from an area of Amathera called Alpagium."

"How far is it from here?"

"In good weather at a steady pace, it takes about ten days. I could fly it faster if I wanted to, but I am in no rush."

"Why are you here?"

"I am waiting to meet someone."

"In a starter zone."

"They are not from here."

Reflecting on his words, SJ could only think of one person who would bring a dragon to the starter area. "Are you here to see Fizzlewick?"

"How do you know who Fizzlewick is?" the dragon asked, raising an eyebrow.

"I am his apprentice."

The dragon looked at her, frowning slightly, deep-set wrinkles appearing across its brow. "You are the reason. I see now."

"I am the reason?"

"The reason he asked me to come here."

SJ could still not get past the resonating bass that thumped into her every time he spoke. It was very disconcerting. "Why would you be down here because of me?"

"I am going to do something. Don't be alarmed."

Her heart raced as the dragon muttered a few words in his unknown tongue. A ball of blue glittering light appeared in front of him, and SJ watched in amazement as it grew larger until it became almost her size. In an instant, it shot towards her.

She screamed in terror as the ball hit her and the light surrounded her, her vision shifting as though she'd donned blue-tinted glasses. She felt a warm sensation envelop her, with no pain. It felt as though she was being wrapped in a fluffy blanket, and the light faded as fast as it appeared.

"What was that?" she said in amazement.

"Just something for me to get to know you better." Bob opened his mouth.

SJ stepped back before realising that he must be smiling. His teeth were huge, and she shivered seeing them. The damage they could render against anything would be insane, never mind that he could shoot lightning from his nostrils that crisped anything it touched.

"What did you do to me? I felt warm when it enveloped me."

"It is like your identification skill."

"How do you know I have that skill?" SJ asked in surprise.

"My spell informed me. I also know your class. Very interesting indeed. I have known several fae but never one of that class before."

SJ stood, open-mouthed.

"Umm. You are not very skilled yet, are you?"

SJ spluttered a response. "I—well, I am only Level 5. How can you see all the details about my skills?"

"Oh. Your skill will do the same eventually when it levels high enough and you get your other skills developed as well."

Bob had vibrant, deep, golden eyes with sharp black pupils, and they appeared to drill into SJ's soul as she stood there.

"I am not sure why I was directed to see you. I had an event appear." SJ was not sure why she was even telling Bob the details of why she had come to the meadow.

"As I say, I am here because of Fizzlewick and you. You are special."

"Special how?"

"Fizzlewick did not tell me everything when he messaged me, but enough to indicate that you were bringing change, and looking at your class, I can see why he thinks so. It is the rarity of your race and class combination and the skill paths you have chosen and are likely to choose. I have known many assassins over the years and still have a couple of assassin acquaintances. I have never met an assassin who chose subterfuge as their specialisation."

"You know assassins?"

"Yes."

"What are they like?"

"Cold-blooded killers. Their existence revolves around their next victim, planning, and plotting. You, on the other hand, do not seem to be that way inclined," Bob replied. "Very strange, very strange indeed." He appeared to be talking thoughtfully to himself.

SJ could not take her gaze from Bob, his beautifully coloured scales and golden detailing. This close, there appeared to be a coppery green undertone. Bob's scales reminded her of overlapping scale armour, and the appearance matched the armour's name. Bob suddenly moved, making SJ jump from her trance-like state, and he sat up on his forelegs, stretching his neck into the air. As he did, he let out a deep rumbling groan. The whole meadow seemed to shudder this time.

Bob looked down at SJ. "I think we are going to have an interesting future together," he finally said.

"Together?" Surprise etched onto SJ's face.

"I will be here for a few more days while I wait for Fizzlewick to see me, although I think the crafty old goat may have engineered this encounter."

"I still do not know why he would want you to meet me. I heard what you said, but it still doesn't make sense. I am only one person. How can I effect change by myself?"

"You won't be by yourself. That dress you wear is the first sign of that. Gods do not give gifts lightly, and only those they deem worthy of the investment receive anything, and they are unique. Never again will a dress like your own be given or received by another. If Fizzlewick thought you were not special or able, he never would have given it to you."

The whole scenario made SJ's head spin, and she felt nauseous from the continual battering of the bass of Bob's voice. Bob unfolded his wings. Their leathery form and span were enormous, and they reminded SJ of a bat.

"I will leave you with a parting gift. It has no value to any other and will only work for you." Bob uttered more words, and a small blue-and-gold box appeared in the meadow before her. It reminded her of a small jewellery box she'd had as a child. SJ bent and picked up the box. The surface shimmered in her hands.

"May I?" she asked.

"Please do."

Opening the box, SJ revealed a small vial. Inside the vial was a bright golden liquid with blue speckles. "What is this?"

Dave had been silent the whole time Bob had been speaking, and SJ had completely forgotten about him in the briefest period since arriving, too busy being in awe of the powerful beast before her—until now.

"Holy boils on a freaking orc's bulbous nose," Dave sputtered. "It can't be."

SJ dared not reply to Dave.

"If that is what I think it is, then I will—I will—I have no idea what I will do . . ." He trailed off.

"It is something special that will help you with your growth. I believe I understand why Fizzlewick is interested in you, and I am now as well. There could be some intriguing times ahead if what I think he hopes will happen happens. I can't say, so don't ask," Bob said, smiling again.

SJ removed the small vial from the box and held it in her hand. The bottle felt warm to the touch, and the liquid inside swirled as she moved it.

"I assume I drink this?"

"You would assume right. I must go for now. I sense others approaching the meadow and do not wish to scare anyone else today. I will see you again, SJ, and one last note before I depart: If you meet any more of my kind, don't worry." With that, Bob forced his wings down rapidly. The downdraft flattened the grasses and sent SJ falling onto her rear, still holding the vial and box in her hands. Sitting on the ground, she watched as Bob lifted from the ground and flew swiftly away towards the mountain peaks, staying just above the tree-line.

"Dave," SJ said as soon as Bob disappeared over the trees.

"Hang on," the reply came back.

"Hang on for what?"

"Shh. A minute, will you?"

Feeling completely overwhelmed from speaking to a dragon, she was not in the mood to be silenced by Dave.

"HOW DARE YOU SHUSH ME," she snapped in a loud tone.

"Okay. Okay. Drink it."

"Drink it? What even is it?"

"Just drink it. Believe me when I say it will be the best decision you ever make in your new life." The excitement in Dave's voice was palpable.

Frowning, she lifted the vial, examining its swirling liquid contents, which seemed to have a life of their own. She placed the small box into her inventory and then, pinching the small glass stopper on the top of the vial, removed it. The smell from the liquid was that of a crisp, cold winter morning. It was the strangest smell in the world from a liquid that felt warm through the vial.

Cautiously, SJ drew the vial to her lips.

"Don't waste a drop," Dave said.

The vial could hold no more than one drop of whatever the substance was. Tilting the vial back, she allowed the liquid to fall onto her tongue. It gave the strangest sensation, the liquid feeling hot and cold all at once. It seemed to pulse in her mouth, and she held it momentarily before swallowing.

As the liquid travelled down her throat, an intensity of feelings hit her like a crescendo of waves. Happiness, sadness, pleasure, pain, life, death, hot, cold, relief, anxiety. The emotions and depth of feeling increased in intensity. SJ had fallen backwards and lay on her back, her eyes closed as her body contested and then adjusted to this foreign matter that was now inside her. It seemed to permeate every cell. She could feel it moving, adapting, and combining.

She let out a gasp. "What is happening to me?" she said through gritted teeth.

"You will see, if I think what is happening is happening" were Dave's only words. He sounded as though he was in the distance but in awe of whatever it was.

As SJ lay there, absorbed by the emotional pleasure and pain of the ride, her mind drifted. Visions flashed in front of her closed eyes as though she was watching a cinema screen, fleeting and so brief she could see no details. They subsided, her body tingling and her senses heightened. Opening her eyes, she sat up, feeling weary and drained. Looking around the meadow, everything seemed to have a new clarity.

"How do you feel?" Dave asked.

"I don't know. Strange, I suppose. I feel like me but not me," SJ said as she looked at her hands and the small vial with its stopper she was still holding. She placed the lid back on the vial, recalled the small box from her inventory, placed it inside, and returned them. A sharp pain flared in her head. She grimaced, scrunching her eyes closed and grasping at her temples. She groaned loudly. The pain subsided again, and she opened her eyes. Her display triggered.

> Symbiotic Relationship Established
> You've received a gift few have, let alone survived.
> Details:
> Brotuliosteryiweqmanprubloreb, the greatest of his kind, has gifted you a drop of his blood. Only the blood of the purest being can be used for symbiosis.

"It—it was dragon blood?" SJ stammered.

"Yes."

"And what has it done to me?"

"Open your character sheet and see what it says. I do not know what it may grant."

SJ pulled up her sheet.

Symbiosis
Dragon Sense—your senses (touch, hearing, smell, and sight) are heightened.
Precognition—foreknowledge due to increased perception will allow you to evade a killing blow. (24-hour cool-down)
Divine Lightning—your blood is combined with that of a blue dragon, increasing healing speed while out of combat.

"Wow" was the only word that came to SJ.

"Wow. Are you kidding me? That is freaking awesome! You have survived symbiosis with dragon's blood. Do you know how rare that is?"

"How rare . . . and what do you mean *survived*? The message said something about that but no details."

"The last successful symbiosis was between a necromancer and a demonic lord. Only creatures of a certain standing and level can offer the gift, a once-in-a-lifetime opportunity. Bob has granted you the most powerful gift he could. Most who have ever tried to complete symbiosis have died in the process of transforming bloodlines due to them not being compatible or aligned. Bob must have sensed something in you even to have attempted it."

Dave continued. "I wasn't talking to you when you spoke to Bob because I was talking to the System."

"You told me to just drink it. When it had a chance of killing me?"

"It was worth the risk," Dave answered.

"And you spoke to the System?"

"Yes. They spoke to me directly, which is very strange, actually almost unheard of, since I am like a thorn in their side. I think they would have preferred it if you hadn't let me stay, and they could have reformatted me! The System was as confused as I was that the dragon would give you a drop of its blood, and was worried. I don't know what is happening, but your status is causing serious concern. They are restricted from doing anything because of their agreement with you about no increased threat repercussions, but they will watch you carefully."

"I am more confused than anyone else. Why are so many suddenly interested in me?"

"I don't think this is sudden. I think a larger game is at play here, and we have not even started it yet."

"What game?"

"Fizzlewick hinted at change, and your new life will define your path, but I think it will be different this time."

"What do I do now, then?"

"We go back and do what we were going to do. Quest, level, earn reputation, and turn you into the best assassin Amathera has ever seen," Dave said jovially.

Standing in the beautiful meadow with two streaks of blackened earth caused by a dragon's sneezes, SJ had no idea what this meant.

"Wait a minute. The dragon arrived the day I arrived on Amathera. He said it took him ten days to travel here. How was it here before I arrived?"

"Ah. That will be the time-lapse. You remember I said there was a time difference between accepting your choices and arriving in Amathera. Even though you wouldn't have noticed, as it appears instantaneous. On Amathera, you arrived two weeks after your details were uploaded into the system," Dave said.

After the details of the time-lapse were revealed, SJ could not muster words to explain her thought process. It begged a whole new conversation that she was not ready for at the moment.

Turning, she began the trip back to town. When she reached the meadow's edge, there appeared three hunters from the town who she recognised from the inn, where they often met. After exchanging pleasantries, they came to a standstill as they saw the streaks in the meadow.

"What happened here?" one asked, confused.

"I have no idea. It was like that when I came through," SJ replied, smiling as she left them.

CHAPTER THIRTY-SIX

Announcements

When they returned to town, it was late afternoon. The town square was packed. "What's going on?" SJ whispered.

"Let's find out."

A very angry-looking mayor stood on one of the empty vending stands, the table creaking under his massive form. He began to speak, and the crowd who had gathered fell silent.

"Thank you to those who have come to attend the town meeting," Mayor Maxwell said. "I know that rumours have already been spread, and some of our members have panicked, thinking of leaving town, but I have some news."

Whispers and comments began amongst those in the crowd.

"First point of note: There is no GoblinPox. I will say again, the rumours about GoblinPox are unfounded. The poor goblin suspected of violating quarantine has been released from jail and reunited with his family. Several of you are friends with him and will be happy to hear the news. Also, I hope it stops any more panicking and people thinking about leaving."

A few in the crowd cheered at the comments.

"The second point is much more serious and has not happened in Killic for over a decade."

The crowd fell silent again at the mayor's sombre and serious tone.

"There has been a murder."

Audible gasps and muttering erupted from those gathered, and general conversations broke out. Several in the crowd shouted, asking who.

"Quiet down, quiet down." The mayor waited for silence before he continued. "A body was found this morning down by the mill near the mage academy. It is that of a human male. A human male Legionnaire."

The mention of a Legionnaire sent a fresh round of muttering and comments through the crowd, and a couple creatures turned and looked at her. She felt her nerves tingling and could feel her ears burning; she was glad she had long hair as it helped hide the nervous expression she must have had on her face.

"SILENCE," Mayor Maxwell shouted, again waiting. "There has been an investigation ongoing since this morning, and as things stand, we still have no suspect.

The wounds look like the claws of an animal caused them, but there are no animals that we know of in town who could cause such damage. Before anyone asks, we have checked all the lycanthrope. As you can expect, they were our primary suspects and have been checked this morning against the wounds. The body, having been found where it was, is the area of confusion. The Legionnaire rented a house on Hutret Street on the other side of town, and it is known that he frequented establishments with a poor reputation. There was no reason for him to be by the mill."

SJ noticed several in the crowd had suddenly looked down, making it obvious who had visited there or visited often.

"Barney Jiilrew," a female voice cried out, making everyone turn and look, "as my husband, you better haven't been visiting that place, or I will have your guts for garters."

SJ saw a large orc standing with his head down. "I only went once, love. I got dragged by the boys," he replied.

His orc wife balled her fist and hit him square in his nose, making it explode, before she turned and stormed off. Several in the crowd cheered for her while others laughed at the spectacle. The large orc, now highly embarrassed and holding his bleeding nose, hurried down the street after his wife, pleading.

"Quiet down," Mayor Maxwell said. Even his demeanour had changed slightly after the spectacle. "The suspected murder victim ran an alchemy shop, and there have been rumours today that he may have started the GoblinPox scare. We have no confirmation yet, but it is coincidental if that is the case. I am asking all town members to be extra wary over the next few days while we get to the bottom of this, and there will be an increased patrol until we resolve the issue."

More muttering.

"If you know or have seen anything, please come forward and report to the barracks. Captain Broadaxe is overseeing the investigation. Rest assured, we will find the guilty party and deal with them. Thank you for your time." As the mayor stepped down from the stall, he glanced across and noticed SJ standing to the side of the crowd where she had entered the town square late.

Many turned and made their way into the Hogling Arms, and SJ had turned to follow when she heard the mayor's voice. "Excuse me," he called.

SJ glanced back, fear coursing through her veins as the gigantic man walked over. Knowing he was a were-bear did not help her nerves.

"Yes," she replied, her voice a little higher-pitched than usual.

The mayor walked up to her, standing close, not in an intimidating way, but it didn't help how SJ was feeling. "SJ, wasn't it?" he asked.

"Yes. How can I help you, Mayor Maxwell?"

"Please call me Zigferd."

"Zigferd. What can I do for you?"

"I just wished to say thank you for this morning. Yesterday was a long day with the fear of GoblinPox, and I need to apologise for my lack of thought. Thanks to you, it has been confirmed that it is not GoblinPox and is a rather rare case of this Torpu you mentioned. Which will hopefully end any more panic or issues."

"It is all I can do to help," SJ said, smiling as best she could. Her heart was still hammering in her chest.

"Setu mentioned you saw the alchemist last night. Can I ask where you saw him?"

"It was at his shop. Setu had shown me where he lived, and I saw him return with his half-orc friend. They had been to the Wandering Ogre, and both appeared rather drunk. I eventually got him to play me at cards after talking my way in and offering myself as a bet."

Mayor Maxwell's eyes opened wide at the comment.

"Thankfully, I won, getting Setu's deed back."

"He was alive at what time?"

"I am unsure, but I returned to the inn before midnight. I ordered some food and went straight to bed until Gary told me about Setu this morning."

"Okay. Thank you for answering my questions."

"It is a pleasure. If you need any other help, please let me know. I must get Setu his deed—I can return it to him now he is free."

The mayor coloured slightly at the last comment and bid farewell, returning to the barracks area.

SJ went into the inn. It was heaving. Looking at the state of some of the patrons, several looked like mages and were slumped in chairs and across tables. It did not look like they had left since the call to aid at the docks. The town meeting had now added to the crowd. SJ wove through and headed straight up the stairs to her room.

"Oh my god," she said, sighing in relief as she sat on the sofa.

"That was a close one," Dave said.

"Close. I thought I was going to be dragged off for murder."

"You could have told him you killed him. I doubt anything would have been done. It may have affected your chances of earning a reputation in the town, but it is unlikely to have any other impact, apart from you being banned. Starter towns are always strange places. You would get dragged up on charges in larger towns and cities, but not here."

"*Doubt* does not fill me with much confidence." SJ sat there and began her wing exercises.

"Well, I can't say for definite, but the chances would be slim. The worst they would have done anyway is ban you from the town. There is no way a starter town would do anything severe to a Legionnaire. They get paid bonuses for Legionnaires who successfully integrate into Amathera."

"Why are there so few of us here, then?" SJ grunted.

"If you consider the number of starter towns and the number of Legionnaires worldwide, there are probably only a few in each one at most."

"Do you not know how many, then?"

"Not exactly. There are new arrivals and departures often enough to keep ticking things over."

"Will everyone always know that I am a Legionnaire?"

"No. Not once you start to level more. It is obvious when outsiders come to starter towns, and as I say, many initial rebirths occur in the towns themselves. It was unusual for you to start outside the way you did."

"I don't understand the way this all happens."

"Nor do I, and I have been doing the job a long time," Dave chuckled.

"Not very helpful," SJ moaned, rolling her shoulders to ease her tightening muscles. "These exercises are torture. I have only done them twice today."

"The sooner the better."

SJ sighed again and did another round of exercises, resting her arms at her sides as best as possible. When she finished, she stretched off and walked to the wardrobe. She emptied the contents from her inventory but kept her waterskin, rations, and the box from Bob. She then picked up Darjey's lockbox and set of keys.

Sitting back on the sofa, she tried the keys until one slipped in and opened it. Inside were three pouches. Picking them out, she heard the jangle of coins and opened the leather ties that held them closed. The first pouch only had thirty-two copper in it. The second was better, holding fourteen silver. The third felt empty, and she was just about to drop it back in the lockbox when she picked it up and felt a coin in it. Opening the pouch, she gasped. Tipping it into her hand, she stared in awe at the bright gold coin.

"Holy snoozle burgers," Dave said in amazement. "He must have been running a very successful scheme to have made that much."

A beautifully detailed dragon face adorned one side of the coin, with a large number one on the other.

"At least I can give Setu his money back now."

"For someone who is supposed to be good with figures, your math hasn't worked this time, has it?"

"What do you mean? Setu needs forty silver."

"No, he doesn't. He needs fifteen silver and the deed to cover the twenty-five."

"With the twelve I got from Darjey and the fourteen here, I have more than enough, then."

"More than enough. You are seriously well off for your level. Just think, you could buy an upgraded profession basket already."

SJ remembered that a good was only ten silver, and a rare was one gold. Not that she was planning on spending one gold on it straight away. She added the coins and lockbox to her inventory, as she would need to dispose of the lockbox and the keys.

"I still need to find this cottage at some point."

"Yep."

"Right, let's go and see Setu and give him his money and deed back."

* * *

When she arrived at the docks, they were still active, and as SJ walked across the bridge to the small island, she could hear the shouts and calls from the fishermen by the jetty. SJ headed straight over to Setu's and was just reaching to knock on the door when it opened, and a large orc walked out, nearly walking into her.

He jumped in surprise at coming face-to-face with SJ.

"Gary?"

"SJ. You scared me half to death. What are you doing here?"

"SJ," Setu called and ran out of the house. His four-foot-high frame grabbed her in a hug. "Thank you so much for your help. If it weren't for you, I wouldn't be back home with my Margu and the sproglings."

"It's okay," SJ replied as Setu stepped back, a huge grin on his face. "I brought you this back."

She removed the deed from her inventory, handed it to him, and was just about to hand over the fifteen silver pieces when Dave spoke.

"How did you get the silver?" Dave said.

SJ hadn't thought of that and stopped herself just before she retrieved it. She took out three silver coins instead and handed them to Setu. Setu's eyes opened in amazement.

"What is the silver for?"

"To help you get sorted. I know you lost another fifteen with the alchemist conning you."

Setu's cheeks reddened slightly.

"Glad he is dead," Gary said emphatically.

"I heard. I was in the town square when the mayor announced it."

"I am not surprised after the number of people he conned. We found a journal in his house containing names and people who owed him money. It seems he and his half-orc friend had a decent scheme going."

"Oh?"

"Yeah, and the half orc has disappeared. No one has seen him since the body was found. We checked all the places we know he goes to, and there is no sign of him. Captain Broadaxe thinks he may have killed him and run off with the money. It could have totalled a couple of gold at least."

"The mayor said they didn't have anyone as a suspect?" SJ queried.

"We don't because we can't find him. It doesn't mean he isn't the prime suspect, though."

"I see."

"It is good that the half orc has disappeared. You would have only ended up having to kill him otherwise," Dave said.

"SJ. Can I get you anything while you are here?" Setu asked.

"I don't suppose you have coffee, do you?"

"Coffee, I certainly do. Please come in, and I will make one."

"Right, I need to head off to work. I have patrol duty tonight," Gary said. "SJ, I mentioned martial arts to Lorna. She said she would be happy to train you. There is a small fee—donations to the Guards' Retirement Fund, nothing too expensive."

"That sounds amazing. When can I start that?"

"Call in and see her. She is often at the sparring grounds if not the barracks."

"Where are they?"

"Behind the barracks. There is the jail yard, and next to it are the sparring grounds."

"That sounds great. Thanks, Gary," SJ replied, smiling.

"No problem. See you tomorrow, Setu."

"Bye, Gary."

SJ followed Setu into the house. She could see none of the sproglings in the front room, which was empty. "Where are the kids?"

Setu turned and frowned. "Kids?"

"Sproglings."

"Oh. Their Aunt Suuqu has collected them for the day."

SJ walked into the kitchen area. On her last visit, it had been in a state, but it was now pristine. Everything was cleaned and put away where it should be. SJ smiled.

"Looks like you cleaned up, then?"

Setu went red again. "Yes. When I got back."

"It looks nice."

Setu made coffee, and they went to sit in the front room. They passed small talk for some time, and Setu explained the fishing quota rules and how he could provide fish for Margu to sell on top of the usual rates he had to fish for the town. The economy that operated in the town impressed SJ, and it appeared that all services were covered through the town's coffers and that it maintained a steady economy due to it. SJ thought the money must just end up being recycled rather than an actual profit being made by most. It was a strange concept to consider.

According to Setu, most people in the town were happy with their status and what they did daily, enjoying their work and their roles. Setu had asked SJ about herself, and she hadn't divulged any details, being very vague with her comments until they reached a comfortable impasse and sat sipping their second coffees. Eventually, SJ said she needed to leave, and Setu thanked her again, giving her another hug and saying she must come and visit when Margu was better so he could introduce her. She promised she would and left. As she walked down the path, leaving Setu, her display triggered.

Congratulations! Your reputation with Setu was raised to Liked.

Quest: Save a Soul Part 2—Complete
You have returned Margu's title deed, and Setu has been freed.
Rewards: 150xp + 20% = 180xp awarded

> Congratulations! Your reputation with the town of Killic was raised to Friendly after you prevented the departure of its residents because of the fear of GoblinPox. All future town interactions will offer a 20% experience bonus for quests completed.

"That's good," SJ said as she crossed back over the bridge.

"Good? That's great. It will speed up your levelling process."

"How does reputation work fully?"

"It is one of the easier systems out of most in Amathera. There are six ranks: unknown, friendly, liked, popular, honoured, and revered. There are negative reputations as well. For each level gained up to honoured, your earning potential and bonus experience increase by 20 percent per level. Once you reach revered with a town or city, any quests can earn 100 percent bonuses. The problem is that many will never reach revered because of the level cap for experience due to the territory the towns are in, which can make it a pointless exercise to pursue."

"That makes sense."

"Capitals, on the other hand, do not have restrictive territory caps, so they can continue to offer quests, which is why so many flock to them."

SJ checked her experience.

> Experience: 521 of 600

"Only another seventy-nine experience needed to Level 6," SJ said happily.

Her increases and improvements were coming along well; this one quest, which had taken her just under a day to complete, had earned her a combined total of 480xp. If she kept going at her current rate, she would soon reach Level 10.

"I am going to see Lythonian while I can."

"What about your tailoring?"

"I will do that when we get back later. I said I would call to see him about his problem, so I better do."

CHAPTER THIRTY-SEVEN

Discovery

The streets of town were still busy in the early evening, and traders were just packing their stalls up for the day. Many stayed open late with the days as long as they were. Reaching the outskirts of the town, SJ approached the church. The sun's evening rays shone brightly on the multitude of flowers that decorated the graveyard's grounds, their petals open, bathing in its warmth. SJ had always found it surreal to see the clash of life and death in one place.

As she approached the door to the church, it opened. Lythonian was just leaving.

"Hi, Lythonian," SJ said, smiling.

"Hey, SJ." Lythonian returned the smile with his toothy grin. "How can I help you? I was just locking up for the night."

"I have come to look at the ledgers for you if you wish. Sorry I didn't return immediately; I have been a little busy."

"That's okay. Let me go and grab them."

SJ followed Lythonian back into the church and collected the journals. There were six heavy leather-bound affairs.

"These are all the church's financial details from the past four years. I thought it may help if I gave you some from before I started."

"That could be useful, thank you. I will start looking through them and see if anything stands out."

"I have always been meticulous in my record-keeping, so I hope it is not an error I have made," Lythonian said with a worried look.

SJ picked up the heavy books and added them to her inventory, thankfully removing the need to carry them. Her display triggered.

Quest: Find the Source
Locate the discrepancy in funds and find out what is happening.
Rewards: 200xp + Reputation
Would you like to accept the quest? **Yes/No**

SJ accepted. Noticing a small icon on her display she hadn't seen before, she selected it. A quest log screen opened, displaying a list of quests either in progress or completed. That would make tracking things easier, and she remembered Dave had mentioned that displays could be altered and that she would have to investigate the interface more to see what else it had available.

"I will return the books as soon as I can."

"I have just started a new ledger today, so I do not require those back immediately."

"I hope I can understand it before you are dragged away to answer charges."

"Thank you. I was just going to get some food; would you like to join me?"

"That would be nice." SJ hadn't eaten today, and her stomach growled.

Lythonian locked the church, and they walked back to the rectory. The small house on the edge of town was one of the plainest SJ had seen. There was nothing ostentatious about it, and it was obvious that Lythonian didn't live a life of luxury. He fussed in the kitchen for a while before bringing out two bowls of stew.

"What is it?" SJ asked.

"Vegetable stew. It is home-cooked, and I grow the vegetables in the garden."

SJ picked up a wooden spoon she had been given and tasted the food. It was delicious and reminded her of the stews her mum made in wintertime. It was strange to have it on a summer day, but the weather here didn't change much.

After finishing the meal and wishing Lythonian a good evening, she returned to the inn. It was still heaving and filled with the sounds of laughing and singing as she approached. It really was the hub of the town. After walking to the bar and getting a coffee, she went to her room. Removing the books from her inventory and placing them on a table, she began the laborious task of reading through them.

"I need a pencil and paper," SJ said suddenly.

Dave had remained quiet throughout her time with Lythonian and only spoke up now.

"For what?" he said, yawning.

"Why are you yawning? You don't sleep."

"Do you know how boring it is watching someone read through ledgers and look at numbers for so long, randomly muttering to herself?"

"It hasn't been that long," SJ replied, then looked at the time on her display. She had been going through them for nearly four hours, and the light had faded outside. It brought back memories of her work, when colleagues frequently reminded her to take breaks in the evenings. When she got focused, she lost all track of time. "Okay. A little longer than I expected, perhaps. It's fascinating, though, seeing how everything has been recorded. Just glancing at the difference between the years before Lythonian took over and now . . . his records are so thorough, I can see why he is confused at where any loss may have come from."

"This has to be one of the most boring quests I have ever witnessed."

"It's not boring. Numbers are fascinating." SJ smiled.

"For you, maybe. They are not for me."

"Are you not an AI who talks about altering his code, which is basically just ones and zeros?"

"Oh no. Coding is much more than that. Imagine a DNA string made up of multiple strands of detailed information. Now, that is interesting."

SJ had never got her head around coding. It had always seemed like a foreign language to her. Some of SJ's friends had thought her passion for her work a little strange, but she had always loved numbers and working with them. If she hadn't become a forensic accountant, she was pretty sure she would have been an accountant anyway. The economics behind the financial sector had always interested her, and listening to Setu describe the town's way of working had enthralled her.

"I still need a pencil and paper to make notes, though."

Just then, there was a knock at the door, and she heard an excited voice outside.

"SJ? Are you there?"

She didn't recognise the voice straight away.

"Who is it?"

"Fhyliss."

SJ opened the door and saw Fhyliss standing before her with a grinning face.

"Hi, Fhyliss. What's wrong?"

"Oh. Nothing is wrong. I just came to say thank you."

"Thank you for what?"

"Mayor Maxwell told us that if it wasn't for you, we might have ended up in lockdown again."

"Oh, he did?" SJ was surprised that he had admitted his shortcomings, and she felt a new level of respect for him.

"Mum says that you can stay with us next week for free. That is if you were planning on staying here longer?"

"That would be amazing, and yes, I plan on staying. I don't suppose you know where I can get a pencil and paper, do you?"

"Sure. I can get you some; follow me."

SJ left the room, locked the door, and followed Fhyliss farther down the hallway. She had never even walked to the end of the hall, only ever stopping at her door. The hall turned a corner and came to another door. Taking a key from her pocket, Fhyliss opened the door and let SJ inside.

"Is this where you live?"

"Yes. This is home," Fhyliss replied.

The area must have taken up nearly half the floor space of the inn below, and there was a large open living room and then bedrooms off the main room. There was no kitchen area, which made sense with the kitchen downstairs. Fhyliss walked to one of the doors and opened it. SJ expected a bedroom, but she was completely taken aback by what she saw. The inside of the small room was an artist's paradise. Pictures and paintings were everywhere, from creatures to landscapes to people.

"Wow. Are these yours?" SJ asked in amazement.

"Yes. I paint and draw in my spare time." Fhyliss walked over to a small table and rifled through a drawer before removing a notebook and then picking up a pencil from a pot on her desk. "Here you go, this should do you," she said, handing them to SJ.

"Thank you. I will get them back to you when I'm finished."

"No, keep them. I have loads of spares, and just let me know if you need any more."

"You should put your artwork on display in the inn."

"Do you think so?"

"Yes. It's amazing."

"I may speak to Mum and see what she thinks."

"I bet you could sell some of those quite easily."

"I have never thought about selling any of them. I just paint and draw because I enjoy it."

Wishing Fhyliss a good night, SJ went back to her room. It was coming close to midnight, but by the sounds of the bar, things were still in full swing, and Fhyliss had to get back to help. SJ's display triggered.

> Congratulations! Your reputation with Fhyliss was raised to Friendly.

SJ went back into her room and continued looking through the ledgers.

"SJ!" Dave shouted.

SJ woke, realising she had fallen asleep while still working through the ledgers. She sat upright, stretching and standing from the desk.

"Morning. I can't believe I fell asleep at the desk."

"You were snoring well," Dave chuckled.

SJ looked at the time. It was 08:05. She had no idea when she fell asleep. She had some suspicions over what may have happened to the money and needed to start investigating. She had written a list of individuals from the ledger accounts she wanted to speak to. It felt just like being back on Earth; her passion for getting to the truth burned inside her.

"Exercises, breakfast, and then off to work," SJ said cheerily.

"You sound happy this morning."

"I have things to do and people to see."

With a quick wash in the cold water from the pump, she freshened herself up and left the inn, heading to the meadow. The early morning sun shone brightly on the picturesque scene, and she got straight into her training regime. Returning to the inn shortly after, she felt much better this morning.

"Please remind me to do my wing exercises later," she told Dave as she ate breakfast. She had gone for a bowl of porridge with sweet honey this morning, and SJ had no idea how Floretta made porridge taste so amazing. Drinking the last of her coffee, she went up to the room, gathered the notebook and pencil, and then left to begin her rounds of speaking to people.

It was later in the afternoon before SJ returned to the inn, having spoken to half a dozen town members about various things related to the church. She had not said what she was doing but had got snippets of information from the people she spoke to. Due to this, she had started to draw suspicions about two of them. One was a female elf named Lorian, and the other was a male dwarf named Cet. There were minor anomalies in the journals about the charity donations that had been recorded and transferred to town members. Reading the journals had brought to light that the town's economy was not as affluent as it seemed and that several had to survive through donations.

The elf and dwarf oversaw the church's food bank. It was funded through charitable donations, but when SJ investigated the income and expenditure, small anomalies showed payments had been made without reference to goods received. She had realised that it was not just Lythonian who filled the ledgers; several church congregation members helped complete them.

"The town is not as well off as it seems. I had my suspicions when we went to the jail, but they are even more apparent now," SJ said.

"I must agree. On the surface, the town seems like everything works well, and everyone is happy, but I think there is a darker side to it," Dave replied.

"I am going to visit some of the areas of town where these food bank donations are stated as being delivered."

SJ was only aware of the one area of town, near the barracks, where the buildings had seemed poorer, but when reviewing the journal, there were several neighborhoods. She asked for directions to one of the named streets, and a kind old kobold told her where to go.

The location was towards the east of town, and she had not been there before. The streets were much closer, the thatches almost touching, and as she walked down the street, she was stared at by several of the occupants. Feeling a little uncomfortable, she looked for the address she had noted down and went straight to it. Two large gnolls were standing down the street, and it looked like they were drinking. Several small groups were on the streets, and it reminded SJ of film scenes of the streets in some cities. People stood or sat outside calling and shouting to each other. She expected to see a car suddenly drive down the road and a shooting start.

Knocking on the door, she waited a few moments before the door was opened by an ancient, shabbily dressed, and emaciated-looking dwarf. All dwarves she had seen were what she would describe as typical: large, barrel-chested, with muscular arms and chests. This dwarf was anything but.

"Can I help you?" he said, coughing.

"Hi. I just want to check that your deliveries have been getting to you okay."

"Deliveries?"

"From the food bank," SJ said quietly, not wishing to be overheard by anyone nearby.

"I get something once a fortnight. It's not much, but better than nothing, and since I can't work anymore, it helps."

"Once a fortnight? Is that all?" SJ said, a little surprised.

The dwarf coughed again, covering his mouth. "Sorry. This damn illness."

"What do you suffer with, if you don't mind me asking?"

"LitRPG."

"What is that?"

"Lithium Respiratory Poisoning Gasteyli."

"That sounds serious."

"It is incurable. Once you catch the bug, you can't get rid of it. I worked in the mithril mines of Horhtuji for years, and no one knew that there was a lithium vein until years after we had been mining there."

"You poor thing."

"I am lucky compared to many who worked there. Several have lost their lives since. I moved away and initially came here because my sister lived here, but I have been by myself since she passed away."

"You have no other family?"

"No. I have always been chasing the mithril dream. Mining was everything to me, and now I am too old and frail to do anything beneficial for the town."

SJ felt sorry for the old dwarf; her heartstrings were pulled by his tale.

"LitRPG is one of only a few incurable illnesses on Amathera," Dave said.

The ledgers recorded deliveries to this dwarf three times per week, yet he had said he only received fortnightly supplies. Each transaction had been recorded in the journals, and this was where things didn't add up. The expenditure for the food that was being purchased did not match what was listed. Everything seemed to have been overpriced. She had spent the morning walking around the market traders and checking the food prices and knew that all this copper would soon add up. At least fifty individuals or families received support through the church.

"Can I help you with anything while I am here?" SJ asked.

"No. I have what I need: a bed, a roof over my head, and food when it comes."

"Thanks for your time, then," SJ said, smiling at the old dwarf.

"It was nice to get a visit, especially by such a pretty face," he replied, smiling back before another bout of coughing hit him.

Walking away, SJ whispered to Dave. "I think I know what they have been doing. I need to check with another few families before I can confirm."

"It sounds like you have a plan."

"I am not sure what to do about it yet, but if I can get enough evidence, I should be able to challenge those I believe are responsible."

"You think it's the elf or dwarf?"

"I think both. I don't think that one could be doing it without the other. One shows the food bank's income, and the other shows the outgoings. If I have reviewed the logs properly, they are skimming a significant amount of funds weekly. They have also run food drives, which seem to have not been directed to those who need it."

"You enjoy this sort of work, don't you?"

"Yes."

She spent the rest of the afternoon visiting other families and individuals listed in the ledgers. Two she was alarmed to find out no longer even lived in the town. Everyone she visited told her the same: They received fortnightly deliveries, although everyone had several weekly deliveries listed. It was soon adding up by looking at the differences in funding to outlay and then considering what was being taken in total.

There were a hundred twenty-four people named across all the entries, including individual family members. One family made up a significant number of the list. That was Little Stuart's. She had called in to visit, finding the small three-room property overrun with ratkin. She wondered how they survived and now understood how hard it must be for Little Stuart and why his bellpop capturing was so important.

SJ returned to the inn and ordered food, feeling guilty when it arrived and was placed in front of her. It tasted divine, like her other meals, but she only picked at it half-heartedly. Unable to finish the food, she grabbed a coffee and headed back upstairs.

Dave reminded her to do her exercises, and she sat on the sofa, completing her fourth set for the day. The burning lessened each time she did them, and she could feel slight improvements in her wing movements.

After running herself a bath and climbing in, she made mental calculations about the potential money being siphoned from the church.

One hundred twenty-four people miss five deliveries a fortnight . . . Say an average of 5 copper per meal, which equates to 3,100 copper. Then, over two years, multiplying by a further fifty-two for the fortnightly consideration, it comes to 161,200 copper, which translates to 16 gold and 12 silver. If the church said it was 12 gold short in funding, this 16 gold would easily cover the shortfall.

The difference was in the way the transactions were recorded for overpriced goods. She had seen a similar practise back on Earth, where people buy cheap and sell high or buy high and sell cheap, depending on the fund movement between parties.

She knew she had gathered enough evidence, but what to do with it?

CHAPTER THIRTY-EIGHT

Heresy

Breakfast was hogling rashers, hogling sausages, and two fried eggs. The only thing it needed was mushrooms and baked beans. SJ mopped up the final bit of egg yolk with her bread. Smacking her lips in satisfaction, she let out a fulfilled sigh. The inn was quiet, with only a couple of patrons eating breakfast. Picking up her coffee, she walked to the hatch.

"Morning, Floretta." SJ was sure she didn't sleep.

"Morning, SJ. Everything okay?"

"Delicious as always. I have a favour to ask."

"Of course."

"Do you have any mushrooms at all here in Amathera? They would go a treat fried up with the rest for breakfast."

"Umm. We do. I have never even thought of it. The forest ones would go well. I will get some and see how they turn out. Thanks for the suggestion."

"No problem." SJ smiled and put her now-empty coffee mug on the bar as she walked towards her daily training routine.

After finishing her kata practise and first wing exercises, she lay back in the early morning sun, soaking in its rays.

"I have been thinking what to do next," she said.

"And what have you decided?" Dave asked.

"I have all the paperwork evidence and the information from the food bank recipients, but I have no physical evidence that they are doing anything wrong."

"So, what is your plan?"

"I am going to do a stake-out."

"OOOO. That sounds fun. Just like in the movies."

"I am not sure how fun it will be, but I have references for the food vendors in the ledgers, and if I keep an eye on them, I may be able to witness some transactions."

"This is much better than reading pages of numbers," Dave said, finishing in a bored, droning voice.

"I wouldn't be thinking about it without the boring numbers."

"When you see them do something wrong, you can swoop in and arrest them like they do in the films."

"I don't have any powers to arrest anyone."

"Okay. Just swoop in and kill them, then."

"I can't just randomly kill people!"

"You are an assassin . . . It's your calling."

"I will only kill people if I have to or if they are evil."

"Thieves are not evil, then?"

SJ didn't reply.

As they headed back to the inn, Dave was whispering in her head about his favourite stake-out scenes from films. SJ headed upstairs and changed into the clothes she had bought from Fizzlewick, including the cloak. Pulling the cloak up around her face and looking in the mirror, she was hardly recognisable compared to the beautiful dress she usually wore. She went to place her dress in the wardrobe and then decided against it, placing it in her inventory instead. To her surprise, it fit into one of the tailoring slots. If she needed to change into it for better protection, she would.

She began her investigation by making sure she could remember the names of the stall-holders from whom the two suspects had purchased. No one paid any attention to her as she went downstairs and left the inn, and although she had got to know several people in the town by sight, they didn't seem to notice her as she walked down the streets with her head dropped so that her face didn't show fully.

Enough people were going about their daily lives, and another person walking in a cloak was nothing special. The whole day was spent moving from trader to trader on the list, and it was not until very late that afternoon, when one of the fresh produce traders was packing up, that the elf she knew as Lorian approached the goblin stall-holder.

SJ was standing in a small alley. No one noticed her watching in the shadows. The goblin began to fill a couple of the crates with older produce for the elf. SJ watched as money changed hands and Lorian walked away, the goblin saying he would drop them off at the church hall later.

SJ had not even realised there was a church hall and now had to find it, but first, she needed to speak to the goblin.

"Hi, there," she said as she approached the stall.

"Sorry. I am closing for the day. I have a delivery to make."

"It's about the purchase that elf just made."

"What about it?" the goblin said, turning for the first time and seeming slightly surprised to see SJ's face under the hood of her cloak.

SJ smiled at the goblin sweetly, and he squirmed a little from her gaze. She was, after all, a beautiful fae.

"How much did she buy?"

"Everything is going past its best. She regularly pops in and purchases it, which saves it from going to waste."

"That's generous of her."

"She works for the church, delivering food parcels."

"That's a noble sacrifice."

"She is a good one, Lorian."

"You know her well?"

"Not that well, but she is always helping with the church."

"I would like to reimburse her for her continual generosity. Could you let me know how much she paid?"

"Of course. She bought all the old stock for twelve copper. I need to go and deliver two whole crates' worth so they can be sent out."

"Thanks for your help, and don't tell her if you see her. I want it to be a surprise when I reimburse her."

The goblin smiled at SJ, and she turned and left.

It took SJ another two days to investigate her suspects before she witnessed further purchases. Not all stall-holders had fallen for her reimbursement comment. A couple said she could just donate to the church instead. She knew how much the elf and dwarf had spent on the other goods, though, so she headed to the church at the end of day three.

Lythonian was in the vestry when she arrived.

"Welcome, SJ. How are you getting on?"

"Very well, I hope. I just need to finalise a few details. Do you have the current ledger available?"

"Of course." Lythonian reached behind him to a bookcase, withdrew the ledger, and handed it to her.

"I see that it is not just you who enters information."

"No. There are several who help."

SJ flipped the ledger open to the last page, reading through the entered information, and the evidence was there. Both of her suspects had entered the entries she was looking for by hand. Lorian's purchase, which she had witnessed two days prior, showed she had paid out eighty-four copper. That was seventy-two more than she had actually paid for the produce. There were entries from the dwarf with differing numbers as well.

"Got you," she said excitedly.

"Got me?" Lythonian asked, confused.

"No. Sorry. I have the evidence to prove what is happening to the money."

"Really?" Lythonian said with surprise.

"Yes. The question is, how do we now challenge them?"

"With blades and violence," Dave interrupted.

"What have you discovered?" Lythonian asked.

"Both Lorian and Cet are skimming from the books."

"Skimming?"

"They have been saying they have spent more than they have and registering false amounts in the ledger. They have been purchasing old food and not delivering what they say they have been."

"What? How do you know?" Lythonian was shocked to hear the information.

SJ explained what she had found and witnessed and the information she had gathered. Her case was solid, with only one outstanding question still confusing her.

"Do they take money from the church's coffers to pay for the goods?"

"Yes. They both have access to the money."

"Where is it kept?"

"Here in the vestry."

"How much should be in there now?"

Lythonian turned the ledger around and scanned the totals. "Should be 2 gold, 74 silver, 289 copper."

"How often do you check the total?"

Lythonian went quiet for a moment. "I just keep the tally in the ledger," he eventually said, blushing.

"You don't check?"

"The volunteers have been congregation members longer than I have. They know more about everything than I do."

"You have been here two years, though!" SJ exclaimed.

Lythonian was embarrassed. "I will check it now." He coughed, stood, and walked to a small cupboard. Inside, he withdrew a small chest and, placing it on the table, removed a key from under his armour and opened it.

The coins were counted and stacked in neat piles on his desk a while later. It was forty-two silver and eighty-nine copper down. Lythonian was in turmoil over the shortfall.

"How often do they access it?"

"Almost daily because of the food they purchase."

"And when does it get emptied?"

"The church receives a monthly stipend. Recently, we have been low on funds to pay it all."

"How much do you pay monthly?"

"Four gold; it is based on expected contributions."

Four gold was a significant sum, and SJ was surprised the church made so much. Everything had fallen into place over what had happened, and SJ needed to confront the pair now.

"Do you know where they will be now?"

"They are usually at the church hall sorting out deliveries. I never really go there as I am busy running the various services here."

"Well, shall we go and visit?"

They left the church after Lythonian locked everything up, and she followed him right out of the church. SJ had never been down this way before, and after several hundred feet, they came to a single-storey building with a sign advertising it as the CHURCH OF AMATHERA COMMUNITY HALL.

They entered the hall. Inside were rows of tables with small crates on top of them. Two young kobolds were busy splitting food down into the crates.

"Have you seen Lorian or Cet?" Lythonian asked.

They pointed towards the back room. Lythonian walked up to the door and tried the handle. It was locked, so he knocked on the door. "Lorian, Cet, are you there?"

There was movement behind the door, and after a few moments, they heard a key turn, and the door was pulled open. Cet stood there. "Lythonian, what brings you here away from your important work at the church?" he said, grinning at him.

"I need to ask some questions. Is that okay?"

"Please come in."

They walked inside. The room was about half the size of the main hall area, and there were a couple of large desks and two sofas. SJ thought it was very well-furnished for the back room of a church hall. Lorian sat lounging on one of the sofas.

"Take a seat, my friend, and what can we do for you both?"

Lorian smiled charmingly at Lythonian, and SJ was sure he looked away shyly. SJ placed her hand on Lythonian's shoulder, and the large draconian turned and looked at her.

"Allow me." SJ had faced down many people like this before. "It has become apparent that the church is losing money. I was asked to investigate this issue and have concluded my findings. I will ask you both now if you have anything you wish to say. It will be best for you if it's stated now."

Since SJ had drunk the dragon's blood, her senses had heightened. She could feel an immediate tension in the air and noticed the smallest of glances between the two.

"I am not sure what you are referring to," Cet replied, frowning.

SJ explained her findings and was in the process of commencing her conclusion to the issues when her senses went into overdrive. She had felt nothing like it before and noticed the slightest movement from Lorian's hand. She dived sideways as the bolt of ice shot at where she had been standing. Her display flashed.

Precognition triggered—cool-down 24 hours

The gigantic bolt would have torn her in two. Lythonian gasped in shock as the bolt of ice penetrated the room's wooden wall easily. Screams from the kobold children in the main hall could be heard. In the same instant, Cet drew an axe from his belt and charged at Lythonian. SJ triggered identification.

Cetius Hillgrinder	
Race:	Dwarf
Level:	7
Hit Points:	75
Mana Points:	35
Attacks:	Chop, Cleave

Lorian Mercanji	
Race:	Elf
Level:	8
Hit Points:	45
Mana Points:	35 of 85
Attacks:	Ice Magic, Stab

Lythonian Waryista	
Race:	Draconian
Level:	13
Hit Points:	70
Mana Points:	140
Attacks:	Holy Smite, Strike

SJ was shocked that Lythonian was Level 13. Considering his mannerisms and being in a starter town, she had thought he was much lower. As SJ watched, a spiked mace and a shield appeared in his hands. The shield was brilliant white and emblazoned with the church's emblem.

"For the church," Lythonian screamed as he intercepted Cet's attack.

SJ ran towards Lorian. She was dangerous as a mage, but looking at her mana, she had already thrown her most powerful spell. As SJ moved, her blades appeared on her hands. She was about twenty feet from Lorian when Cet brought his axe down on Lythonian's shield with the loud clang of metal on metal.

Lythonian took the strike with no movement in his shield arm and swung his mace with speed and precision, smashing it into the side of Cet's body. The power behind the strike was immense, and Cet was knocked sideways, his shorter, stocky form hurled across the room. He gathered himself again and went at Lythonian.

SJ reached Lorian, and her dagger appeared in her hand. She went to stab SJ. Ignoring the weapon, SJ moved in close to get within striking range. There was no way that Lorian could cast with SJ so close to her, and she lashed out with her blades. A shimmer appeared around Lorian as she struck, and her blades came up short against a blue glow, casting sparks around her fist.

Lorian's blade scraped against SJ's side, making her wince in pain. Stepping back from the mage, she identified Lorian again. Her mana was now down to 10. SJ kicked out her foot, coming up short against the blue shield again. Lorian attacked again, extending her arm outside of her shield. This time, SJ moved back and defensively swept down with her blades. Her blades cut deep into Lorian's arm, causing slashing damage, and she dropped her blade.

SJ heard a roar and saw Cet powering at Lythonian, swinging his axe in a wild frenzy. SJ thought he must be a berserker. Lythonian took the assault on his shield, looking calm and patient. Lorian cried out, pulling her bleeding arm back and holding it across her body. The strike had taken a third off her health. SJ was not finished and kicked out again. The shield flared, but its colour was dimming. Striking out with quick successive punches, she powered them into the shield. It flickered and flared at the strikes, sparks flying from it as her claws struck, and then it gave way.

Lorian had not attacked again, simply backing up and allowing SJ to strike her shield. As the shield dropped, the mage took a last stand, firing a missile at SJ at close range. She had no time to react, and the magical bolt flew deep into her chest. Screaming in pain, she staggered backwards, reaching up to her chest as the bolt vanished from existence once it had done its damage. Her health from the dagger and the bolt was now down to twelve hit points.

Lorian rushed SJ with her dagger swinging wildly. It was obvious Lorian was not a mêlée combatant. Even with the fog of the pain from the magic bolt, SJ could defend, parrying her strikes with relative ease. SJ saw an opening and struck, ducking and striking with her kick at Lorian's knee. The kick was true, and Lorian cried in pain as her knee gave out. She stumbled sideways, and SJ saw a blue bottle in her hand.

It had to be mana, and SJ had to stop her from drinking it. As she raised the bottle to her lips, SJ lunged forward, striking with the blades. They dug deep into her side, and Lorian gasped, almost dropping the bottle. SJ heard a terrifying scream and glanced to see the mace of Lythonian coming down on Cet's head. The crunching and cracking sounds were sickening.

Lorian kicked out herself at SJ, catching her in her midriff again, and tried to drink the bottle. The furniture in the room had been scattered in the fight, a sofa overturned and a table broken in half from either a mace or axe blow. SJ suddenly felt warmth flood her body and, turning, saw a white streaming light erupting from Lythonian's outstretched hand. Her pain lessened, and she watched as her health rapidly increased back to full.

SJ grinned at the sensation and stepped in to finish Lorian. Swipes and strikes rained towards the mage, and she too busy trying to dodge the blows to drink her potion. SJ again struck true, puncturing her in her shoulder with a forward punch. Lorian coughed up blood. Her health was down to the last couple of hit points now. She fell to her knees, holding her lacerated shoulder with one hand and her punctured side with the other. The blue bottle was now resting on the floor, spilling its liquid.

Lythonian stepped forward, towering over the now-quaking mage.

"Lorian. I have relied on your support for the past two years, and you have gone against me, the church, and the good people of this town. Through the Order of Amathera, I charge you with the crime of heresy and sentence you to death."

SJ watched in stunned amazement as Lythonian swung his mace at her head.

CHAPTER THIRTY-NINE

A Bolt from the Blue

Lorian's dead body fell sideways to the floor. Lythonian stood still, watching the light fade from her eyes before he turned.

"Are you okay?"

SJ was shocked at the icy demeanour that Lythonian had shown; she'd never expected the cleric who spent his days praying and providing services for so many gods to be so ruthless and effective. He did not look as though Cet had even landed one strike on him, and his cloak and clothes still shone with the bright white of his order.

"I am fine."

"Good. I will need to report this to the mayor."

"Will you not get in trouble?"

"No. This is church property, and I am the leading member of the Order in town. I will only do it out of politeness."

"That was awesome. Did you see how great Lythonian was?" Dave asked.

SJ didn't reply, instead looking at the state the room was now in, with blood covering various areas and the furniture destroyed.

"At least you now have the evidence to clear your name."

"I do, and it is thanks to you," Lythonian said.

SJ heard the crying from the other room and turned to glance at the door.

Lythonian said, "I will speak to the children. They will be traumatised if they witnessed the fight at all."

There was an enormous gaping hole in the wall where the huge ice spike had shot through it. Lythonian turned to walk to the door. SJ removed her blades and bent to loot Lorian's corpse.

> 70xp awarded for the death of Lorian Mercanji
> 2 x Light Mana Potions, 1 x Dagger of Piercing, 1 x Robes of the Wanderer, 4 x Gold, 17 x Silver, 23 x Copper

SJ gawped at the amount of gold, knowing its value, especially in the town, and then identified the dagger and robes.

> **Dagger of Piercing**
> Quality: Good
> Damage: 5–8

> **Robes of the Wanderer**
> Grade: Rare
> Quality: Rare
> Durability: Good
> Enchantment Slots: 1
> Armour Class: 5
> Attributes: Improves mana regeneration by 100% when out of combat

Lythonian walked back through.

"I have looted Lorian. She has some of your missing gold." SJ called the four gold and the seventeen silver from her inventory and handed them to Lythonian.

"Thank you," Lythonian said, and walked over to loot Cet's body. "Another seven gold and four silver. That is nearly all twelve returned. I should be okay with the remainder to balance the books."

"At least that is one good thing to have come out of this."

"Do you need any of the equipment?" Lythonian asked.

"I don't know what he has."

"Chain-mail armour—it's a decent set, dwarven-made, with an axe + 2, rations, and a backpack."

"No. I am fine."

"I will sell it for the church, then. The axe should raise a few silver, at least."

"I got some robes and a dagger from Lorian."

"Keep them if you wish. I have no need for mage items."

SJ quickly searched the room. There was nothing else of value, so she and Lythonian left the hall. Lythonian locked up after them, and they returned to the church. Once in the vestry, Lythonian removed the chest and placed the gold and silver inside. As Lythonian closed the lid, SJ's display triggered.

> **Quest: Find the Source—Complete**
> You located and dealt with the heretics undermining the church's work.
> Rewards: 200xp + 20% = 240xp awarded

> Congratulations on reaching Level 6
> You have been awarded the following:
> 5 hit points
> 5 mana points
> +1 Dexterity
> +2 free points to distribute as you wish

SJ added +1 each to Charisma and Wisdom, which made all her base attributes at least ten and boosted her secondary bonus, meaning all her attributes earned minor bonuses.

↻Level: 6	
Experience:	231 of 800
Hit Points:	39
Mana Points:	35
Dexterity:	16
Wisdom:	10
Charisma:	11

"You are progressing really well," Dave said proudly.

"Thank you again for your help, SJ," Lythonian said. "If you require healing at any time, do not hesitate to come and see me."

"I will, and may I ask you a favour?"

"Of course, what is it?"

"Could you possibly not include me in the story with the mayor? I would prefer to stay out of the limelight if that is possible."

"If you wish. Although I am sure he would wish to thank you for helping remove trash from the town."

"I just want to level quietly if I can," SJ replied, smiling.

"Don't worry. I will not say you were involved if that is what you wish."

"Thank you. I'm heading back to the inn. If you need anything, please let me know."

"I will, and thank you again. You have saved me from a lot of trouble."

> Congratulations! Your reputation with Lythonian was raised to Liked.

"Your knitting is coming along," Dave said.

SJ had just finished the fourth pair of woollen socks. They looked more like open-ended tubes rather than socks, but they had registered as poor-quality items and counted as four of the five she needed to complete her tailoring quest. Alongside the morning training routine and wing exercises, she had spent almost all the next day on them.

"I am not sure I can call these *coming along*," she said, picking up one of the tubes and pulling it onto her arm. It was more like the woollen sleeves she had owned back on Earth, and she could poke her fingers through the larger holes she had left.

"Only one pair left, and then onto Level 3."

"I need to finish this last pair," SJ replied, picking up the knitting needles and continuing. She had been getting faster with each pair. Another hour passed before she eventually finished the fifth.

"It took a whole day to make five pairs of socks," SJ said as she placed the last pair down. This last pair looked like they had a heel, and when she identified them, they showed a common quality.

> Congratulations! Tailoring Apprentice Level 2 completed.
> Quest: Tailoring Apprentice—Level 3
> Collect 10 bundles of cloth.
> Would you like to accept the quest? **Yes/No**

"I think I need to see Fizzlewick again."

SJ looked at her profession screen and noticed the list of potential recipes had increased. She could now learn various woollen item recipes, plus cloth gloves. SJ thought it must be the next crafting recipe she would need to make. It was early evening when SJ headed towards the tailor's shop. She was not sure it would even be open. Upon arriving, she discovered her apprehensions were right; a sign on the door read CLOSED.

"Damn. I wanted to get the cloth bundles and get to Level 4."

"We can come back in the morning. It isn't as if you don't have time," Dave said.

"I know. I know," SJ sighed.

Heading back into the centre of the town, SJ's senses tingled. Her increased senses felt so strange, and considering what had happened the last time they had triggered like this, she scanned the area, looking for a potential threat. She could not see anything or anyone.

"I sensed something," she whispered as she continued down the street.

"I can't see anything," Dave replied.

"I know. It's strange, though. Something doesn't feel right."

The scream came from off to her left. SJ turned and ran towards the sound. Running down a side street, she came out onto the street behind the tailor's shop and saw a group of townsfolk standing around something on the ground. SJ walked over and tried to gently elbow her way through the gathering crowd. A deep voice boomed out.

"Step back. Give me room."

SJ saw Captain Broadaxe's stocky and powerful form making its way through the parting crowd. Lying on the ground was the form of a dryad, blood covering the cobbles where she lay. SJ could see a bolt sticking out from her chest. Captain Broadaxe bent down next to the still form and felt for a pulse.

More of the guards arrived and pushed the crowd back, clearing more room around the body. SJ could hear people muttering in the crowd about a second murder.

Captain Broadaxe spoke to the guards before turning to the gathered crowd.

"Everyone needs to leave and go about their business. Standing here is not helping the situation."

A voice cried from the crowd. "That's another murder. Why haven't you found the suspect yet?" More muttering and grumbling supported the call, and SJ could see the frustration etched on Captain Broadaxe's face.

"I SAID EVERYONE NEEDS TO LEAVE," he bellowed, anger visible on his face, his beard twitching.

SJ was moving away from the area when she saw a face she recognised.

"Gary."

Gary turned from where he was ushering townsfolk away. "Hi, SJ. I'm a little busy, sorry. Come on, you heard the captain. Move back and on your way," he said loudly.

SJ turned to leave and made her way back towards the inn. "Another dead body," she whispered.

"Yes. It's strange in a starter town for there to be a murder."

"I haven't helped."

"Yours was legitimate."

"It still doesn't feel good."

"Meh. It's your job and calling now, remember? I am not sure who would have killed a dryad. They are usually among the most respected races because of their natural skills at supporting town growth by providing crops and the like."

The news arrived at the inn before SJ. One thing that was apparent in the town was the speed of gossip. It was like an information highway, and if SJ hadn't known better, she could have sworn they all had mobiles and messaged each other. The room was even more crowded than usual; it was a gossipmonger's paradise. SJ stood at the bar and waited patiently to order a coffee while listening to the chatter.

The dryad who had been found dead was a farmer. She spent her days in the fields caring for the crops and was well-liked and revered by the town. The fact that she had been shot with a bolt just by the edge of town had started the tongues wagging that it may have been someone from outside who killed her. The thing was, no one could work out why she would be targeted.

One story mentioned she had had an affair with an elf's husband, but this was quickly refuted, and the comment almost caused a brawl until Bert stepped in to calm everyone down. Looking at Bert, you would expect he would be the strong arm of the inn, but it appeared more feared Kerys when she raised her voice than Bert.

"Coffee, please," SJ called to Kerys over the growing din.

"Sure," she called back, grabbing a mug and bringing the pot over. SJ had realised that she was the only one who ever seemed to drink coffee in the evenings, and Kerys left her with the pot so she could serve herself.

Kerys was alone at the moment and run off her feet, trying to contend with the growing crowd. It seemed she had not expected such an influx so early. "You need a hand?" SJ called to her.

Kerys glanced at her briefly. "If you could grab some empties, that would be helpful. Fhyliss is on her break for another thirty minutes yet."

SJ smiled in response. After savouring one more bitter swig from her coffee, she put her mug and coffee-pot on the bar and made her way around the room. She collected empty glasses off several tables, which earned her confused but grateful nods from several of the patrons. She was a beautiful fae, after all, and several of the males' eyes lingered on her a little longer than they would if their wives or loved ones had been around.

The thirty minutes passed quickly, and soon, Fhyliss appeared back in the bar area and took over from SJ, who returned to the end of the bar where she had left her coffee mug and poured herself another cup. Kerys briefly thanked her before being dragged away to serve more customers.

It was not long after that Gary and Setu arrived at the bar. They walked up to order drinks, and when Setu saw SJ, he came over to her, grinning.

"Hi, SJ. I have been waiting to see you," he said.

"Hi, Setu. Why, what's wrong?"

"Nothing. Margu has been awake for two days now, and after I explained everything you did to help, she said she wants you to come around for dinner."

"That would be very nice. When?"

"Tomorrow okay for you? She said she would cook hogling steaks as a treat."

"They aren't cheap," SJ replied.

"It's a special occasion. Without your help, we would not even have a stall now."

"Tell her I accept, and I look forward to it."

"Great. Do you want to come and sit with us?"

Gary smiled at SJ.

"Sure."

They walked over and took a table near the end of the bar, which was a little quieter.

Gary pulled a deck of cards from his pocket. "You ever played Hangman's Noose?"

"No. I have never heard of it," SJ replied.

"Time to learn, then," Gary said, and he dealt three piles of cards on the table.

It took SJ a while to pick up the rules of the game, but the cards were like cards from back on Earth; the only difference was the face cards. The Hangman's Noose was the name of the ace cards, and the jack was a knight, the queen an empress, and the king an emperor. The values were otherwise the same.

After a few practise hands, Gary suggested they play for copper. SJ declined and said she would watch the pair of them play. As they played, they discussed what had happened with the dryad.

"They think the bolt is hob."

"What?" Setu said in shock.

"Yup. They don't think it was an aimed shot. Looking at the angle at which it hit Florina, it was on its way down."

"But a bolt being fired randomly towards town? They have never done that before."

"They?" SJ asked.

"Hobgoblins from the valley. It has been a while since they last hit, and it was probably a scouting party or similar."

"How often do they attack?"

"Not very, but they are often out scouting. That's why we have so little on that side of town field-wise. Most farmers are based on the far side, so the town is between where the hobs would come from. No one wants to get caught up in a hobgoblin raid if they can help it."

"Why do you not have a wall?"

"It has been suggested many times, but Mayor Maxwell has always resisted it."

"Why would he not want to defend the town better?" SJ asked in surprise.

"It's not that he doesn't want to. It's more the cost involved. The town doesn't have endless coffers. We don't get many Legionnaires through here, so we rarely get the bonus payments for growth that other towns might."

"This is all down to this false economy, isn't it?"

"What do you mean by that?" Gary questioned, frowning.

"The town's economy seems to be self-sufficient. The movement of money seems to occur cyclically. It doesn't seem like wealth grows. Rather, the economy stays constant."

Gary's frown deepened, still unsure what SJ meant. Setu smiled, replying, "Like our fishing conversation. I agree, SJ. After we spoke about it, I think that is a pretty good view."

"I think that the money the town has seems to go from one to the next, then back into the town coffers as tax, and then regurgitated again. I don't think there is much the town can do to bring in more money without increasing the town's population."

"I think I understand what you mean," Gary eventually replied, after scratching his head thoughtfully.

It was obvious to SJ that Setu was the more intelligent of the two friends and understood much more about the town's economy.

"What is the plan with the hobs?"

"There is no plan, just increased guard presence on the town's borders."

"How far are your borders?"

"The edge of the first field out of the east of town is the general town border. That is why the Wandering Ogre is outside the town's jurisdiction. It is built past the boundary."

"Doesn't it get attacked by the hobs as well?"

"I am not aware it ever has been. It would not surprise me if Niweq had a deal struck with them. He is a crafty sod at the best of times."

"I met Niweq when I went looking for the alchemist."

"Careful," Dave suddenly said.

SJ, suddenly realising she mentioned she had been to the inn, changed the subject. "Talking about the alchemist, any more news on a suspect?"

"The half orc has never returned. That means we have no other suspects. Captain Broadaxe spoke to Mayor Maxwell today about closing that investigation down. Especially now that we will also have Florina's death to deal with."

"I see. From what you said, he sounds like the prime candidate." Thankfully, neither Setu nor Gary had noticed her slip.

"Captain Broadaxe said it was too much of a coincidence for him to go missing at the same time. Especially now we know about the scheme they were running."

The time passed quickly, watching Setu and Gary play. Setu came out as the overall winner between the pair, but it was all in good humour, unlike the last time SJ had seen them play.

"I need to get going," Gary said, downing the last of his ale.

"I should go as well," Setu said, hiccupping. He had been drinking honey wine and was on his third glass. Standing, he swayed gently.

"I am going to head to bed now myself. Tell Margu I will be there tomorrow."

SJ watched as Gary steadied Setu, supporting him as they left the bar. SJ smiled. It was nice having friends again.

CHAPTER FORTY

Martial Arts

Walking through the town's streets the following day, SJ felt as though there was uncertainty about everything after the dryad's death. The usually boisterous vendors seemed quieter. After waking, she had completed her daily training regime and decided it was a sparring day. She still had not progressed in her martial arts and could not advance her kata until she sought training. Following Gary's directions towards the barracks, she went around the side.

There was a fenced-in area made from wood standing fifteen feet high, and across the tops, metal shards had been placed, making it impossible to climb over without taking damage. It had to be the jail yard. Just beyond it was a small fenced-in compound. It had archery targets and training dummies with crudely drawn faces set up. It reminded SJ of a trip to Warwick Castle, where they put on shows as though it were medieval England.

There were at least twenty creatures training in the compound, whether with bow and arrow, crossbow, or various mêlée weapons. Some guards were sparring with wooden swords; their movements were swift and precise, and the dwarf overseeing them shouted praise or chastised poor form, whichever was deserved. There were grunts and groans and the rhythmic thud of wood on wood.

Across and behind the yard, SJ could see a stable area. It was the first she had seen since being in town, and several horses were being tended to. Spotting a ratkin, she thought it looked like Little Stuart but couldn't be sure.

Several small rings were off to one side of the compound. As SJ approached, she spotted Lorna's bright orange hair. The large, powerful woman grabbed an orc and, tilting her shoulder into him, sent him up and flying over her shoulder. He landed with an audible grunt on his back on the sandy ground.

"I have told you many times, stop leaving yourself open for a throw," Lorna snarled at the orc as he picked himself up.

SJ walked towards the ring. She got several looks from others training but paid them no attention. On reaching the ring, she stood listening to Lorna instructing the six guards being put through their paces.

"I want you all to complete three forms before you finish for the morning. And I mean three full forms," Lorna barked at them. Audible groans escaped the trainees' lips. Turning from the ring, Lorna saw SJ.

"Hello. Can I help you?" Lorna asked.

It was the first time SJ had seen her face, and she was beautiful. Her flowing orange hair looked like flames surrounding her face. She stood tall with a straight back, towering over SJ, and looked exceedingly strong.

SJ cleared her throat, feeling a little intimidated by the woman. "Hi. Gary directed me to speak to you about training."

"Ah, the fae monk."

"Yes. SJ. Nice to meet you."

Lorna stepped forward, holding out her hand and smiling at SJ. It was a disarming smile, and SJ knew behind it was a strength she could not challenge. Not yet, at least. SJ took her hand, and Lorna gently squeezed it. SJ tried not to flinch under the pressure.

"I am Lorna. We don't often get trainees, especially in martial arts. Most would go and see Brother Wilbert, especially considering you are a monk."

"I heard he was full and could not take any more trainees currently."

"Well, then, I need to know a little about you and your current skills if I am going to train you."

"I currently have Level 3 kata."

"At least you have something to start with. I will put you through your paces and see whether you wish to continue training with me. If you do, I ask that you donate to the Guards' Retirement Fund. I don't need to be paid for my time, as the town pays me."

"That sounds great. When would you like to start?"

"Now. First, I would like to see the kata form you have. Do you have something to change into? That dress will get ruined very quickly."

"Don't worry about the dress. It will be fine." SJ smiled.

Lorna raised an eyebrow in response. "If you say so, but don't blame me if it gets torn."

"It won't; don't worry."

"Kata, then?"

Lorna was not wasting any time, and SJ was shown to one of the training rings and got underway performing her katas. She had already completed them first thing, and they were so natural to her again now, she glided from one step to the next. Lorna watched in silence until she had finished.

"Very unusual style. I have not seen that before. Where did you start training?"

"I trained as a young girl and have not done it for a long time."

"The form is very defensive. There are strikes, but it is not an offensive style. Here, we train in a form known as Amar Ti. It is the most common of the styles and offers a much more offensive stance and approach. It is all about incapacitating and finishing the enemy quickly. Particularly good for open combat situations."

"I am happy to learn something new."

"Good. We will start with the basics and see how you get on."

By the time the training ground broke for lunch, SJ had been shown the basic stages of new katas, and she didn't know where the time had gone. The new forms allowed her to use her Dexterity to perform the moves with fluidity. SJ was impressed with Lorna and her instruction. She guided with precision and expertise and instructed SJ to emphasise mental discipline and resilience.

SJ quickly mastered the first two new kata forms. The style was much more aggressive, as Lorna had said. It worked on power and strike rate, and its potential excited SJ. She sat and joined the guards for a bowl of stew and water before returning to the training ring. She was already feeling the burn in her muscles and wasn't sure if she could keep this up all day.

The afternoon session was gruelling. It was no longer just the katas' forms but strength training. Her Dexterity was fine, but to gain the power that Lorna showed with her moves, she might have to invest some of her points in Constitution to prevent the pain from the strikes she performed. She joined the other trainees for part of their session as Lorna took them through different kicks and punches, and by the time the training ended, she was thoroughly exhausted.

SJ could not remember a time in her life when she had completed so much physical exercise in one day.

"Will you be back tomorrow?" Lorna asked, smiling at SJ as they left the training ground.

"Tomorrow?" SJ asked, surprised.

"We train most days with rest days as needed to develop and grow quickly. I am guessing you aim to train hard and fast."

Letting out a groan as she flexed her shoulders, she smiled weakly. "I'll be here . . . if I can move in the morning."

"You need some Dryac."

"What is Dryac?"

"It's a cream. You rub it on your sore muscles, and it soothes them. Works wonders."

"Where can I get some?"

"There is a healer near the town square. A gnoll called Grewlas runs the shop. He is an alchemist by trade but specialises in healing tonics and lotions. The best in town. His prices can be steep, but I would pay for his Dryac any day of the week compared to many others. Few specialise in specific areas of alchemy, and he has them down to a fine art."

"I will look into it. How do I go about donating to the fund?"

"If you see Captain Broadaxe, he is in charge of the retirement fund."

"Great. I will try to catch him tomorrow. Thanks for today; although I'm knackered, I did enjoy it."

Dave had been quiet most of the day and spoke once they walked away. "She is good."

"Good?"

"Her level is quite low, but her dedication to her art has meant that she is way beyond what you would expect."

"What level is she?"

"Level 17."

"That high? I never realised."

"The skill she shows in martial arts is what I would expect for someone in their thirties."

"Oh. That is impressive, then."

"Very. I think she has been away from the region to level at some point but returned, as she won't gain experience around here now to progress. That has not stopped her dedication to her skill, though."

"It is good to know she is that proficient." SJ was pleased with the revelation that she was being trained by someone knowledgeable. "I think I will visit Fizzlewick before seeing if I can get some Dryac and then a bath and bed."

It didn't take long to reach the tailor's shop, and the sign again showed CLOSED.

"I wonder where he is." SJ frowned.

"We could go and buy cloth somewhere else?"

"I suppose, but I need the recipes as well."

"We better wait, then."

A question had been bugging SJ for some time, and she needed to know the answer. "Dave."

"Yes."

"Why can't I identify more people and increase my identification skills faster?"

"You could identify more people if you wanted. It is just frowned upon."

"Why?"

"Most won't know you are doing it, but anyone with the skill or sometimes even a high enough Wisdom can pick up on it being done to them. Many who do class it as invading their privacy."

"Bob inspected me."

"That's a little different. Bob did prewarn you he was going to do something, and would you try and stop a Level 88 blue dragon doing what it wanted to do?"

"Fair point. I wish I could level it faster, though. Each level has benefits, but I can't start branching into other skills until it levels higher."

"You could always ask people if they mind. I am sure many won't, but just be prepared that some may take offence to it. That means that it can impact your reputation. I know I mentioned that there were only six levels. There are only six positive levels. There are also negative levels."

"Oh. You mentioned them but never detailed them."

"Similar steps as on the positive side: Neutral, Mistrusted, Against, Disliked, Hated, Detested."

"Can I set levels?"

"I am not sure. I have never known a Legionnaire to do it before." Surprise was etched in his voice.

"If people could do it to me, I would think I could do it back."

Silence.

"Nope. Impossible. It would be classed as playing the System. Theoretically, you could set everyone to revered and try to influence them to amend their status towards you. Only Amathereans are allowed to, and it is not a whimsical decision. It comes purely through interaction."

"That is a shame."

"I agree, but unfortunately, we can do nothing about that. Although it's another worthy attempt at finding a loophole," Dave said. "I do like how your brain works occasionally. Not very often, I might add, but definitely on occasion."

SJ folded her arms and shook her head. As she approached the town square, she could hear shouting and screams.

"What's going on?" SJ said.

"No idea," Dave said.

SJ broke into a jog to find out what the issue was. As she entered the square where all the vendor stalls were, she suddenly had to jump backwards as a wagon being pulled by two horses clattered past on the cobbles. The square was chaotic. The careering wagon had hit three stalls, and no one was driving. The horses looked spooked, snorting and flaring their nostrils as they circled around the square. Vendors and customers alike were getting out of their way.

A female dryad ran out of the inn as the out-of-control wagon swung past. SJ watched as the dryad threw her hands before her, pointing at the wagon and horses. The instant she did, the horses reacted, slowing down and, within a short distance, coming to a stop, still shying and snorting. The dryad walked towards them with her hand held out and gently ran her fingers over the neck of the first horse she reached. It calmed, its breathing easing. She then repeated the exercise with the other, which stopped stomping.

SJ was amazed at the spectacle.

"Druids. Hmph," Dave said.

"The control she has over them is amazing," SJ whispered.

"I suppose it wasn't too bad," Dave said grumpily.

"What do you have against druids?"

"Fluffy nature lovers. I prefer death and glory."

"Hopefully not in that order!"

"As long as it's not your death, then yes."

"You are a little psychotic, aren't you?"

"My latest personality test said I have psychopathic tendencies, so I can't argue."

SJ shook her head, not replying, and wondered what questions he had been asked to get that answer as an AI, never mind why an AI would even complete a personality test.

The apparent wagon owner approached the dryad, and though SJ was too far away to hear what was said, the gnome dropped his head, seemingly scolded. The vendors and affected people were glaring, and some were shouting at the gnome. The dryad stood there watching with a slight smile on her lips. Now that the horses were calmed, she turned and walked back towards the inn, arriving at the door at the same time SJ did.

The dryad was beautiful; she had long dark brown hair and wore a pale yellow dress that fit her perfectly and matching jewellery around her wrists and neck. A large gem hung on the necklace. SJ thought it might be amber or similar.

"Sorry," the dryad said as she let SJ enter before her.

"Thanks. Impressive work with the horses."

"In my trade, it helps."

"What trade is that?"

"I am the local wagonista."

"Wagonista? What is that?"

"Oh, you must be new," she said, smiling. "I own and run the local wagon merchants. We provide most of the wagons and carts in town, and being able to work with horses is a must."

"I see," SJ said, surprised.

As they entered, SJ noticed a movement from the corner of her eye and turned to see a shape on the dryad's shoulder. Something was moving, hidden under her long brown hair. The dryad walked to a table, where she sat at a plate with half-eaten food. She'd clearly left it to stop the antics in the square.

Walking to the bar, SJ kept watching the dryad, wondering what the movement was. The dryad picked up something that looked similar to a pine nut and lifted it towards her shoulder. Two furry little paws appeared and grabbed it before disappearing again.

"What the hell was that?" SJ whispered.

"What?" Dave asked, confused.

"There is something on her shoulder."

"Ohhhh. She has a familiar."

SJ knew what familiars were. "I wonder what it is?"

"Go and ask."

"A little rude to just walk up and ask, *Hey. I don't know your name, but what's that thing sitting on your shoulder?*"

"Hey, SJ," Fhyliss said, getting her attention.

"Hi, Fhyliss. Can I please get a coffee? Do you also have anything light food-wise today?"

"I will check the menu, although Floretta can whip you up something if you wish."

"I would like just a salad, if that's possible?"

"Sure, no problem. I will go ask."

A few moments later, with a large mug of coffee and confirmation of a salad being made, SJ stood, still staring at the dryad.

"I have to ask," SJ whispered.

Walking over to where the dryad was sitting, she waited for her to notice her standing there.

"Can I help you?"

"I am wondering how much a cart and horse costs."

The dryad's eyes lit up. "Please take a seat." She proffered SJ an empty chair, and SJ took it. "It all depends on what you are after, to be honest. Are you looking for a wagon for just an in-town runaround or something more long-distance capable?"

SJ hadn't been expecting a response like that and, within minutes, was tied into visiting the wagonistas to see what they had on offer. She had agreed to go the next day after training. The dryad had finished eating and stood to leave. "When you get down tomorrow, just ask for Katiyanna."

"Okay. I'm SJ. I will see you tomorrow."

The dryad left, leaving SJ rubbing her head, baffled by how the conversation had just turned. She had been getting excited talking about the carts and wagons, picking up on the passion from the dryad, and had completely forgotten to ask about the familiar.

"I think you better leave your gold in your room tomorrow," Dave said.

"Why?" she whispered.

"If you go there with gold, you won't return with it. She had you drawn in on every word."

SJ frowned, unable to deny that the conversation had entranced her. "I did get a little excited."

"That dryad is very good at her job by all accounts. Wagonista sales-people are renowned for being good, but she is *very* good and must have a high Charisma for her charm to be so strong."

"I was charmed?"

"Not magically, but yes, you were charmed by her."

SJ was tired, a little uncertain about the conversation, and sore from the training. She had forgotten to visit the healers for the Dryac that Lorna had mentioned. Fhyliss brought over a large plate full of all kinds of salad; SJ thanked Fhyliss, picked up the plate, and headed to her room.

"You remember you are supposed to be going to see Setu and Margu this evening?" Dave asked.

SJ had completely forgotten and wished she had not confirmed an exact date.

"Thanks, Dave. I had forgotten. I better get ready." SJ sighed. All she wanted to do was get a bath and go to bed, but she knew she had to keep her promise.

CHAPTER FORTY-ONE

Not So Familiar

By the time SJ had returned from visiting Setu and Margu, it was past midnight, and she was exhausted after the day's training. Returning to her room, she stripped off, walked to the bedroom, and collapsed on her bed.

"I will wake you in the morning," Dave said.

"Do you have to?" SJ groaned.

"Training grounds," Dave chirped.

She let out a deep groan, pulled the pillow over her head, and soon fell asleep.

The next morning came too soon, and when SJ went to move after Dave's not-so-melodic voice rang in her head, she moaned. She felt stiff all over. The only part of her that didn't feel as though it was throbbing was her head.

"God, I ache," SJ said.

"Fizzlewick isn't here to help you," Dave said sarcastically.

"Urgh. I wish I had gone to collect the Dryac Lorna mentioned."

"Get some this morning."

"That is if I can even make it that far," she said, and slowly climbed from the bed and bent at the waist, trying to touch her toes and stretching her back off as much as she could.

"It's not even eight o'clock yet. Why wake me so early?" she complained.

"You have things to do."

"Yes. Training."

"Wing exercises. You're almost there now and should be able to attempt flying soon."

SJ had not attempted to fly since starting her wing exercises, but she was determined to ensure she was fully prepared. With an audible sigh, she sat on the edge of the bed and performed her routine. The pain that coursed through her body within moments was horrendous. The exercises from the training ground had probably done her wing muscles more good than she was willing to accept as she huffed and groaned with each bout.

It was still early when she reached the training grounds, and only a few trainees were around. She sat down on a barrel at the side of the training ground and relaxed, soaking up the sun. She had called in at the healer's as suggested by Lorna and picked up a pot of the Dryac cream. It cost seventy copper, the most expensive item she had bought since arriving. She had rubbed the cream into her worst aching muscles, and the relief had been almost instantaneous. She wished she had got some the night before.

"Morning," Lorna called as she walked across to the rings. "Nice to see you here so early and keen to learn."

SJ smiled. "Morning. I feel a little better since I got some of the Dryac this morning. If it hadn't started working so quickly, I am not sure I would have been training today."

"It's good stuff, isn't it?"

"It's amazing."

"You may as well start with the basic katas. If you can remember them from yesterday, get started while we wait and see if anyone else arrives today."

Still feeling stiffness in various muscles, SJ slowly began a warm-up, completing exercises she had done during her gymnastics days. She was amazed at how flexible she was compared to before she had arrived in Amathera, and it had to be down to her increased Dexterity. After the warm-up, she started the new katas. Lorna watched her intently, advising her where she could tighten her stance, adjust her moves, and in general, improve her basic technique. The aggression in this form SJ could see would be formidable.

Finishing her routine, she asked Lorna, "How easy is it to advance kata?"

"It depends on your ability. I can teach you all the katas, but how well you can perform the routines will dictate how fast you can advance the skill."

"I know the first two now. What is the third one?"

"You must learn a couple of the kicks before performing the kata."

"Okay. It's like my previous style, then." SJ wanted to reach the Level 3 kata in Amar Ti to continue pushing and progressing. "Could you show me while we are waiting for the others?"

"Considering no one else has arrived yet, it may just be you today."

SJ was not sure she wanted to have Lorna's complete focus. She had been able to relax slightly yesterday while she spoke to other trainees, but with only her, there would be no respite.

By the time they broke for lunch, SJ was drenched. She must have lost litres of water in sweat. Drinking deeply from her waterskin, she sat on the ground.

"Your dress always looks immaculate. I assume it is magical?" Lorna asked.

"Yes. That is why I am not worried about it getting dirty."

"That can't have been cheap."

Not wanting to say it was a gift from a god, she wasn't sure how to respond to the statement. Eventually, she just said, "No."

The afternoon session was even worse than the first day; the strength training took a new level of effort, and various leg, stomach, and arm exercises left her muscles quivering. The amount of money it would have cost back on Earth to have a personal trainer like Lorna would have been astronomical considering the focus and details she went into explaining the benefits and requirements for each exercise that SJ completed.

Her Strength was lagging, and it became increasingly apparent she needed to improve it. Her katas were physical forms, not just agility-based moves; hitting accurately would be one thing, but having the power to support the precision would be critical.

"Back tomorrow?" Lorna asked, grinning at SJ as she moaned and straightened from where she had been performing cool-down exercises.

"If the Dryac does its job, I should be. Not sure I can do this every day, though."

"We only train in three-day cycles; the fourth day is always rest."

"One more day of torment and torture before a day's rest is what you're telling me?"

"Only if you are up to it," Lorna said, laughing.

"I need to level my skills, so I have to be," SJ said, a little concerned about the training ahead of her. None of this was like the games she had played on Earth; the movement was physical and intense, not just click and accept.

"I need to finish planning the rosters. Have you seen Captain Broadaxe yet?"

"No. I still need to catch him."

"He should be in the barracks now for handover."

The pair made their way to the front of the barracks. SJ hadn't been inside before and was surprised at what she saw when she entered. It was set up more like a police station than a residential building. There was a front desk, and then behind were various sections and desks laid out.

"This looks a little strange," she whispered after Lorna wished her farewell and walked through the back of the barracks.

"Why strange?" Dave queried.

"Just not what I expected. There are so many desks."

"Different departments."

"They have different departments?"

"Of course, what did you expect?"

"Honestly, I just expected a guard room and some beds."

"The barracks are the hub of the town. The mayor's offices are upstairs."

"It's like a town hall?"

"Comparing it to Earth, it would be similar. It is not just guards that work here."

"That makes a little more sense. I wondered why there were so many sitting at desks."

"Shift change in five minutes." Captain Broadaxe's deep voice could be heard as he walked down a flight of stairs into the main office area. Several creature sitting on benches at the side of the room began to stand and move. Each was dressed like a fighter, and they must have been on the oncoming guard shift. There were about twenty different people, and SJ was surprised there were so many.

Captain Broadaxe approached the front desk and picked up a sheet of parchment as the group formed. "Tonight, the following is needed." He listed the tasks that had to be completed by the various pairs he had assigned. It was very comprehensive, and SJ was utterly impressed with the professionalism. Once he had finished his briefing, the teams dispersed from the barracks, leaving Captain Broadaxe chatting to an elderly-looking orc at the front desk.

SJ walked up. "Hi."

The orc and Captain Broadaxe turned to look at her. "Can I help you, miss?" the orc asked.

"I am here to see Captain Broadaxe."

"What can I do for you, then?" the captain asked, smiling.

"We briefly met in the jail the other day with Gary."

"Ah. Yes, how could I forget?"

"I came to see you to donate to the fund as Lorna is starting to train me."

"I see. If you follow me—" He walked to open a small swinging gate that separated the front from the back area.

SJ walked through, and the captain approached the room's rear office. Walking inside, Captain Broadaxe offered SJ a chair to sit on opposite him on the other side of a large desk covered in paperwork and what looked like maps.

"Training donations all go to the Guards' Retirement Fund. How much you donate is up to you. There is no set amount." He leaned forward, opened one of his desk drawers, and removed a small chest. Placing the chest on the desk, he opened it with a key from his belt. SJ could not see the contents from where she sat.

SJ had been trying to think of a suitable amount to donate. She had been struggling with the expectations for many things since arriving. She eventually removed a silver piece from her inventory and offered it to the Captain.

He grinned at her, took the silver from her hand, deposited it into the chest, and secured it again. "Very generous of you," he said.

"I have no idea what the going rate is."

"It is whatever you feel is appropriate; as I say, there are no set amounts as it is voluntary."

"Well, Lorna has been amazing since I started yesterday."

"If you are training in martial arts, that is a hard discipline to learn."

"I hope to excel, eventually."

"I will stick to my great axe. Chop and cleave." He chuckled.

Until now, SJ had not even noticed the huge great axe he indicated as he spoke. The dwarf was about five feet tall, and the axe looked almost as large. It was no wonder he had such massive arms and chest if he spent his time lugging something that size around with him.

"I don't think I could even pick that up," SJ said honestly.

"Ha. It's light. It looks worse than it is. Anyway, I must go and do some rounds. Thank you for your donation."

"Of course, sorry." SJ stood to leave.

"If you are after some work at all, we sometimes post quests on the noticeboard at the inn, and we pay a fair rate."

"I will keep an eye out. Thank you for your time."

"No. Thank you."

Following Captain Broadaxe back to the front, she wished him a good day and headed outside.

"I need to visit the wagonista," she whispered.

"It will be by the stables on the other side of the training grounds. Wagonistas are almost always by the stables."

"Okay," SJ said, turning back towards the rear of the building and heading over to the stables she had seen.

The stables looked like any other she could ever remember seeing in the many films she had seen over the years: a low-fronted, slanted roof affair with open spacing and individual wooden stalls. As she approached, several people were working, mucking out and busily tacking several horses for a couple of waiting clients. A female troll walked from the stable, leading one of the most enormous horses SJ had ever seen. It reminded her of a Shire horse but on an even larger scale. It must have stood almost ten feet tall at the shoulder. It was making SJ feel as though she was in her miniature form. The troll swung herself up and onto its back, and the horse whinnied in protest initially before relaxing and walking off. The troll being on its back made it look like a normal-sized horse.

It was still amazing to consider all the different races that worked amicably together. It was nothing like she had expected before her arrival. Walking over to an orc who was busy tacking a horse, she asked for directions to the wagonistas and was directed to an area farther away from the main stable front. Walking around the side of the stables, SJ was amazed to see a large open space with a gazebo-style covering. On display underneath the overhanging canopy were various carts and wagons. SJ spotted Katiyanna and headed over.

SJ was adamant that she wouldn't purchase anything and decreed that she would only visit because she had promised to. Katiyanna wore a pale blue dress today, again with matching jewellery. She was a beautiful creature. Her delicate features and pristine appearance added to her charismatic charm.

As SJ neared the area, an orc dressed in smart attire approached her.

"Hello. Welcome to Amathera's premier wagonistas. How can I help you today?"

Taken aback by the orc who stood smiling at her, she stumbled over her reply.

"Erm. I am here to see Katiyanna?"

"I see. Please wait here, and I will confirm she is available."

Katiyanna stood talking to two other orcs, both dressed in similar attire to the one that had greeted her. The orc approached her and talked to her briefly. Katiyanna turned.

"Hello, SJ. I am so glad you came to visit," she said, grinning, her face even more beautiful when she did.

"Hi."

"Have you had any thoughts on what you may like?"

"I haven't. I do not know about different carts or wagons."

"Well, you have come to the perfect place to learn," she said. "Let me show you around."

Following Katiyanna, SJ was shown around various carts and wagons, all with slightly different specifications relating to their uses and, particularly, their comfort. She was amazed at the level of detail and construction that went into them. Most of the carts looked like general-purpose carts she had seen being moved around the town; others had awnings or extra storage space on them. The wagons were even more detailed, and one of the display models even had a frame that reminded SJ of old Romani caravans. She had politely asked questions about the various models, and Katiyanna was so enthusiastic that she was caught up in the moment.

"You left the gold in your room. Didn't you?" Dave said.

Ignoring Dave's remark, SJ looked at a particular wagon with a covering, a small bed, and other furnishings.

"This is one of our better range models," Katiyanna said. "It is used by many who take to the open road, providing storage and comfort for your possessions as you travel. It is also able to be magically imbued."

"Magically imbued?"

"Yes. Many dislike leaving their wagons unattended in larger towns and cities, so they will have the latest antitheft magic imbued on them."

"Oh," SJ said in surprise. It was mind-boggling that it was just like walking into any car sales room on Earth.

"This particular model is perfect for an individual. It is not too large or too small and can be pulled by a single horse, although it is advised to use two for swifter travel."

Dave had mentioned previously that due to inventory limitations, many parties took carts into dungeons with them, and looking at the size of the wagon, it would not be very practical. One of the orcs came over and whispered to Katiyanna.

"Excuse me a minute," she said. Turning, Katiyanna quickly walked over to a rather angry-looking draconian in a heated discussion with one of the other orcs.

"You are thinking of buying one, aren't you?" Dave said.

"I am. Why?"

"You know you can get coaches between the various towns and cities rather than buying a wagon to travel in."

"That is good to know, but this one here is almost perfect. Look at it." SJ indicated with her hands.

"It's a wagon!"

"Yes, but the finish . . . and it has improved suspension for the bumpy roads."

"Do you hear yourself?!" Dave exclaimed.

"What?"

Dave tutted, and she could imagine him shaking his head in dismay at her.

"It looks nice," SJ said pleadingly.

"You haven't even asked how much it is yet!"

"No, but I can."

Dave sighed. "You would need horses, and then you have tack, feed, and stable fees to consider."

Honestly, she hadn't even considered the extra costs that might be involved.

"How much are horses normally?"

"Depends upon breed and type. Mules or ponies are cheaper than actual horses. Dungeon divers would just take a mule and cart for loot collection. You can then go all the way up to the chargers. Prices will vary, but you are looking at a few silver for decent ones of excellent stock."

"A few silver? That expensive?"

"It's an investment. There are loaners in most towns, but they are unreliable and not always fit for purpose."

Climbing into the back of the wagon, SJ looked through the various fittings and heard a commotion. Looking over, she saw the still-angry face of the draconian, who was now raising his voice and shouting at Katiyanna. One of the orcs put his hand towards the draconian, who batted it away and pointed viciously at the dryad. Katiyanna was standing there with a smile on her face, replying in a calm voice. The draconian wouldn't have any of it and was getting even more animated. Another of the orcs walked forward, and they both had to forcefully grab the draconian and move him away from the area. As he walked away, SJ saw the funniest scene. A tiny furry paw appeared amongst Katiyanna's hair. She was certain that it gave the draconian the universal sign of contempt.

"Did you see that?" SJ said, startled.

Dave was busy laughing.

"That creature, whatever it is, just gave the draconian the finger."

"It has an attitude for sure," Dave chuckled.

A few moments later, Katiyanna walked back over. "I am sorry about that. Unfortunately, you can't please all customers. He was trying to blame our wagon for damage to the goods he was transporting. He is known as a careless driver. There have been several complaints in town about his driving."

It reminded SJ of all the social media posts she used to see about drivers in and around where she lived in London. Someone was always being complained about, and photos were splashed all over. The similarities between the two worlds were uncanny.

"Have you decided on anything you like in particular?"

SJ could not stop staring at the side of Katiyanna's face, where she had seen the little paw appear.

"I have to ask, what is that on your shoulder?"

Katiyanna laughed. "You mean Lubearius." She reached up and pulled her hair to one side. SJ heard immediate chittering and saw a small bright red squirrel sitting on her shoulder. It looked so cute.

"Lubearius? That's a strange name."

"He has a bit of an attitude, and I am sure he thinks he is a bear rather than a squirrel."

The squirrel chittered away unhappily at being revealed from its hiding place. Its eyes narrowed, and it stared in disgust at SJ.

"I can see that," SJ chuckled.

Katiyanna reached up, grabbed Lubearius, and lifted him down. He squeaked in protest but didn't try to bite or fight.

"May I?" SJ asked, lifting her hand towards the tiny creature.

"Of course."

As SJ's hand came in range to stroke his furry head, he whipped around with his rather sharp incisors and bit into the end of her finger. SJ yelped, pulling her hand back, and saw blood dripping from her punctured finger.

"Lubearius. What have I told you before? You never bite a customer," Katiyanna scolded him. "You are not getting any nuts today now." Looking back at SJ, she apologised, "I am so sorry for his behaviour."

SJ could see the little beastie suddenly shrink and drop its shoulders. It turned to look at SJ with wide, pleading eyes. "My finger is fine. There is nothing to worry about," SJ said, wiping the end of her finger on her dress, knowing it would self-clean and the wound would heal soon enough.

"Please accept my apologies. He is not normally that aggressive."

"He is a feisty little one, isn't he?" SJ said, smiling.

Katiyanna smiled back, and the small squirrel looked as though it was proud of itself at the comment. "He has got me in trouble occasionally, unfortunately," she replied as she placed Lubearius back on her shoulder, the squirrel disappearing back to hide behind her hair, holding it apart with its little paws so it could look at SJ still.

Dave was busy laughing hysterically in her head, gasping for breath at her finger being bitten.

"How much is this wagon?" SJ asked, indicating the one she'd climbed back down from as Katiyanna had returned.

"This model comes in three forms. Single or double tack, and then the optional imbuement and detailing package is available."

"Detailing?"

"Sign writing and luxuries. You can get one fully furnished with bedding and the essentials. Pots, pans, the usual traveller's needs."

"What do they cost?"

"The basic model, unfurnished single tack, costs twenty silver. Then we have the thirty silver upgraded dual tack, and the imbuement package, which costs forty-five silver. This model is dual tack as standard."

"What about the additional packages?"

"Sign writing and luxuries cost an extra two silver. So, for a top-of-the-range model, it is thirty-two silver. We can offer finance deals to suit most needs."

"How do they work?" SJ had the funds to buy one but wasn't willing to do so without knowing the associated costs for horses and feed.

"Finance can be arranged by paying monthly fees at any local branch of Amathera Bank. They have offices in larger towns and cities. All wagons are magically assigned until the last payment is made, and missed payments will result in reclaim. On receipt of the final payment, the wagon's deed will be transferred, giving you full ownership."

It was amazing that the overarching economy included banks. Dave had not mentioned them, and she would need to talk with him. He had mentioned auction houses before and assumed they must be similar.

"Can I have some time to think about it?"

"Of course. For the next seven days, we have a promotion offering all new purchases free annual servicing and retreatment to protect them from the elements for the next three years. It's available at any of our branches."

"That is good to know. I will think about it and might be back. Thanks for your time."

"No problem, and please call anytime if you have more questions."

As SJ went to turn, she saw the little face of the squirrel appear in Katiyanna's hair.

"Bye, Lubearius," SJ said to the small familiar.

The squirrel watched her quizzically as she began to move away before sticking its tongue out. Dave erupted into fits of laughter again.

CHAPTER FORTY-TWO

Up, Up, and Away

The next day passed in a blur of training again with Lorna. SJ's form was improving, and she hoped she would soon trigger the next kata level the way she was going. Lorna had informed her she could not train at the training grounds the following day because of their rules around rest. She decided to look around the town more and pick up some quests. Fizzlewick had still not returned to the tailor's yet, and she was a little concerned about where he had gone. Knowing that Bob had been waiting to see him probably meant he was on the mountain. The form of the massive blue dragon could still be seen back at its peak again.

"Flying day," SJ said excitedly. She had followed the exercise regime Fran had told her about, and she knew just from the exercises that her wing muscles had been improving significantly.

"Great. Let's get you miniature and flying around battling the birds, then."

"You mentioned birds deliberately, didn't you?" SJ frowned, recalling the huge raven that had grabbed her from the sky.

"Would I do something so cruel?" Dave stated innocently.

"Yes."

"I am hurt," he said, giggling.

"Sounds like it." SJ was in her room and began her transformation, standing at her six-inch height moments later. It had been a few days since she had altered her size, and the perspective of everything changed so substantially in miniature form.

"This is going to be fun. Hopefully, you won't face-plant."

Shaking her head at Dave's comment, she slowly moved her wings. She could already feel the difference in scale of her wings between her two forms, and they moved naturally. Her muscles didn't throb like they had when using a single movement, and she slowly got used to the rhythm she needed to follow.

"Okay. Here goes!" SJ moved her wings in their rhythmic pattern, increasing the speed, until without realising it, she was suddenly several inches from the ground. "This is so much easier," she said happily with a huge grin on her face.

"Let's see you fly, then."

"I am flying."

"No, properly. Acrobatics, spins, swoops; come on, don't be shy."

SJ gritted her teeth as she focused on the movements and slowly lifted higher into the air. She was now at least three feet above the floor and adjusted her beat slightly, changing her position. There was none of the leaning backwards and forwards she had been attempting previously, and she could stay virtually upright as she turned. Slow and directed movements made her turn in the air with ease. Gradually reducing her beat, she lowered herself gently back to the floor.

"That was amazing," she said excitedly.

"Boring, more like."

"What do you mean *boring*? I flew."

"You flew before."

"Not properly, though. I also don't ache at all. It felt so natural."

"You still need to actually try to fly somewhere."

"I could get a decent look of the town from the air."

"You could if you actually flew."

"I did fly. Stop trying to burst my bubble."

"I'm just saying. Watching you take off and land after a couple of turns isn't exactly what I would classify as flying."

"Fine." SJ huffed and beat her wings again, lifting off the floor much faster than before. Dave had annoyed her with his hypocritical remarks, and she would prove him wrong. She moved forward and continued to rise. In moments, she was up by the heavy, thick cross-beams of the room's high ceiling, where she startled a small mouse sitting and happily eating. It scurried across the beam and disappeared into the adjoining room.

Turning and looking down, she suddenly got a strong sense of vertigo, her stomach somersaulting.

"Ew. Not good," SJ said.

"What isn't?" Dave asked, confused.

"Vertigo."

"You haven't suffered from it before."

"I have never flown this high before. It's a long way down when you are six inches tall." She moved to the beam and landed on it, resting for a moment until her stomach stopped fluttering so badly.

"Was it really a great idea to select a race that can fly if you suffer from vertigo?" Dave sarcastically replied.

"I've never had vertigo before!"

"Not a good time to start, then, is it?"

Taking a deep breath, SJ steadied herself before starting again and returning from the beam. She slowly circled the room, gradually gaining more confidence in her ability and the subtle movements needed with her wing beats to adjust her flight path. It was strange how it seemed so natural now that her muscles were working independently and not moving simultaneously. The last couple of training days had been more than enough to support her daily schedule of wing development.

"I need to see Fran," SJ said, grinning from ear to ear. Now she could move and fly so easily in comparison to her first attempts.

"Sounds like a good idea. No time like the present."

Looking towards the open window, SJ suddenly felt panic. "What if there are birds that will attack me?"

"You can actually fly now and move out of their way."

SJ wasn't so sure and hovered by the open window.

"Come on, stop acting like a bugbear cub," Dave said.

Growling in response, she started out the window.

The sun, as it had been every day, was blazing down onto the town, and as she left the inn window and lifted towards the roof, she couldn't stop looking around at all the goings on. Her eyesight was perfect since her transformation, and the view of the square was completely different and much more interesting than walking at street level. She could understand why so many people had always gone on about helicopter and balloon flights back on Earth.

Lifting over the inn's roof, she began heading towards the windmill she could see down by the lake-side. She felt amazing flying, watching the day-to-day activities, and could hear the banging of the smithy. She could see the smoke rising from its chimney. She felt free. The warm sun bathed her wings, and her back was not aching in the slightest. Gradually picking up speed as she flew, she was soon travelling much faster than she had ever done before.

The windmill sails spun easily, and it was then that she realised there was quite a breeze coming off the surface of the lake. Not having noticed it in the town, it became apparent now that she had left the streets and was crossing an open field. The breeze hit her, and she could feel herself being pushed off course slightly. Adjusting her flight path, she corrected her direction and continued. As she neared the mage apprentice building, there were several outside training, casting various spells, and that was when the gust hit her.

One of the mages must have been an air mage; the wind whipped up, and her small body was suddenly caught in a tornado. She saw the spiralling air at the same time as it hit her. Squealing in shock, she was suddenly thrown through the air as though she weighed nothing, completely out of control and at the mercy of the power of the mage's magic. The tornado was rising rapidly in the air, and she had no control over where she was going as she was spun around like a sock in a washing machine.

The wind carried her higher and higher across the lake's surface. Her head spun, and she felt exceedingly dizzy. She'd stopped moving her wings in the panic. It was then that the wind suddenly died. In absolute panic, she plummeted towards the lake she was now over—by maybe a hundred feet. Trying to beat her wings frantically became even harder while she tried not to throw up due to how dizzy she had become.

"Dive and glide," Dave shouted in her head.

Struggling to align her body, she tilted down, extending her wings to the sides, the air buffeting her as she tried to steady her fall. Angling slowly upwards, she gradually glided at the speed of a bullet—but at least she was gliding. She tried adjusting her wings slightly, mimicking, as best she could, the flaps on a plane, and it worked enough to calm her descent so she could better control her movement. Still, the crop fields surrounding the mill were approaching too fast.

Hurtling between the windmill sails, only just missing one, she careered towards the field. Trying to slow herself down as best as she could, she crashed into the tops of the ears of corn. She eventually hit the ground, tumbling end over end until she came to a rest on her back, panting.

"Impressive crash landing. Nine out of ten," Dave said.

Staring up through the corn at the sky above, she thanked her lucky stars she was now back on the ground. She slowly climbed to her feet, brushing off the cornstalks that had stuck to her.

"That wasn't fun."

"You were doing well until that spell hit you."

"Wish you got warnings about spells!"

Her dress flowed perfectly as normal around her, and the dirt stains from her crash landing vanished magically.

"I think I will walk the rest of the way," SJ said as she grew to her normal size in the middle of the field of corn. She made her way towards the fence near the windmill.

"What are you doing in there?" a voice called from the mill. "Can't you see the signs?"

SJ looked over at the mill, and a round, portly man was calling over to her in the doorway.

"Sorry. I crashed here," she said, smiling at the man as she approached the fence and hopped over.

"Crashed?" he said with a confused look on his face.

"Yes. I was flying and got hit by a gust of wind. I didn't mean to cause a problem." She saw signs on the fence saying not to enter.

"You have just walked through the centre of a fresh field. You have probably contaminated the entire crop."

"Contaminated?"

"With your filthy fae form."

SJ's temper flared. "Pardon?"

"You heard me. All you fae do is cause mischief and mayhem. Due to your kind, I have lost so many crops over the years."

SJ growled, looking at the man. "How dare you be so rude? You do not even know me, and you accuse me of an issue because of an accident."

"How dare you walk through my field?" the man snapped back.

A large, portly woman appeared next to the man at the door. "Hubert, dear. Please go inside. You know you get yourself all wound up."

The man grumbled as he turned and walked back into the mill.

The woman said to SJ, "I am sorry, dear. I heard you say you crashed?"

"Yes. I was flying to see Mistress Fransisca, got caught in a spell, and lost control. I am sorry if I've caused an issue."

"Oh. Don't worry about Hubert. His bark is worse than his bite. It would not matter if you had been a fae, a goblin, or an elf."

"That isn't how it sounded," SJ said firmly, still furious at Hubert's remarks.

"Come get a glass of milk," the woman said, smiling brightly at SJ. Her face reminded SJ of her grandmother: *wrinkled skin and a big grin*, as she was fondly known in the family.

SJ approached the woman, still scowling. She had not drunk milk since arriving in Amathera, and she was surprised when the woman removed a large pitcher of milk and two glasses from out of nowhere and placed them on a small table sat by the mill entrance. SJ picked up one of the chilled glasses and drank. It reminded her of her childhood when she used to get the full-fat milk at school. It was creamy and delicious, and she downed it.

"You may wish to wipe your mouth, dear," the woman said, chuckling.

She assumed she had a white moustache her top lip. Wiping it on her sleeve, she said, "Thank you. That was delicious."

"My pleasure. Nubbins does produce some of the best milk in town."

"Nubbins?"

"Our cow," the woman said, pointing to the side of the mill, where there was a small field. SJ could not see the cow from where she stood.

"I see. That is why it tastes so fresh."

"Every morning, I go out to milk her for a fresh jug."

"Can I ask your name?"

"I am Gladys. You have already met my grumpy other half, Hubert," Gladys said, chuckling.

"SJ," she said, smiling, the milk placating her anger.

"You look like one of those adventuring types."

"I am. Is there something you need me to do?"

"We do. Have you heard of the cottages?"

The mention of cottages suddenly reminded SJ about the deed, which she had not even looked into yet. "I haven't. Can I ask what you need exactly?"

"We have a cottage to the north of town through the crags and into the valley below. It is one of three tucked away into the woods. It is a beautiful area with a fishing lake. We bought it as our retirement home but have not managed to go down there for a while, as a group of undead have been in the area. Mayor Maxwell won't send the guard as it is outside the town jurisdiction, and he definitely won't after the death of Florina because of the fear of a hob raid."

"I could go and investigate. I am free today but have a busy schedule with training again tomorrow."

"That would be fantastic, if you could. The road splits as you follow it into the valley. If you follow it right, you will come to the cottages down by the lake-side. Ours is the second one. There is a third one farther around, but we only saw the owner of it once, and they disappeared."

SJ's display triggered.

> **Quest: Investigate the Cottages**
> Clear the cottages of the undead infestation and find the source.
> Rewards: 200xp, Gift from Gladys
> Would you like to accept the quest? **Yes/No**

SJ smiled, selecting Yes.

"I will head on over and see what I can find out."

"Thank you and please return for your reward once you have found something out." Walking away from the mill's entrance, SJ was trying to get her bearings.

"Which way is it, Dave?" she said, once she was far away enough.

"It will be back across the meadow where you met Bob and through the crags."

"I am lost. Which way is that from here? I wish the map worked."

"Not till Level 10. Head back towards the smithy, then follow the road back through the fields again. You could probably just follow the lake-side, but at least you have been that route before."

Checking her inventory, she still had her waterskin, rations, and lockbox and keys from Darjey. This would be an opportunity for her to get rid of the lockbox while out of town. She didn't fancy dumping possible incriminating evidence anywhere near Killic itself. She didn't regret giving up on speaking to Fran today after her fraught flight since she had no desire to bump into the mage who had caused her to crash-land; in all honesty, she felt both embarrassed and angry. And so, following Dave's directions, she started towards the meadow. As she passed through the forested area, she again saw and heard plenty of signs of life in the trees and bushes. The scenery reminded her of the picture books of woodland she used to read as a child.

It took her just over an hour to reach the edge of the meadow, the scorched patches of Earth still visible where Bob had stained the earth with his lightning sneezes. Walking down the path in the middle, SJ noticed a group of deer along the lake's edge. SJ was amazed at their beauty, causing her to stop and watch them for a few minutes. As they moved through the clearing, SJ noticed that one of them was limping slightly. *I wonder . . .* she thought as she turned to head towards them.

"Where are you going?" Dave asked.

"Just checking on something. I think that may be the doe I saved."

As she neared the group of deer, the large bucks stood alert and looked towards her. She kept walking forward, not rushing or making any threatening movements or sounds. The doe that had been limping glanced up from its drinking, saw SJ, and bleated before heading towards her. SJ held her hand out as the doe approached. The larger of the bucks snorted but didn't challenge. The doe walked up and sniffed SJ's hand before licking it. The doe's limp was the only visible sign left from the wolf attack.

She felt bad for the doe and wished she could help heal it fully. The one thing about being an assassin was she had no skills or ability to heal. She knew she would have to invest in some healing potions, lotions, or similar things going forward after spending a few minutes with the doe. The group moved away once she continued across the meadow.

Passing through the woods on the far side, she reached the craggy outcrop and the split in the rock face. The path was still clear and well-travelled. Crossing between the rock faces, she looked down into a huge, wide valley below.

CHAPTER FORTY-THREE

The Not Living, Living

The scene before her as she looked into the valley was stunning. Birds flew above the deep, rich forested areas, and a river crossed the valley. In the distance, SJ could make out some structures, but she could not tell what they were. The path twisted down the mountainside towards the valley floor several hundred feet below.

"This is going to be a trek back up," SJ said.

"Maybe you should have bought a wagon."

"I wasn't expecting to go so far today."

She continued the descent to the valley floor. The air at the valley's base was slightly cooler, which surprised SJ, who thought it would have got warmer, trapping the sun's heat. Reaching the bottom, she followed the main track that led through the centre. She had not been travelling long when they found a fork in the trail. The split turned right slightly before turning more sharply into a wooded area.

Another thirty minutes or so later, the path became worse. It was still a track but saw little traffic. It curved down through a wooded glade, and on the far side, it opened into a large open meadow. In the distance, SJ could see some buildings, so she headed towards them. As she approached, her senses heightened; she felt like she was being watched.

"This doesn't feel right," she whispered.

"I can't see anything."

"Nor I yet."

At that moment, an arrow came whizzing towards her from the buildings; thankfully, it was not very accurate and sailed past her. Diving to the ground instinctively, she then lay still, listening. "From the direction of the building," she said.

"Yeah. I saw something, but I'm not sure what."

SJ shrank to her miniature form. If she was going to be pinned down, then she would not be an easy target. Edging away from where she had dived, she started moving towards the buildings. She heard footsteps approaching through the grass.

"Where did it go?" a female voice said.

"No idea. Did you hit it?" a male voice said.

"Not sure."

"We can't have any creatures snooping around here. The boss will go mad if we're seen."

"I know."

SJ heard the swish of what could have been a sword or something similar chopping through the long grasses to the left of where she was now. As she continued away from the two voices, Dave spoke in her ear.

"Two skeletons. One archer, one fighter by the looks of them."

"They must be the undead that Gladys mentioned."

"Only saw them briefly, so didn't see any details."

"Okay," SJ said as she continued. As she neared the buildings, she could hear more voices; in total including those in the field there had to be at least four, possibly five. The closest building was now just ahead of her, and she moved to the edge of the long grass, peering out carefully. There was a gap of twenty feet of hard-packed ground before she could get to the side of the building.

"I am going to fly to the roof," she said determinedly, and flapped her wings, slowly lifting from the ground. The one good thing about her flight was it was silent: Her wings made no sound. As soon as she was hovering, she crept higher above the grass line and then, seeing it was clear, lifted higher and headed straight over to the roof. She landed gently on the patchy thatching, which clearly needed repairs. She could hear the skeletons talking below her. Creeping to the far edge of the thatch, taking care of where she placed her feet, she lay down and peered over.

Just below her, she could see the tops of two heads; one was wearing a metal helmet, and the other had the plain white skull of a skeleton with a random wisp of hair attached to it. The sound of one of the voices confused SJ. It wasn't a skeleton, but a strange-looking being slightly away from the building that didn't seem to have much of a body, floating rather than walking.

"What is it?" SJ whispered.

"Phantom. An undead minion mainly used to cause fear rather than damage. They are usually very weak to fire," Dave said.

The phantom made a sound like a deep moan.

"I know, we have to move the gear," a huge skeleton complained. "At least this delivery can be loaded straight onto the boat rather than messing about storing it first."

Moaning again, the phantom pointed at the barrels next to the building. Sighing, the large skeleton moved towards the barrels, bent, and picked one of them up before moving it over to where a cart was situated. It loaded the barrel in the back as SJ watched the return of the two other skeletons, who had gone out towards the field where she had been. A third skeleton also walked from inside the building she was on top of. There were five skeletons and the phantom in total.

"Anything?"

"No sign. Whoever it was has disappeared."

"We need to keep an eye out while we finish packing up."

"Yeah. Charlotte, can you keep watch?"

The skeleton with the bow and arrow said, "Yeah, I'll keep watch."

SJ watched as four of the skeletons finished moving the barrels. The fifth, with the bow, Charlotte, stood by the edge of the building, looking back across the meadow where the track was. Once the cart had been packed, the four skeletons moved to the front of it, and as they picked up the cart handles on either side, the phantom let out a deep moan.

"Coming," Charlotte said as the others began to pull the cart off down a track leading towards the lake ahead of them, about two hundred feet from where SJ was on the roof. When they reached it, they began loading the barrels from the cart onto a rowing boat bobbing in the water. Once the boat was full, two skeletons rowed across the lake. The others then turned, grabbed the cart handles, and dragged the empty cart along a path farther down the lake-side.

"I wonder what they are doing," SJ said.

"No idea, but they must be under the influence of a necromancer."

"Why do you say that?"

"They have to do what they are instructed, and I think the phantom is in charge of them."

"A necromancer will assign a leader?"

"Some do. Some do it all themselves, but it's easier if they have minions who do the work for them."

The beings were now a fair distance from the building, and she slowly stood, flapping her wings before making her way to the ground. Considering her initial trouble, the fact flight was now feeling natural was quite disconcerting. The building she was now in front of looked run-down and derelict. The front door was hanging on by a single hinge. Its surroundings would have made it a beautiful home at one time, but it would need a lot of work to return to that standard. SJ could only assume that she was in the right area where the cottages were supposed to be from Gladys's directions.

"Let's see what they have been doing here." Entering the building, SJ immediately saw destroyed furnishings: Tables, chairs, and cupboards had all been ransacked, damaged, or smashed. Based on the state of the inside, it must have been derelict for a very long time. Thick cobwebs coated the rafters, making SJ shudder and reminding her of her crypt visit. Searching around the small cottage, she found nothing of value or interest that may have indicated what they were doing here.

"I can't find anything."

"I haven't seen anything unusual either. I do not know what was in those barrels. Maybe check around outside."

Walking back out of the small cottage, SJ searched the immediate area. A small shed had its door open, and broken baskets and pottery pieces littered the floor. There was no sign of what they had been doing or what was in the barrels they were moving. The only signs were the fresh marks on the earth where they had stood and the tracks the cart had created in the dirt path leading down to the lake.

"We need to follow them. Your quest says to clear the cottages, and this has to be the first one. Gladys said hers was the second, never mind the third one she mentioned."

"Yeah. I will stay miniature for now; it will be easier not to be seen." Taking off, she cut diagonally across the field in the direction the cart had been pulled along the lake-side. It didn't take long to reach the lake, and looking right, she could see another building farther down, slightly around a bend in the lake. Taking her time and staying low to the grasses, she flew towards it.

As she neared the building, she heard the voices of the skeletons.

"Brian. Get a move on. We haven't got all day."

"Shut it, Terence. I'm moving as fast as I can."

"Try moving faster. I want to get back at some point."

"Why, what do you have planned? A nice dinner, perhaps."

"Very funny."

Charlotte joined in, laughing with Brain. The phantom moaned, and the other two skeletons moved towards where Brian was to help him do whatever he was doing.

SJ flew upwards slightly to give herself a better angle and could see this cottage was in much better condition. It had a small white picket fence surrounding it, and the grass was overgrown, but she suspected it had been cared for until recently. From what SJ could tell, at the side of the small cottage was the entrance to a storm cellar, and one of the skeletons was moving a barrel out from it.

"What are they up to?" she whispered.

"No idea."

"I wish I knew what was in the barrels. One of them mentioned that it had not been long since they had a delivery. Delivery of what? And why store it and not take it straight back to wherever they have come from?"

"I still have no idea."

"I thought you were all-knowing."

"Very funny. Haha," Dave said.

"Be careful, Terence," Brian cried to the largest skeleton as a barrel toppled off the back of the cart. It thudded heavily to the ground, and a red liquid leaked from it. "Damn it, Terence. It's leaking."

Looking at the large skeleton, SJ could see the telltale signs of an orc's tusks. It was strange to realise that the skeletons were not all human.

"It's not my fault the cart wasn't level."

"The pair of you just stop and get it picked up. We will have to stash it on its side to stop it leaking anymore," Charlotte chimed in.

"I am going to use identification," SJ whispered.

"Be careful. You don't know what Wisdom they have."

"I don't care, and I am only small. They still won't see me that easily at this range." Hovering above the grass, she cast her identification skill at the skeletons and phantom.

"The sneaky assassin is learning. You know what, I must admit I have been a little silly."

"Why?"

"The chances of you being spotted identifying people, unless they have a direct identification skill themselves, is very slim when you are miniature."

"Now you tell me!"

"I hadn't thought about it before, never having had a fae Legionnaire."

SJ sighed.

"Sorry," Dave said.

"Did you just apologise?" SJ said, mocking shock.

"Maybe, but don't get used to it."

Smiling, SJ read the results on her display and checked her skill progression.

Subterfuge: Identification Level 3 (19 of 30 to reach Level 4)

Skeletal Archer	
Race:	Undead
Level:	7
Hit Points:	35
Mana Points:	35
Attacks:	Pierce

Skeletal Fighter	
Race:	Undead
Level:	8
Hit Points:	50
Mana Points:	40
Attacks:	Slash, Thrust

Skeletal Rogue	
Race:	Undead
Level:	6
Hit Points:	30
Mana Points:	30
Attacks:	Stab, Slash

Phantom	
Race:	Undead
Level:	10
Hit Points:	55
Mana Points:	100
Attacks:	Confusion, Fear

"There is no way I can take on four of them, at the levels they are."

"Knowing how necromancers work, if you took out the phantom, the chances are the others wouldn't do anything."

"What makes you say that?"

"They are instructed. The phantom is directing them and making sure they do their work. I bet if you can take it out, they would only attack if you attacked them. They are probably out of range of the necromancer directly."

"I'm not a gambler and don't fancy betting on them not attacking me."

"That was a low blow!" Dave grumbled.

"I didn't mean it that way, but if the truth hurts . . ."

"Hmph."

"I will just watch for now and see what they do and where they go."

Moving towards the side of the field and the tree-line, SJ positioned herself so she could see the happenings more easily. She flew to a branch and gently landed on it. The cart was being loaded with more barrels from the cellar.

"At least we should be finished for now," one of the skeletons said.

"It's been nice being away from the boss, though."

"I can't disagree."

"What does he even need with all this?"

"No idea. Knowing him, he will have some mad scheme he is trying to cook up. He never leaves his laboratory most days."

"The gnoll hunters we have been collecting it from must have slaughtered an entire forest to provide so much blood."

SJ gasped at hearing that the barrels were full of blood. Thankfully, she was far enough away for her not to be heard.

"Blood!" she whispered.

"Probably trying to create a new being."

"What sort of being would need barrels of blood?"

"Meh. Necromancers are a strange breed. They are always trying to create new horrors."

SJ had witnessed at least seven barrels being loaded onto the rowing boat, and now a further six had been loaded onto the cart. That was a lot of blood. Each barrel reminded SJ of the ones she used to see in the micropubs around London. There had to be litres, and she had no idea how many barrels had been delivered previously.

The skeletons began moving the cart away from the building and headed back towards the rowing boat. SJ watched them leave and flew to the cottage, landing on the ground by the red-stained earth. She glanced around the area but didn't see anything. This cottage had been left untouched apart from its cellar being used for storage, by the looks of it. Checking that the skeletons and phantom had moved out of sight, she grew to her normal size and tried the cottage's front door. It was secure and didn't look like anyone had even attempted to open it.

Moving round to the storm cellar, she made her way down. The inside was damp and musty, and just enough natural light leaked in from the open entrance to allow her night vision to make out the empty cellar. There was nothing of interest. Walking back out, she glanced over towards the direction they had gone.

"I need to see where they are going," she said as she shrank again.

"It sounded like they were finished doing what they were doing here. So I doubt they will be back for now."

"The quest said to clear the cottages and find the source. The first part of it seems a little easy now if they are leaving."

"Don't complain."

"I'm not. I was just expecting to have to fight them."

"You may yet. I wouldn't get so confident that you won't. You still must find the source, which means finding the necromancer."

Making her way back towards the lake-side, she stopped in the grass and looked towards where the cart had been taken. SJ could see the skeletons and their phantom leader now waiting near where the rowing boat had left. She watched for some time before she noticed the rowing boat moving back across the lake's surface. It arrived and was loaded with the barrels again before departing and heading once again across the lake. SJ then watched the strangest sight. The three skeletons left behind walked into the lake until they disappeared under the surface, leaving the cart behind. The phantom floated out across the lake, accompanying the rowing boat.

"I wasn't expecting that."

"The joys of not having lungs or needing air," Dave said.

SJ could not clearly see across the lake from where she was, so she flew into the air to give herself a better view. Across the lake, she could vaguely make out a small building, and as she watched, the rowing boat headed towards it. To the left and right, the lake was quite large, and it would take her some time to work around it.

"I should just fly across."

"Perhaps, but you will be quite easy to spot above the water."

"If I stay low, though?"

"I wouldn't advise it. You saw what happened to you over the river with the fish that wanted to snack on you. There is no telling what is in the lake."

"Good point. I will go around." Turning, SJ flew down to the lake's edge and followed it towards the far side. Her flying speed was naturally increasing, and as she moved around the lake-side, she travelled at least as quickly as a fast run on land. It was a fantastic feeling, the air whipping her hair and dress out behind her. Glancing over towards where the rowing boat had been unloading and noticing the large fir tree that had been near it, she could tell she was making good time. Off to her right, as she flew along the edge of the lake, she came upon the third cottage. Just ahead, she could see a small jetty suitable for tying a boat up and a path that led back into the woods slightly.

"Dave. Can you please note this and remind me to check it later?" SJ asked as she flew past.

"Will do."

SJ continued around the side of the lake. It was small compared to the enormous lake that Killic sat on the side of, and it didn't take her too long to move around to the other side. Slowing down as she saw the building up ahead, she cut off into the tree-line across a small open area and moved towards it. Reaching the closest she could in the woods, she landed on a branch again and looked down towards the building.

There was a jetty and what looked like a storage building, and that was it; there was no sign of the skeletons or the barrels from the now-empty rowing boat. The phantom was nowhere to be seen either. Looking at the dirt-packed track that led away from the lake, she could see the furrows of a cart or wagon cut into it. SJ fluttered down from the tree, landed by the building, and peered into its open frame. There was nothing inside.

She turned and was about to start down the track when she heard a splash from the lake. Hiding behind the side of the building, she peeked around the edge and saw the skeletons emerging from the lake that they had walked across. Water drained from their clothing and weapons; one of them picked some green plant fibre from its ribcage that had been caught as it waded across the bottom.

"That never gets normal," the one she thought was named Brian said.

"It's fun, though," Charlotte said.

The larger orc skeleton shook its bones off like a dog flinging water everywhere. It was a strange sight to behold, three skeletons conversing, never mind watching them walk out of a lake. The three began moving away from the lake-side and headed down the track.

"Let's go see where it takes us," SJ said as she followed the skeletons at a distance.

CHAPTER FORTY-FOUR

Adjudicator

The three skeletons continued down the track for quite a distance before they came to a crossroads. Turning right, they started following the track leading towards the valley side. Watching from a distance, SJ hovered low by some bushes. The three had been talking as they walked, not saying much of interest that SJ could pick up but enough to let her know they had been here for some time now. The track followed a slight gradient as it approached the steep valley wall, and the ground was becoming more broken and uneven.

At no point had SJ even considered how much she had been flying nor felt any tiredness in her back, the subtle movements allowing her to move without any strain. The skeletons reached the brow of a hill and dropped out of view. SJ followed slowly and approached with caution while they were out of sight. Skimming along the edge of the track, she arrived at the brow and heard the phantom moan. Stopping, she slowly dropped to the ground and walked to the ridge through the grass.

Looking down into the depression before the steep valley side, she could see the area she could only assume housed the necromancer and its minions. There were three buildings, all of which were a single storey, two smaller and then one much larger. Smoke was billowing out of the chimney of the larger building. Around the buildings, rocks had been piled to create a crude defensive wall. It only stood a few feet high and would not have been challenging for most races to cross.

The skeletons were all outside one of the buildings. The five stood together now, including the two she had seen rowing the boat. The strange sight was the two beasts towing an open-backed wagon. They looked half lizard and half horse, and SJ watched as one of the skeletons fed them a chunk of meat each. Triggering her identification skill, she read the details of the group. Only the ones she had not previously identified added to her skill growth.

Subterfuge: Identification Level 3 (23 of 30 to reach Level 4)

Skeletal Fighter	
Race:	Undead
Level:	6
Hit Points:	40
Mana Points:	30
Attacks:	Slash, Thrust

Skeletal Fighter	
Race:	Undead
Level:	5
Hit Points:	25
Mana Points:	25
Attacks:	Slash, Thrust

2 x Lizorse Level 2	
Hit Points:	20
Mana Points:	0
Attacks:	Bite, Claws

"Those creatures look much stronger than they are," she whispered.

"Lizorse are renowned for having bad tempers. They are very strong for pulling wagons and carts but not user-friendly. Very few races use them because they habitually bite chunks from their owners. Not an issue for skeletons, though," Dave chuckled.

"I don't think I would like them pulling my wagon."

"Your wagon? You don't own one."

"Yet."

Dave sighed.

A figure appeared at the entrance to the larger building. All SJ could see from a distance was a black-robed arm that pointed as they spoke. The voice was that of a male. "Bring me those barrels. I want the pool filling," he called, before disappearing back inside again.

The phantom moaned, and the skeletons moved to where the barrels brought from the lake stood. Audible groans came from the skeletons as they grabbed the barrels and took them inside.

"How am I supposed to do anything about this place?"

"Not easily, by all accounts."

"There are too many to attempt to fight alone."

"Unless you can pick them off."

"How? I have no idea how to kill a skeleton."

"You can't kill them. They are already dead." Dave chuckled at his joke.

Rolling her eyes at his poor humour, SJ watched as the phantom moved towards the lizorse. As it neared, the lizorse flared up, stomping their lizard feet, flicking their forked tongues, and baring their teeth. The phantom put one of its shadowy arms out and placed it on the side of the nearest lizorse. It hissed in resistance before becoming still.

"What is it doing?"

"Feeding, I think. They feed on fear."

SJ shuddered at the thought of the formless being touching her skin. As she stood watching the skeletons move the barrels into the building, her display triggered.

Quest: Investigate the Cottages—Complete

The cottages are clear as the undead have left the area, and the source has been located. You may claim your reward for identifying the source and location of the necromancer behind the recent events.

Rewards: 200xp + 20% = 240xp. -50% as cleared without interaction = 120xp awarded

Return to Gladys to receive your gift.

"That's unfair," SJ whispered harshly.

"It's the System, unfortunately."

"It's not my fault they left the cottages."

"It happens with quests. When set, the parameters can change because of natural or other occurrences, and the System will adjust outcomes."

"Hang on. I read that in the terms and conditions."

"Yes, you did. Oooooh, again, another anomaly."

"I didn't agree with their amendment rule; therefore, they can't adjust a value offered, can they?"

"In theory, no, they shouldn't. In practise, once a quest is in play and accepted, other administrators will track and monitor the deliverables and adjust them as required. They are unlikely to even know your status, considering they will have hundreds of thousands of quests they monitor and adjust."

The thought of a load of AI administrators who were purely monitoring the outcomes of quests added another layer of complexity to Amathera.

"Can I do anything about it?"

"Let me check."

Several moments passed before Dave spoke again.

"I have raised a support ticket with the quest team. It is case number 00000001."

"It's the first case ever raised?"

"Yes. No one has ever questioned the quest system previously."

"What have you said?"

"I have stated that as you never agreed to the terms and conditions, you don't accept reduced rewards for quests as stated. Therefore, you expect the full amount of quest experience as offered initially, irrespective of the reasons behind the parameter changes."

"That sounds quite a fair statement. Thank you for doing that," SJ said sincerely.

"It is my pleasure, my YLF."

"When do you think you will get a response?"

"No idea. Hang on. I just got one!"

"What have they said?"

Silence.

"Dave?"

"Now, this is interesting."

"What is?"

Silence.

"Dave?"

"Hang on."

It again took several moments before Dave responded.

"It has been raised to the System. I have just had one of the adjudicators contact me directly."

"Adjudicators?"

"Yup."

"I never thought you would have such a thing."

"They preside over any disputes and investigate any issues over protocol concerns, et cetera."

"So that happened to you before, then?"

"Erm. Well, yes."

"Are you the best person to speak to an adjudicator, then?"

"I am invulnerable to them with you taking me as your administrator. They cannot amend or change an administrator once a Legionnaire lives in Amathera. All the rules are designed around the expectations of standard acceptance, and I am finding out as I go along with you on this journey that I can do and say more than I have ever been able to before. The relative freedom is quite invigorating."

"Can they not just speak to me?"

"No. That would buck the System. As I said, many administrators don't even talk to their Legionnaires apart from basic guidance information at major level amendments. One of the main reasons I got into gambling was to pass the time."

"If they wanted to, they could, though?"

"Thinking about it, I'm not sure they could. Administrators have specific integration coding, which allows our projected consciousness to be heard. I don't believe an adjudicator could be designed to deal with internal issues or ever be client-facing. They are the prudes of our world, always straight laced and very boring to talk to."

Struggling to understand the life of an AI administrator, which was classed as a race, with a societal structure complete with a Gamblers Anonymous organization, never mind internal adjudicators for protocol analysis and checks, was another level of confusion that SJ would have to try to fully understand in time. For now, she just wanted an answer about her quest experience.

"Okay. Let me know when you get a response, please."

"Of course. This is so much fun compared to normal," Dave happily replied.

Her display triggered.

> **Quest: Necromantic Prevention**
> Investigate what the necromancer is doing and stop its scheme.
> Rewards: 550xp
> Would you like to accept the quest? **Yes/No**

SJ looked at her experience, which currently sat at 231 of 800. If she could complete the new quest, even with only half the reward for the cottage quest, she would reach Level 7.

"That's a lot of experience," SJ said.

"It is, especially for a Level 6 quest. I would normally expect only two or three hundred to be offered, at a maximum."

"That's good, then," SJ said, happy with how things were working out.

"Not necessarily."

"Why?"

"You already wondered how you could take on the skeletons and the phantom, and now we're adding the necromancer as well. Plus, we don't know yet if there are even more minions inside. It seems like a deliberate hook quest."

"Hook quest?"

"Yes. Some quests will be offered at lower levels that are actually for much higher levels or for parties to complete."

"I shouldn't accept it, then?"

"You can accept it. I just wouldn't complete it by yourself at Level 6."

"I would need to find someone to help me?"

"Definitely, or wait until you are at a higher level. If you accept it, no one else can be offered the same quest unless you leave a territory. If you recruit help, it would mean that experience would be shared, but you would also receive individual experience from any kills and potential loot."

"Leave a territory?"

"Yes. When you cross territory borders, unless the quest is specifically stated as working towards a larger aim and needs you to cross borders, then quests are all released, freeing them for others to complete."

"If I did not accept the quest, I could go back to town, let others know, and they could come here and complete the quest, then?"

"Yes. If you wish to, you could just not disclose the location in the hope no one else discovers it until you are strong enough to accept the quest."

"I don't like the sound of that idea."

"I wouldn't advise it, because when you leave a starter territory you may end up with hundreds of quests to choose from. That is when picking and choosing the quests you wish to complete requires thought. There will be limitations on the number that may be accepted."

"I didn't know that."

"It gets more complex in relation to quests and availability."

SJ was just about to respond when her attention refocused on the phantom, which let out a deep moan. She was too far away to hear a response from the skeletons that were now back outside, but one of them stood from where it had been sitting, walked over to one of the other buildings, and disappeared inside. Minutes later, two elves were dragged from the building entrance. They both appeared to be wearing basic farmers' clothes, and nothing about them indicated they were fighters or adventurers.

The skeleton forced them to their knees, and as SJ watched, another skeleton led the lizorse towards them.

"They aren't being fed to them, are they?" SJ asked in shock.

"I don't think so. Watch," Dave said.

The elves wailed in fear as the animals approached. One of them appeared to faint. Once the lizorse were several feet away, they stopped, and the phantom walked forward. It reached them and placed its hand on the conscious, screaming elf. The screaming became hysterical and then ceased after several moments, and its body seemed to go limp.

"It's feeding off prisoners." There was anger in SJ's whisper.

"The lizorse didn't seem that fearful of it, so it probably needs more sustenance."

"That is sick and evil."

"It's Amathera. Every race or creature has its own things. Feeding off fear, for a phantom, is like eating a hogling roast."

"It may be, but using prisoners . . . !"

"Okay, maybe I agree that is a little evil, although I have witnessed much worse over the years."

"I don't think I want to know."

Once the phantom had finished feeding from the elves, their limp forms were dragged back inside the building again.

"I am going to free them."

"How?" Dave asked.

"I must do something; I can't just leave them there."

"We just discussed not moments ago the dangers of higher levels and taking on so many, and now you want to free two elves."

"Not by attacking them all. I will wait until they are asleep tonight."

"You are forgetting one slight problem with your cunning plan."

"What?"

"They are undead. They never sleep."

"Damn." Although SJ thought it might be the case when she saw Floretta in the inn, she never confirmed it.

"If I were you, I would either accept the quest and get help, or accept and come back when you are stronger."

"Okay," SJ said, and accepted the quest. "Let's get out of here. I want to return as soon as possible with support and turn this place into dust."

"That sounds like fun."

Turning and moving back from the ridge of the valley, SJ soon began to fly back towards the lake. It didn't take long to fly there, though she was too distracted to pay much attention to how much time had passed. Anger zipping through her, she was thinking through who she could get to help her. She had three creatures in mind: Zej, Fran, and Lythonian. Considering that the quest involved the undead, she would speak to Lythonian before the others. His healing skills as a cleric would also benefit her.

"Do parties have size limits?" she asked.

"No. The larger a party, though, the less the experience you earn since it is shared."

Skirting around the lake, she reached the jetty by the track leading towards the third cottage.

"I am going to check it out quickly," she said, turning and heading that way. Flying swiftly, the ground flashing beneath her, she felt amazing and free. The path twisted into the wood and then opened into a clearing. Stood in the middle of the clearing was a beautiful small cottage. It reminded her of a fairy tale. The thatched roof looked well kept, and the two small windows framed on either side of a wooden door appeared to smile as she approached. There was a small outhouse, a shed to one side, and a well. It looked peaceful and pristine. She could understand why the skeletons hadn't used it, as it was farther from the lake than the other two cottages.

The area around the clearing was overgrown, and a few vines had started to grow up its side, adding an extra charm to its appearance. She slowed as she neared, and landed, growing to her normal size. On the door was a sign: FARLECK COTTAGE.

"We found it!" SJ said excitedly.

"Found what?"

"Farleck Cottage, the one I have the deed for."

"Oh. Yeah. Sorry, I was a little distracted."

"Doing what?"

"It is my weekly AIGA meeting."

"Oh. You should have said."

"No. It's okay. I remote in so we can all say how well we are doing. It's almost over now."

It was hard to understand how an AI could have meetings for Gamblers Anonymous, but Dave had stated that administrators were classed as a race. Walking to the cottage door, SJ tried the handle, but it was locked. Remembering she had brought the keys from Darjey, she took them out and tried them. To her delight, one key fit, and she unlocked the cottage door and walked inside.

Everything was covered in dust, but the quaint room, with its thick-beamed ceiling and the fireplace built into the back wall, looked homely. On one side of the room was a bed-frame and a wardrobe, and on the other, a small kitchen area with a stove, table, and chairs. In the centre of the small cottage was a sofa facing the fireplace. Apart from the large furnishings, any belongings had been removed from the cottage, but it wouldn't take much to get it back to a cosy and liveable state. Removing the key to the door from the remainder, she placed it back into her inventory after locking the door and exiting. She would have to come back here with the deed and claim ownership. This would be a beautiful place to stay.

"Okay. Let's get back to town and see who we can get to help," SJ said as she continued her journey back.

CHAPTER FORTY-FIVE

Breakfast at the Hogling Arms

By the time SJ reached the outskirts of town, several hours had passed, and she had not realised how long she had been gone. Checking her display, it was late afternoon. Walking across the last field to the edge of town, she heard the familiar sound of the smithy, and the smell of iron and fire rolled across the field, carried by the lake's light breeze.

"I will not go to the mill until we hear about the quest," SJ said as she headed down the main path towards town.

"No. I would wait and see what they say. I have had no further response since I addressed it and an adjudicator was assigned. I will chase it for you if I haven't heard anything by later today."

"That would be great. Thanks," SJ said. Dave had become more and more helpful over the past few days. Whether this had just been a natural progression in their relationship, SJ couldn't be sure, but she was happy with how they were working and getting along. Dave was still as sarcastic as ever, but it was fun and never with malice, and the more she listened to him, the more he reminded her of her Uncle Dave. She hoped his operation had gone well but knew she would never know. It was strange when she occasionally thought back to Earth and her life before coming to Amathera. With its vibrancy and cultural differences, this new world, never mind fantastical creatures, felt more and more like the home she should always have been a part of.

Nearing the smithy, she could hear Zej's usual booming voice, and it sounded like he was reprimanding someone again. When she walked around the side to the open-fronted building, a large orc was standing at the forge, hammering away at an enormous piece of glowing metal. Zej was busy at a table. It looked like he was shaping metal with a file for some weapon variant.

"Hi, Zej," SJ called as she approached.

Looking up, the broad-chested dwarf broke into a grin. "Hi, SJ. What brings you back to my hot paradise?"

"I wanted to ask if you ever have time off?"

"Occasionally . . . Why?" he asked, raising one eyebrow and smirking.

"Not—not like that," SJ stammered, feeling her cheeks redden.

"And there was me thinking that a pretty little fae was asking me out for an ale," he said, chuckling.

The heat burned in her cheeks even hotter. "I *wondered*," she pressed on, "if you wanted to help with a quest."

"It's been several years since I quested or even considered it."

SJ suddenly realised that she had no idea what level Zej was at. "Can I ask a personal question?"

"Aye. What is it?" Zej inquired, and seemed interested in what she wished to ask.

"Can I inspect you?"

"If you wish. It doesn't bother me."

SJ triggered her identification skill and opened her mouth when her skill results returned.

> You are unable to identify over ten levels above your own.

That meant that Zej was at least Level 16.

"It won't work."

"What level are you?"

"I am 6."

"I assume your identification skill isn't very high yet?"

"No, not Level 4 yet."

"That is why; at Level 5, you will receive ten more levels in identifying higher levels."

"Oh. I had no idea."

"If you have been around as long as I have, you learn a few things, even if I don't have the skill myself."

"Do you mind if I ask you, then?"

"Ha. No. Not at all. I will save you the trouble. I am two hundred thirty-one years old and a Level 19 fighter."

"Level 19!" SJ exclaimed in shock.

"Aye. I haven't been questing in almost fifty years now," Zej said, laughing heartily.

"Never mind your age."

"I don't suppose you are very aware of the ages of my kind, being so young in Amathera. Dwarves can live until we are in our four hundreds. I am still a youngster."

Although SJ was aware of the vast differences in age of all those around her, she couldn't help but be shocked that Zej was two hundred thirty-one years old even though his face looked no older than early thirties; though, she thought, she supposed he was just in his *two* thirties.

"I am still trying to get used to the age differences," SJ said apologetically.

Dave suddenly spoke. "This starter town gets even stranger. I can understand a few being higher levels, but a Level 19 fighter in a starter town is very unusual, even if he has hung up his sword."

"What is it you need help with?" Zej asked.

SJ looked over at the orc hammering away at the forge.

"Can we go outside?" SJ motioned to move away from prying ears, not that he would have heard over the hammering.

Following SJ outside, Zej turned to walk up the steps. "Come, let's get a drink and chat."

The steps at the side of the smithy led up to where she had assumed Zej lived. When Zej reached the top and opened the door with several keys, she suddenly thought it might not just be a home. He stepped aside, letting SJ in. What beset her eyes was an amazing array of armour and weaponry. The area above the smithy here must be his shop. Standing on mannequins were beautifully crafted and shiny armour sets, posed with various weapons.

"Wow. These are amazing," SJ said, scanning the interior and taking it all in.

"Ah, these are just a few showpieces," Zej said, smiling. Walking across the initial room and past a small counter, he went to another door and unlocked it, allowing SJ inside. The next room was his personal area. She entered a lounge with a large sofa and comfy armchairs, where Zej offered her a seat. The room felt warm and snug, and the heat from the forge below acted as a heat source for the building. Zej walked to a small set of drawers with a few bottles on them and took two glasses, pouring a dark golden liquid into each before returning, handing SJ one, and sitting in an armchair.

"Hentrot, duh," he said, lifting his glass before him. "It means *good health*," he said after seeing SJ's confused expression.

"Hentrot, duh," SJ said, lifting the glass to her lips and taking a sip. The golden liquid felt like pure fire touching her lips and tongue. Coughing violently as she swallowed it, she squeaked, "Woah. That's strong."

"Ha. Dwarven brandy. So, what's the problem?"

Once the burning sensation eased, SJ said, "I have discovered a necromancer in the next valley over and have a quest to get rid of it. I can't do it alone as there are too many of its minions."

"A necromancer, you say. Now, that's unusual, being that close to here. I can't remember the last time one even came near the area," he said, frowning. "You say there are many of them. How many?"

"I saw five skeletons and a phantom. I believe it is trying to create another creature, as it had received a shipment of blood."

"In the name of Killoc, that cannot be allowed to happen. Why have you not spoken to Captain Broadaxe or the mayor?"

"I have only just returned, and you were the first that came to mind," she said, smiling.

"Well, I could dust my armour off and take Betty for a swing."

"Betty?"

Zej stood and walked to the side of the room, where a metal pole rested in the corner. When Zej picked it up, she realised that it wasn't a pole after all but the handle of a huge, two-handed war hammer. "Betty," he said, smiling.

The war hammer was pure black. Its front face was flat and smooth, but there was a sharp spike at its rear. It looked lethal.

"That's one nice-looking weapon," SJ said, admiring the finely crafted engravings on its surface.

"She has made me proud," Zej said, looking lovingly at the hammer.

"If you could help, that would be amazing."

"I can. It's been a while, and I only normally get to use her when we get attacked by the hobs."

"You help defend?"

"Anybody in the town can do it if it's a hob raid. They come in numbers, so the more to defend, the better."

"I had no idea there were that many issues here."

"It's not often, but on occasion, they try to raid the town."

"Hopefully that's kept you in practise enough to take down some skeletons?"

"I expect so. When would you want to go?"

"It's too late today, but tomorrow, if you are able?"

"I am. Now drink up and let's celebrate your first battle."

SJ smiled, taking another swig of the brandy, which again sent her into a coughing fit. Once she had arranged for them to meet at the inn for breakfast before setting out in the morning, she bid farewell. She couldn't believe her luck that she had managed to find a Level 19 fighter to support her on her quest.

"How does the experience work with level differences?" SJ whispered to Dave as she walked towards the church to see Lythonian.

"It doesn't make a difference—if it's just the two of you in a party when you complete the quest, the experience will be split into halves. That also means that any coin is split equally in a party and that any loot can be shared out between party members as chosen and agreed. Depending upon who sets the party up, who has overall control of the loot assignment will decide."

"If that's the case, how do parties work? Are there bonuses or buffs?"

"It's your quest, so you should set the party. Some party members may still provide boosts during combat."

"That sounds great."

It didn't take long to work through town to the church. The doors were open, but there was no sign of Lythonian. An elderly gnome was busy replacing the flowers around the vestry.

"Excuse me. Do you know where Lythonian is?"

"Hello, dear. He is down in the crypt. That poor dryad girl who was killed the other day is being entombed."

"Oh. I will not interrupt him, then."

"He won't be long."

Although SJ had been in the church several times, she hadn't spent long looking around, and she took the opportunity to study the space and look at all the various statues. The intricate detailing and sculpting of the stone were phenomenal, and on closer inspection, they looked almost lifelike in appearance. The gnome sang as she moved from vase to vase with fresh flowers. Her voice was carried by the arched ceiling, which made SJ feel at peace. The lyrics told a tale of the valour and pride of a fallen hero.

The time passed quickly listening to the singing, and Lythonian soon returned.

"Hello, SJ," he said, upon seeing her standing and looking at the immaculate sculpture of one of the gods.

"Hi," she said brightly. "These are amazing."

"They were created long before my time. The sculptor was a famous dwarven stonemason."

"They are so lifelike."

Lythonian smiled. "I do appreciate the detail in them. Anyway, what brings you back here so soon?"

"I have a question to ask of you. Is that okay?"

"Please do."

SJ spent the next few minutes explaining what she had discovered about the necromancer and its following. She watched as Lythonian's face went from shock to outright anger by the time she had finished.

Lythonian did not mess about with his response. "When are we leaving?"

"You are willing to help me? I don't want to pull you away from your duties."

"Disposing of a necromancer is more important than my duties here for a day. I can't abide their art."

"I am meeting Zej at the inn for breakfast, and then we can set off, if that's okay with you."

"I will be there first thing. Do you have transport?"

"I was going to walk."

"I will bring the cart."

"That would be easier. Thank you."

"Not at all."

After bidding Lythonian farewell, she left the church and headed back to town.

"With Lythonian and Zej, I don't think you will need anyone else," Dave said.

"Are you sure? There are at least seven of them."

"A Level 19, 13, and yourself. I doubt you would have even needed Lythonian with you, although having a cleric is always beneficial in a party, especially with the undead."

"That's good to know. We have no idea what level the necromancer is currently at. I didn't see it clearly enough to identify it."

"I would have stopped you attempting to identify it anyway. Necromancers usually have high Intelligence and Wisdom, and Wisdom is your enemy when it comes to your skill being sensed."

"I was in miniature form, though."

"I am just advising you that identifying any of the robed classes is going to be more challenging in general because of their Wisdom levels."

"I am sure you said when we first came here that everything should be balanced to it being a starter town."

"I did, but since arriving, I have realised this is not a normal starter town, nor is what is happening normal."

"What do you mean?"

"A god and a dragon for a start, both of whom you have interacted with, and then the higher levels that reside here as well. I could not find anything in the archives about this town either. It really does seem as though it is rarely used. Yet, it has still evolved well without Legionnaires being present. It's an anomaly on its own."

"Let's go see if Fizzlewick is back yet," SJ said, heading towards the tailor's.

Everything was dark inside the shop, and the closed sign was still hanging on the door.

"I hope he is back soon," SJ grumbled.

"I am sure he will be, eventually. He is a god, though, and works on his own timing, so there are never any guarantees."

Feeling a little dejected about the prospect of not being able to progress her tailoring skills, she headed to the vendors. She had seen several in the town that sold materials and headed to one. "If we don't know when Fizzlewick will return, I'm going to get the cloth bundles, at least."

An hour later, she returned to the inn with ten bundles of cloth in her inventory and picked up some other clothing items to wear in her room, including a nightdress, all for fifty copper. After speaking to Kerys and arranging breakfast for three the next morning at first light, she returned to her room. Training would have to be missed tomorrow because of the quest. SJ felt obliged to let Lorna know she wouldn't attend and found herself missing mobile technology, which had become such a part of everyday life back on Earth. Instead of updating her in seconds, SJ resigned herself to heading over to speak to Lorna in person at the barracks.

Walking down the stairs the next morning, SJ smiled at seeing a table laid out as she had requested. Three places were set, and a large coffee pot stood in the middle of the table. Fhyliss was busy sweeping the floor from the previous evening's activities and waved at SJ as she entered. Sitting at the table, SJ poured herself a large glass of coffee and sipped it while she waited for Lythonian and Zej to arrive.

Lythonian entered first, wearing his usual attire. His gleaming chain-mail and white cloak clashed with the inn's darker tones. Sitting at the table with SJ, he poured himself a coffee after exchanging pleasantries. Fhyliss had raised her eyebrow at seeing Lythonian enter the inn, which implied that he rarely frequented the establishment. Not long after, the inn doors burst open, and Zej walked in.

The vision of pure power that oozed from the dwarf was immense. Wearing a suit of dark blue, full plate armour and holding Betty's impressive form over his broad shoulder, Zej stole SJ's greeting from her lips.

"Lythonian," Zej said as he walked to the table, thudding Betty on the floor next to it.

"Zej, my friend. I have not seen you at a service in a long while."

"Apologies, but I have been busy recently. We had an influx of apprentices that I am slowly whittling down," he said, chuckling. "I was unaware you would be joining us on this adventure?"

"That is my fault, Zej. I only spoke to Lythonian after I saw you. It's not a problem, is it?" SJ said.

"Not at all. Lythonian and I have fought together before, and I know how adept he is with that mace."

"Anything for the path of righteousness," Lythonian responded.

Feeling completely outdone by both of her recruited members, SJ was uncertain of what to do or say. Because they were such high-level fighters in comparison, she could not advise or offer guidance to either of them.

"Would you both like food before we depart?"

"Aye. That sounds good. Floretta cooks a mean breakfast."

"Fhyliss?"

Fhyliss walked over.

"Would it be possible to get three breakfasts, please?" SJ asked, smiling.

"Of course," Fhyliss said, and walked to the serving hatch.

"Fhyliss, can you make mine a double, please?" Zej called after Fhyliss, who turned and smiled in response.

A while later, Zej finished his double portion of breakfast. Floretta had added mushrooms, which tasted divine fried, as SJ had suggested.

"Shall we go?" SJ asked.

"Let's. While the day is still young." Lythonian said, standing.

Walking out of the inn door, Lythonian introduced SJ to Humberto, his horse, who was pulling a cart with enough room for the three of them to sit comfortably. Even with Zej in his plate armour, the horse had no problem pulling the cart. It was the first morning since her arrival that the sun was not blazing.

"Looks like we will have rain this evening or tomorrow," Zej said, looking at the pale blue sky.

Looking up, SJ could see nothing to make her believe it would rain apart from it being a slightly cooler day, but she had no reference.

"I hope we are back by this evening if we make good time getting there."

"I would like to hope so as well," Lythonian added.

"I am sure we can be back for this evening. I don't see a necromancer being too problematic." Zej answered, smiling.

The enthusiasm of the two older warriors affected SJ, and she felt safe and secure knowing that she had two stronger members in the party to support her in completing the quest. As they began the drive to the valley, Zej and Lythonian recounted some of their previous tales of battle and questing.

CHAPTER FORTY-SIX

Compound

After a couple of hours of travel, they reached the lake and cottages in the valley, the track becoming more difficult to traverse as they approached.

"I think we should leave the cart here," Lythonian suggested as they approached Gladys and Hubert's cottage. SJ had brought the deed for Farleck Cottage with her and wanted to claim it, but she was still determining whether she should do so with Zej and Lythonian present. After mulling it over, she decided she would.

"I own a cottage just farther down the lake," SJ said.

"You do?" Zej said, a little surprised.

"Yes. It was given to me."

Zej did not press the matter, and Lythonian did not comment further. SJ now felt uncertain whether she had done the right thing.

Lythonian drove Humberto along the track until SJ indicated the cottage that was hers. It looked as beautiful and idyllic as the first time she had visited it, and hopping down from the cart, she walked over to the door, removed her key, and opened it. Lythonian and Zej were busily untacking Humberto from the cart, and she removed the deed to check that her name was now active on it, which it was. As she smiled to herself, Dave suddenly piped up in her head.

"Did you want to let them know you have a cottage?"

"I trust them," she whispered.

"Trust is earned. Lythonian, you have a reputation with. Zej, you don't. You need to consider your standings before divulging information in the future."

"Okay. Point taken."

Outside, Humberto nibbled on some tall flowers by the side of the cottage. Zej was looking at the roof of the cottage.

"This is a lovely little place," Zej said. "The chimney needs realigning, though."

SJ followed Zej's gaze to where the chimney stood proudly over the rear of the roof; she couldn't see anything wrong with it from her position.

"Does it?"

"Yes. My father was a stonemason, and although I broke the family tradition by becoming a blacksmith, I know a fair bit about the trade."

"Is it safe?"

"Oh, it's safe enough for now. This place has stood empty for a while."

"I have never stayed here. I only just acquired it."

"You can tell by the moss on the chimney. The heat from the chimney would normally keep it clear, as it would dry and fall away. It wouldn't take much to sort it out, but it needs doing at some point."

"Thanks. I will keep that in mind."

"A few masons in town could fix it for you. It shouldn't be too expensive unless they need to acquire new stone."

"Is stone expensive?"

"Not very, but it must be shaped properly, which takes time."

"Oh, I see." SJ was still getting used to the time factor, which became more apparent with everything in Amathera. It was not as though she could just call into a local builders' yard and pick up a hob of bricks.

"Do you mind if I ask how you acquired it?" Zej asked.

SJ felt a rush of panic flood her. How could she explain she got the deed from Darjey or provide any other suitable explanation?

"Tell the truth," Dave said.

How can I tell the truth? she thought.

"Just say what happened. You are a Legionnaire and do not fall under the same remit as townsfolk, remember," Dave continued.

SJ bit her lip and cautiously looked at Zej. Lythonian stood now, listening while brushing the side of Humberto's mane.

"I acquired it through a quest."

"A quest. It's a decent reward for a quest. It must have been challenging."

"It was. It was one of my first."

"What did you have to do?" Zej asked.

"That's the harder part to explain," SJ replied shyly.

"Hard to explain why?"

"It was related to the GoblinPox scare and was my first job for my class."

"Oh. What did it relate to?"

"It's a little hard for me to say."

"Why?" Zej said, frowning.

"It was my first kill."

Zej's eyes shot open at her comment. "You had a kill quest at such a low level. That is a rarity. I didn't get my first one until I was Level 12."

"You have had them also?"

"They are quite standard at times."

"I had no idea. I am still trying to learn about my new life."

"You will in time. You are already doing well for the short time you have been here."

SJ looked surprised at the comment. "What do you mean?"

"I haven't always lived in Killic. I was brought up in the capital, and I have met many Legionnaires over my time. You are a refreshing change compared to many."

"Oh. I didn't realise."

"Who was your target?"

"Another Legionnaire."

"Ahhhh. It is starting to make sense now."

SJ could feel a bead of sweat run down her back, she was so nervous talking to Zej about this.

"Sorry?"

"The Legionnaire found by the mill. Was that your handy work?"

"Not in full, no. I didn't move the body," she stammered.

Lythonian stood by SJ, reaching out and touching her shoulder. "Do not be afraid to speak the truth. I know your true class, and you assisted the church in driving out those who were taking advantage."

SJ looked up at the tall draconian's face before she replied.

"You know my class?"

"Of course. Only one of your kind would use those blades."

The thought had never crossed her mind, and she felt light-headed.

"I thought you were a monk," Zej said, questioning her.

"You are safe here. You can say," Lythonian said.

"I am an assassin."

It was Zej's time to be shocked at her revelation. "An assassin?"

"Yes." SJ dropped her head in shame.

"What an amazing choice! I have never, in my lifetime, met a fae assassin. I would not be surprised if you are unique."

"You think so?" SJ asked.

"If not unique, exceedingly rare," Zej said.

Lythonian smiled at her. "Show Zej your blades."

SJ looked between them before she called her blades to her hands. Zej whistled in appreciation.

"They are a fine-looking set of claws. Do you mind if I inspect them?" Zej asked.

SJ gently removed one of her gloves and handed it to Zej. Carefully taking the weapon and turning it in his hand, he let out another whistle. "These are very impressive. It's a rare weapon at such a low level. How did you acquire them?"

"From a Berserker Badger drop."

"You have something special here. When you level, and they become less useful to you, these will sell for a hefty sum at the auction house."

"Really?"

"Yes. A weapon like this is rare, never mind the bleed effect they possess. You have something to treasure here. Have you been training with them?"

"I have been training in martial arts but not with my claws out. I have not wanted to advertise my class."

"You should do. There will be adjustments you can make to your style to improve your combat ability."

"I thought assassins were frowned upon?"

"No." Lythonian said, "An assassin is a class, after all. It's how you use your class that matters. Even rogues can be good."

"It feels nice to talk to you both about it. I have been so nervous about anyone finding out."

"Some frown upon different classes. It's no different from myself and necromancers," Lythonian said, turning and spitting.

Seeing the draconian spit in anger was more alarming than anything she had witnessed.

"So you think it's all right to tell people I'm an assassin?"

"I wouldn't openly advertise it, but if you trust the people you are speaking to, then there is no harm," Lythonian said. "When you assisted me at the church hall, it was obvious what your class was. A monk never uses a weapon, as they have specific abilities that strengthen their martial arts skills."

"I am sorry I lied to you, Zej," SJ said.

"There is no need to apologise. I would have been as cautious as you have been," he said, smiling and returning her glove.

SJ was relieved at her revelation and felt like a weight had been lifted from her shoulders. She now had people she could talk to.

"Thank you for your honesty and trust," Zej stated.

> Congratulations! Reputation with Zej has increased to Friendly.

"Now we have started to be more truthful . . . what happened with this Legionnaire?" Zej asked with a broad grin.

It took another twenty minutes or so for SJ to fully explain what had happened during her quest to help the town and free Setu. Zej asked her questions about specific aspects while Lythonian stood listening quietly.

"You have had an unusual start to a new life here," Lythonian said.

"Why is that?" SJ asked.

"Your quests are already aligned to a higher path than I can ever remember."

"Higher path?"

"If I didn't know better, I would think the gods look down on you fondly."

SJ felt her cheeks redden at the comment. There was no way she would mention Fizzlewick or Bob to them. At least not yet.

Lythonian walked over to Humberto, grabbed his reins, moved him to a small tree to the side of the cottage, and tied him up. He had had his fill of flower heads.

"Shall we continue to this necromancer, then?" Zej asked.

"Let's," SJ said, smiling with newfound confidence.

Dave was talking in her head as they began to walk towards the location.

"The interactions you have just had are, again, another anomaly. I have witnessed similar before in much larger towns or cities, but never in a starter town.

I am starting to believe that everything about you is different. It is as though you are at a higher level in all interactions, yet you aren't. Not signing the T's and C's has completely changed the dynamics so that you have Amatherean freedom with Legionnaire potential."

SJ could not respond, so she simply listened to his musings.

"The fact that you can openly discuss your class as an assassin without repercussions and directly understand the influences of the class systems that people choose is very strange, yet not when considering how everyday Amathereans interact. Only the emphasis of a Legionnaire would generally equate to the levels of concern. This whole novel approach is nothing I have ever handled before."

"I am as new to this as you are. I have only ever had to contend with standard approaches, and we know, as your waiver status suggests, that you do not fall under anything that has existed before in the world.

"We will achieve great things in time, which again is something you have plenty of. You may one day reach Level 100," Dave finished.

Reaching a crossroads on the track, SJ informed Zej and Lythonian that the area was pretty close now.

"How do we want to handle this?" SJ asked, nervous tension building in her. She felt her hands shake slightly with the trepidation of what was to come.

"First, you need to form a party," Zej said.

"How?"

"I'm not sure what you have as a Legionnaire. I can try to explain and see if it helps. On your display, there should be a small set of three dots. Do you see them?"

"Yes."

"Select them, and there should be an invitation feature."

SJ checked, and there, indeed, was an invitation feature. Selecting the option, she then chose Lythonian and Zej and added them. Within moments, her display triggered; they'd both accepted her invitation. On her display, there were three bars. Each showed the health of other party members, including the numerical values.

"Wow," SJ said, looking at their health compared to herself. "You have a lot of health."

"Tank build." Zej grinned.

"Defensive build for myself," Lythonian said.

Compared to SJ's paltry health, Zej's at Level 19 was nearly 300. His Constitution must have been high alongside his Strength to boost his stats so high. Lythonian's at Level 13 was much higher than her own, standing at 70.

"Are you able to scout ahead?" Lythonian asked, looking at SJ.

"Sure," she said, shrinking to her miniature form.

"It always amazes me every time I witness that," Zej said, smiling now and looking down at SJ's six-inch form. Beating her wings, SJ took off and continued down the track ahead of her friends. Reaching the brow of the depression, she looked down to where she could only see two skeletons. She watched for a few minutes before returning to where Lythonian and Zej had stopped at a distance from the brow.

"Only two outside," she reported.

"You said five and a phantom plus the necromancer?"

"That is all I saw. Yes."

"Okay," Zej said. "We want to avoid fighting them indoors if we can help it. I prefer to be in the open. Betty is not the easiest weapon to use in a confined space."

"I agree. I would prefer to draw them out," Lythonian added.

"There is a wall around the compound. It is not very tall, but it would still slow you down approaching them."

"Based on the information you provided about their levels, I have no concerns about attacking directly," Zej replied.

"I am much weaker than you are, though."

"I will taunt them, don't worry. It is a tank trait that should draw their attention."

"Stay small and wait for an opportunity," Lythonian advised.

"Okay," SJ said.

"Also, if possible, do not destroy the skeletons. They are in servitude, after all. The necromancer's death can free them, and then we can see what alignment they hold and decide how to handle them," Lythonian said.

"Understood," Zej said.

"Give me a minute to get closer if that's okay?" SJ asked.

"We will approach in three minutes," Zej said.

SJ flitted back towards the brow and moved around the edge of the depression, staying out of sight of the buildings until she was aligned towards the back of the building the necromancer had been inside. Thick black smoke was pouring from the main building's chimney, and as SJ edged towards the building's rear, she heard a deep moaning sound. It didn't sound like the phantom.

She reached the corner just as the first sign of Lythonian and Zej appeared on the track. She watched as a bright light enveloped Zej, and he began to walk towards the compound, Betty still casually slung over his shoulder. The skeletons noticed them almost immediately and shouted. The door opened to one of the other buildings where SJ had seen the prisoners being kept, and two more skeletons appeared. She then heard the voice of the necromancer. She could not see it from where she was behind the building.

"Who dares disturb my work?" it cried in anger.

"Those who cleanse Amathera of your dark kind," Lythonian said in a thundering draconian voice. It shocked SJ to see the expression of pure hatred that now covered his face as he looked into the compound. SJ edged farther around, flying over the wall and landing on the ground, then moving to the corner of the building.

Zej walked calmly and deliberately towards the compound entrance with

Lythonian close behind him. Neither showed any sign of concern or hesitation as they approached.

"Destroy them," the necromancer shouted. The fifth skeleton had appeared from inside the main building behind the necromancer and the phantom. The skeletons and phantom formed up and approached Zej.

The archer fired an arrow at him. At the short range they were away, it struck his armour with a resounding ping, bouncing off harmlessly. Zej, walking with his full plate armour and plumed helm, looked stunning with the sun's rays reflecting off its highly glossed surface. One skeleton vanished from view. The archer kept firing at Zej, who paid no attention to its feeble arrows that could not penetrate his thick armour. The phantom wailed as it swooped forward, and reaching out, a black strand left its hand and flew at Zej. He raised his hand in defence, catching the black stream as it hit him. He pulled his arm back slightly, and Lythonian suddenly cast a bright ray of light at the phantom. It wailed in response, dropping its attack and leaping away from Lythonian's.

The first of the skeletons reached Zej as the phantom withdrew, and it swung its sword towards the armour-clad fighter. Zej swung Betty in defence, bringing her around in a sweeping arc and battering its strike away as the others moved in to attack. Zej, after parrying the blow of the first skeleton, then swung Betty in a low and swift strike, catching the leg of a skeleton. The strike sent its lower limb flying, and the skeleton fell sideways to the ground, incapacitated.

Lythonian had moved forward and tried hitting the phantom again with another bolt of light. SJ was still standing, dumbfounded, watching the fight unfold, when she heard the chanting of the necromancer. Dave's voice exploded in her head.

"That necromancer is Level 21," he screamed in a warning tone.

"Damn. How come it is so high?" SJ whispered.

"I have no idea. It shouldn't even be in this territory," Dave replied.

The necromancer's hand formed a cloud of mist as it chanted.

"Stop that spell if you can," Dave said.

SJ moved into action, spurred by Dave's comment. The moment she was behind the necromancer, she landed and grew. Her claws equipped, she struck at its back, plunging both sets into its robed body. The necromancer cried out in pain as its health bar dropped slightly. She could not tell by how much as she had not identified it. As soon as she struck, she reduced her size again. She had disrupted its casting, but it spun to see who attacked it.

The face that looked on SJ as she shrank was that of pure evil. A gnarled face and sunken eyes with black rings and pitted skin stared at her as she finished transforming. Taking off, she flew away as fast as she could. The fact that it had seen her meant she could no longer hide, and she flew back to the corner of the building quickly.

The necromancer cried out as a bolt of energy left its hand aimed straight for her. She saw it at the last moment and threw her flying form onto the ground; the bolt just missed her. Crashing down, only six inches tall, with a Level 21 necromancer focusing his wrath on her, was not good. That was when Lythonian arrived.

Charging towards the necromancer, shield up and mace held high, he swung at its distracted form, and his mace caught the necromancer on its side. The necromancer howled in pain, again its health only dropping by a small amount as it spun on Lythonian and grabbed for his arm. Lythonian stepped backwards as it did.

"Don't let him touch you," Lythonian called with intensity in his voice.

SJ picked herself up from the ground and took off again, flying away from the necromancer, who was now focusing on Lythonian. The necromancer chanted again, and a new cloud formed in its hand.

Zej had disabled three of the five skeletons, all of which were fighters. The phantom was again trying to drain or do something to him, and he walked towards it, grimacing as the dark light struck him. SJ noticed that Zej's health was slowly being drained by whatever the phantom was hitting him with, but only by small increments. Zej got in range and brought Betty around in a violent and decisive motion. The phantom, still attempting to drain Zej even so close, was caught by the hammer's flat face, and it rippled when struck, its body unaffected by the impact.

Lythonian noticed it happen and, while backing away from the necromancer, called out, "Switch. Watch its touch!"

He and Lythonian swapped places, and the armour-clad powerhouse that was Zej moved quickly towards the necromancer. SJ had moved to the archer, who was busy trying to hit either of them when she could. An arrow struck Lythonian in his shoulder, and he cried out as it found a weakness in his chain-mail; the arrow now stood protruding from it. Lythonian finished the spell he had been casting, and as he did, the skies seemed to open and a bright light suddenly enveloped the phantom.

As soon as the light struck the phantom, it wailed and moaned, its body bathed in what SJ could only assume was holy light. Its form shrank, and a fine yellow strand escape from its dark-robed form. In amazement, SJ watched as it suddenly grew into a ball of light and flew upwards into the sky, the phantom's robes falling to the ground where it had stood.

The cloud the necromancer had been forming suddenly burst forth and struck Zej. Zej held Betty in front of himself, trying to shield himself from the blast, but to no avail. The cloud hit him, and he screamed as SJ saw his skin turn a green colour from the spell. Lythonian, hearing the scream, turned and started chanting towards Zej.

SJ had reached the archer now and grew behind her. On reaching her full height, she not only struck at her legs with a sweeping kick but also swung her claws at the bow. They sizzled through the air and cut through its string, making the partly pulled arrow ping off harmlessly as the skeleton's legs were removed from under it. It fell on the ground with a clattering of its bones.

That was when SJ felt a sharp, searing pain in her shoulder. The fifth skeleton, the rogue that had disappeared from view, must have been waiting for an opening and had pierced her shoulder with its vicious strike. Taking nine damage, she winced in pain and turned to face it. She could not focus on Zej and Lythonian; now she had a fight to win. Stomping down on the skeletal archer's shoulder, she made sure it could not react and snarled at the rogue standing before her.

CHAPTER FORTY-SEVEN

Burn, Baby, Burn

The rogue slashed at her, and SJ's Dexterity was the only thing that saved her from being cut across the face.

Withdrawing a couple of paces, she moved into her martial arts stance, her claws ready in front of her. Using bladed weapons against a skeletal body was possibly not the best, but if she punched and kicked, it would hopefully still have the desired effect.

The skeleton stepped in and jabbed forward with its blade, attempting to stab at her chest. She instinctively brought her hand upwards, blocking the attack, and drove her foot towards the skeleton. She was slightly wide where she would normally have met the fleshy feeling of a thigh, and her strike only brushed its femur. Cursing, she drew back as it again slashed its blade towards her body.

She could not read the skeleton's emotions, and it was strange hearing it groan and grunt as it tried to attack her. She stepped back yet again as it continued towards her. She wanted to incapacitate it rather than try to break it, so she kicked, aiming for its side. The attack caught the skeleton on its ribs, and it made a sound as though the air had just been forced from its lungs, which was obviously impossible.

Stepping back, it composed itself before attacking again, moving in and slashing repeatedly towards her. She parried its blade with her arms and claws. Her training with Lorna and the new martial arts style with the adapted stance left her more open than she was used to, and she needed to adjust. Switching it up, she went on the offensive. As the blade swept towards her face, she moved into the strike, catching the forearm of the skeleton on her raised arm and punching forward with her free hand. Her fist clattered into its sternum.

Her claws were useless in this fight, on more than one occasion missing completely as she struggled to compensate for the narrow target of a bone rather than flesh. The claws had already caused a punch to glance off its ribcage, reducing the impact, so she recalled them to her inventory as she continued her attack. Completing a series of swift punches and kicks, she powered the skeleton backwards and away from her. Her fists had been hurting from the strikes against solid bone even wearing the gloves, and now her knuckles felt every strike, making her wince. She would need to increase her Constitution to punch more freely without the pain she was incurring—but there was nothing she could do at the moment. She was still trying not to destroy it and at no point aimed for its skull, only focusing on trying to take out one of its legs.

It staggered backwards from her onslaught until she stepped back again, giving herself more room. The skeleton shook its head and made the motion of cracking its neck before it moved forward again. With only fist and foot strikes, she wasn't doing much damage at all, although its health had fallen slightly from her onslaught. As it stepped in again, holding its blade, SJ swept low and brought her shin into contact with its own. The sweep connected with power and precision this time.

She heard a crack as the rogue's ankle bone snapped from the impact. The skeleton stumbled forward, crashing into her, and its dagger, held out in front of it, caught SJ in her arm as it fell on top of her, causing her a further five damage. The skeleton had groaned in pain from its dislodged ankle, and she scrambled frantically from underneath it, trying to push it off her while watching for the blade it still held. Rolling away, she went to stand again and backed away from it. The skeleton was trying to stand, but with its broken ankle, it could not support its own weight, falling back down to one knee. Resting its hand on the ground, still holding the dagger, it stared at SJ.

The archer she had taken out was lying on the floor, its shoulder having been dislodged, meaning it could not have used the bow even if it didn't have a cut string. SJ was panting from the fight with the skeleton and glanced at Lythonian and Zej to see how they were faring. The kneeling skeleton threw itself towards SJ, pushing up with its one good leg as it tried to lunge at her. She noticed the movement, stepped back again, and allowed it to miss and flounder onto the ground again. It cursed at her.

SJ ignored it again, turning to glance at the others. The necromancer's health was down to a quarter, but so was Zej's. Lythonian was doing better, but he had still taken damage. In shock at Zej's health level, she could not help but support him. Her own health was down to two-thirds.

"Be careful," Dave said. "If a curse hits you, it is likely to kill you."

"I won't get hit, then," SJ snarled as she ran at the back of the necromancer, equipping her blades.

The skeleton yelled to the necromancer as she neared, and it glanced back but not in enough time to prevent SJ from leaping forward and kicking it square in its lower back. The necromancer groaned from the impact, not taking any damage but knocked off balance by her attack. She lunged forward, her claws striking at it as it staggered to regain its balance. In the same instant, Zej swung Betty. Hammering into the side of the necromancer, its staggering form increased the momentum of the impact between Betty and its side.

Screaming in pain, the necromancer's health plummeted from the attack. SJ swiped her clawed hands across its unprotected back as it recoiled from the force and carried Betty back towards her. Her blades sliced through its robes easily, and she noticed the greying, withered skin beneath as they cut deeply. It was now down to its last few hit points. It turned and reached out to touch SJ, and she recoiled backwards.

The scream that erupted from Lythonian was deafening as he charged straight at the necromancer with his shield held high. The necromancer, with three foes surrounding it, could not react to them all at once, and the shield slammed into it, lifting it from its feet and, with the draconian's height advantage, carrying it backwards. Lythonian kept powering his legs with the necromancer across his shield straight into the side of the building. With a sickening thud, its head bounced off the wall as its body was crushed against it—its health fell to zero.

When Lythonian stepped back, the crumpled remains of the necromancer slithered to the ground at the base of the wall. Its hood fell backwards, revealing its horrific face and head for the first time. It looked as though it had been scalded and burned with acid. Its withered and mottled grey skin stretched taught with various scars. As its body struck the ground, SJ's display triggered.

Quest: Necromantic Prevention—Complete
You have defeated the evil necromancer and disabled his minions.
Rewards: 550xp, shared between party members = 185xp awarded

Combined experience gained for the death of the evil necromancer and phantom 630xp, shared between party members = 210xp awarded

---

SJ checked her experience gains.

Experience:	626 of 800

If the adjudicator ever replied, she might still earn enough to reach Level 7.

The five skeletons that had been disabled during the fight were now sitting on the ground, looking around at each other as though unsure of what to do. Lythonian turned to Zej, removed a blue bottle from his inventory, and drank it. As soon as he finished it, he chanted, and a band of white light similar to what SJ had received in the church hall struck Zej. The green tint on his face from the necromancer's curse faded, and his health increased.

"He was much higher-level than I expected," Zej said, standing with Betty resting on the ground beside him. His face was covered in beads of sweat. Removing his helm, he placed it on Betty's handle and turned to look at the skeletons.

"Now, then, what are we going to do with you five?" he asked them.

The female archer, now sitting and holding her displaced shoulder, spoke before the others. "You have made my dream come true. Now I am no longer under his entrapment, I feel as though my soul has been returned," Charlotte said.

"Lythonian. What do you think?" Zej asked.

As he finished streaming his healing into Zej, whose health was nearly back up to half, Lythonian looked at the skeletons before replying, "I will check their alignments. Depending upon what I read, I will decide whether they live or are sent to their permanent afterlife."

Two of the skeletal fighters, who'd each lost one or both of their legs to Zej's war hammer, began to crawl away from where they lay.

"I think we have an answer for two of you already," Zej said. Lifting his helm from Betty, he handed it to SJ, who took it as he hefted Betty again and walked towards them. They screamed as the war hammer was brought down on their skulls, crushing them into fragments, the light in their eyes dimming and fading for the last time.

The three remaining skeletons watched the show, and if they could have displayed terror on their faces, SJ believed they would have. The large orc fighter was still lying on the ground with his displaced leg some fifteen feet away.

"I, for one, am glad to be free also," he said, groaning as he pulled himself across the ground towards his leg.

The rogue had not replied and just sat silently on the ground. Lythonian removed a small device from his inventory and, saying a few words, held it in front of the rogue. It looked like a magnifying glass in design, but as he spoke an incantation, the glass changed colour. It turned a dark blue, and Lythonian raised a draconian eyebrow.

"I have not met many rogues of your alignment before. Chaotic good," Lythonian said, before walking to the archer and the fighter and doing the same. This time the glass turned an orange colour, which Lythonian announced meant they were true neutral.

After finishing his inspections, Lythonian stated, "I see no reason they can't be trusted to return to society."

"That settles it, then," Zej said, smiling. "Now, would one of you like to tell me what you have been doing here?"

The archer replied first. "We got here two months or so ago. I have been in the necromancer's charge for several years. He has been attempting to create an abomination. We had been collecting blood from a gnoll hunting tribe based on the other side of the valley and bringing it back here."

"What about you two?" Zej asked.

The fighter replied, saying he had been in his service for a year, and the rogue was the most recent addition, having only been part of the necromancer's group for three months. The two fighters Zej had destroyed were long-term minions of the necromancer, as was the phantom Lythonian had banished.

"If we do free you and let you go, where will you go?" Lythonian asked.

"I don't know, being honest," the orc said. "I am not even sure where we are."

"You are close to Killic," Zej answered.

"Killic! We have travelled that far south," the rogue said, a little startled.

SJ had been watching this all unfold when she suddenly remembered about the prisoners.

"Where are the prisoners?" she said.

"In the building over there." The rogue pointed towards the building SJ had seen them taken into previously. Leaving Lythonian and Zej with the skeletons, she walked over to the building and entered.

The stench that hit her nostrils of unclean and unkempt bodies made her gag. Inside was dimly lit, with a single candle burning on the top of a bottle on a small table. The windows were all boarded up, and six cages were inside the building. Two of the cages were occupied, and SJ removed a torch from her inventory and lit it with the candle's flickering flame, which illuminated the forms of the two elves she had seen huddled at the rear of their cages.

"Are you okay?" she asked softly, walking towards them.

The closest elf turned to look at her with terror-filled eyes that made it look half crazy. The elf in the second cage also turned and spoke with a gravelly, parched throat. "Who are you?"

"I am here to free you both," SJ said in a calm and gentle tone.

"Free us," the crazed-looking elf said as it chuckled. It seemed to have lost its mind during its time at the compound.

"Yes, free you," SJ said, walking to the cage door. The crazed elf moved as far away as possible and curled up in the corner. The cage floors were covered in straw, and the elves had been kept as though they were livestock. In each cage was a wooden bowl containing water and a bucket. They both appeared to be emaciated. Each of the cage doors was locked with a padlock.

"I will find the keys," SJ said.

Zej was busy placing the orc's leg by his side as SJ walked outside.

"Where are the cage keys?" SJ called.

Zej looked around where he stood and saw a set on the belt of a skeleton he had crushed the skull of. He picked them up and threw them to SJ, who caught them before returning to the cages. The smell again hit her as she entered. Walking straight to the doors, she unlocked them both. The second elf hurried from the cage, looking at SJ with suspicion but not as much fear as the one still curled in the corner, jabbering to themself.

"Come on, you are free. You can leave here," SJ said in a kind voice.

"Leave. No, I must stay. I am food. I am food for the phantom."

"No. The phantom is dead. You are free to live your life again," SJ said. "Do you know them?" This she directed to the other elf.

"Only since being here. We are not from the same village," he said.

"Lythonian," SJ called out the door.

Moments later, the large draconian walked into the building. If the smell affected him, he did not show it.

"They will not leave the cage. They say they are phantom food and must stay."

"I will speak to them. You take the other outside."

SJ led the freed elf back into the sunlight. He squinted as his eyes adjusted to the brightness. The elf scanned over the dead necromancer, the empty robes of the phantom, and the broken skeletons on the ground.

"Why are they still alive?" he asked, staring at the three sitting on the ground.

Zej stepped towards the elf. "They have been freed of their master. Our cleric friend has checked their alignments, and there is no reason they should not be able to return to their professions or trades and live a life as a reborn."

The elf was dressed in tattered clothes, his dishevelled state even more apparent in the light of day.

Going into her inventory, SJ removed some of her dry rations and waterskin and handed them to the elf.

"Thank you," he said, smiling at her.

"Where did you come from?" SJ asked.

"A small village a day's travel from here, on the other side of the valley towards Asterfal. We have both been here a couple of months. I was just walking home when I was feared by the phantom and grabbed by the skeletons."

The rogue, hearing what the elf said, spoke. "I am sorry that I captured you. I had no option but to do as instructed."

The elf looked at the rogue warily. SJ doubted he would ever trust an undead again.

"I am guessing you will head back home?" SJ asked.

"I will. My family will have wondered what has happened to me."

Hearing the elf mention his family and how they had missed him hit SJ like a freight train. She thought again of her own family and supposed they must have been upset by her death, however far away she had grown from them over the years. Feeling anger and frustration brewing, she kicked out at a pebble, sending it spinning across the ground and clonking the orc's leg, which was still sitting by his side.

"Sorry," SJ said. The orc was just looking at her. "What's inside?" she asked the archer, pointing towards the main building.

"The necromancer's labs and quarters. We rarely went in there unless it needed things moved."

Making her way to the entrance, she peered into the gloom of the arched door. Thankfully, there were torches lining the walls. Inside, she entered an open room with three doors leading from it. The building on the outside had a large rectangular shape, and the entrance was offset to the left. Walking to the first room and trying the door, SJ found it opened into what must have been a kitchen at some point. Empty plates and bowls littered the area, and there was a stove that didn't look like it had been lit for a very long time. The stone walls had a layer of grime, and thick cobwebs hung from the room's corners and across the ceiling rafters.

She went to the second door opposite and opened it into a bedchamber. The room's centrepiece was a large, dishevelled double bed with stained sheets, and a desk and chair stood to one side. It must have been where the necromancer slept. The room smelt stale, like the scent mouldy fruit gives off, as though something had been decomposing in it. She walked to the desk, which was covered in pieces of parchment filled with tiny scribbles and drawings that SJ couldn't quite read in the torchlight. It was then she noticed the boarded window. Moving to it, she pulled the boards away, pried the shutter open, and forced the window that was stuck in its frame wide, flooding the inside with light and fresh air.

Searching the room, SJ found nothing of interest, but she still gathered and placed all the parchment notes in her inventory. The one thing she made sure she picked up was the ink-well and feather the necromancer had used for writing. The ink-well was a small silver pot with clawed feet, and she was sure it would be worth a few coins at least. Leaving the room, she went to the last door at the end of the entrance room. Through the doorway, it turned right and opened into a much larger room, which, based on the building's appearance from outside, took up most of the interior. The room was again lit by torchlight. There were tables around the room, and several body parts of animals and what she believed to be humanoid forms lay on their surfaces.

One table was covered in jars and vials of various liquids and several unrecognisable body parts; all SJ could identify, her stomach turning, were a heart and a liver. The main thing that drew her attention was the malformed body that was lying in a huge bath of blood. Its head seemed to have been created from at least two different beasts, and its body was also made of mismatched parts. This had to be the abomination the necromancer had been trying to create. She shuddered involuntarily at its deformed and grotesque shape. It was approximately ten feet long from its head to its clawed feet.

The stench was over-powering and SJ forced open the darkened windows to clear the air before she searched the remainder of the room. The abomination looked as though it had everything it needed anatomically, and she noticed scribbling on the floor surrounding the bath comprising runes and symbols. She could only guess that the necromancer had been preparing to perform a ritual. Thankfully, by all accounts, they had got it before it had risen.

A few items looked valuable, so she dropped them into her inventory, although she would also check with Lythonian and Zej. Walking back out into the fresh air from the macabre quarters of the necromancer was more refreshing than she expected, and she stood in the entranceway, taking a couple of deep lungfuls of air.

"Are you okay?" Zej asked, concern etched on his face.

"I am fine. I think we got here just in time, based on what is lying inside there."

Zej raised his eyebrows and walked over. "I will go see."

SJ stepped aside and let him in. Several minutes later, he walked back outside carrying a small chest.

"Where was that? I didn't see it."

"Under the bed."

"Oh, I never looked. Glad you did."

"That abomination is horrendous. If it had arisen, god forbid what damage it may have done."

Lythonian appeared in the other building's doorway, supporting the elf by his arm and speaking softly. He then walked him towards the other elf, who handed him some of SJ's rations.

The skeletons had all moved to each other now, with the archer being the most mobile.

"Have you looted the corpse yet?" Lythonian asked, walking over to them.

"No. Go ahead," SJ said.

Lythonian moved to loot the corpse of the necromancer. SJ's display was triggered, presumably because they were a party.

> 1 x Poisoned Dagger +4, 1 x Body Bag—10 slots, 1 x Robes of the Damned +3, 1 x Ring of Mana Regeneration +2, 3 x Lesser Mana Potions, 2 x Lesser Healing Potions, 83 x Copper, 23 x Silver

"I hate necromancers so much," Lythonian growled.

"Take what you want from the loot, and we can split the coin," SJ said.

"I would take the ring and the mana potions, if that's all right?"

"Sure. What about you, Zej?"

"You take the loot. I am fine with the coin split." As he spoke, he was busy digging the tip of Betty's spike into the chest lid, prising it open.

"What are these?" Zej said. He tilted the chest forward to show them three large, knobbly, blue-green eggs sitting on top of a silken cushion.

"Holy goblin spawns." Dave's voice suddenly erupted in her head.

He'd been silent for so long that SJ jumped slightly at the sudden intrusion.

"Those are miniature wyvern eggs," Dave shouted excitedly. "They can be hatched and trained from birth. There are specialist druids who are skilled in their training. Having a miniature wyvern as a pet is an awesome thing. They are highly sought after and valuable. I would not sell them. You need to locate a trainer. There may be one in Asterfal, the closest city."

Lythonian bent over, looking at the eggs. "If they belonged to the necromancer, we should destroy them," he said emphatically.

"NO," SJ shouted a little louder than she meant to. "I know what they are. They're miniature wyvern eggs. They can be hatched and trained as valuable pets."

"Wyvern eggs. Why would a necromancer have those, and how do you know?" Zej asked.

"They were mentioned in the quest, but I had forgotten about them. I have no idea why a necromancer had them," SJ said, "but we can't destroy them. They are valuable."

"If you say so. I have never heard of them before. I know of wyverns but not miniatures."

"Well, there are three, so we have one each," SJ said, smiling at them both. Lythonian just shrugged in response, not very taken by the eggs.

SJ collected the loot items and split the coin between them.

Zej was heading to the third building they had not entered yet. It had a large set of double doors. "Wait," SJ called as he went to open them.

"What?" He turned, looking at her.

"I think the lizorse are in there. They had a wagon and lizorse when I came the first time."

Zej paused his hand on the handle and looked at the skeletons on the ground. "Are they?"

"Yes," the archer responded.

"Are they tethered?"

"Yes, why?"

"Is the wagon any good?"

"It's just a basic model."

"Ah. I won't bother, then," Zej said, letting go of the handle.

"We need to burn this place and leave," Lythonian said, looking skywards. "The rain is coming."

SJ looked up at the still-clear sky, confused by the comment, but again would not question the locals.

"What do we do about them?" SJ asked, looking at the elves and skeletons.

"We head back to the cottage. Then from there, we can use the cart to transport them back to town. They can make their way from there," Lythonian responded.

"Can you heal the skeletons so they can walk?" SJ asked.

"I can. I have been waiting for my mana to regenerate," he replied.

A while later, all three skeletons were back on their feet, the orc bowing to Lythonian and singing his praises for healing his leg. It took a little longer to get the elf that Lythonian had calmed to accompany them. Still, eventually, the group returned to the cottage, leaving the now-burning remains of the necromancer's building behind them.

CHAPTER FORTY-EIGHT

When It Rains, It Pours

They reached the cottage after a couple of hours. During the return journey, SJ had learned the elves names. Jasitu was the elf that she had freed and the other was called Disarus who Lythonian kept having to deal with. He had tried to run off several times, wanting to return to the compound. But they all made it to SJ's cottage, where Humberto neighed at Lythonian, who walked straight up to him, patted him, and whispered in his ear.

"What are you going to do now you are free?" SJ asked the skeletons while they all waited for Lythonian to attach Humberto to the cart.

"I have no idea. I never believed I would be free again," the archer said.

"What did you do before as a profession?" SJ asked.

"I was a gardener."

"And you two?" SJ asked the others.

"My profession was as a carpenter," the orc replied.

The rogue looked away slightly and whispered a response.

"Sorry? I didn't hear you," SJ asked.

"I was a sweeper."

"A sweeper?"

"A chimney-sweep."

Considering all the buildings had fireplaces, it made perfect sense they would have chimney-sweeps. "What's wrong with that?" SJ asked, frowning.

Dave replied, "Chimney-sweeping is a profession forced on those caught thieving. It is classed as a criminal profession. A skeletal chimney-sweep is very novel, though."

SJ didn't push the rogue into elaborating now that Dave had provided context. Instead, she changed the conversation's direction: "I suppose now that you have another chance at eternal life, you could learn another profession?"

"Unfortunately, no," Zej said. "Undead can no longer learn new professions."

"Couldn't they still learn something new even if they can't level it, though?"

"I suppose it's possible. I've just never heard of anyone doing it before."

The small well by the cottage had a rope and bucket attached, and SJ needed to refill her waterskin. The two elves had drunk most of it. Turning the handle on the well, the wooden gears spun freely, and the bucket did not rise.

"Damn," she cursed.

The skeletal orc, having seen what she was doing, walked over. "I can sort that out. It won't take too long to make some new cogs for it. The whole frame could do with being replaced, looking at how worn it is."

"Could you? That would be amazing. Actually, I have an idea," SJ said, smiling at the orc and then turning to look at the other two skeletons.

"What?" the archer asked.

"Why don't you three stop here for now? I know you don't need food, so it's not as though you will go hungry, and you can sort yourselves out and decide what you want to do going forward."

"Whose cottage is this?" the rogue asked.

"Mine," SJ said.

"You would be happy for us to stay here?" the orc said, surprised.

"Yes. At least, I don't plan on living here now, and it needs to be furnished properly. Before considering living here, I must bring supplies from town."

The archer looked at the rogue and the fighter before returning her gaze to SJ. "I think we would all be very grateful to stay here for now, if that's really okay."

"Of course. Make yourselves at home. I would ask a favour, though," SJ said.

"Yes?" the orc asked.

"Would you tidy the place up a little while I'm gone? The garden is overgrown and messy, and the well could be repaired, as you mentioned. There is also a second cottage down the lake-side that could use some attention."

"That sounds a fair exchange," the orc said with what SJ assumed was a smile. Even the rogue appeared to be happy with that idea.

"If you go down past the next cottage, there is another abandoned and derelict cottage. I don't know if there is still a deed for it, but it is in a shocking state. If you repaired that one, you may have somewhere you could even make your own."

"We will prioritise your cottage before any others," the archer responded.

SJ removed the key from her inventory and opened the door to the cottage. There was nothing inside of value, so she couldn't lose anything by them staying here. In fact, it might benefit her, if they repaired the well and sorted things out.

"What are all your names, by the way?" SJ asked.

"I am Charlotte," the archer said, "and this is Terence"—she indicated the giant orc skeleton—"and Brian"—she pointed to the rogue.

"It is nice to meet you all officially. I am SJ, if you hadn't already guessed."

Lythonian had finished attaching Humberto to the cart, and with a bit of strong-armed persuasion, Disarus was eventually made to climb into it. The other elf sat next to him to keep him calm.

"I think we are ready to head back," Zej said.

SJ walked over to Charlotte and handed her the cottage key. "Here. I will return in a few days and see how you progress."

"Thank you, and we will do what we can to sort things out," Charlotte said.

The three skeletons watched as the cart moved down the track away from Farleck Cottage. "Very generous of you to let them stay there," Lythonian said as they distanced themselves.

"I have no need for it at the moment, and if they can look after it and sort things out, it benefits both sides."

"I agree. It's just that Legionnaires are not known for being as concerned about Amathereans as you are. You are a breath of fresh air compared to many."

SJ blushed, feeling the heat in her cheeks. She believed she was acting no different to how she had always been back on Earth. Yes, it was a different world, but her grandfather had always told her to treat others as she wished to be treated.

"Thank you," she replied shyly.

The journey back to town was uneventful. Thankfully, Disarus did not escape from the cart. As they reached the valley's top and passed through the meadow, the skies darkened. It was as though someone had instantly turned a light off. SJ looked across the meadow and towards the lake and saw heavy dark clouds building over its surface.

"Won't be long now," Zej said.

"The skies looked clear this morning. How did you know it was going to rain?" SJ asked.

"The temperature; as soon as the sun weakens, we know rain is due."

It wasn't as if they had a meteorology department sending the latest weather alerts.

"We should be back before it starts," Lythonian added, spurring Humberto on now they were back on relatively flat ground.

As they neared the edge of town, the first raindrops fell. The air temperature had dropped, and the breeze slowly built in force. After dropping Zej at the smithy and thanking him for his help, SJ and Lythonian continued to the church.

"What do we do with the elves?" SJ asked Lythonian quietly.

"I will need to spend time with Disarus who is still affected, but Jasitu can hopefully return to his village as soon as possible."

Pulling up outside the church hall, SJ jumped down and helped the elves from the back of the cart. She removed a silver coin from her inventory and handed it to the sane elf.

"Here, take this. It will allow you to get clothes, food, and drink, and hopefully passage back to your village."

"Thank you so much for your kindness and for freeing us," the elf said, bowing deeply. "If you are ever near the village of Cuopi, please do call in. It's only a small village, and we don't have much to offer, but you will always be welcome."

Congratulations! Reputation with Jasitu increased to Friendly.

"Thank you. If I am ever in the area, I will call in. I wish you good luck," SJ said. "I will stop by to see you tomorrow, Lythonian."

"No problem. Thank you for the adventure. It has been a few years, and I enjoyed myself today," the draconian said, smiling fondly at her.

The side of Lythonian SJ had seen was that of a righteous defender, and his stalwart behaviour and gentle manner had again been shown to hide a warrior at heart.

> Congratulations! Reputation with Lythonian has increased to Popular.

SJ headed back towards the inn, and the rain fell heavier as she did. Many of the usual vendors were no longer present on the streets, and the usual open stalls were closed or empty. On reaching the inn, she was amazed to see how busy it was inside. According to her display, it was only mid-afternoon, yet it looked as it usually did in the early evenings. Seeing Bert standing by the bar, she waved and went upstairs to her room. The large troll smiled back at her.

In her room, she emptied her inventory and placed the items on the table. Zej had given her the chest that had held the miniature wyvern eggs. She opened the lid and admired the beautiful colour of their shells, the iridescent shimmering fixing her gaze.

"I am trying to find out their value," Dave said.

"How can you do that?"

"Secret."

"We have no secrets. We are best friends," SJ said.

Silence.

"Dave? Are you there?"

Silence.

"Dave?"

"Thank you," Dave said suddenly.

"Thank you for what?" SJ said, confused.

"For what you just said."

"What?"

"You said we are best friends," Dave replied with a sniff.

Realising she hadn't even considered the implication of what she said made her feel that Dave really was her best friend. They were inseparable, after all, and their growing camaraderie and exchanges had developed a trust and understanding during the time they were together. They were both outsiders in their ways, she being an anomalous Legionnaire and him a thorn in the System's side. Dave was always looking out for her, guiding her. He had screamed the warning about the necromancer, and he didn't need to. He had informed her about the miniature wyvern eggs, which Lythonian would have been happy to smash. So many small and subtle interactions had added up.

SJ felt a tear roll down her cheek, and she reached up, wiping it away.

"Are you okay?" Dave asked, concern in his voice.

"I am, yes."

"Then why are you crying?"

"I'm happy."

"Oh!"

Silence ensued for several moments before they both started talking at the same time. Unable to understand or hear what the other had said, they both laughed.

SJ spent the remainder of the afternoon talking to Dave and reviewing all the items she had collected, including the new loot from the necromancer. Dave confirmed that some of the items would sell well in the auction house or a city where there would likely be people with the coins available to purchase them. It was while they were sitting talking that the heavens opened fully.

The window to the room had been open since she had arrived, and she had never bothered closing it. The rain got heavier as the skies continued to darken, and there was still enough natural light to allow her to see with her improved vision despite the darkened skies. The sudden clap of thunder made her jump out of her skin as she hadn't been paying the weather any attention. Upon standing and looking out the window, she saw the rain bouncing off the cobbled street below. The town square was empty, with no one in sight, and most of the buildings had all their windows closed, and some even had shutters pulled across them.

The inn's roof overhang protected her window from the rain, and she leaned on the windowsill, resting on her elbows with her face in her hands as she watched the rain gather in pools amongst the cobbles. The streets didn't have gutters or a sewer system to carry the excess water away, and she noticed the small rivulets of water that ran down the streets towards the lake.

There was a bright flash off across the lake to her right, and she saw the lightning dispersing as though it had hit the lake surface, followed in moments by another deep boom as the thunder rolled in. The intensity of the rain increased, coming down almost vertically, and the weight and size of the drops striking the barrels and crates lined up by the roadside sounded like war drums beating. The awnings of the vendor stalls, which usually kept the intense sun off the wares, were filled with pools of water.

"This is one serious downpour. It reminds me of my last day on Earth," SJ said.

"It's quite a heavy storm. I have no idea how long it will last."

"I am going to get some food."

Downstairs, the inn's crowd had only grown. Moving to the corner of the bar, she waited to be served and listened to the locals' various conversations.

"This reminds me of the storm fifteen years ago," a male half elf said to his companion.

"It does. I expect it will last a while," his female companion said.

"It's a good job we packed up when we did, or the clothes would have been ruined," he said.

Many of the usual vendors had migrated to the inn, and as she stood waiting, the bard appeared on his small stage by the fireplace. Soon, the inn was filled with music and laughter as he told his tales. SJ had joined the singing, having picked up a few of the lines from previous evenings, when the inn door flew open. Gary stood in the doorway, water dripping from his clothing as he bellowed.

"Hobs are advancing."

The music stopped instantly, and SJ stared at him, not quite comprehending his comment.

"Hobs are advancing. All those able are asked to accompany the guard to the town line."

He turned again and ran back outside. Murmurs were soon replaced with shouts and cries as patrons downed their drinks before running from the bar, braving the torrential rains to defend the town. SJ watched as the crowd thinned out, then hurried back upstairs and grabbed her cloak from her room. Throwing it on, she left the inn with her hood pulled up and moved towards the barracks.

Many of the streets had now been turned into rivers, and she sloshed through the water-covered streets against the heavy, drumming rain. There was no let-up in the torrent that was hitting the ground. As she neared the barracks, she could hear the shouts of orders over the downpour. She watched as the mage she had seen make announcements walked onto a platform next to where Mayor Maxwell now stood. The crowd anxiously looked at him as the mage's voice cut over the storm.

"THANK YOU FOR COMING. USUAL POSITIONS FOR PRECONFIGURED GROUPS. ALL STREET ENTRANCES ARE TO BE BLOCKED BY WAGONS, AND HEALERS AND MAGES ARE REQUIRED AT EACH LOCATION IN SUPPORT OF ARCHERS AND FIGHTERS."

The crowd was splitting into groups, and SJ watched as the first started moving away from the barracks, heading towards the southern edge of town. Where the field finished, so did the town boundary. SJ noticed Lythonian and Zej in the crowd, wearing the same attire as on their recent quest. As she headed towards them, they began to jog off with another group.

SJ redirected towards the platform, where Mayor Maxwell and Captain Broadaxe were in deep conversation. A large gnoll approached her. "Where are you assigned?"

"I am not. I am new, so I have no idea where I am needed," SJ said.

"Join the group on Timber Street if you can. They are down a mage," the gnoll said.

SJ was about to reply that she wasn't a mage when the gnoll turned to talk to another who had just arrived, ignoring her.

She headed towards the edge of town, having yet to learn where Timber Street was. Across all the streets she came to, large wagons had been drawn as she reached the edge, blocking the roads. These were not standard wagons and had been fitted with wooden panelling that covered the gap underneath them, and archers were now standing in the backs of them looking out across the field. The rain had not eased, and there were shouts and calls as people still made their way to whichever group they needed to reach.

A young-looking kobold was running past her towards the closest group, and SJ called out, asking where Timber Street was. He pointed, saying that it was two streets over. Shouting her thanks, she jogged away. The same setup existed on what she assumed must be the right street. Wagons blocked the entrance, and archers stood waiting. Stood slightly away from the main area was a small awning that had been hurriedly thrown up, and under a raised poncho, several creatures dressed in robes stood. It had to be the mages, healers, or both.

Staying back from the leading group, SJ watched and listened, and as those assigned to groups eventually reached their locations, an unnatural silence fell across the town. There were no more calls or shouts, just the silent anticipation of conflict. SJ had no way of supporting with ranged attacks and, unsure what benefit she could bring here, stood behind the wagons. She moved off to an alley close to the blocked entrance.

"I can't do anything from here," she whispered.

"What's your plan, then?" Dave asked.

"I think I am going to see what is coming," SJ said as she shrugged off her cloak and transformed into her miniature form. The rain that hammered down now felt more like being pelted by huge water bombs. She wasn't going to be deterred, though, and flapping her wings and staying close to the edge of a building out of the worst of the rain, she made her way to the roof.

Once she'd landed, she moved over to the outer edge of the building and then flew the short distance to the next building, the gap between them not large enough even to be called an alleyway. She stood by the chimney of the building closest to the fields, and standing behind it where she was protected from the downpour, she looked out across the fields. The skies were dark and grim, mottled dark greys covering the usually blazing skies she had been used to since her arrival in Amathera. Squinting with her hands cupped around her eyes to keep the rain off, she peered into the afternoon's gloom. She could see nothing out of the ordinary, and there was no sight of anything crossing the fields.

"I wonder how far away they were spotted?" SJ said.

"I assume they must be close. Otherwise, nothing would have been done. Especially in weather like this. I can feel the water in my circuits."

"Really!" SJ replied, shaking her head in dismay at his comment.

"Well, it's not very nice out, is it?"

"You are an AI talking inside my head. Unlike me, you cannot feel the weather."

"I can imagine it, though. The cold, damp water seeping into every orifice, your hair plastered to your head, your dress clinging to your legs, and your boots full of water."

"The rain is not cold, my boots are perfectly dry, and my dress is not stuck to me at all. The only factual thing about that statement is that my hair is plastered to my head."

"I was being artistic in my appraisal of the situation."

"It was more along the lines of doom and gloom."

"I will have you know I performed very well in my theatrical thesis."

"Your what now?" SJ said, surprise etched on her face.

"My thesis."

"What thesis?"

"I completed an AIA in Dramatic Arts."

"Now, that begins to explain a great deal," SJ chuckled. "I am confused about why an AI would need to complete a thesis, never mind about something like theatre."

"As I have told you before, being an administrator is a highly sought-after job. You don't stand a chance at selection if you don't have a degree."

The world of the administrators was more confusing than ever, and rather than bits of data flying around in the everlasting ether, SJ imagined little robots all sitting in cubicles. As her mind drifted, another flash of lightning brightened the gloom of the storm. In the flash, SJ thought she saw something across the fields.

"I think I saw something," she said as the thunderclap followed the flash. The storm was overhead and wasn't moving quickly.

"I didn't. Sorry," Dave replied.

"I am going to investigate," she said as she approached the roof's edge. The wind wasn't very powerful but was certainly stronger than the breezes she had flown in so far, apart from when the mage's spell caught her. Cautiously, she lifted off the roof and, staying high, moved out across the field. The raindrops hammered against her small form. Gritting her teeth against the monstrous water droplets, she flew over the field as fast as possible. Flying at that height, with the hammering rain, she doubted anyone would see her, but to be safe, she moved to the right, approaching the water's edge of the lake, instead of staying directly in the middle of the open area.

Reaching the tree-line across the field, SJ swooped low and into the branches. The canopy of the trees gave her little reprieve from the rain. Under the canopy, she couldn't hear anything apart from the thundering droplets battering the leaves. Working her way between the branches, she approached the original path on which she had initially arrived at Killic. Slowing and dropping onto a branch, she peered between the branches and down the path that led there. What she saw sent fear pulsing through her.

CHAPTER FORTY-NINE

Bordon the Brandisher

The line of hobgoblins filled the path leading through the woodland. They were marching four abreast. SJ couldn't tell how far back they went because the path curved, but there must have been over thirty rows, meaning there were at least a hundred twenty. Stood in the middle of the slow marching line were three other creatures: a vast, monstrous creature SJ recognised from her gaming days as an ogre, a larger hobgoblin wearing the robes of a mage, and a person whose face sent pure anger flaring through her. It was the face of Malcolm the half orc.

The line was moving slowly forward. As it reached the field opening, the lines split, heading to each side and spreading out as they faced towards the town along the lengths of the cornfield. From this side of the field, SJ could just see the town and the blocked streets with the wagons and could vaguely make out a head above the barriers that had been created. The huge ogre was passing beneath her now, and she could hear Malcolm's voice.

"I told you it would be the best time to attack. They wouldn't have been expecting it now," he said.

The monstrous form of the ogre looked at him but didn't respond. Instead, it stepped towards the edge of the open fields, its massive form blocking SJ's vision back towards the town. The hobs that had split along the field's edge slowly moved through the tall corn-stalks. She wished the wind had been even stronger to flatten them and make the hobs more visible as they crouched and moved towards the town. The ogre didn't enter the field and instead just stood as it gave some commands in a language SJ didn't understand. It moved to the side so its bulk was nearer the tree-line.

"I need to get back and warn them," SJ said.

"This is a very organised attack. I can see why the town is prepared to defend against them if they have been hit before," Dave said.

"At least Malcolm is wrong. The town is aware." SJ spat his name angrily.

There were still more hobs filing down the path. There must have been nearer three hundred, at least in the raiding party. Remembering that she could, she triggered her identification skill at the line that was still advancing. Her display flooded with information before it began to combine and lessen. The sensation made her feel light-headed, and she grabbed the tree-trunk to maintain her balance.

> 36 x Hobgoblin Fighter—Levels 5–12
> 25 x Hobgoblin Berserker—Levels 8–11
> 31 x Hobgoblin Archer 1—Levels 6–9

> Congratulations! You have reached Identification Level 4.
> Congratulations! You have reached Identification Level 5. You may now identify creatures twenty levels higher than yourself.
> Subterfuge: Identification Level 5 (45 of 50 to reach Level 6)

"Well, that is one way to level your skill. Next time, I would suggest being a little more careful. Most people select individual targets. Group data above twenty doesn't give you much information," Dave said.

"And at what point did you ever tell me that?" SJ hissed, still clearing her head.

"Erm. Maybe I forgot that part," Dave laughed nervously.

SJ looked at the back of the ogre and triggered her skill again, this time focusing only on it.

Bordon the Brandisher	
Race:	Ogre
Level:	23
Hit Points:	480
Mana Points:	55
Armour Class:	28
Attacks:	Bash, Charge
Special:	Rage

As the details appeared on her screen, the ogre turned around and stared directly towards where SJ was hiding amongst the branches. She couldn't hear what he said but noticed the robed figure move in her direction.

"Damn," she cursed. She began to fly back through the tree branches. There was no way the ogre could have seen her, but it knew it had been identified.

"Told you to be careful," Dave said.

SJ ignored his comment and flew back towards the lake's edge through the canopy. The first line of hobs was probably halfway across the field now, and she could make out several carrying crossbows as they lifted them, pointing towards the street entrances. There were six in total, and the town defenders were formed, blocking the hobs' advance.

"That ogre is a monster at Level 23," SJ said.

"He is exceedingly high for a starter town. The necromancer's being 21 was bad, but a Level 23 ogre is insane to even be anywhere near here. Then again, we do have a Level 88 dragon sitting on a mountaintop not far away, not to mention a god in town."

Wiping her face to clear the rain from her eyes, SJ looked over the field. She was only Level 6 and one higher than the weakest hobs she had identified. She felt helpless and distraught at what was going to happen. The lightning flashed in the sky again, and this time, as it did, it was followed by the deep sound of a horn being blown from the direction of the town. The hobs must have been spotted as balls of light were cast into the air. From several locations along the town's front, brilliant light suddenly appeared, floating over the fields.

"Yes," SJ said, clenching her fist.

As the glowing balls moved over the fields, the gloom from the storm was reduced with almost daylight conditions because of their brilliance shining down. One of the hobs turned and aimed his crossbow at one of the balls, firing at it. The bolt sailed towards it to pass harmlessly through. They were magical, after all, and not something that a bolt could damage. SJ had not seen the cloaked hob since she had moved away through the branches but realised it must be near the field again. A dark bolt shot towards one of the balls of light, and upon hitting it, extinguished it.

"I need to do something," SJ said.

"I think this is a perfect opportunity for you to train."

"Train! During a battle?"

"The hobs won't expect anything to attack them from behind, so you can take advantage."

"How do you suppose I do that?"

"Hit-and-run tactics."

Contemplating Dave's comments, SJ looked to the end of the hobs' line nearest the lake. It was some distance away from her, but at least focusing on one end would stop her from being caught in the middle of everything if things went wrong. Lifting from the branch and dropping low, she skirted the field's edge before rising and heading towards her target.

There was a cry from her right as she flew, and she turned to see the massive ogre now standing in the centre of the main track and slowly moving forward. He was still out of range of any arrows from the township. His cry cut over the thundering rain, and on his command, the hobs stood, releasing their flight of bolts towards the town's defences. The whistling sound of bolts and twanging strings was lost in the storm.

A cry of pain reached SJ across the field; someone defending the town had been hit. SJ grimaced at the thought of the almost-silent lances of death flying towards the town unseen. A whistling sound suddenly reached her ears, and as she neared the side end of the hobs' line, she realised what it was. The archers from the town had returned fire.

Glancing upwards, she noticed a stream of tiny flashes of dark streaking through the sky. The storm affected their parabolic flight. None came close to her position, but there were sounds from along the hob line as the falling shafts of death struck more than one.

Reaching the last hob on the line, SJ identified it.

Fighter	
Race:	Hobgoblin
Level:	7
Hit Points:	45
Mana Points:	40
Armour Class:	10
Attacks:	Slash, Stab
Special:	Nil

Its back was to her, and she was about four feet away from it. There was another hob to her right, about fifteen feet farther away, leading this hob slightly as it focused on sneaking closer to the town.

Landing and ducking down, she allowed herself to grow, equipping her claws as she did. The hob moved no more than six feet from her now, and she crept towards it until she could have reached out to touch its back. It wore rough-looking leather armour, its green arms uncovered except for bracers on its wrists with matching leather greaves on its calves. Thinking through her options and not knowing what healing the hobs had, she considered disabling enemies rather than going for kills. She knew her damage would not be high enough to kill them without hand to hand fighting, and she couldn't chance being caught against more than one. She just wasn't strong or skilled enough yet.

The way the hob stooped in a crouching position revealed the backs of its ankles, and with a decisive and swift strike, SJ brought her blades down across them. The shock at being struck from behind made it flash forward, standing as it did. The damage she had wrought caused it to fall. Immediately shrinking again, she moved left and flew away again towards the lake's edge. Nothing followed or came for her, and as she turned to see the outcome, her display triggered.

> Congratulations, the bleed has been applied.

Another hob had moved over to the downed one and snarled, saying something in their tongue that she didn't understand.

"He called him a useless piece of troll dung," Dave said.

"Thanks," SJ said, her body tingling from the adrenaline.

"One out of the fight, at least."

"Too many to go through."

Turning, SJ flew back behind the line and along the path, which was a natural break between the end of the field and the woods. There was nothing on the track as everything approached the town. Shouts and cries had started as both sides had begun to call orders as the battle commenced. SJ flew above the corn, and not forty feet from her was the back of a person she recognised. The half orc Malcolm stood at the rear of all the hobs, well away from the front line advancing.

"He is mine," SJ hissed under her breath, temper flaring.

"Be careful. I will watch your six," Dave said.

SJ changed her direction, heading straight to where Malcolm was standing. He was holding a large two-handed sword with his back to her. Nothing was near him, as he had allowed himself to fall behind. Bordon was walking forward, showing no concern as another rain of arrows came down. Bordon lifted the huge club he was holding above his head as they did, and a couple struck it, sticking in.

Landing a few feet from Malcolm, SJ grew again, still crouching. When she had first fought him in the town, he had worn a breastplate, and she hoped he was again. She identified him as she moved to strike.

	Malcolm Kilgore
Race:	Half Orc
Age:	20
Level:	6
Hit Points:	36
Mana Points:	30
Armour Class:	10
Attacks:	Slash, Charge
Special:	Nil

The only change he had achieved was reaching age twenty. The level increase in her identification skill allowing her to see further details. With both her fists clenched, she drove her blades deep into his lower back. At the same moment, a clap of thunder sounded overhead. Malcolm's body clenched forward, his back arching and his scream covered by the rolling thunder. Removing one of her blades, she struck again higher up his back. His health had dropped by two-thirds from her first dual strike, and as her second strike punctured the centre of his upper back, his health dropped to zero. Anger and hatred fuelled SJ; she withdrew her blades and allowed his now-lifeless form to fall to the floor. How dare he bring hostiles to the town?

"Small," yelled Dave.

SJ snapped from her trance and shrank again. Thankfully, no one had noticed because of the sounds of battle that had commenced and the thunder above. Turning, she flew low and fast back to the road.

"That was a clinical finish. Very impressive," Dave said.

"Good riddance to bad rubbish." SJ had just performed her first real assassination. She felt no regrets in ending Malcolm's second life after what he had brought to the town. As the realisation set in, she rose and scanned the battlefield. The hobs were now closing in on the town, and archers were still trying to pick off approaching forms. SJ could hear cries and moaning from around the field at various locations. The mage stood nearer the back of the group, with Bordon still walking calmly forward down the central track leading to the main street.

Looking right, SJ saw some hobs moving back across the field. One of them was limping with an arrow sticking through its thigh. Another supported it as it moved to the track before dropping it down, turning, and running back towards the town. The injured hob was now lying a short distance from her. Moving into the woods, she approached where it lay, triggering identification as she neared.

	Archer
Race:	Hobgoblin
Level:	8
Hit Points:	31 of 45
Mana Points:	45
Armour Class:	8
Attacks:	Bolt
Special:	Nil

The archer struggled, trying to remove the arrow from its thigh. It cried in pain as the arrow's head was caught and would not pull free. He let go of the arrow, hitting the earth with its clenched fists, unhappy about not being able to partake in the battle. SJ grew and stayed behind a tree, looking at its back. Sneaking from the wood's edge, she again struck with precision. Her blades tore into its neck, and it would have screamed if it was able as its arm flew up, trying to grasp her hand. Her other blades then plunged into its back, similar to what she had done to Malcolm. Its health had dropped to a sliver, and as it grabbed her arm and tried to wrestle her forward, she withdrew her claws from its back and struck again, removing the last of its resistance. Immediately, she shrank and again changed position and moved away back into the woods.

Three corpses now lay on the field from her hand. She felt no remorse as her display triggered.

Congratulations on reaching Level 7
You have been awarded the following:
5 hit points
5 mana points
+1 Dexterity
+2 free points to distribute as you wish

She opened her character sheet and immediately assigned her two free points to Constitution to support her martial arts training and improve her health. With her significant points gain compared to many, she could soon start to benefit from being able to balance her attribute growth bonuses.

	↻ Level: 7
Experience:	36 of 1000
Hit Points:	52
Mana Points:	40
Dexterity:	17
Constitution:	12
Subterfuge:	Identification Level 5 (49 of 50 to reach Level 6)

"I am heading towards town. They are too close now. I will see what I can do to help," she said.

"You are doing so well back here, though," Dave said.

SJ flew swiftly across the top of the cornfield, the rain still hammering into her smaller form, and the occasional drop made her adjust her position. The hobs had started to reach the wagon barriers broken up by the buildings acting as the town walls, and as she neared, she could hear the clash of steel as hand to hand combat commenced. Looking over, she watched the monstrous ogre still strolling slowly towards the main entrance.

SJ could do nothing to stop the Level 23. Something with that many hit points and armour class would be like striking a mountain at her level. Moving forward between the natural break in the line where the hobs had moved to attack one of the wagon positions, she flew up and over onto the rooftop of the nearest building—flying to the edge and landing, she surveyed the wagons below her. A fierce battle was underway between a group of hobs who had managed to force their way over the top of one of the wagons and the citizens of Killic. Swords clattered, and axes swung. Both sides took injuries, and the number of casualties increased.

A dwarf who SJ had seen in the inn on several occasions took a nasty slash to its face from the axe of a hob and fell to the ground wailing. As it did, a stream of light burst forth and struck him. His cries of pain lessened as the healing spell did its job. It was absolute chaos everywhere she looked. She was at least a street from the centre and swiftly flew across to the next building. To her left, Bordon was approaching the wagons. The hobs moved out of his way as he swung his huge club and smashed one of the wagon's sides, sending splinters flying. He roared in anger.

Just down the street, SJ noticed movement: Mayor Maxwell was transforming. He was a large man standing at least seven feet tall, but the beast he turned into was on a whole new scale. Mayor Maxwell stood up on his hind legs as the largest grizzly bear SJ had ever seen. Bordon must have stood nearly twelve feet tall, and the mayor stood just as tall, if not taller, on his hind legs. When he dropped to all fours, his shoulder must still have been nearly six feet. Roaring in anger, spittle flying from its mouth, the grizzly charged at Bordon.

The next clap of thunder could not have been better timed as the two monstrous forms crashed into each other. Bordon tried to swing his club at the mayor as he leapt at him. Their bodies collided, and the momentum forced Bordon to stagger backwards from the blow as the grizzly raked its huge claws down the front of the breastplate Bordon wore. The metal tore open as if it were a tin of soup. Bordon roared in response and brought his club round, crashing into the side of the mayor's head. Dropping back to the ground, the mayor stood and roared again at Bordon, who roared back. The two goliaths stared each other down, awaiting the other's next move. While the behemoths fought, the remainder of the armies were fighting for their own survival.

SJ watched as Captain Broadaxe withdrew his axe from what had once been a hobgoblin and was no longer recognisable, it had been cleaved so cleanly. He let out a battle-cry, and a bright flash of blue light encircled him as he sprinted forward through the now-open entrance to the street, meeting the hobgoblins who were pushing their way through. A bolt of blue flashed forward from the field, and SJ noticed the hobgoblin mage directing attacks at those defending. SJ decided on her next target.

CHAPTER FIFTY

Distracted

The hobgoblin mage cast a bolt of blue light towards an unsuspecting fighter engaged in combat with another hob. As the light struck him, his body froze as if he'd been turned into a statue. The effect was that he was unable to parry or block the sword stroke that cut into his abdomen. After several moments, the spell wore off, and the victim fell forward, grasping at his wound.

Snarling, getting angry, and seeing the mage's underhand techniques, SJ took off from the roof, flying in a circular pattern, and moved around and behind the mage. She triggered her identification skill as she was coming in to land.

Iratu the Mad	
Race:	Hobgoblin
Level:	18
Hit Points:	105
Mana Points:	145 of 270
Armour Class:	20
Attacks:	Magic
Special:	Invulnerability

Congratulations! You have reached Identification Level 6. You may now select your second Subterfuge skill.

SJ had no time to even consider selecting skills and didn't know what to expect of a mage; SJ couldn't tell if it had high or low mana for its class. At least she knew the health it had remaining. As she read the display, the mage spun from where it had been facing and scanned the direction she was in. Diving as fast as she could to enter the cornfield, she felt the mage's gaze track her movement.

"WATCH IT," Dave shouted as a red ball of fire travelled towards her.

Changing her direction and flight path, she turned away from the mage as fast as her wings would carry her.

"Well, that was so stupid, casting identification on him," SJ hissed.

"Not the best. I did say mages usually have high Wisdom."

"Yeah. I know."

Where SJ had been just moments before, there was a small explosion, and the crops burst into flames, ignoring the pelting of the rain because of the fire's magical power. Sweeping around again in an arc, she moved to the mage's side and again began approaching, this time moving much more cautiously through the tall corn. Rubbing her eyes, she peered towards the mage but could not see it. She didn't want to chance flying above the height of the corn because of the ease of her being spotted, so she continued to edge forward.

The cries and shouts of battle continued, and just off to her right, another ball of flame hit the ground and exploded. Considering its direction, this had not come from the mage by all accounts, and she assumed a mage in the town was trying to attack it.

"Damn. I also need to watch out for friendly fire," she said.

"No one knows you are out here. Anything currently outside the town limits is thought to be hostile."

"I know," SJ growled.

Not being able to see the mage was not helping, so she gently lifted to peek over the top of the corn. The mage was busy preparing another spell, looking towards the town, and she took the opportunity to move closer again, quickly flying at an angle leading behind it. As she got within ten feet, she crashed into a barrier. Not expecting the impact, she hit it head first. Sparks flew, and her momentum sent her spinning and crashing to the ground a couple of feet below. Lying on the ground, stunned, shaking her head to clear it, she noticed her health had suffered; she'd lost ten hit points from the impact.

There was no way she could force her way through the barrier that surrounded the mage. Getting to her feet and moving with her claws in front of her, she prodded until she reached a point where she felt resistance. Cursing under her breath, she had no way of getting through. Small arcs of power came off the barrier as her claws touched. The mage turned from facing the town, and SJ pulled her claws away as it did. Standing still, she prayed it hadn't seen her.

A bright blue bolt struck its shield, sizzling over its surface, and the mage turned towards the town again. SJ picked a small pebble from the ground and threw it at the barrier away from where she stood. The stone, tiny even in her miniature size, sizzled as it touched the barrier and bounced off it. Another bolt flew from the town's direction, this time yellow, and crashed into the dome surrounding the mage, the combatting magic arcing off across its surface again. The dome was not visible unless something touched it.

"How do I penetrate that?" SJ asked.

"It will be taking damage like the personal shield the mage used on the church hall. There will be a damage limit before it wears out. That is when you can take advantage."

"I can't just stay here waiting."

"What else can you do?"

"Wear it down," SJ said, pushing her claw out and into the barrier again. Staying low, she began to circle the dome, dragging her claws across its surface. The mage was casting another spell, and she watched a red bolt fly from its hand and strike an archer trying to shoot at it. She heard the archer scream as the bolt hit it in the chest, catapulting it backwards from the wagon it stood on.

Looking towards town, SJ saw the massive forms of Bordon and the mayor slugging it out against each other. The hobs' numbers were slowly dwindling, but so were the defenders'. Three wagons had been used to block the road at the main entrance, where the widest street was. Only one remained, with archers still trying to fire at close range at the hobs. Mêlée combat was taking place, and she heard a scream of rage as a hob spun wildly, slashing its axe around as though possessed. It had to be a berserker, and in its enraged state, she saw it take out one of its own with a strike across its back, as it didn't care who or what was near it.

The mage turned and saw her moving around the dome, dragging her claws and creating a trail of sparks as she did. She hoped her claws damaged the shield, but she couldn't tell for sure. The mage growled and shouted something at her in its tongue.

"Oooo. That wasn't very nice. He deserves to have his mouth washed out," Dave said.

That was all the translation SJ needed, giving her the confidence that she was impacting it. Moving as fast as she could in a circle, she was visible but, at the moment, didn't care. The mage shouted something, and one of the closest hobs ran towards her. She flapped her wings, taking off, switching her path, moving up and keeping her distance, then heading to the other side. The dome did not affect the charging hob, and it passed through the shield and swung towards SJ's miniature form with a sword. Seeing the wild swing coming a mile off with her enhanced senses, she jinked upwards, the sword blade sweeping underneath where she had been. She felt the draft of the blade as it passed within inches of her.

"You are taking serious risks," Dave said as the hob turned and came after her. Her small form and level of agility meant she could fly quickly, and it could not reach her with a swing before she was out of the way again. A red ball of fire suddenly hit the hob chasing her, sending it crashing backwards towards the mage. Its leather armour scorched from the impact of the spell. Growling, it got back to its feet and, rather than chasing SJ, waited for her to move in its direction. That was when the barrier failed.

The sparks and resistance suddenly cut out, and the hob mage screamed what she could only imagine was a curse in response. Seeing the barrier was down, she immediately turned and headed away. She could not take the chance to attempt to land and grow with the fighter and mage present. Weaving in and out of the cornstalks, she moved several feet before cutting back through them and towards where she hoped the mage's back would be. Taking a chance, she rose and noticed she was a little off target, then realigned herself. The mage seemed to be busy concentrating on the town again. The hob that had come to defend it was standing nearby, still scouring the field.

She was now positioned behind the hob warrior, which looked to be flagging since it had taken the hit from the fireball. She quickly triggered her identification skill.

Fighter	
Race:	Hobgoblin
Level:	8
Hit Points:	21 of 50
Mana Points:	45
Armour Class:	9
Attacks:	Slash, Thrust
Special:	Nil

As it was a normal fighter with only twenty-one hit points remaining, SJ felt confident she could take it. Switching her path, she flew straight at its back, and as she neared, she dropped and grew and was in a full run as she reached it. Her claws extended as she stabbed into its side with her left hand while slashing with her right. The hob wailed in pain at the surprise attack and pulled away, swinging its blade around in defence. SJ moved her arm, catching the blade swing on her claws, sparks flying, and only parrying it just enough to stop it from striking her. She stepped back as the hob staggered. Its health was now showing as a sliver on her display. Not considering anything around her, she focused on finishing the hob.

The mage struck. There was no warning. At such close range, the bolt pierced her side an instant after being cast. Crying from the impact, SJ stumbled sideways, her health reducing by twenty more. There was little choice remaining for her now. She had to fight, even if it meant her death. Kicking out at the hobgoblin, she caught its thigh with her foot, and it staggered from the blow. She proceeded to step in, punching with her clawed fist. The hob was so close that it could not get its sword up to defend itself, and she hit it square in its chest. The scream filled her ears as it fell to the ground.

Not paying it any further attention, she spun to face the mage. It had moved away, creating more distance from her. It was circling, its hand in the process of creating a spell, a red glow beginning to form. There was no way that she could survive a fireball at close range. At the speed they travelled, she would not get out of the way in time. It took her less than a split-second to run at the mage.

The mage was looking at her, and its eyes widened slightly in surprise as it saw her move towards it rather than away. Screaming, she charged, closing the distance as the mage tried to finish its spell before she reached it. The mage pushed the red ball of energy coursing at her with its hand. Her senses went wild; her body reacting without her knowledge, it unnaturally dived forwards and down at the mage's side as the energy crackled within an inch of her body. Automatically rolling, she sprang up, and her display triggered.

> Precognition triggered—cool-down 24 hours

Knowing the only reason she had survived was because of the dragon blood inside her, she felt a renewed vigour. Standing, she launched at the mage, kicks and punches hurtling at its robed body. The mage was not in any way prepared for mêlée combat, and she hammered into it, striking and kicking with fierce abandon. This could be the last thing she attempted in this life, and in a moment of absolute stupidity, as thoughts rushed through her mind, she shouted.

"Record!"

"Hang on," came a very excited Dave in reply.

Punching, kicking, twirling, pressing against the mage, she continued her onslaught, the new techniques taught by Lorna paying off in an offensive fight. Her claws did little damage to the mage compared to the lower-level hobs, but they were gradually picking away at its health. When the beam of light hit her, she initially thought she was about to die.

"It's Lythonian!" Dave screamed.

Though she couldn't even consider looking for the draconian, she could see her health increasing as the light struck her. She spun to the side of the mage, and as she did, the light cut out. She was back to over half her health now. It hadn't healed her greatly, but it gave her the confidence to continue.

A dagger appeared in the mage's hand, and he struck out, unable to cast a spell against the barrage of attacks he was receiving. SJ didn't see it at first, and he swept the blade across her, cutting into her arm. She winced in pain from the strike, taking minimal damage, and her display triggered again.

> You have been poisoned.

The initial damage was nothing, but she knew that if she was poisoned, she would need more healing.

"Damn," Dave suddenly said. "Break off now. I can't believe it poisoned you."

SJ kept pressing.

"NOW," Dave screamed.

SJ saw a shape moving, and her senses triggered, noticing the towering form of Bordon in her peripheral vision. She had been so focused she had not noticed the turn in the battle. The hobs were beginning to flee and move back across the field. Bordon was leading their retreat. He did not stop and careered into her, not paying her any attention with his massive twelve feet in height. She was catapulted across the field, tumbling through the corn-stalks. Her health plummeted again, and she had less than ten hit points remaining. The mage had been going down, and as her senses returned from the impact, she saw it running across the field behind Bordon. It glanced back at her with a look of hatred.

> Commiserations! Your reputation with Iratu the Mad has been reduced to Disliked.

She lay back in the cornfield with her body feeling like a charging rhino had hit it.

"Stay awake," Dave said.

Her eyes felt heavy, and her health was ticking down from the poison as she felt it burn inside her. She only had four hit points remaining, and unless she received healing, she would die. As her health reached two hit points, she spoke to Dave.

"I will see you in the white room," she said.

"No, you won't," Dave said. "You are now out of active combat."

"What?" SJ said groggily.

"Look at your health."

Her health remained at two.

"What's happening?"

"It's your blood, the healing symbiosis. Thankfully, the poison is not as strong as many can be."

Having completely forgotten about the increased healing she had earned from the dragon blood, she suddenly realised it was keeping her alive, counteracting the poison's damage.

Hearing shouting and calls, she tried to stand but was unable to do so in her battered state. She realised that her leg was pointing at a rather obscure angle. Shouting weakly, she called out as bodies from the town moved out into the field. She lay her head back on the soaked earth, the still-heavy rain splashing her face, but she didn't care now; she just wanted to lie there. Pain seeped through her body, the poison setting her nerves on fire as it tried to attack and her dragon blood fought back. It felt as though small explosions erupted inside her.

A face appeared above her, one she didn't recognise, but it cried out. "I found her, over here, quick."

Another face peered down, this one belonging to a human with a thick beard and moustache of brilliant white. The man was wearing plate armour and carrying a spear, and he chanted, placing his hand on her chest. She felt the warmth seeping into her, her health improving slowly but not as expected.

"She is poisoned," the man said. "Get Tilly here now."

SJ couldn't focus properly; the pain was too intense. She was forcibly sat upright, crying in pain at the movement as the cold of a glass vial met her lips. A sweet liquid was being poured into her mouth. It smelt of cotton candy, and SJ drank greedily.

"She will be good in a moment. Then you can heal her again," a female voice said.

The white-haired man again placed his hand on her chest, and the warmth returned to her body, this time flooding her. It felt as though she had been hit with an adrenaline shot. Her leg realigned, miraculously painlessly, and her health increased rapidly. It took moments for her to be brought back up to her maximum hit points. Feeling energised beyond anything she had felt before, she suddenly sprang up.

"There we go," the white-haired man said, chuckling. "That's the reaction I expect."

With wide-open eyes, SJ stared at the man. "Thank you."

"I haven't seen that in a long time," Dave said.

SJ couldn't reply with three people literally within a foot of her.

"Are you feeling okay now?" the female asked.

"Yes. I think so. I feel like I have just drunk two pots of coffee," SJ said, the words pouring quickly out of her.

"That will wear off in a moment," she said.

As she took in the scenes of the cornfield, SJ realised that a line of townsfolk was slowly working their way across it. They had now passed by where she had been lying. Standing in the centre of the line was Captain Broadaxe. She watched as he suddenly swung his great axe down and heard a scream before silence again.

"After battle is never pleasant," Dave said, seeming to pick up on what SJ had been thinking.

The giddiness of the healing spell began to fade, and her vision cleared fully, her head calming.

"Thank you all for healing me," SJ said, looking at the three standing by her.

"The thanks go to you. If you had not distracted that mage, the mayor wouldn't have got to Bordon. The mage always casts some form of invulnerability on him. It didn't matter what we hit Bordon with, we couldn't break his skin. As soon as the mage's shield failed, he lost it, and the mayor could damage him, forcing him to pull back and retreat."

"Oh!" SJ exclaimed in shock at the revelation. She'd had no concept of her impact on the battle.

"Mayor Maxwell is just being treated but asked that you be brought to the barracks as soon as you are fit," the human man said.

Looking back at the line still moving across the field in the pouring rain, she considered her response. "I should go help."

"You have done enough," the woman said, taking her by the elbow and slowly turning her back towards town.

"I stopped recording and watched it back," Dave said. "You were a whirling dervish—very impressive for your level! I can't wait for you to get stronger. Hopefully, one day, you will be able to watch it back, and I will definitely be sharing it on our social network."

SJ smiled at his comment as she began walking back into town.

The raid had been thwarted, but the hobs were still out there.

CHAPTER FIFTY-ONE

Thanks

As SJ entered the top of the main street, the aftermath of the battle was ever present; the splintered remains of two wagons were being cleared away. A group was in the process of cleaning up and picking debris from the street. Blood-red puddles could be seen amongst the debris. A few injured creatures were still being cared for by healers as they topped up their health. SJ spotted Lorna walking from one of the side streets.

"Hi, Lorna," SJ called.

Lorna looked over, smiling, and came to greet her. "I saw what you did from the other street. That was either incredibly brave or incredibly stupid of you. I have no idea how that fireball didn't hit you."

"I think I got lucky," SJ said, not wanting to mention symbiosis with a dragon. "How did you get on?"

"They are repelled for now but will be back—they always are. The attack wasn't as bad as it has been in the past. The fact that the mayor could injure Bordon for a change helped."

"Has that mage always been present?"

"Yes. It was always protecting him. I don't know what you were doing, but to drain the shield that quickly has never happened before. Even with mages concentrating fire at it."

"Oh. I was hitting it with my . . ." SJ paused.

"Claws, I think you meant to say," Lorna said, smiling.

SJ flushed.

"At least I know what class you are now," Lorna said, winking.

"I—I'm sorry," SJ stammered, "I should have said."

"No need to apologise. I know monks never use weapons, so you can only really be one of two classes, Rogue or Assassin, as I can discount fighters since you wear no armour. You don't look like a ranger or use a bow, so the process of elimination with your claws only gives me the assassin choice left."

"I didn't want to advertise it."

"An assassin is an unusual class. I have met a few before, but many are not like you. They aren't as open and friendly."

Blushing even more from the compliment, SJ wasn't sure how to respond.

"Where are you heading?" Lorna asked.

"The mayor wants to see me at the barracks."

"I'm heading back to report in. I'll join you."

The rain still pounded the cobbles. The volume of rain had created small rivers that now flowed freely towards the lake.

"How long does the rain usually last?" SJ asked.

"When it comes, it stays for a while. I would expect another few hours before it starts to clear again," Lorna replied.

"Is it always like this when it rains?"

"Yes. It's clear most of the time, but when it does rain, it pours. It will do the crops well."

"Lorna," a gnoll called as he approached.

"Oscaray. How did you fair?"

"Well, the main hobs were still pushing the main street, so we didn't get the same quantity attacking Hillier Street. Unfortunately, we lost one. Young Wesley fell before Alex could heal him."

"Have you reported in yet?"

"Just returning. The mayor is after some fae or other, wants to speak to her."

"You mean SJ," Lorna said, indicating to her.

Oscaray noticed SJ for the first time as she stood to the side of Lorna.

"That will be her, then," Oscaray responded. "Is it true that you brought the mage shield down?" he asked.

"Yes. With the help of the mages," SJ replied.

Lorna scoffed. "She is being modest. It would have been up much longer without her draining it."

"My thanks to you, then," Oscaray said, smiling. "It probably saved several lives today."

A clap of thunder erupted, and SJ jumped, it being the first one in a while, and the rain seemed to increase in intensity.

"Anyway, I am heading back to report in," Lorna said.

"No problem. I assume you will be at the Arms later?" Oscaray asked.

"We will have our usual table reserved," Lorna said.

When the two women reached the barracks, the building was busy. The old orc on the desk didn't even pay any attention to Lorna or SJ as they walked straight through the swinging barrier, too busy dealing with the influx of townsfolk. Lorna led SJ to the wide staircase at the side of the room. On the first floor, there was a large, open set-up similar to downstairs, with two offices situated at the other end. In the middle of the large room was a wooden table with a perfect replica of the town sitting on it. The details were immaculate, and two gnomes were busily shaping and adjusting some of the buildings at the table.

SJ stood looking at it in awe. It was unbelievably detailed, even on closer inspection; the signs for the shops even swung on little posts. Lorna led SJ around the table and walked towards the double doors at the end of the room. They were open, and inside, SJ could see the impressive form of the mayor standing in bear form still. A female dryad dressed in a white robe stood talking to the mayor.

"I want the wagons replaced as soon as possible. Speak to Katiyanna, and if she tries to spin her line about payment and finance, quietly remind her that I oversee the businesses that can operate in this town and that she still owes pitch rent. We will hold a service tomorrow at the church for those who have lost their lives today. I have already spoken to Lythonian. Finally, once we have the damages totalled, inform any inquiring parties that compensation will be confirmed within five days."

"Anything else?" the dryad asked.

"Could you get a message to Magius? My shoulder still doesn't feel right."

"Of course, Mayor," she replied, and she turned and smiled at Lorna and SJ as they walked in.

"Mayor," Lorna said, nodding her head.

Seeing the huge grizzly bear this close was quite nerve-wracking, never mind the fact it was talking in perfect common. "Lorna. And I see SJ is with you," the mayor said. SJ guessed the bear was smiling, though it was hard to tell. "Please come in and take a seat while I change."

The mayor's body shuddered, and his limbs shifted from the huge paws they were back into hands. The clothing he had been wearing was restored as he changed.

"Please sit," he said, definitely smiling now at SJ, who had not got past the office threshold and was standing, open-mouthed.

"Sorry," she blustered, walking into the room and sitting in one of several large armchairs facing a huge wooden desk. The mayor didn't walk around the desk but instead stepped over to a cupboard at the side of the office, opened it, and took out a decanter and three glasses. Back by the armchairs, he placed the glasses on the edge of his desk and poured three before handing one each to Lorna and SJ. He then sat in another armchair instead of behind the desk.

"First, we toast," he said.

SJ held the glass containing red liquid in her hand. She could smell a spice coming from it.

"To our fallen brethren," he said, lifting his glass and drinking it in one.

"The fallen," Lorna said, doing the same.

"The fallen," SJ copied, and drank the liquid. It had a strange taste the flavour of cinnamon and root beer. It did not have the harshness of Zej's dwarven brandy and went down easily.

"Now, then, SJ. I and we, the town, owe you a thank you," the mayor stated.

"I am not sure what for. I only did what anyone would have done," she said, feeling a little nervous next to this beast. Now that her identity as an assassin was assumed, she worried that people might start adding two and two together about Darjey's death.

"You are a low-level Legionnaire, but you took no thought in throwing yourself in peril to defend the town. That is not something we are used to witnessing. Especially considering it was against the mage. That mage is powerful and has ended several over the months."

"Months!" SJ exclaimed in shock.

"Yes. We have been fighting the hobs for a long time."

"I had no idea."

"Thankfully, it is not a regular occurrence, but still too frequent for my liking."

"I see."

"If you had not managed to take down the mage's shield today, I am unsure how long I could have fought Bordon while he was invulnerable. Thankfully, it isn't very often that he comes to attack himself. At least our scouts got the message back before they arrived."

At that comment, a large bird similar to a raven but with red plumage landed on the windowsill of the mayor's office and tapped on the window. The mayor stood and walked over, opening the window. When he did, it hopped inside.

"Rex, Alice has just left," the mayor said as Rex ruffled its feathers and sprayed water from its body.

"That must be a scout of the druids," Dave said.

Rex squawked at the mayor.

"You know, I don't understand what you are saying. She was going to the wagonistas, if it was urgent. If not, stay out of the rain for a while. I am guessing her window was closed."

Squawking again, Rex preened its feathers. The mayor returned to sit down.

"Sorry about that," he said.

"Not at all," SJ said.

"Now, back to business. Without you taking the mage shield down so quickly today, we may easily have lost many more before pushing them back. Can I ask how you did it?"

"I was just hitting it."

"Hitting it? Did you not take damage?" the mayor asked, frowning.

"No. I used my claws."

His eyebrows raised, and a half-smile appeared on his face. "Claws, you say."

SJ's nerves were on edge. She had mentioned her claws to the mayor, but it was too late now. By all accounts, she had been seen by too many during the battle. "Yes. I use claws to fight."

"Do you mind if I see them?"

Sitting nervously, SJ lifted her hands from where they had been resting on her knees. Feeling her palms were sweaty, she called her blades. The gloves appeared instantly on her hands, with their four black claws on each.

"I see, and I wonder why you didn't take damage from the shield. Those who have hit it before have always been shocked. Are they magical?"

"They are +3."

"That is not a great deal," he replied, frowning again.

"They also have a bleed effect that can trigger."

"Now, that is interesting. I wonder if that is what prevented you from harm."

SJ had no idea. She had been shocked when she crashed into the dome but had never even considered that she would have got shocked using the claws.

"It's your boots," Dave said.

SJ had never even looked at her boots since first putting them on. Quickly checking their details, she saw the changes.

Boots of the Assassin
Grade: Epic
Quality: Perfect
Durability: Excellent
Enchantment Slots: 2
Armour Class: 5
Attributes: Protection from Lightning—Going to slit a mage's throat? Sneak along a trapped corridor? You don't want to be shocked in the process by crafty defences. Feet must be grounded.

"It's the same reason the mage's personal shield in the church hall didn't affect you. Most mages can give off a nasty belt from their shields, as you found out crashing into it," Dave said.

"It's my boots," SJ said aloud. "They give me protection."

"That's interesting to know. What sort?" the mayor asked.

SJ felt uncomfortable and uncertain under the spotlight.

"It's fine. It's normal to discuss skills, abilities, and bonuses," Dave said. "Many use them as bragging rights to try to earn better positions, and that is not just Legionnaires. Look at Lorna and her ability in martial arts or Fran at the mage academy. They wouldn't have got their roles without others knowing their capabilities.."

She resolved herself to the fact that she was here now, and with Dave's supporting words, she answered the question.

"They protect against lightning."

"Excellent. I am sure one of the enchanters may be able to consider enchanting some of our guards' equipment with that attribute if that's the case. If not, maybe Mistress Francisca could do it. Being able to attack the mage with mêlée rather than trying to wear its shield down with spells would be significant."

"I volunteer for that," Lorna said.

"Ha. I bet you would." The mayor smiled. "I may even offer my own boots as well. Anyway, I wished to see you not just to say thank you."

SJ felt a trickle of sweat run down her back.

"What was the reason, then?" SJ asked nervously.

The mayor stood and walked around the desk, opening a drawer and returning with a small box. He handed the box to SJ. "I wished to also gift you this for what you did today. As I say, you saved lives with your bravery."

SJ took the box, feeling relief and embarrassment all at once. She felt her cheeks go red.

"I didn't expect anything," she replied.

"It's nothing large, don't worry, but I thought you might like it as it matches your dress," he said.

Opening the small box, SJ gently lifted out a green choker. Hanging down at the front of the choker was a beautiful large green stone. It was identical to her dress's colour. SJ turned it in her hands in amazement.

"This is too much," she said, flabbergasted.

"Nonsense. It's not much. It is just a thank you from the town for what you did today."

SJ met Lorna's smiling eyes, and the tigress just shrugged, indicating she should take it.

"Thank you so much."

"That is an Arcavian Earth Stone," Dave said. "It is quite common, but that cut is especially good. You may be able to get it enchanted. Identify it and see what it says."

Choker of the Earth Stone
Grade: Uncommon
Quality: Flawless
Durability: Excellent
Enchantment Slots: 1
Hidden: Alignment Fae (1 of 5)

"Oh my god," Dave said in shock. Knowing SJ couldn't reply, he continued excitedly. "Most pieces of jewellery have one enchantment slot, so there is nothing unusual there. Enchanters use jewellery items often to hone their skills. It's that hidden part. I have only had two Legionnaires before who have ever got set items, and neither were five-piece sets. A five-piece set is ridiculously rare. There is no guarantee that you will ever get the other pieces. What is mind-blowing, even for my amazing level of knowledge, is the fact that it is aligned to fae only. The chances of you being here at this time in this place and then being offered a piece of jewellery as thanks for what you have done for a starter town with a much higher-level structure than any other starter town I have ever seen has a probability of 0.0001."

SJ placed the choker around her neck and brushed it with her fingers, looking down. "May I?" SJ asked, indicating to a tall mirror at the side of the office.

"Please," the mayor replied.

She walked over and looked at herself. The choker finished off the top half of her outfit perfectly. The large green gem shone and twinkled in the lantern lights in the office, which fought off the dimness of the storm-clouds. She couldn't help but smile at her appearance. She was a beautiful creature as a fae.

"Thank you so much. This is lovely," SJ said.

"It is only a trinket, nothing special," the mayor said, smiling.

"What little he knows," Dave said.

"Lorna. You have an update for me?"

"Yes, Mayor. The street held its ground, one wagon damaged but repairable. Five casualties are all being healed. We will require a new supply of potions for the spell casters. Supplies are starting to run low."

"Excellent news, and there is no problem with the potions. Oscaray stated the same, so I have already asked Alice to instruct Master Rui and Constance to start producing them," the mayor said.

It was a surprise to listen to the report and see how everything seemed to be aligned throughout various areas of the town. It was so efficient, discussing combat and then logistics straight after a battle while still cleaning up the chaos that it left behind.

"SJ, can you join us this evening in the Arms? We will toast our fallen and fill our bellies," the mayor said.

It wasn't really putting her out since she was living in the inn. "Of course. I would love to join you."

"Excellent. We will see you this evening."

The gathering came and went. They spent time talking about all the members of the town who had lost their lives, which totalled six. After a toast to their bravery, the bard had sung, bringing many of the inn to tears with tales of valour and lost love. The food was served. Roast hoglings were placed on the tables, which had been rearranged to accommodate the much larger groups. Once those invited had eaten, the tables were moved again, and the drinking began.

As the evening went on, it seemed as though half the town was in the inn. It was so crowded, and by the time SJ eventually excused herself and retreated upstairs, she was feeling a little worse for wear, having joined in with too many toasts to the fallen. It was a memorable evening, but she hoped it would not be repeated for a very long time.

CHAPTER FIFTY-TWO

Looking Down

When SJ awoke the next morning, her head felt like she had a herd of elephants stomping in it. Groaning loudly, she sat up.

"Are you okay?" Dave asked.

"My head," SJ said, holding it in her hands. She didn't think she had drunk that much the previous evening, but it was still enough to make her feel bad.

"Drink a potion. You have one from Darjey's loot in the wardrobe."

"It's a bit extreme using a potion to get rid of a headache."

"It's not a headache; it's a hangover. Your body is dehydrated, and it's only a minor. They only heal one to eight health; the lessers you got are better at eight to sixteen, but unless you have potions of rejuvenation, which basically rebuild your cells, it's the fastest cure."

Walking over to the wardrobe, she took out one of the smaller vials, uncorked it, and drank. The potion didn't take long to work. Her body felt more invigorated, and the thumping in her head faded. In under a minute, she felt as right as rain again.

"I wonder if that is how Darjey and Malcolm had been drinking so much. Using potions to heal themselves between drinking bouts?"

"I don't think they were ever sober enough to even consider them," Dave replied.

Walking to the window, she looked out into the town square. The rain had stopped at some point overnight, and the cobbles appeared to be steaming as the remaining water slowly evaporated from them. The usual bright, clear skies had returned, and the sun blazed down. The street vendors moved crates and barrels and tipped the excess water from their stall awnings, while the shop owners opened their shopfronts, letting in the sun's rays.

"I need to sort out the loot I have. See Fran and Fizzlewick. Go and train and pick up some more quests."

"We have much to investigate and discuss," Dave added.

"What do we need to discuss?"

"Everything. What is happening here is not normal. Every day, the mechanics of what should be a starter town are being challenged. I am trying to investigate the code to see what is happening, but I still haven't fully sorted out my loophole since the emergency patch."

"You mentioned that before, but everyone in town was here long before I arrived, so it has to be a normal starter town."

"I spoke to Malcolm's AI last night before he was reassigned. He said he had also noticed strange things with levels and the general town function. A starter town having a hostile settlement so close is unheard of. It leads us to believe that the System is losing more and more control over what it implemented thousands of years ago. Autonomy is taking over, realigning things more. I think that it is part of natural balance and that because of the good nature of the town, the hobs appeared as a balancing act."

"This must have happened before, if that is the case."

"Not that we are aware of. It seems to be a recent change. I have messaged some of the AIs on other continents, but they won't be able to respond about their actual Legionnaires until they pass. Being able to talk about you and your experiences with other AI while I still support you is only because of the waiver. I am not held to account."

"Won't that anger the System, though?"

"They can't do anything about it now. Interference with an existing AI is one of the primary taboos. They would have to break their own rules to do so. That reminds me, I completely forgot: I heard from the adjudicator."

"Oh. What did they say?"

"They accepted your statement. Therefore, the initial full experience will be assigned upon completion of the quest."

"That means I can see Gladys this morning, then," SJ said, smiling. Yesterday, when she had come upstairs and walked into the bedroom, she had removed the choker. Picking it up from the bedside table, she walked back through to put it on in front of the mirror. It was a beautiful piece.

"Okay. It's time to complete the quest and see if Fran is free to check in about flying."

"I am not sure you need to. Your flying is natural now."

"I know, but she said she would like to go on a flight with another fae again."

After grabbing some breakfast, SJ began the walk over to the mill. She could have flown, but after yesterday's deluge, she enjoyed walking in the morning sun. Several of the townsfolk waved to her this morning as she walked along; she recognised some of them from yesterday's battle and time in the inn but didn't know everyone's names. She smiled back, offering pleasantries in response to greetings.

"You are getting popular. I am surprised . . ."

SJ's display triggered.

Congratulations! Your reputation with the town of Killic was raised to Liked after you supported the town during the recent hobgoblin raid.

All future town interactions will offer a 40% experience bonus for quests completed.

". . . And there it is," Dave finished, chuckling.

"Yes," SJ whispered ecstatically.

"That will help speed things up again."

"I need to get more quests once I complete this one."

The mill's sails were slowly turning, and Hubert was busy moving bags of flour onto the back of a wagon.

"Morning. Would you like a hand?" SJ asked, smiling.

Hubert turned to look at her, slightly taken aback, not hearing her approach. "You!"

"Yes. Me," SJ replied, getting ready for a confrontation.

"Lucinda told me what you did yesterday."

"Lucinda?" SJ asked, not recognising the name.

"Mrs. Larper, she runs the best bakery in town. You were fighting on the front line."

"I was."

"Well, thank you," Hubert said.

"I only did what anyone else would have done."

"Not of your kind," he said, throwing another sack onto the wagon. "Gladys is inside," he stated, climbing onto the wagon and moving towards town.

SJ wasn't sure if he meant fae or Legionnaire by his statement, but she didn't want to challenge him and cause an argument. The mill door was open, and when she looked inside, SJ could see the mechanism she remembered from a school trip to an old mill back on Earth. A large mill bin sat at the bottom of a wooden chute, and up on the inside, she could see the large grinding stones slowly crushing the grains. The grinding stone and creaking of the wooden structure were loud in the confined space of the insides. She noticed Gladys on the floor above.

"Hi, Gladys."

On seeing SJ, the woman hurried down the ladder.

"Hello, dear. I'm so glad you're back. I heard what you did yesterday in town. I received the notification that the cottages were clear. Thank you so much."

SJ's display triggered.

Quest: Investigate the Cottages—Complete

The cottages are clear as the undead have left the area, and the source has been located. You may claim your reward for identifying the source and location of the necromancer behind the recent events.

Rewards: 200xp + 40% = 280xp awarded

Return to Gladys to receive your gift.

SJ smiled at seeing the increased experience gained because of her new reputation level with the town.

"Here, please take this," Gladys said, handing SJ a small vial of liquid.

"What is it?" SJ asked, peering at the pale white liquid.

"It's a cure potion. It will treat any toxins or poisons that you have suffered."

"That's amazing, thank you."

"I heard what happened to you during the battle yesterday and thought it may benefit you more than the coin I had planned."

"You heard about me being poisoned?"

"The whole town has. You are the talk of it."

"I am? I noticed more people waving to me today, but I didn't think I had done that much, and no more than those who gave their lives."

"We probably would have lost many more if it wasn't for you, though."

"Thank you. I have something to tell you as well."

"What?" Gladys asked.

"With Zej and Lythonian's help, we cleared the necromancer from over the other side of the lake. That is where the undead had come from. Three of the skeletons have been freed and are currently staying in one of the cottages. I have asked them to take care of your cottage while they are there. I am planning to revisit them in a few days. Lythonian checked all their alignments so they can all be trusted," SJ finished, seeing that a worried look had started to appear on Gladys's face.

"If the venerable Lythonian checked them, then that makes me feel better," Gladys said, now smiling again.

"I am going to see Mistress Francisca at the academy while I am over this way."

"Thank you for what you have done. I will visit the cottage in a few days myself and see what state it was left in."

"Oh. They had never entered it. They were using the storm cellar for storage."

"That is a relief," Gladys said.

"Let me know if you need anything else done at any time," SJ said as she turned to leave.

"I will, and see you soon."

Walking the short distance from the mill to the mage training grounds, SJ took in the wonder of the magic being demonstrated as she approached. Various coloured lights could be seen competing against the bright sun. There were many more mages outside compared to her initial visit, and Fran stood in front of them all, giving instructions.

"We need to improve our offensive strategy. I know many of you are new mages, but our weaknesses were revealed yesterday. We should be able to stop the hobs in their tracks, yet every time, we suffer due to too many defensive spells rather than offensive ones. Today, we train offensively. Now I want you to break off into pairs and practise with each other, and I will check in and see how you are getting on."

SJ walked over to where Fran stood, speaking to the goblin clerk.

"Hi, Mistress Francisca," she said as she approached.

When Fran turned, her gaze drifted immediately down to her choker. Her eyes grew a little wider before she hurried towards her. Without saying a word, she took her by her elbow and turned her, walking into the main building. SJ was taken aback but didn't resist allowing herself to be ushered.

The inside of the building was different from what SJ had expected. She had images of alchemy sets and bottles and potions lying everywhere, and instead of a laboratory setting, she was met with a common room with sofas, a dining area, and then a corridor that ran down the centre of the building. It was nicely furnished, and there was no clutter. Fran led her to a side door and opened it, showing her inside.

"Sit," she said sternly.

SJ did as she was asked and sat down. Fran walked to the other side of a desk and sat.

"Are you okay?" SJ asked, a little concerned.

"Where did you get it?" Fran asked flatly.

"Get what?"

"The choker."

"Oh. Mayor Maxwell gave it to me for helping yesterday as a thank-you gift."

"Do you know what it is?"

"I have identified it, yes."

"So, you know it is fae?"

"I wonder what her problem is?" Dave said, sounding concerned.

"I do. Is there a problem?"

"That is the Choker of the Earth Stone, right?"

"Yes. How do you know?"

"It is a lost treasure of the fae. It has been missing for centuries. It is one piece of a set lost during the dark elf wars."

"You recognise it?"

Fran took out a key and unlocked a drawer in the desk, lifting out a parchment. Placing it on the table, she unrolled it. On the parchment was a list of various items and pictures of each one neatly drawn and painted. In total, the parchment had nearly thirty items listed. Halfway down the page was the image of the choker SJ now wore. It was identical. Beneath it were four other items which made the set. The Tiara of the Earth Stone, the Earrings of the Earth Stone, the Earthen Breast, and the Belt of the Earth Stone.

SJ was amazed to see her choker and the four other items. "What does this mean exactly?"

"You are wearing a fae heirloom. Its true power is unknown, to my knowledge. It has been centuries since the set was combined."

"Oh. Do I need to return it to someone?"

"No. It cannot be taken from you now you have worn it, not without you being killed. It is soul-bound."

Looking at the item details again, she noticed a new comment next to where it had stated it was one of five in a set.

Soul-Bound

"I had not realised."

"The fact that it is now back in the hands of a fae is the best we could hope for. The chances of finding the other pieces to the set are virtually zero. There have been sightings of various heirlooms over the years, but this is the first time I am aware that one has reappeared again in fae hands."

SJ's display triggered.

Quest: Earth Sentry
The fae heirlooms have been missing for centuries. You have received one of five pieces of the Earth Sentry set. Find the other four remaining pieces to complete the set. This is a racial quest and has no territory limitations.
Progress: 1 of 5
Rewards: Earth Sentry status

"Now, that is a proper quest," Dave said.

Ignoring Dave, SJ looked at Fran, a little concerned that she may have painted a target on her back. "Does this mean others will hunt me down?"

"Hunted down, no. Be looked at differently by fae . . . perhaps, but only if they know what you wear. I know because of my position as an enchanter and my previous time in the fae capital, but the heirlooms have been missing for so long that many have forgotten about them."

"I didn't realise you were an enchanter."

"I am, and Mayor Maxwell sent a message yesterday about lightning protection on your boots stopping the mage's shield from damaging you. I am currently looking into learning it so we can enchant more gear."

"The mayor thinks it would help significantly, having mêlée fighters able to attack."

"It would. One of the biggest issues is that using mage spells against magic shields is like using a thimble to extinguish a fire. Especially the shield that the hobgoblin mage uses. It is arcane dark magic, not elemental like most mages."

"I have no idea about how different magics interact. There are a lot of mages here, though; I would have thought you would be able to do the hobs much more damage."

"Most of the mages here are below Level 5. They may have a barrier spell, which you would have seen at the docks, but they don't have offensive capabilities. When you consider a mage, having a barrier or personal shield is their priority over anything else. Many mages never even learn offensive magic, as they have no need for it. They focus more on magic that helps with normal everyday life."

"I automatically assumed mages would cast fireballs or lightning bolts everywhere."

"Ha, no." Fran smiled. "Most are learning work skills. Water mages are highly sought after in the desert regions. Fire mages in the ice regions, et cetera. Many learn only to support."

SJ was surprised at this information, having assumed that all mages would be combat oriented. Given the lack of sciences she had witnessed so far, it made sense that they would be more of a support class.

"Are any combat focused?"

"Some are, but it's a rarity. Those that are usually work for the larger cities as protectors."

"Could you not have created a shield to protect the town from the hobs, blocking them from approaching?"

"It is not as easy as you may think, especially with the lower-level mages we have. They can only hold it for a short period before it dissipates, and due to limited mana, they then become useless without potions. The hobgoblin mage is very skilled. He has a permanent invulnerability shield that, once cast, remains until it is destroyed and projects a personal skin shield to Bordon."

"Are you not as powerful?"

"No way near. I have also split my elemental alignments, not focusing on one specific element to the same degree. Although I am a water mage, most of my spells are support based."

The revelations of the mages' class system were not what SJ had expected, but they did make sense of why they had not been very effective in combatting the hob raid.

"The reason I came to see you is that I have been flying," SJ said, changing the conversation.

"Excellent. How have you been getting on?"

"Great, I think, at least. There are no aches or pains, and it feels so natural."

"Show me, then."

SJ stood from her chair before changing to her miniature form, then took off and hovered.

"Great." Fran transformed herself and flew over the desk. "Shall we go for a flight?"

"Do you not need to watch the apprentices?"

"I should, but they can keep practising. They will need to keep allowing their mana to recharge, so it is a process that takes time. We don't just have limitless mana potions available. We save them for the raids."

There was a window at the rear of the office, and Fran flew over and lifted the latch. It pushed open easily, and she flew outside. "Come on, then."

SJ followed. Once outside, Fran set off steadily, flying over the training ground. The mages below were busy testing each other, and SJ watched the spectacle as they flew over. After glancing at SJ and seeing that she was coping with her speed, Fran slowly picked up the pace. SJ hadn't paid attention to the speeds she had been flying at before, but now she realised how fast the ground was starting to flash below her.

"Let's go higher." Fran suddenly changed direction and flew straight up. SJ could not turn as swiftly, and aligning and following took her a moment. Trailing Fran and trying to chase her down, she increased her speed again. Fran moved quite a distance away straight up before stopping, and SJ pushed hard to reach her.

She realised she was now panting from the exertion and came to a hover at her side. "That was harder than I thought it would be."

"Your speed will increase over time; you are already very fast for a new flyer," Fran said, smiling.

Looking down for the first time since chasing Fran, the realisation of how high they were made her feel giddy. "Whoa. This is high," SJ said, her eyes wide as she stared at the ground far below. They must have flown a few hundred feet straight up. "Do we have limits?"

"Limits in height we can fly? No. The only thing that would stop us is air temperature. If we went much higher than we are now, since we are in the mountains, we would soon start to feel it."

Understanding the general physics of Earth and altitude, it made sense that Amathera would have similar conditions even if it were larger than Earth. From their height, SJ could see over the mountains and across the wide-open forest area and farmland that surrounded the town. The width of the lake from this height was truly awesome. The town now looked like the model on Mayor Maxwell's table.

"This view is amazing."

"It is rather beautiful and peaceful up here," Fran said.

SJ looked over at the mountaintop in the distance, where the considerable form of Bob had been, and realised that he was no longer there.

"I wonder when the dragon left," SJ said.

"I saw him leave yesterday before the rain came. He took off heading north again."

"That will stop you from having to protect yourself from the lake surge."

"It will. We only just managed to stop the first one. The second surge we were better equipped for."

"I saw you at the docks. It was an amazing sight."

"You would have seen the shields, then. That is all many mages can do apart from throwing the occasional minor offensive spell. The timing of the shields was critical, and several mages suffered from serious mana fatigue afterwards."

SJ had heard about mana fatigue from games she had played and books she had read, so she didn't need to ask what Fran meant.

"Seven o'clock, up three hundred feet," Dave suddenly said.

SJ turned, looking upwards, and saw a large bird in the distance. Fran followed her gaze.

"You must have strong senses," Fran said, raising her eyebrows.

Not responding, SJ watched as the bird adjusted its flight and started to align with them.

"That looks like a falcon. We better head down." Fran said.

Fran turned and descended, SJ followed.

"It's moved off," Dave said.

Looking backwards, SJ saw it had indeed changed direction and was flying over the lake towards the thick forest on the far side.

"It's stopped following," SJ said.

"I should get back anyway," Fran responded.

The descent was gentler than the ascent, and flying back over the training ground again, they entered Fran's office through the window before transforming back into their larger forms.

"I enjoyed that. I last flew with a fae many years ago. You are very natural, and your speed will increase more. Over the next few months, you will learn your limits."

"Thank you. I would never have got to where I am without your help."

"It is my pleasure," Fran said. "I better check on the apprentices."

Walking out of the building, SJ noticed two mages arguing. Fran immediately headed over to them.

"Thanks," SJ called. Fran waved briefly before turning back to speak to the apprentices.

"That was invigorating," SJ said, "and thanks for the warning."

"No need to thank me," Dave said.

Dave's naturally warning her about the bird made SJ feel happy, and a grin broke out on her face.

"Wind again?" Dave asked.

CHAPTER FIFTY-THREE

Broken Heart

Considering yesterday's raid on the town and the bad weather, the streets were bustling quite normally by the time she returned to the centre.

"THE SERVICE OF REMEMBRANCE WILL COMMENCE AT FOURTEEN HUNDRED HOURS TODAY. ALL THOSE WISHING TO PAY THEIR RESPECTS TO THE FALLEN, PLEASE ATTEND PROMPTLY." The now-common sound of the mage who made the announcements rang out. It was only mid-morning, and SJ still had plenty of time before the service. Although she didn't know those who had been lost, she still felt obliged to attend.

As she walked along, a small gnoll child ran into SJ's leg, nearly taking her off her feet. The gnoll had been knocked to the cobbles and was shaking her head, sending her pink hair ribbons swaying, tears running down her cheeks.

Kneeling down, SJ asked, "Are you okay?"

"No. My daddy is dead," the girl wailed.

"You poor thing. Where is your mother?"

"I don't have one."

This surprised SJ, filling her heart with sorrow. "Oh dear. Who is looking after you?"

"I was collected from home last night when Dad didn't return and taken to the orphanage."

Reeling from the news that the town had an orphanage, SJ was lost for words for a moment.

"Where are you going?" she finally asked.

"Away."

"Away where?"

"As far away as I can get."

"You are too small to take care of yourself."

The young gnoll looked at her resolutely and snapped, "I'm not too small." She growled, showing her rather sharp teeth. She reminded SJ of a small puppy rather than the young child she was.

"But how will you get food?"

"I will hunt, just like Mum and Dad used to."

"Hunting is a good profession," SJ smiled, trying to gain rapport with the young gnoll. "I am sure you will become a great hunter one day, but you need to train and learn the profession."

"I will train. I will learn to hunt and kill, and then when those horrible creatures return, I will kill them all."

"Which horrible creatures?"

"The ones that attacked the town."

"Did you see them?"

"No. But I know where they live. Dad always told me they come from the valley."

"Have you eaten today?"

The girl met her eyes for the first time, and when she saw SJ's kind and concerned face, she replied, "You are very pretty."

SJ blushed. "Thank you. You are pretty as well."

The girl looked down at herself where she still sat on the cobbled street, frowning. "Do you think so?"

"I do, yes. I think you will grow up to be a beautiful young lady." SJ noticed her face relax, and the tears stopped flowing for the first time since she had run into her. "You can't grow up alone, though. You need people to help you; otherwise, you will struggle. To be a hunter, you need to fight hoglings. I have fought hoglings, and I know how difficult they can be to kill."

"You have hunted hoglings?"

"I have. Yes."

"Could you teach me how?"

"I am no expert, and you are a little small still. They are not small creatures."

"But I need to be a hunter. I need to. I need to learn how to kill." The anger that appeared on the girl's face was heart-wrenching. SJ's emotions were being taken on a rollercoaster listening to her and her determination to become a hunter and seek revenge. The hobs had a lot to answer for.

"Have you eaten today?" she asked again.

"No. When I woke up, I snuck out."

"They will be worried sick wondering where you are."

"I need to learn, though. I need to make a coin. Dad always said coin must be earned."

"Your dad sounds as though he was a wise gnoll."

"He was the best," the girl replied, sniffing, and a fresh tear ran down her cheek.

"Would you like some food?"

The young gnoll placed her hands on her stomach.

"Come on. Let's get you some food, and then we will get you back," SJ said, offering her hand.

The gnoll looked at her hand momentarily before reaching out and taking it. SJ stood, helping her to her feet. Glancing around, she saw food stalls in the market, but she knew exactly where she would take her.

The inn was quiet at this time of day, and only a few patrons sat at tables. She walked up to the bar with the gnoll, who stared around the inn. It was obvious she had never been there before. Kerys was polishing glasses behind the bar and saw SJ and the young gnoll.

"Who do we have here, then?" she asked, smiling.

"She ran into me in the street, and I said I would get her some food. Is there any breakfast left?"

"I can check," Kerys replied.

SJ led the gnoll to a table in the corner of the inn and sat her down. "I will be back in a minute," she said, smiling sweetly at her.

She didn't respond, and SJ turned, heading back to the bar.

"Who is she?" Kerys asked as she approached.

"No idea. She is from the orphanage; her dad was killed yesterday, apparently, and she has no mother."

"Oh dear. That must be little Cristy. Dawkins' daughter. He was one of the town's best hunters. Bordon killed him yesterday during the raid. He was trying to protect the mayor when he got knocked down."

SJ remembered the name being mentioned last night. The comments had been that he had fought bravely but was no match for the power of the ogre.

"I am going to feed her and then take her back," SJ said.

"We still have breakfast leftovers; I will get Floretta to plate some up."

"How much?"

"Nothing, it's on me." Kerys smiled.

SJ walked back over and sat with Cristy. "I am SJ, by the way. What is your name?"

"Cristy," she replied, confirming that she was Dawkins' daughter.

"Nice to meet you, Cristy. That is a pretty name."

Cristy made the faintest smile at the compliment.

It didn't take long for Kerys to walk over with a child-sized portion of a full breakfast. It even had mushrooms, which, since being added, made it even more wholesome. She returned a minute later with a large glass of fresh milk.

"Coffee?" Kerys asked.

"I may as well while Cristy eats," SJ replied.

Cristy was not planning on hanging around and wolfed the breakfast down and polished off the glass of milk in quick order. SJ hadn't even drunk half a cup before the young gnoll was finished. Cristy released a small burp and covered her mouth in embarrassment. SJ chuckled at her.

"Sorry," she replied.

"No need to apologise. In some places, it is polite to burp after a meal."

"Is it? My dad always said it was bad manners."

"Oh. If that's the case, then maybe I am wrong," SJ replied, not wanting to tarnish the vision she had of her father. "Shall we go back to the orphanage?"

"I will be all alone there."

"I am sure you can make friends there, and I promise I will come and visit you as well."

"Will you? Will you also teach me how to hunt?"

"I may in time, but for now, you need to grow stronger by exercising regularly and learning."

"Learning?"

"Yes. Learning, getting educated."

"What's educated?"

"Reading, writing, maths. Learn what you can and become intelligent and strong all at the same time."

"Do you think I can?"

"I do, yes. I think you can do whatever you put your mind to in time. It may not always be easy, and at times you may struggle, but the more you can do, the better you will become."

Taking SJ by surprise, Cristy hugged her.

"Thank you," Cristy said, squeezing her tightly.

SJ hugged her back and held her tight for a few moments, her heart almost breaking at the courage and bravery of the young gnoll.

"That has to be one of the most beautiful scenes I have seen in a long time," Dave said in a caring tone.

After asking Kerys for directions to the orphanage, SJ escorted Cristy back. The grandmotherly dwarf who ran the orphanage had been worried sick when she found that Cristy had gone missing, and had even informed the town guard to look out for her. SJ explained to her what she had said and that she had promised to come and visit. The dwarf, whose name was Madeline, promised to take special care of her. SJ asked about education, and Madeline told her that they were taught the basics once they were old enough, but they were restricted by what they could do at the orphanage.

It reminded SJ of the social care system in the UK and their hands being tied usually due to lack of finances. Madeline informed her that hiring one of the local scribes would require a monthly fee once she had learned the basics. It cost forty copper a term, which the orphanage couldn't afford, and SJ didn't hesitate to take out two silver and forty copper to pay for her first year.

It wasn't even midday when SJ left the orphanage, promising Cristy she would come and see her in a couple of days.

"What you have done today has, above all other actions, made me the proudest to be your administrator," Dave said as SJ walked off, continuing her original journey to find Fizzlewick.

SJ could feel the heat in her cheeks from the compliment. "Thanks," SJ replied, feeling thoroughly embarrassed.

"In all my years, that has been one of the most genuine interactions I have witnessed. I only say what I see."

"Enough, please, Dave. I didn't do it for compliments. Then again, since it is a compliment from you, maybe I should be grateful and take it while I can," SJ said, grinning.

"I agree you should. Aye, hang on, that's not fair. I do compliment you."

"Do you?"

"I gave you a nine out of ten. That was a compliment."

"Which you then changed to a seven, if I remember rightly."

Silence.

"Dave?"

"Yes," he replied, grumbling.

"Thank you. It is appreciated."

"My pleasure," he replied in a gentle tone.

Reaching the tailor's shop, SJ was delighted to see that it didn't have the usual closed sign she had got used to seeing. Opening the door, the bell tinkled, and walking in, the front of the shop was empty, with no sign of Fizzlewick's quarterling form.

"Fizzlewick?" SJ called, walking towards the counter.

Hearing movement in the back room, she waited patiently until the beads moved. It was funny knowing that the wizened old quarterling who wandered through was, in fact, a god.

"SJ," Fizzlewick said, a smile breaking the wizened face. With a flourish of his hand, the shutters closed, and the front door locked. Fizzlewick transformed before her.

"Hi, Fizzlewick," she said excitedly. Finally, she would be able to progress in her tailoring skills.

"I see you are now Apprentice Level 3. I am guessing you need more recipes?"

"I do, yes. I also have some questions."

"Indeed, I bet you do," he replied, chuckling. "Bob was very complimentary of you."

"So, you did go and see him."

"Yes. We had a long old chat. It has been a century or more since we last had a chance to catch up properly."

The periods still amazed SJ. She still hadn't even been in Amathera for a month, and it already felt like she had done so much. Considering what she might do in a century made her head hurt.

"Did Bob tell you what he gave me?"

"He did, and I am glad you are still alive. It was very risky for him, although I had to accept his judgement on that. Even as a god, I was not fully aware of how the symbiosis works with dragons. You are both very fortunate, and you must have done something to impress Bob. He has had the opportunity over his life to have chosen a bond before, and after meeting you for the first time, he decided to share his most precious gift."

"He mentioned that he could see why you had asked him to come down here."

"He needed a holiday. After all, he is the ruler of the northern ice regions and doesn't get away very often. It was about time his daughter stepped up and took some responsibility. I just hope she didn't cause too many problems while he was away. For a blue dragon, she does have rather a temper."

Trying to comprehend the family dynamics of dragons was not something SJ was quite ready to consider.

"Ruler, you say?"

"Yes. Bob oversees the northern territories. The ice mountains, in particular. The dragons are in constant conflict with the ice giants and elementals that live there. It has been an ongoing feud for over five centuries."

SJ had images of huge ice giants and dragons duking it out. She bet it would be a sight to behold.

"I need the cloth gloves recipe. I also had loads of the woollen recipes become available."

"Yes, yes. That's normal practise. Let's go downstairs, and we can start sorting you out."

Once they were in the cellar, sitting in the luxurious chairs that Fizzlewick had made appear, he presented various recipes. SJ had fourteen woollen recipes she could learn for various clothing items and cloth gloves.

"How much do these all cost?"

"All woollen recipes are a copper each. Cloth starts at ten copper but increases in price depending upon the item."

SJ counted out twenty-four copper and handed them to Fizzlewick. He took them, making them disappear. Picking up the cloth recipe, SJ opened it and read what she would require. The needles were not a problem as they were in her tailoring set. She needed to purchase thread and buttons, though. Looking at the design, they seemed like standard gloves with a small button and loop that could be fastened at the wrist to help them stay on.

"Can I get all the extra materials I need, please?"

"Of course. Here you go." The required items all appeared on the table. "Three more copper for the lot."

Paying Fizzlewick, SJ picked the items up and added them to her inventory, then did the same with the recipes. Every recipe took up an individual slot, meaning she would need to carry some of them with the other items she was still carrying. They did fit into the tailoring slots in her inventory, but fifteen recipes plus the three slots for the buttons and different threads and the items she carried as standard meant it was again already full.

"I really need to get a larger inventory. These recipes take up so much room for being a roll of parchment," SJ said.

"Recipes can be combined into one slot," Dave interjected.

"How?" SJ said.

Fizzlewick smiled, knowing she was replying to Dave. It was nice being able to talk openly to Dave in the presence of the god.

"In the tailoring inventory slots, you have various settings, one called a bookcase. Do you see the three dots?"

SJ looked at her display, saw the dots, and selected them. She found the option to turn a specific slot into a bookcase. She selected her first tailoring slot and chose the option. She then noticed a sort button. Selecting it, her vision flashed as the recipes all got moved around, and in place of the single recipe in the first slot, there was now the image of a book. Selecting it, a sub-window appeared listing all the recipes. When she selected one, the recipe appeared in her hand.

"That is amazingly useful." SJ smiled, happy at the new information.

"It appears your friend is very supportive," Fizzlewick said.

"He is."

"Aww shucks, you'll embarrass me," Dave said.

Laughing at Dave's comment, SJ felt relief for the first time since yesterday's raid. It was amazing how the small things brought happiness.

"Is there a way to learn tailoring techniques that I may need in the future?" SJ asked.

Fizzlewick narrowed his eyes slightly at her question. "You mean advanced techniques?" he asked.

"Not necessarily advanced. I mean, currently, I have only made the woollen socks, and I had to learn the knitting method required in Amathera from the recipe. Is there something that shows you all the various techniques you can practise before they become part of a recipe? I suppose like an instruction manual of knitting or sewing or whatever all the other requirements are."

"Manuals are held in the libraries of some cities. They are not normally mentioned as the recipes have details for each design."

"I understand. That it would just be nice to practise some of the other techniques before I potentially have to use them on a recipe, making it easier when I do."

"That is a very diligent approach. The tailors' guild would be very happy with someone with your thought process. The problem you have with that is that without a recipe to follow, what would you do?"

SJ remembered her days in school when, as part of her design technology and art lessons, she had spent several lessons just performing various stitches in nice, neat rows on cards to showcase her skills. She hadn't taken it for one of her education choices, never thinking she would need the knowledge she had learned again. Thinking about the various things she had learned during her short time on Earth, many of those she had given up would have been much more useful than she gave them credit for.

Being one of the technology and e-commerce age where everything was only one click away on a screen, she never had to consider the manufacturing requirements or time needed to become proficient in many areas. It made her consider her missed opportunities. Another example would have been cooking. She had cooked a little back on Earth, but most of her life she had spent eating out.

"I can just practise the different stitches; I don't need to have something to make to sew."

"You are correct, you don't." Fizzlewick smiled. He waved his hand, and a rolled piece of cloth appeared on the table. "Please."

SJ picked up the piece of cloth and unrolled it. It was the size of a hand towel, and in neat little rows on the surface were many different stitches and approaches. Each one had a small, neatly sewn label above it.

"This is exactly what I meant," SJ said. "I can create something similar and practise each of the styles."

"You can indeed. Would you like to keep that as a reference?"

"Are you sure? It is pristine."

"Ha. I hope so. I am a god and a Grand Master, after all." Flicking his hands, he produced a new piece of plain cloth with a golden needle and thread.

"What is that thread?" SJ asked in amazement.

"Oh. This is nothing special, really. It's just imbued to prevent knotting."

SJ watched in amazement as Fizzlewick sewed quickly and precisely the first of the various techniques, completing it in no time. "See, making a new one doesn't take long."

"I think it would take me a very long time."

"If you keep training, you will become proficient. One day, you may even become a Grand Master."

"I hope to. I have a long way to go; those woollen socks took so long."

The whole time Fizzlewick was talking, he continued to sew with an unnerving speed and precision.

"Can I ask about Bob?"

"What do you want to know?"

"Why was he here? He said it may be because of me."

"You would be right. It was because of you," replied Fizzlewick matter-of-factly.

"Why would he be here because of me?"

"I asked him to come and see me, and you just happened to visit him." Fizzlewick smiled.

"Was the event because of you?"

"I can't give away the secrets of the gods," he replied, winking.

"Why would you do that?"

"I have already told you. We gods are very excited about you and your potential, not being held to the terms and conditions. Bob is one of the strongest and most respected across the continents. He is also one of the few dragons with the gods' respect. He has brought relative peace to the north since he took over his reign, and if there is one person for you to know in your long journey ahead, it would be one of such high standing."

"I am so new and such a low level. What could I possibly bring to aid?"

"Nothing as yet, but in time, those who align with you will, I believe, see the benefits."

"What benefits?" SJ asked, feeling daunted and confused.

"I cannot say at this time."

"Why not at this time? Isn't it right that I should know, if it's something about me?"

"Unfortunately, no. As you grow and become stronger, you will realise that what we started in this town called Killic may eventually lead to great things for this continent and even Amathera as a whole."

The thought of her having an everlasting impact on Amathera filled her with dread, fear, trepidation, and excitement in equal amounts. Could she really have the impact that Fizzlewick believed could happen? The waiver was one thing, but what could she do as a single person to affect the workings of a world, and in what way?

She sat in silence, watching Fizzlewick sew, his hands a blur. After what seemed like no time, he held the cloth up before him, smiling. "There we go."

Checking her display, SJ noticed that there was only an hour until the service would start at the church. "I better go. I want to make sure I get to the service on time."

"Of course. I understand," Fizzlewick said, nodding his head.

SJ stood to leave when a question entered her mind. "Do you mind if I ask you something?"

"Please do."

"Were you here yesterday?"

"No. I returned this morning. Why?"

"I wondered if you could help defend the town or not."

"Unfortunately, no. If I did, that would be considered interference, and we would come under the System's scrutiny. The gods exist with the freedom they have because we must follow certain rules, one of which is that we may not directly join any combat situation."

"That is a shame."

"If I had, the chances are another god would do the same for the hobs, and then it just gets overly political. The last time it happened, it led to one of the worst wars this continent has ever seen, which is why the System amended its laws."

"What was that?"

"The Scrug Wars. I may tell you about it one day. It was a dark time. Anyway, you better go if you don't want to be late. I almost forgot—nice choker," he casually added, winking.

SJ smiled nervously, knowing he knew exactly what it was. "Thanks, and I will be back soon." SJ left and began the solemn walk to the church.

CHAPTER FIFTY-FOUR

Emotional Progress

The small churchyard was already getting crowded, with a great many of the town's citizens arriving for the service. SJ felt a little uncertain about her presence as she had known none of the victims, but she felt obligated to be there. Lythonian stood at the entrance, welcoming the family members of those who had lost a loved one. Bright bouquets were positioned in large pots lining the path towards the entrance. Although people spoke, they did so in hushed and respectful tones. As SJ stood silently watching the proceedings, she was suddenly hit in her leg. The small form of Cristy had run to her and now clung tightly around her calf. Madeline, the kindly dwarf from the orphanage, walked over.

"Cristy."

The small gnoll looked up at SJ. Her face already had streaks from the tears she had shed. She sniffed loudly. "Will you come with me?" she asked with pleading eyes.

The crippling feeling of despair hit SJ like a bullet, and she could feel tears in her own eyes forming as she looked down at her. "Come where?" SJ asked.

"To the church. Will you sit with me, please?" she begged.

SJ looked over at Madeline, who smiled kindly, shrugging.

"If you want me to, I will, of course," SJ replied.

SJ offered Cristy her hand, and she held it tightly as they walked up the path to the entrance. SJ could feel eyes on her as she did. She hadn't planned on entering the church and just wished to be present to show her respect. Now she felt in the spotlight. Her beauty and green dress contrasted with many who wore darker colours. Cristy wore a pale pink dress and matching pink ribbons in her hair. Holding her gaze down, not wanting to meet the eyes of those lining the path, SJ led Cristy to the entrance.

"Cristy, my dear child," Lythonian said as they approached the steps. "SJ, will you be accompanying her?"

SJ turned again to see Madeline, who just nodded. Turning back, she responded, "Yes. I will be with Cristy."

"You are seated on the front left pew at the end nearest the wall," Lythonian replied, smiling kindly.

"Thank you."

Leading Cristy, SJ entered the church. Having been there several times, she wasn't expecting what she was now met with. The inside was packed; virtually every pew was full. Consciously, she walked down the central aisle before turning and leading Cristy to the left, showing her a seat next to a kobold and her children. Cristy did not release her grip on SJ's hand and, once sat, leaned into her.

Music began filling the church, from a goblin playing an instrument SJ did not recognise, which sounded similar to pipe music. Several townsfolk stood in white robes at the front of the church, and as the tune changed, they began to sing. SJ recognised the old gnome she had seen replacing the flowers in the church previously, and she appeared to be the group's lead as their soft lilt filled the church's eaves. The choir's sound brought a sense of comfort and solace to the occasion.

Lythonian walked to the altar. As the music and singing ended, silence filled the proceedings except for the gentle sobs of several gathered within the church. The individual grief and communal support were insurmountable.

"I stand here today with a heavy heart. It is seldom that we must gather for such an event as the loss of six members of our community at one time. Losing someone dear to us is never easy. As we gather here today, we are joined by a profound sense of loss but also by the enduring memories and love that will forever live on in our hearts. Today, we come together to honour the lives of Sarwick, Zefir, Lotti, Porewi, Kas, and Henrick to celebrate the moments we shared and to find solace in the legacy they leave behind.

"As we reflect on their lives, let us take time to consider their loved ones, many of whom are here today with us in the congregation. Let us keep their memories dear; remember the shared laughter and moments that will be etched in our hearts forever. Though they may no longer be with us in body, their spirits continue to burn fiercely and will illuminate their next lives.

"Though I stand here with a heavy heart, let us find strength in each other during this challenging time and comfort in those around us, friends, family and strangers alike, as we bid them farewell. Let us all stand as those fallen are brought to their final resting place."

Music and song started again as six caskets were carried into the church and laid out on the floor before the altar. Then SJ watched as several stood and walked forward, placing flowers on their tops. SJ could feel Cristy's tears soaking through her dress where her face was hidden and the sobs that wracked her slight frame. She felt a tear on her own cheek but didn't wipe it away.

Once the caskets were in and the music stopped, Lythonian addressed everyone again. "Several wish to speak today in memory of our fallen heroes. Mayor Maxwell, will you kindly proceed?" he asked.

SJ turned and saw the mayor stand a couple of rows back and make his way to the altar. He was wearing plain black garb, not his usual clothes. His huge frame seemed to be trying to break out of the material. After the mayor made his speech, several more took their turns until everyone who had lost their lives had been spoken about. Their lives, loves, and laughs were all discussed.

The speeches in the inn the previous evening had nowhere near the same emotional impact as today's service and eulogies. SJ held Cristy tight to her side and stroked her head gently, soothing her. Cristy was brave enough to turn and look at the orc hunter who spoke fondly about her father when her name was mentioned. She even managed a very weak smile of thanks before the grief had taken her again with a new fit of sobbing.

By the time the service had ended and the caskets were removed for burial, SJ felt both emotionally and physically drained. She had attended funerals before, but the raw emotion of all present, not just family members, had torn at her insides. This emotion had turned to anger as she had sat there considering the hobs and Bordon. SJ knew she wanted to seek revenge for those fallen.

As she sat waiting for the congregation to leave before escorting the tiny innocent form of Cristy outside, her display triggered.

> **Quest: Vengeance**
> You have witnessed the heartache and torment caused by the evil that resides in Amathera. You may seek vengeance on those guilty of crimes against the town.
> Kill Bordon the Brandisher: 1000xp
> Kill Iratu the Mad: 700xp
> Prevent any further hobgoblin raids on Killic.
> Rewards: 1500xp, reputation with Killic. Usual level kill experience awards apply.
> Would you like to accept the quest? **Yes/No**

SJ couldn't help her eyes going wide. The experience rewards alone were huge, but to attempt to kill such high-level opponents . . . She had no idea if she could even consider it.

"Wow. That is huge!" Dave exclaimed; he had been silent through the whole service until now.

Ignoring the quest offer, SJ stood slowly, lifting Cristy and holding her tiny form in her arms. She carried her from the church. The young gnoll rested her head on her shoulder and gripped her tightly around her neck. Outside, the sun streaked down into the churchyard, and SJ walked over to the six freshly dug plots in the grounds and stood watching as the caskets were gently lowered. After a while, the crowd thinned. Lythonian spoke to each of the family members present, showing his deep level of care and offering personal support at this trying time. Madeline had joined SJ by the graveside, and she felt Cristy's grip lessen around her neck and heard her breathing become heavier.

"She is asleep," SJ whispered to Madeline.

"I will get her home and tucked up in bed. The poor little thing is exhausted."

SJ carefully untangled Cristy's small arms from her neck, and with a few low grumbles, she rearranged her still-sleeping form around Madeline's neck.

"Tell her I will call in and see her soon," SJ said, bidding farewell to Madeline as she carried Cristy from the churchyard. SJ followed the main group of townsfolk as they left the church and filtered back into town, many of them heading to the Hogling Arms.

It didn't take long for the inn to be even busier than the previous evening, and SJ noticed that many of the vendors who would normally be out all hours seemed to have closed up early to attend. The quiet affair became livelier as the afternoon became evening. By the time the night arrived, the sombre mood had been replaced by laughter and singing as they celebrated and drank in respect to those lost.

Several townsfolk had spoken to her throughout the evening, and Gary, Setu, and Margu had arrived. One of the unfortunate lost, Lotti, was Margu's cousin. SJ expressed her condolences, and then Margu hit the ale. It was Setu's night to stay sober as his wife shared in the loss of her relative with family and friends. They played cards as Gary and Setu did most nights, and Margu showed she was exceedingly skilled and beat them both hands down. By the time they departed, Setu and Gary had to support her.

SJ stayed off alcohol and only drank coffee, and it was nearing midnight by the time she eventually went to her room. As she climbed into bed, thinking about the hobs and Bordon stirred her anger back up.

"I will accept the quest and find a way to end their terror," SJ said.

"A noble cause. Have you any thoughts on how you may do it?" Dave said.

"Not yet. I will need to scout their settlement soon, but I will train for now. The fights I have had since learning the new techniques from Lorna have been one thing, but I need to level and unlock more skills if I am going to be able to fight them."

"The quest doesn't say it is solo. You don't have to do it alone."

"I know, but enough have already died due to them."

"Unfortunately, that is part of life in Amathera. There are always conflicts underway."

"This world is no different to Earth."

"There are many similarities, yes."

"I need to improve the use of my claws," SJ said with determination.

"You are an assassin, after all, and with Lorna and several in the town knowing your class, they may be able to provide weapons training."

"I know my claws are good, but as I level, I wonder what Zej might be able to make."

"He is a skilled blacksmith, so you could ask him. Although, at your level, your claws are quite adequate currently. It is more down to using them more efficiently when you fight."

"I know you mentioned there were weapon damage charts. I still haven't looked at any of them yet."

"If you look where your primary weapon shows on your display, you will see the three dots, which is the menu standard."

SJ selected the dots, and a menu appeared showing her various pieces of information. Damage charts appeared, and looking at the graphical data that was shown was remarkably complex. There were selectors for every variant of base weapon type, and you could see the respective damage expectations depending on level, attribute, and damage type. The primary weapon damage could be selected, and the table would be altered. Everything was worked on a median value from minimum to maximum damage permissible.

The comprehensive details allowed armour class inclusion to see comparative hit requirements. The caveat that covered all the information was that the position where a strike occurred on a body could not be predefined. Then, there were both racial and class characteristics, which also came into play. It was a minefield of information, and SJ could have spent hours looking through all the comparative tables and charts.

It even allowed you to add your current weapons statistics, which she did for her blades, and compare them to other weapons at the same level. She was pleased that her claws sat in the top 5 percent of damage-dealing ability. This was the most helpful information, allowing her to see as she progressed when she needed to upgrade them.

"I completely forgot in the emotions of the past couple of days that I can select a new subterfuge skill," SJ said. She selected her skill page and read the details.

Subterfuge: Identification Level 6 (0 of 100 to reach Level 7)

The jump in identification requirement to Level 7 was huge.

"Let's see what skill choices I now have," SJ said excitedly.

Opening her display, she reviewed her options.

Subterfuge
Shroud—as an assassin, you may hide in the shadows; when you are shrouded in darkness, damage is reduced temporarily. The skill lasts thirty seconds per level, up to five minutes at Level 10. (No base attribute)
Disguise—you can become the unknown. At early levels, basic appearance can be altered slightly, obscuring the vision and mind of those looking at you. Did they see a dwarf or a kobold? At higher levels, clothing can be adjusted to hide in the crowd. (Base attribute Charisma; counter Wisdom)
Charm—a good assassin can work their way into the heart of their enemy before presenting them with their death. At Level 1, you may charm that vendor for a better deal. At Level 10, rulers will be at your beck and call. (Base attribute Charisma; counter Intelligence)

> **Discovery**—increased Identification and reduced chance of being detected by analysing another. Reduces willpower adjustments by five per level. At Level 10, no one will ever know you are watching them. (Base attribute Intelligence; counter Wisdom)
>
> **Infiltration**—having control of your emotions is vital. Infiltration allows you to naturally present as a person expects, following their mannerisms and beliefs, hiding your thoughts from being visible. Successful application will last for twenty-four hours. At Level 10, you can sit with your most hated enemy, laughing at their jokes while plotting their demise, and they will never know what is going on inside your mind. (Base attribute Charisma; counter Intelligence)

"These choices all have benefits that could be huge long-term," SJ said.

"They do. The subterfuge skills branch is quite impressive for those who can master the techniques."

"How do they level? Is it through experience gain?"

"Once you reach Level 10 in your character development, you get skill points you can assign, which give hard increases. Alongside hard skill gains, you can also improve them through use, but at lower levels, it can be much more difficult to achieve results successfully. An example is Disguise. At Level 1, while talking to someone, if you trigger the skill during a conversation, there is a slight chance that they may not fully remember who they had just been speaking to or be able to describe your appearance. Your problem is that even if they didn't remember what you discussed, they would remember what you look like, especially with your unique dress. There is a table that shows you success rates and the bonuses through attribute enhancement."

SJ checked her display and found the subtable Dave had mentioned. Again, her display flooded with tables of data. This time, the information was much easier to configure and understand as it automatically adjusted depending on her attribute levels. The level increase and success mechanism were the same for all the skills with an associated base attribute rather than her character level attribute adjustments, which gave her a 10 percent addition to her hit points for Constitution per point starting from ten. The attribute adjustments only added a 1 percent increase in success rate per skill level in comparison.

At Level 1 of a skill, each one had a 10 percent success rate. Then, considering her Charisma was currently only at ten, there was currently no additional bonus. If she adjusted the value to twenty on the table, she had a further 10 percent boost to success. The subterfuge skills required SJ to focus on adding points to her Charisma or Intelligence to get boosted benefits. All the skills reached Level 10, showing a 100 percent success rate.

Then, there were the counter attributes. With a skill with a 10 percent success rate and no bonuses, if a target had ten attribute points above her own, they would remove 10 percent of the success rate, meaning that it would never work against specific targets. So, even if a skill reached Level 10, it could still be negated depending upon the attributes of a target.

"How high do the attributes of higher levels reach?" SJ asked.

"Being a Level 50 fighter, for example, with level increases in Strength, each level would mean that most would have at least sixty Strength at Level 50. Therefore, to negate a Strength-based attack using a skill such as shield block, the skill would be compared directly against the Strength of the defender using the skill. So, at Level 50 with a base Strength of sixty, the defender would require a Level 7 skill minimum, still only granting a 10 percent success rate if they had a Strength of only ten. Their Strength attributes would obviously compare against their attacker and counter each other accordingly. It does start to get complex again with class and environment bonuses for combat skills.

"Your subterfuge skills are much easier to calculate if you know a person's class. This will allow you to consider their attribute bonuses, and once identified, the basic details are shown. With discovery, you start to be given their attribute levels and specific skills. It is like the advanced identification spell Bob used on you; with the bonus, it often isn't discoverable when triggered. I say often because there are always exceptions depending upon counter skills that other classes may know."

"Thanks. I will sleep on it and decide tomorrow how I will progress. I need to get to Level 6 in my kata to improve my martial arts skills. Night, Dave," SJ said as she settled on her pillow.

"Night, SJ, sleep well," Dave said.

After such an emotional day filled with solemn ceremonies, heartfelt conversations, and the transition from mourning to celebration, SJ felt drained. She would seek vengeance against those who had fallen defending the town. The ogre and mage would suffer for their evil. As she lay listening to the sounds of patrons leaving the inn and singing in the streets, it created a sense of familiarity, providing a comforting backdrop for SJ as she fell asleep.

Dave was working through his latest report as he watched SJ sleep soundly in her bed. His initial time in Amathera with her had been more than interesting. As he read through his submission, he was in awe of her current progress regarding her reputation and how she interacted with those around her. She was unlike any previous Legionnaire, and he felt closer to her than he had any other. If he had a heart, it would have broken with Cristy's loss. He had never been so emotionally tied to a Legionnaire or those of Amathera before.

Watching the blanket that covered her chest rise and lower slowly as she slept, his thoughts drifted to what adventures might lay ahead.

Author's Note

Time for the plug. In the indomitable words of Dave:
Silence.

It appears Dave has given up for today, so I will take over. I hope you have thoroughly enjoyed what you have read, and if possible, please write a review. If you want to keep up with what is happening in Amathera before book two is released, please catch up on Royal Road.

I also release early chapters for Patreon members with varying tiers and access at www.patreon.com/Bosloe.

I can be found on social media platforms under @bosloe or @bosloemcanu, or on my Bosloe McAnu author page on Facebook.

To learn more about LitRPG, talk to authors (including myself), and simply have an awesome time, please join The LitRPG Group by Aleron Kong on Facebook. Another two of my favourite Facebook groups are LitRPG Books and LitRPG Legion, where you can gain a fountain of knowledge and recommendations.

Acknowledgements

So many amazing authors in the genre have guided me on my journey or just been there to listen to me rant. To name a few, and if I miss anyone, I am sorry:

Ryan Maxwell—Thanks for all the encouragement and the push. TJ Lombardi—Thanks, bro, bro. Lars Machmüller, Dawn Chapman, Maria D'Mim, Aoife Wai and Rachel A Cooper, and a special thanks to Geneva Agnos for the continuing work she does in the LitRPG community.

I can't finish without passing a huge thanks to all those who have read and supported my creativity since I began writing *One Flew Over the Dragon's Nest*. Several I wish to mention are listed below:

Anonymous, Azgaroth, Edward Ravenbear, Erik Bekke, Falxie, Kyle Anderson, LS, Nyx, Onean, PickledTink, Sgt Jiffy, Simon Hoerder, Aalan, Dragonzrule, Kasidya, Lorddarkai, majorsilver99, Penthero, Samantha Nelson, Swebby, Yawonnoway, zehalper, Raizuto, Basically_God, and ptb_ptb.

About the Author

Bosloe is a math teacher with a military and business background. His passion for teaching comes from a desire to give something back. Born in Northwest England, he discovered a passion for storytelling early on but only recently began writing himself. Inspired by the fantasy and LitRPG genres, he wrote the Amatherean Tales as his debut series. Bosloe lives in Oxfordshire with his wife and fur babies.

Podium

DISCOVER MORE
STORIES UNBOUND

PodiumEntertainment.com

www.ingramcontent.com/pod-product-compliance
Ingram Content Group UK Ltd.
Pitfield, Milton Keynes, MK11 3LW, UK
UKHW041953060625
459351UK00003B/15